THE ONLY EASY DAY WAS
YESTERDAY

THE STORY OF THE MAKING OF THE FIRST
UNITED STATES NAVY WOMAN SEAL

STEPHEN ENNA

authorHOUSE®

AuthorHouse™
1663 Liberty Drive
Bloomington, IN 47403
www.authorhouse.com
Phone: 1 (800) 839-8640

Published by AuthorHouse 08/05/2019

ISBN: 978-1-7283-2184-4 (sc)
ISBN: 978-1-7283-2185-1 (hc)
ISBN: 978-1-7283-2186-8 (e)

Library of Congress Control Number: 2019911042

Print information available on the last page.

THIS BOOK IS DEDICATED TO MY
THREE GRANDCHILDREN
HADLEY, ELLA AND NOAH

KEEP CLIMBING THE MOUNTAIN
UNTIL YOU CAN REACH OUT AND
TOUCH THE RAINBOW

LOVE PAPA

CHAPTER 1

THE BEGINNING

On a high plateau above the city of Portland, the Alameda neighborhood sits on the 1859 land claim of William C. Bowering and his wife, Isabelle. The area became known as Gravelly Hill Road for the gravel pit at NE 33rd and Fremont. In 1909 The Alameda Land Company laid out the exclusive Alameda Park subdivision that was then added to the City of Portland.

The Alameda today is a neighborhood where you will find tree-lined streets, older architecturally significant and view homes, neighborhood shops, coffee places, and a high level of community involvement.

The Alameda Ridge is a large gravel bar that was formed between 15,000 and 13,000 years ago at the end of the last ice age. It occured when the ice dam containing Glacial Lake Missoula collapsed some 40 times, causing some of the largest floods known on earth.

The flood waters spilled across Idaho and eastern Washington, surged down the Columbia River and through the Gorge, flooding the Willamette Valley as far south as Eugene, Oregon.

These floods covered the city of Portland in approximately 400 feet of water, carving out Sullivan's Gulch, the large ravine that holds interstate 84, and depositing large volumes of unconsolidated silt, sand, gravel and boulders.

As the west flowing waters rushed around Rocky Butte, sediments were deposited on the west side of the Butte, forming an approximately 100 to 150 foot high bar that became Alameda Ridge

The Alameda Ridge runs through the Madison South, Roseway, Rose City Park, Beaumont-Wilshire, Alameda and Sabin neighborhoods. Today it is the home of a number of Portland's most expensive homes.

It was here on the Alameda Ridge that Jim Jamison and his wife, Sarah, bought their dream home in 1990.

The home was done in an English Tudor style with expansive views out towards the downtown city of Portland, Oregon. The home had a commanding view of the West Hills, the Willamette River and downtown Portland. At night it was one of the best views in the city.

Jim and his wife grew up in Portland and, like so many Oregonians, they remained in their state for their entire educational experience. Jim and Sarah both attended Beaumont Grade School, Grant High School, and the University of Oregon.

Both Jim and Sarah were athletes in college. Jim played basketball for the Oregon Ducks, and Sarah was a member of the gymnastic team. Jim was 6'4 inches tall and had played basketball his entire life. He was captain of the Grant High School team and was recruited to the University of Oregon with a partial scholarship.

Sarah began taking tumbling at the age of 3 and had continued with gymnastics throughout her childhood. She was also recruited to attending Oregon and was given a partial scholarship as well.

The couple's first home was an apartment on the east side of Portland. They remained in the apartment for three years, and if you ask either of them, they would tell you that that period of their life was a total blur. Their life seemed to consist of work, eating on the run, and saving every dime they could.

After three years they found and purchased their first home. It was a small bungalow on the Northeast side of Portland. It was in their old neighborhood and not far from Grant High School. The home was small but comfortable, with no view and little lawn.

Both Jim and Sarah commuted to downtown Portland, but neither found that to be difficult. They remained in the bungalow home for six years, living the same type of lifestyle they had during their apartment days.

They worked, ate on the run, and saved every penny they could.

When their dream home came available it was above the median sales price in Alameda. The median sales price was $675,000, and the price of their dream home was $800,000. They both took a deep breath and went for it. It was the biggest decision of their married life, and they never had a second thought.

In 1992 their first child was born. It was a boy whom they named John James Jamison. John was followed by a girl, who was born four years later in 1996. Her name was Ashley Morgan Jamison.

Jim sat in his family room. It was 7PM, and he had had a long day with two different court appearances. A fire was going in the fireplace and, as is the case in Portland, it was raining outside. It was 1999, and Ashley had turned three the week before. Her brother John was now seven years old and, for the most part, the two got along.

This, however, was not the case this evening. John began to tease his baby sister as is the case with most siblings. The difference, however, was that Ashley did not like to be teased and, when pushed to her limit by her brother, she attacked. Not only did she throw punches, but she would tackle him, and if Jim or Sarah allowed it to continue, Ashley would normally come out the winner, with John heading to his room in tears.

That's enough you two, I've had it, and so has your mother. If you can't get along then you will spend the rest of the night in your bedrooms. And no, I don't want to hear who did what to whom. I'm tired, and so is your mother, so either get along or you're going to a complete evening timeout in your room.

But Dad, he started it. That's not true, Dad, she kept bothering me and she broke down my Lego structure that I worked hard on. Did not, yes you did. I did not, yes you did.

OK you two. I have had it. To your rooms. That is it. John bowed his head and headed for his room as his father requested. Ashley on the other hand said, "I am not going and you can't make me". That was it. Jim picked her up in his arms and lifted her up and carried her to her room. He put her on her bed and closed the door. Don't you even think about coming out, young lady. I have had enough of you and your brother tonight so I want you to think about your attitude and your actions. Ashley just sobbed as she sat in the middle of her bed. After one hour, Sara went to her room only to find Ashley curled up in a ball in the middle of her bed sound asleep. Sarah lifted her up, put her pajamas on her, and put her back to bed.

She walked back into the kitchen, poured a glass of Oregon Pinot Noir, and joined her husband in the family room in front of the fire.

Sarah sat down and let a large sigh out. What are we going to do with those two?

You know, Sarah, I have been watching those two since they were born. My take on them is that John is a pretty normal kid. He seems to get along well with everyone he meets, is doing well in school, and participated in a variety of outside activities with no problem.

Ashley, on the other hand, is a real handful. She seems to be not only strong willed, but she is physically strong and when pushed to the wall she can beat her older brother up. She seems to never be relaxed and only seems to slow down and give herself a rest when she is totally exhausted. I don't know if we have a problem with her or not, but I would be interested to know what you think?

I have watched her as well, Jim. I don't remember seeing a child, let alone a little girl, that had so much determination and push. I agree with you that she cannot sit still and seems to push the boundaries of everything she is involved with. I don't think that she has Attention Deficit Disorder, but perhaps I should have her tested at Oregon Health Sciences.

I'm not sure that I know what ADD is, Sarah. Can you shed some light on it for me?

Sure, I'm no expert, but here is what I know about it from my medical studies. I think the three main issues involve problems paying attention, excessive activity, or difficulty controlling behavior which is not appropriate for a person's age.

As I recall, the symptoms appear before a person is twelve years old, are present for more than six months, and cause problems in at least two settings such as home, school, or recreational activities. I'm told that in children, the problems associated with it may result in poor school performance because of lack of attention. So that is about all I know of it.

Well, dear, I'm not sure that Ashley fits all of the symptoms you have mentioned, but it is clear to me that the excessive activity and behavior that is not necessarily related to her age are two things that jump out at me.

I think that given what I have observed and what you have said, that we should go ahead and have her tested at Oregon Health Sciences. In two years we will be faced with her going to kindergarten, and I think that if we have a problem we should identify it and know what and how to deal with it before we get to that stage.

I am somewhat eased by the fact that we haven't had to deal with problems with her nursery school, but I do remember the teacher's comment at our last session which was, "Ashley

5

is a very strong girl both physically and mentally. As such many of her classmates are a bit afraid of her and tend to shy away from her"

I remember that as well and will pass the comment on to the folks at Oregon Health Sciences.

I will make an appointment when I'm at work tomorrow and we will see what they say. I think that is a good plan, Sarah. For no other reason it will help us to know what we are dealing with here.

Cheers to you. They touched glasses and sat in front of the fire looking out at the Portland view through the rain drops.

TWO DAYS LATER

Jim, arrived home about 6:30 from another long day in court. Hi Hon, how was your day? Well it was long but today was a success. We won our case in court and I am happy to say that the Willamette River will avoid another source of pollution as we look to the future. How about you?

My day was fine, no real issues of importance. I was able to get an appointment for Ashley to meet with Dr. Amy Johnson. She is a specialist in child behavior and an expert on ADD. Our appointment is for Friday. Ashley will miss school but I have the day off so we will make an outing of it.

Sounds great, Hon. What is for dinner? Tonight we are having the kids' favorite: spaghetti and meatballs, green salad and garlic French bread. For you and me there will be a great Oregon Pinot Noir and, for the kids, cold milk.

Sounds great.

THREE DAYS LATER

Mommy, where are we going? How come I'm not going to school? Ashley, Mommy has the day off, and I thought it would be fun to take you to see where I work and then go out to lunch together at a great hamburger place. Wow, that sounds fun. Will we get to meet some of the people that you work with? Yes, you will get to meet Dr. Amy Johnson. She works with all kinds of kids your age, and I have asked her to meet you and get to know you. Wow, that sounds fun.

They arrived at Oregon Health Sciences at 930 AM. Good Morning, Sarah, the receptionist said. This must be Ashley. Ashley looked at her mom and said Mommy, that lady knows us.

Yes, she does, Ashley. Her name is Ida and she is one of Mommy's friends. Please tell her good morning.

Good Morning, Ida. It is nice to meet you. It is nice to meet you as well, Ashley. Sarah, I will let Dr. Johnson know that you are here. In a couple of minutes the door opened and Sarah and Ashley were greeted by Dr. Amy Johnson. Hi Sarah, this must be Ashley. Hi Ashley, I am Doctor Johnson and it is great to meet with you. Please come in.

Wow, this is a fun office, Dr. Johnson. Thanks, Ashley. Would you like to play a couple of games with me? Yes, that would be fun. Mommy, is it OK. Sure, go ahead.

OK. Ashley, the first game is to see how long you can sit still. Do you think you can do that? Yes. OK. I will set this timer for 3 minutes. We can both watch. Let's see if you can sit in the little chair until the buzzer goes off. OK.

The three minutes passed quickly and Ashley didn't move. She stayed totally focused. The buzzer went off and Dr. Johnson said, Ashley that was really good you won our first game. Here is a treat.

Our next game is a puzzle. Do you see this puzzle in front of you? It has nine pieces that all fit together. When I say go, do you think you can put it together? Sure, I want to try.

Ashley focused on the puzzle and within five minutes she had all of the pieces in place. That was great Ashley. Now we have one more test to see how you do. Is that OK? Sure Dr. Johnson, this is fun.

OK. I am going to read you a story, and if you hear anything that you don't understand or don't agree with you can tell me at any time I am reading. Do you understand? Sure.

OK here goes. Dr. Johnson read the story without interruption. Ashley did not blurt out any comments and seemed to have the patience to wait until the story was over before she said anything.

Ashley, you did great. I have a present for you. Dr. Johnson then gave her a stuffed Panda Bear Toy. Ashley jumped up and down with excitement. Ashley, I have asked Ida if she would show you around. Would you like that while I talk to your mother? Yes, that would be great.

The door opened and Ida put out her hand and took Ashley out of the office.

Well Sarah, I am sure that Ashley does not have ADD, but it is very clear that she is strong willed and very focused.

I was looking to see if she was going to fidget or squirm a great deal which she did not. I wanted to watch her work a quiet task, which she did, without any impatience and I wanted to see if she would blurt out comments during the story, which she didn't. So that makes it clear to me that she does not have ADD.

She is, in my opinion, big and more mature for her age than I am use to seeing. In my opinion, you have a real future athlete on your hands and one, that at this early age, needs to stay busy. She is also very strong for her age, and her verbal skills are already well defined.

I would recommend two activities that I think will keep her interested, focused and tired out. I would enroll her in an active swimming program and a junior gymnastic program. She will adapt to both quickly and that should keep her tired enough to avoid trying to beat up her brother.

Thanks, Amy. I am relieved but not sure what the future brings for this girl. I guess only time will tell. I appreciate your time and help. See you soon.

CHAPTER 2

THE EARLY YEARS

Ashley and her brother John were almost four years apart. John was out of grade school at the Alameda grade school when Ashley was only in the 4th grade. John melted right in. He was popular, smart, had good ambition and was a good, but not great, athlete. Grade School was just that for John, "Grade School". He was ready to move on and looked forward to the opportunity to attend Grant High School.

Ashley on the other hand was a mover and shaker. She swam three times per week and had Gymnastics three times a week. The only day she had off to rest was Sunday.

One Saturday morning, Sarah was sitting in the stands at the swimming venue yelling "Go Ash" Go Ash". Ashley was competing in a local meet and as always she was leading her race and on course to break another record. "Go Ash" "Go Ash", Sara yelled.

The race finished and, as was becoming the custom, Ashley hopped out of the pool a winner.

The woman next to Sarah had been sitting quietly watching the race when she turned to Sarah and said, Hi, I am Jean Freemont. My daughter is Morgan Freemont. She has raced against Ashley for the past two years and has never come close to matching her in either time or skill. Your daughter is an amazing athlete.

Thanks very much Jean, it is a pleasure to meet you. I have watched your daughter swim and I think she is quite good. Thanks, Sarah, but quite good is not great. There is a big difference.

Hey we have a couple of hours until their next race. Would you like to get a cup of coffee and get to know each other?

That sounds great. Why don't we go out to the coffee shop next to the Community Center. Great, let's go.

They grabbed a table and each ordered coffee. Tell me a little bit about you and your family, Jean. Well, I've been married to a great guy for 10 years. We have a house in the Wilshire district. It is not far from Prescott street. The kids all go to Beaumont Grade School. Morgan is in the fourth grade, her little brother Robert is in the lst grade, and our oldest daughter, Megan, is in the 5th grade.

Wow, sounds like you have your hands full. That is, at times, an understatement, The good news is I don't work anymore and am now a stay at home, full time Mom.

What about you, Sarah? Well, my husband is an attorney and I am a nurse. We have lived on and off in this area since we were kids. We both went to Grant High School and then to the University Oregon. After a lot of years of hard work and saving we went out on a limb and bought our dream home in the Alameda district. I love the house and feel fortunate to be where we are.

We have two kids, John and Ashley. John is four years older than Ashley, so he will start Grant High School this fall. John is a great kid, pretty much down the center of the road, works hard, brings home good grades and makes friends easily. Ashley has been our challenge. She has always had an energy level that is beyond any of her peers. We had her tested when she was three, thinking she might have ADD or something else. She was so active, strong beyond her years and not an easy kid to keep occupied. One of Doctors at Oregon Health Science tested her and found her to be totally normal but well developed and overactive. She suggested that we get her into a pool and competitive swimming and a strong Gymnastic program.

As a result, Ashley has been swimming at the Matt Dishman Center since she was three, three days per week, and the other three she is at the Children's Gym on Sandy Blvd doing gymnastics.

Well Sarah, I can only say that I have watched her in the pool and she is head and shoulders above everyone else.

In fact, I don't think I have ever seen her lose a race. Yes, I know, at times it has been a bit embarrassing. At her age she already has a huge trophy case at home.

How does she do in gymnastics? She is just as talented. She is strong beyond her years, exceptionally well coordinated and not afraid to try anything. As a result the kid is starting to develop muscles that I didn't know existed.

Well, she appears to me to have lots of opportunities ahead of her, it will be interesting to see which way the wind blows her. Oh wow, look at the time, guess we better get back to watch the next event.

It was great to meet you Jean, thanks for the invite to coffee. My pleasure. I hope it is the first of many.

The two women returned to the swimming centerand watched the next race which Ashley won by half the length of the pool.

Ashley continued on her tough training program in both swimming and gymnastics during her grade school years. The summer between her 7th grade and 8th grade year proved to be another pivotal changing point.

Good Morning, you have reached the Jamison residence, this is Sarah speaking. Hi Sarah, it's Freddie Becker from the Matt Dishman Swim Center. Hi Freddie, what's up? Well as you know, I have been Ashley's coach here since she was three years old and as you can imagine I have never had a student that has excelled to the level she has. She is one of a kind and driven beyond anyone I have ever seen.

As everyone is aware, Ashley has never lost a race and she shows no sign of yielding that record. The purpose of my call is to say I think we have reached the highest level we can coaching her here. She is destined for bigger and better things. I believe that for her to achieve those levels and the recognition that come with them, she needs to move to a higher and more competitive program. And, as sorry as I am to say it, she needs coaches that are far more experienced than I am.

Of course, if you want her to continue with us we are very happy with that, but if she wants' to continue to grow and develop with this sport she will need to move up to a more competitive level.

Well thanks Freddie, you have and continue to be a great coach and mentor for Ashley, and I know personally that she looks up to you and holds you in very high regard. If I am to move her forward what program do you recommend and how do I go about it?

Well Sarah, the good news is most of that is already done. Ashley has already built quite a reputation in the Oregon Swim Community and just this morning I was contacted by the Director of Swimming for Team Unify here in the city.

Team unify is a year round YMCA and USA Competitive Team with a Focus on Youth Development

The program offers affordable and effective training with state wide national and international completion opportunities. The Greater Portland Swim Team also has an extensive strength conditioning program five days a week. They are the only team in the region that competes in both YMCA and USA Swim Leagues. The Director of their program is a woman by the name of Nancy Ages. Nancy was a member of the USA swim team and competed in the last Olympics. It was Nancy who called me and asked if I thought Ashley was ready to take the next step.

If you are interested you should call her at 503 969 8175.

Thanks, Freddy. I will need to talk to my husband first and then have a talk with Ashley. We will see where this all leads. I appreciate your call.

LATER THAT EVENING

Hi hon, how was your day? Mine was fine, Jim, how was yours? No complaints, we moved another step forward in developing the clear water plan for the Willamette River. I must say it never fails to amaze me how some people can find problems with everything including objecting to making our river clean.

Well, pour yourself a glass of Oregon Pinot Noir and have a seat in the family room. I turned on the gas fire just a few minutes ago and I need to have a bit of a quiet time to talk to you. Really, what's up? Let me get a glass of wine and I will join you.

They sat for a moment looking at the fire and at the great view. The sun was just beginning to set over the west hills and the colors that were spread over Portland were a variety of reds, purple and oranges.

OK, I'm now curious, what do we need to discuss? Well, today, I got a call from Ashley's coach at the swim center. Really, what did Freddie want to talk about? I assume that Ashley is not in any trouble. No trouble. Freddie just wanted us to know that he believes that he and the others at the Matt Dishman swim center have done all they can for Ashley and he thinks she has huge potential to achieve a lot in swimming. He told me that he received a call from Nancy Ages this morning. Nancy is the coach and Director of the Team Unify Program which is the highest level swimming program that the YMCA sponsors. It is affiliated with the US Swim Team. Nancy said she has watched Ashley over the years and believes that she has huge potential to move ahead.

As you know, we have worked hard since Ashley was three years old to keep her occupied with swimming and gymnastics, and she has excelled beyond our dreams. I was thinking this afternoon that in all of these years she has never once pushed back, said she wasn't interested, or didn't want to participate.

The girl has no, or very little, social life. She is living the life of an athlete and she is a good one. She continues to grow and well exceeds her age group in both height and weight. Because of her gymnastics, she is strong as an ox. Just the other day her brother told me laughing, "Keep that girl away from me, I'm afraid for my life."

The question I have for you, is what do you think we should do? Well, everything you have told me is positive, which will make my evening a lot better. I think we should let Ashley decide what she wants to do, and if she wants to do it, how much time does she want to spend doing it.

Good, that's what I had hoped you would say I will talk to her after school tomorrow and then let you know tomorrow night what she wants to do. Cheers Hon. They touched glasses and both looked out at the great view.

THE NEXT AFTERNOON

Hi Hon, how was school? It was fine Mom, Mr. Johnson is a nice guy and good teacher. He seems to make 6th grade fun. He also must be teaching me something because I'm having no problems at all with my studies. I have about 1/2 hour before I need to head to gymnastics. Do you know where my tights are? Yes, they are in the laundry room.

Ashley, before you leave, I have something I want to talk to you about. What's up Mom? Well yesterday I got a call from

14

Freddie at the swim center. Don't tell me he doesn't think I'm working hard enough? Far from it, my dear. Freddie wanted me to know that he feels that you have progressed to such a high level that the program at Matt Dishman is no longer providing you the challenge that he believes you need. What does that mean, Mom?

It means that Freddie got a call from a women whose name is Nancy Ages. Nancy is the coach and Director of the advanced swim program at the Y, which is called Team Unify. Oh yeh, I have heard of Team Unify. What did Nancy want?

Well, she has been watching you over the years and believes that you have a rare talent that could lead you to a lot of success in swimming and she ask Freddie if he thought you should think about joining Team Unify. Freddie obviously said yes and called your Dad and I. We talked about it last night and came to the conclusion that it is your life and your choice so I wanted you to know that this opportunity is now available to you if you want to go for it. What do you think?

Would that mean that I would have to leave my friends behind? Well yes, as it relates to swimming, but of course your friends will always be your friends as long as you want to take the time to maintain the relationships.

Where is the pool? The pool is downtown not far from the Max station. You would take Max after school to the swim center at the Y and then take Max home in time for dinner on your training days. How much training would it require? Good question. If you have an interest and want me to explore it I am happy to call Nancy Ages and discuss it and the obligation that goes with it. Well, I guess nothing ventured, nothing gained. I do want you and Nancy to know that I do not want to give up gymnastics and spend my whole life in the pool. I need both for myself. I will be sure to let her know. I will give her a call tomorrow and let you know what she says after you get home from school tomorrow.

Now, you better get going to gymnastics.

Hello, Team Unify, this is Nancy speaking. Hi Nancy, My name is Sarah Jamison. My daughter is Ashley Jamison and she swims for the Matt Dishman community Center. Freddie, who is my daughters coach, suggested that I call you regarding the possibility of Ashley transferring to the swim program at Team Unify.

Hi Mrs. Jamison. Please call me Sarah.

Well Sarah, I want to thank you for calling. I have been watching your daughter swim and win race after race for the past three years.

I believe she is something very special and that she has the opportunity to go very far with our sport.

As Freddie may have told you we have a well established program that is tied to the United States Swimming Program. We look for the type of talent that can be developed into the best our country can produce. While it may be too early to tell we believe that Ashley may have that talent and ability.

Thanks very much, Nancy. Those are very nice things to hear. What would the obligation be if Ashley were to move over to Team Unify? Well, to begin with it would require her to spend four days per week training with us.

We would like to have her more but we know that kids have all kinds of other interests, and thus we set the minimum at four days. Her training would be here at the Y after school. Each session would begin at 4PM and would last until 6PM. Part of the time would be out of the water working with weights and other means of conditioning. We have regular swim meets, generally not more than two per month, and they are on weekends, either Saturday or Sunday, but not both. The cost to be a member is $1000.00 per year. Ashley's training would not be by age but by level of accomplished ability. That keeps a significant competition going with each practice.

Do you require that swimming be her only athletic activity?

No, but we do encourage each of our swimmers to concentrate as much as they can on swimming. In Ashley's case I am well aware of her gymnastic skill and the level at which she performs and I do not want to try to discourage her from that as long as she is comfortable doing both.

OK Nancy, that is what I needed to know. My husband and I will talk with Ashley about it.

As you can imagine, we have a pretty independent and driven daughter. We want her to make her own decisions and to learn to live with the consequences of them, so we will sit down and have a talk with her. I will give you a call back in a couple of days.

Thanks, Sarah. I look forward to hearing from you. Goodbye. Goodbye Nancy.

CHAPTER 3

THE NEXT LEVEL

Ashley was home from school on time but needed to rush to gymnastics so Sarah decided not to mention to her the new swimming opportunity and her discussion with Nancy Ages.

John was at a Grant High School function for the evening, so when Ashley returned home she joined her Mom and Dad for dinner. Hey Mom, what's for dinner? Tonight my dear we are going Italian. I made a Lasagna and it will be served with garlic french bread and green salad. For dessert, you have a choice between apple pie and brownies.

Sounds great, I'm starved. Dad, would you please pass the lasagna? Sure Hon, here you go. Mom, this looks great. Thanks. It's all homemade.

Dinner was great, and just as they were finishing, Sarah said to Ashley, "Ash, I talked to Nancy Ages today. Oh, now I remember. She is the coach of Team Unify. What did she have to say, Mom?.

Well, she made it clear that she has watched you swim for a couple of years and believes that you have good potential. She would like you to swim for Team Unify. What does that mean Mom? Well, it would mean that you would have to train with them four times per week. I told her about your gymnastics, and she already knew about your program and the success you have had with it. Four days per week would be the minimum

THE ONLY EASY DAY WAS YESTERDAY

required to join Team Unify. Each training session lasts 2 hours, from 4 to 6, in the afternoon. The sessions are divided between swimming and weight training. There are approximately two meets per month and they are generally on weekends. I talked to Dad about the weekend obligation, and both of us would be OK with trading off to attend the weekend meets with you.

The team trains at the downtown Y which you can take Max directly to. It would mean that you wouldn't be home until about 7PM each night, which doesn't give you much time to relax, have dinner, and do your home work.

I can handle that part Mom. What do I have to do to try out? From what she told me you would not have to try out. She knows what ability you have and would like you to join as soon as you want.

She did say that the program is not age related but rather ability related, and so to determine where you are and how to place you in the program, she would want you to swim a 200 free against others that are already in the program. Apparently this is a standard means of placing new team members. I assume that would happen shortly after you begin, should you choose to want to do it.

That brings me to the decision that needs to be made. You know that Dad and I want to support you in any way we can, but we realize that for you to continue to grow and develop that the only way to do so is to allow you to make your own decisions from this point on.

Well, thanks to you both for your support. I want to think about this overnight. It would mean that I would be giving up my swimming friends at the center and entering a whole new level of competition. It also will require more time and cut into my gymnastic program. I'm not sure that I can do 4 days of swimming and three days of gymnastics, but I want to think about it.

The other thing I'm thinking about is I am almost 11 and will start the 7th grade next fall. This will mean more homework, which will require additional study. Grades are important to me and have come easily to me thus far, but I know that the free ride I have been enjoying will soon come to an end soon.

No problem Hon, take your time and let us know when you make your decision.

TWO NIGHTS LATER

Ashley was home a little early from swimming.

Her hair was still wet when she came into the kitchen. Hi Mom, what's for dinner? Tonight we are going to have Oregon Trout, wild rice and green beans. I have cheese cake for dessert. That sounds great. I'm going to take a shower and then study a little bit before Dad gets home and we sit down.

See you in a bit.

Hi Hon, how was your day at the hospital? No real issues but the longer I do this the more I am happy with the fact that I am now only working three days per week. What's for dinner? We are having trout. I'm going to bake it with some spices and bacon. That sounds incredible. Is Ash home? Yep, she took a shower and is in studying. She will join us for dinner which I should have ready to go in about l5 minutes.

Great, I will just grab a quick shower and then I will be looking forward to a nice Oregon Pinot Gris. I have one in the wine cooler. I will open it for you. I think it is a Sweet Cheeks Pinot Gris. Sarah pulled the wine from the cooler. She opened it and tasted it. It was light and refreshing and should be perfect with the trout.

It was just about l5 minutes when Sarah called Jim and Ash to dinner. John was home and joined them as well. It was becoming a bit unusual for all of the family to be home on a week night. It seemed like, as the kids got older, Their activities and time schedule made family dinners a thing of the past.

Wow, we are all here, Jim said. Cheers to all of you. Sarah lifted her glass of wine as did the kids, who lifted their sparkling waters.

How was your day, John, Sarah asked. It was fine Mom. Grant High school seems to agree with me. I am not starting but am playing on the Varsity second team in Basketball this year so between that, and my studies, I feel like I have plenty to keep me busy.

How about you Ash, how was your day? It was good, Mom. I had a long talk with my gymnastics coach after practice. She had already talked to Nancy Ages from Team Unify. She told me that my progress in gymnastics is way above the norm but that after she talked with Nancy, she understood better why I should devote a little more to swimming. She did offer to extend my practices by a half hour to help my progress continue. I was fine with that, so after the discussion I made the decision to accept the invitation from Team Unify and start my training with them. Mom, would you call Nancy Ages tomorrow and let her know that I would like to participate and to find out when and what I am suppose to do? Sure Ash, that is no problem.

TWO DAYS LATER

Hi Ash, how was swimming? It was great Mom. I told my friends that I am going to be leaving and joining Team Unify. I think they were all supportive but some actually seemed a bit sad. Freddy, talked to everyone as a group and explained why he felt it would be best if I moved up. After that everyone was fine. they want to have a small party after swimming on Friday for me.

Did you talk to Nancy Ages. Yes I did and she was very happy. You are all set to start with Team Unify on Monday afternoon. She told me that on Monday you would spend your time doing administrative stuff. Dad and I have paid for the first year so you are off and running. You are scheduled for Monday, Wednesday, Friday and Saturday. Gymnastics will continue on Tuesday and Thursday. If you get to the point where it is just too much, then we will talk and adjust your schedule to fit your needs.

After school on Monday, Ashley walked to Max and took the train downtown to the Y. She went in and was met at the reception area by a young girl. She explained that she was here to join Team Unify and that her Mom had spoken with Nancy Ages about it. The young girl ask her to take a seat and called Nancy. Miss Ages, I have a woman here in the lobby by the name of Ashley Jamison.

She said she has an appointment with you. Fine Thanks. Ashley, Miss Ages will be with you in a couple of minutes.

A couple of minutes went by and a tall, slim woman appeared in the lobby and went directly over to Ashley. Hi Ashley, I'm Nancy Ages. It is great to meet you.

Thanks Nancy. Ashley, I am so happy you decided to give Team Unify a go. I think the program will suit you, I believe that our program will help you to reach new levels of success. Please follow me.

Nancy took Ashley back to the locker room area. Waiting at the room was a girl about her age. She was introduced to Ashley as Gina Lombardi. Hi Ashley, I'm Gina. Ashley shook her hand and said nice to meet you.

Ashley, as your Mom may have told you, today is an administrative day for you. We want to give you an orientation to the program, a tour of the facilities, take some basic measurements, and finish all of your paperwork.

I have asked Gina to show you around. When that is over we will meet in the locker room, take some basic measurements and then finish your paperwork. Any questions? No, I'm looking forward to the tour.

OK, let's go then. Gina turned to Ashley and said just follow me. Do you have a nick name, Ashley, or do you go by your real name? Everyone calls me Ash, Gina. Well then, if it is OK with you, I will call you Ash as well.

Let me begin by telling you that I have been here for two years. I am 13 years old and in the eighth grade. Where do you go to school? My parents live in Beaverton so I go to grade school out there. What about you? I am 11 and will turn 12 this fall. I go to Alameda Grade School in north east Portland.

How did you find out our program? I actually didn't. Coach Nancy found me, and the next thing I knew, I was asked to join the swim program.

I'm surprised that you are only 11, Ash. Based on your body I would have guessed that you were already in the eighth grade. Yeh, I've always been a bit big for my age. I compete in gymnastics as well so my muscles are much more developed than my friends at school,

Well, here is the pool. Wow, it is big. How many lanes are there? There are l5 lanes and it is an Olympic size pool. The kids that swim here range in age from 9 to 18. We may have a couple that have stayed beyond high school, but that is not usually the case. If swimmers stay with us that long they generally move on to the US swimming program with an eye on making the US Team, or they are recruited by a University and swim for their school in college.

What about the program? Are there goals etc? Yes our mission is to build exceptional people through excellent swimming. Our vision is to develop a well balanced training program so every member achieves maximum potential both in and out of the pool.

Our program offers a natural progression of levels from the traditional swim team participation to a top level competitive swimming program.

I will say, that after two years, I feel that the program overall offers a supporting environment that is enjoyable and has a disciplined workout structure that works for everyone competing at various levels.

We have a mentor program as well. In the next few days you will meet your mentor. It will probably be one of the older girls that has been here for some time and achieved a great deal. Your mentor will provide you with the peer support that is needed to reach peak performance levels. It is not uncommon for a member of our team to be mentored by someone who simply is not as good as the person they are mentoring. I think this must be hard but it doesn't seem to bother the mentors.

You will also be asked to swim a competitive 200 meter race. That will probably happen in the next few days.

The race is set up for all new members. You will race against a group of our swimmers with the goal being to see where you are at this point. You will then be placed in a group based on your ability and will work out with that group on an ongoing basis. That means that your group will be all over the map in age but the approximate same in ability.

I should also tell you that once every six months, Coach Nancy holds an inspiration day That is a day when we don't swim or work out. She invites a guest to talk to us that provides us inspiration to do the best we possibly can.

For example, last Wednesday was inspiration day. To our surprise the guest speaker was Dana Vollmer. As you may know, Dana is a Olympic gold medalist and former world record holder. At the 2004 summer Olympics, she won a gold medal as a member of the winning United States team in the 4x200 meter freestyle relay, and that group also set the world record in the event. Eight years later at the 2012 Summer Olympics, she set the world record on her way to the gold medal in the 100 meter butterfly. She added to her medal count at the 2016 Summer Olympics, where she won three medals in Rio de Janeiro.

I think one of the most amazing things she talked about was

being an Olympic swimmer and a Mom. She lives in California and has somehow figured out how to balance it all. Pretty inspiring.

Let me show you the locker room now. Gina asked Ash to follow her to the women's locker room. Today you will be assigned your own locker. You can keep your stuff in it and it is yours. So you don't have to drag stuff back and forth. It will all be here for you. You can see we have private showers rather than some big group shower and towels etc are all provided.

There are hair dryers, which nobody cares about, and just about every type of cream you need to keep your skin from drying out.

So that ends my tour. Thanks Gina. That was really helpful. Hi you two, and welcome back, Nancy said, as she walked into the locker room.

What did you think of our facility Ash. I think it is beautiful and the pool is huge.

Yes, we think it is pretty special as well. Next Step is to take some measurements if you don't mind. Will you please take off all of your cloths with the exception of your underwear and walk over here to the scale. Ashley did as she was asked. She didn't wear a bra yet so she stripped down to her panties and walked over to the scale. Nancy weighed her first. Ashley, you weigh 33 lbs. That is big for your age. Young women your age usually come in between 15 and 25 lbs. Let's now check your height. You are 3'2 tall which makes you talker than most your age. We are used to somewhere between 2' 3" and 2' 5",

OK. You can put your clothes back on, and let's move to the weight room and check both your arm and leg strength,

Ashley dressed and followed Coach Nancy to the weight room. Let's start with a few pull-ups. Ash, let me see how many pull-ups you can do at this point. Ashley walked over to the bar just like it was gymnastic training. She reached up and hung on the bar. Then she proceeded to do 15 pull ups perfectly.

My god girl, I have seniors in high school that can't do that. Let me check your arm strength. she ask Ash to lay down on the bench and then put a 25 pound weight in each hand. When I say go, please lift the weights up then down, do as many reps as you can. Ash took the weights, centered her back on the bench, and then did 20 reps as though it was no big deal.

OK girl, you are beyond impressing me. Nancy then checked her leg strength and once again was blown away by the strength of this young woman.

Well that does that, Ash. Thanks. Now we have to finish your paperwork and you will be done for today. Any questions?

There were none and Ashley left the Y, grabbed Max, and she was home in 25 minutes.

CHAPTER 4

GROWING UP

Hi Mom, what's happening? Not much Ash. How was your first day at the Y? Well, it went fine. I took Max both ways which took about 25 minutes each way door to door. I made it on time and was met by Coach Nancy. She was ready for me and introduced me to a young girl who I thought was about my age. Her name was Gina, and as it turns out, she is in the eighth grade and has been involved in the program for the past two years. She was super nice and showed me around the facility to include both the pool, locker rooms and workout facilities.

How were they? First class Mom, everything was new and clean. I think there were 15 lanes in the pool, and there was a complete separate area for diving with two spring boards and three platform structures. Gina told me they have a pretty advanced diving program.

Coach Nancy then took some measurements on me, both weight and height. I was heavier and taller than most kids my age. She also then gave me a bit of a physical test with pull ups and weights. I think I blew her away with my strength. No surprise there Ash. With the amount of gymnastics training you have had I'm sure you are in better shape that way than most kids she sees.

So when do you start real training? I will be in the pool tomorrow and will swim the 200 yard free you told me about on Wednesday. Gina told me that all new members go through the same evaluation and that it helps Coach Nancy know where best to place you. They apparently have different levels that are not driven by age but rather on ability. So if I do well it is possible I could end up in a class with mostly older boys. It will be interesting to see how it all works out.

I'm sure you will do well, Ash. Your Dad just got home and is cleaning up.

John is doing homework so once you have your stuff dropped off come on back as dinner is almost ready. Will do Mom.

TWO DAYS LATER

Ashley, got to the Y on time. She had established her locker the day before and all of her swim stuff was in it. Today would be the 200 free that she was told everyone takes. She wasn't nervous in the least. She had swum so many 200 freestyle races over the past eight years that she really didn't think it would be a challenge. She had no idea who her competition would be, but she knew that as always she would try to win the thing.

Her strategy would be the same as always. She knew that each lap gets slower especially when the swimmer has gone out too hard or does not have a high level of fitness.

The middle laps are the slowest, and most people save during this period to save the energy and speed to swim fast as the end of the race nears.

Ashley had been taught that the secret to swimming the 200 and the 400 was to even split the whole way through the race. She would try to swim the first 50 in about 35 seconds and then to hold 38 seconds for the last three 50's.

She was a strong swimmer and as such she often tried to negative split a race, meaning that the second half of her race would be faster than the first.

She changed into her suit, grabbed a towel and headed for the pool. When she arrived she was surprised to see 10 other swimmers and Coach Nancy. Some were in the water warming up. Others were standing around talking to each other. To her surprise the only once she saw that looked her age was Gina. She walked over and said hi to her and was greeted with a warm smile. Gina introduced her to a couple of others.

There was a real mix of swimmers, but it was clear to her that the boys outnumbered the girls. She guessed it was about 4 girls to 6 or 8 boys. To her surprise a few of the boys looked much older. She guessed perhaps 17 or 18. She also guessed that she was the youngest one swimming.

Coach Nancy came over to her and said Hi and ask her if she was ready to do this. Ash just smiled and nodded her head in the affirmative.

OK Swimmers, please line up, Coach Nancy said. Each swimmer took a lane. Ashley was in one of the middle lanes. Coach Nancy then addressed the group. I want you all to meet Ashley Jamison. Ashley is in lane 5. Ashley is the newest member of our team and this will be her 200 trial. You have all done this before so you know what it is about. When the gun goes off I want you to give me the best 200 you can muster. Does anyone have any questions?

Coach Nancy then said, swimmers take your mark. Ashley moved into position. She had done this many times before so she felt very comfortable.

Swimmers set. Then Coach Nancy fired the start gun and the group dove into the pool. Ashley was off the blocks quickly and kept her pace at a higher level through the first lap. She could see the swimmers on her left and right but not those on the outside. It was clear to her that after the first lap the swimmers on either side of her were not going to be her competition. She backed off a bit on lap two and three but felt that she was moving at about the 38 second pace she wanted.

She felt good making the turn into lap four and did so with extra acceleration. She then kicked it in gear and headed for the finish with the goal to touch the wall before anyone else had. She touched the wall but only to find she was third. Two of the older boys had finished fractions of a second before her.

She shook hands with the girl on one side and the guy on the other. She took her goggles off and hopped up and out of the pool. Coach Nancy was there to greet her. Well Ash, that was some kind of race. Ash just nodded her head but didn't say anything. Inside she was really pissed that she had lost and particularly to a boy. Coach Nancy said, you did an excellent job and your strategy was perfect.

I have watched you race so many times that I will say that you did not surprise or disappoint me. You will be placed in our highest swimming group and will begin your training with that group tomorrow. Thanks, Ash said, before she headed for the locker room.

Ash, before you go I want to ask you something. I don't know you well yet but you seem to be disappointed with your finish. Yeh, I didn't win. Ash, you were only beaten by two boys. One is 18 and the other 17. They have been swimming with us since they were your age and neither of them beat you by more than 1/2 of a second. Your performance was simply over the top. You are 11 years old and have a long way to go. Get your chin up girl, you just accomplished what many in our program would train a lifetime for.

Ash looked at her, nodded her head, and headed for the locker room.

Ash was quiet when she arrived home. Hi Ash, her Mom said. Hi Mom. How was your swimming placement race? It went OK Ash said. You seem a bit down. Did something happen? Not really, other than I lost to two boys. Really, and how old were these boys? One was 18 and the other one was 17. And, how much did you lose to them by? 1/2 of a second. Well, if I am correct, you are still 11 years old, and that is a significant difference in age and experience.

Yes, that's what Coach Nancy said. She said my performance was over the top but you know, Mom, I'm not used to losing and I really don't like it. I particularly don't like losing to men.

Ashley, you are an exceptional athlete. You do the best you can do with every event you participate in. You will reach the top of the heap in this program like you have in every other program you have participated in. Just work hard, keep you noise to the grindstone, and the results you want will always come.

Now go get ready for dinner. Dad should walk in the door at any moment. OK Mom, I'm going to grab a quick shower.

A year went by when one evening Ash went to her Mother and said, Mom, can I talk to you alone? Sure, Sarah said, let's go sit in the family room. Dad isn't home yet and John is involved in some school activity at Grant.

They went into the family room and sat down. What's on your mind? Well, I'm a bit worried, and since you are my Mom, and a nurse, I thought I would tell you what I'm worried about. Go ahead, I'm listening. Well the other day I had this bump appear below each of my boobs. All my friends call them boobs. I'm not sure what the right term is. Boys seem to call them tits and some girls call them breasts but in any event I don't have them yet but these two bumps came out of nowhere and they hurt. Let me see them Ash. She lifted her blouse and her Mom looked at them and then touched them. They were nickel sized lumps under both nipples.

Well, my dear, these are nothing to worry about. They are called Breast buds, and they are typical in girls of your age They are the beginning visible evidence of puberty which means that your body is changing from being a small girl to that of a young woman. My guess is that you also are starting to grow

31

hair in your pubic area. Now that you mention it, Mom, that is happening as well.

Well Ash your body is telling you that you are growing up. You may find that you will begin to gain some weight, but in your case, with all of your athletics, that will probably be minimal.

You will soon face what lot of girls don't understand and that is called Menstruation. Girls often have many misconceptions and unfounded fears about menstruation. My guess is you will begin to experience this in about two years.

Menstruation is a normal body function in young and middle age women. It is all related to our opportunity to give birth in the future. When you're older, you'll have the opportunity to become a mother, if you decide to. Even though that's a long time from now, your body is already getting itself ready for the day when you choose to have a baby.

Your breast bumps signal to us that you are entering puberty. Once your body reaches the age where if feels that menstruation should begin each month one of your two ovaries will release a ripened egg inside you. When the time comes that you want to get pregnant and you have met the man that you want to have children with you will have sex and the man will release sperm in you which will unite with the egg. A women becomes pregnant when that takes place and the fertilized egg attaches itself to the inner lining of the uterus, which is called the womb. This is where the baby lives while it's growing and waiting to be born.

Obviously you are a long ways from that, but the point of my story is to set your mind at ease. We all go through it and it is always better to understand what is going on with your body rather than worrying about things you don't need to worry about. When the time comes for your period to begin I will help you understand how to deal with it on a monthly basis.

In the mean time you can expect your boobs as you call

them to begin to grow. Once that happens we will buy you a training bra and go from there.

Thanks Mom. I was really worried. Happy to help Ash. I'm glad you ask me for my help. Now I'm going to go get dinner going.

TWO YEARS LATER

Hello, You have reached the Jamison residence. This is Sarah speaking. Hi Sarah, it's Nancy Ages. Hi Nancy. What brings you to call me? Pleased don't tell me that my beautiful petite daughter has done something that was not lady like?

No, quite the opposite. First I'm not sure anyone would call your daughter petite. Some might say she has a chance at beautiful but all would agree that you have one hell of an athlete on your hands.

Thanks Nancy. What can I do for you?. Well I wanted you to know that now that Ash is about to start high school that she has a lot of folks following her swimming progress. As you know she is undefeated in her last 10 races, and at this point her competition is no longer on a local level but has now risen to a national level.

She continues to break every barrier that is put in front of her. Hey Nancy, whatever happened to the boys she lost to in the 200 two years ago when she started the program?

Oh, the 18 year old was a young man by the name of Peter Merchant. Peter graduated from Cleveland High School shortly after that race and now is swimming for UCLA at the collegiate level. The other young man who beat Ash that day was Josh Peterson. Josh remained in our program until the end of last year and now swims competitively for Stanford. I should point out that before Josh left us he lost to Ashley the last three times he swam against her. I'm sure it was not good for his ego, but I know that deep down Ashley had some real satisfaction. She may not reveal it on the outside but deep within that girl is a drive and competitiveness that is almost immeasurable.

In any event, the reason I called was I wanted you and your husband to know that lots of people are following Ashley and her success. I include in that group the senior recruiting staff for the US Olympic team, coaches from every major university in the country, and a few specialty programs that are only open to the very elite on an invitation basis only.

I don't think anything will come to the surface for awhile but by the time Ash is a sophomore at Grant she is going to be recruited by a whole bunch of different folks,

i think at some point you and your husband should let her know what she can expect in the next few years. I would suggest that you have the conversation with her early enough so she has time to sort out what direction she wants to move in. This is just meant to be a heads up.

Thanks Nancy, I will put it on my list of the things I need to discuss with Jim. Appreciate the call.

CHAPTER 5

COMMING OF AGE

John finished Grant High School and graduated with a 3.7 accumulative grade point average. While it was not at the top of the class, it was a solid enough performance to allow him the opportunity to apply to a number of different Universities. He chose to stay on the West Coast and picked the University of California at Santa Barbara as his choice and was accepted. Sarah and Jim had no idea why he had settled on that school, but both thought it might have something to do with the beach and that worried them a bit about his future studies.

At the same time, Ashley began her high school program at Grant High School.

Grant opened in September of 1924 with 1,191 students. Many of the schools in the Portland Public School District that were built between 1908 and 1932 were designed by architects Floyd Naramore and George Jones. However, so many schools were being built in Portland in the early 1920's, that the district had to hire another architectural firm to design Grant High School. It was designed in the Classical Revival style by architects Knighton and Howell. In November 1923, the bricklayers working on building Grant went on strike. They were very frustrated that the district tried to cut costs by using maintenance workers to lay bricks.

A two year modernization project of Grant High School,

funded by a $482 million bond measure in 2012, began in June of 2017. The interior of the building was gutted and was completely rebuilt. The project included a new three story common area, a new gymnasium, seismic retrofitting, and additional classroom space.

This is the facility that welcomed Ashley with open arms.

In the summer prior to beginning at Grant, Jim and Sarah decided to talk with Ash about what they believed she would face in the not too distant future.

It was a beautiful summer night in Portland. Jim and Sarah were sitting outside on their back patio with a great glass of Oregon Pinot Gris talking about their day when the door opened and Ashley stepped out.

Hi you two. I'm beat. Gymnastics was over the top today, and my muscles feel like they can't move any more. I made some fresh lemonade and it's in the refrigerator if you want to have a glass and join us.

Wow, thanks Mom. I think I will do that.

Ashley was the epitome of a well bred athlete. She was now 5'8'" tall. She was 140 pounds of pure muscle sitting on a medium frame with a Body Mass Index that was made up of pure muscle. Her total body fat was 14%.

Ashley returned and sat down with her Mom and Dad. So, it is a beautiful evening, how was your day Dad? It was fine, no big issues to deal with, no court session and overall the kind of day I really like and don't get much of. How about you Mom? Well, today was baby day. I assisted at Oregon Health Sciences with four new babies. The good news is they all came out as they were suppose to and all are healthy. That means that four new families will wake up tomorrow with a responsibility they never dreamed they would have.

Babies, that is the last thing I would want at this point in my life, and frankly, I'm not sure if that will ever be in the cards for me. I have no idea where the future will take me, but I am going to make sure it is not to baby land until I am really ready for that to happen.

Hey Ash, that brings me to something I wanted to talk to you about. You wanted to talk to me about babies Dad? No, not at all. I did, however, want to talk to you briefly about your future. Last year Mom and I were contacted by Nancy Ages. Nancy called to give us a heads up regarding you. No, you didn't do anything wrong.

She wanted us to know that, given your swimming success, a lot of eyes were watching you, and she felt that by the time you were a sophomore in high school that those eyes would start letting you know of their interest in you.

Since your success has continued over the past year, we thought we would let you know what Nancy told us and let you be the judge of what happens should those interested start to approach you. Nancy mentioned the best swimming schools in the United States, the US Swim Team and a host of specialty programs that are geared toward developing the next Olympic Champions, These are the groups she thought might approach you.

Well, I'm not surprised as I have heard from Nancy and some around her that my swimming success could open a few doors for me that might otherwise be difficult to open.

I am not looking that far ahead but have made some decisions. Number one is I am not going to participate in any of the Grant athletic activities. Frankly, I'm just too busy with what I've got to handle, and I want to devote my school time to studying. I know I will miss lots of things by doing so, but I think it may be more fun for me to sit in the bleachers and root for the team.

If and when some folks contact me, we will as a family talk about it and hopefully come to agreement on what may be best for me. In the meantime, it is business as usual.

Pretty mature way to look at it, Ash. We will just wait and

see what shows up around the next corner. Now I need another glass of Pinot Gris.

Ashley entered Grant High School as a freshman. She was big for her age but still felt the pangs of being the lowest guy on the totem pool.

Her freshman and sophomore years were not eventful. She continued with her swimming and gymnastics training outside of school.

She did not play athletics for Grant High School. She enjoyed the activities which Grant provided as a student not as a participating athlete. She was a regular with her friends at the Friday night football games and also enjoyed the evening basketball games. Athletics that went on during the day like track and field and wrestling she rarely had an opportunity to see. Her social life was nothing to write home about.

She had a few dates here and there. Enjoyed and didn't enjoy a few kisses that were few and far between but managed to make sure no relationship of any significance developed. She simply didn't have time to develop much of a social life. When asked by a friend what were the kisses like, she simply said most were dry and not worth discussing, a couple were wet and sloppy, and I could have done without them.

By the end of her sophomore year Ash was very well developed and a very strong athlete. She was known throughout the high school as an athlete that was special and above the norm. Not many had seen her swim or work the high bar in gymnastics, but those that had seen her perform were so far beyond impressed they couldn't actually describe her abilities to friends. They just said she was unbelievable.

It was the summer between her sophomore and junior year in high school when Sarah picked up the phone call one afternoon. Hi Sarah, it's Nancy Ages. Oh Hi Nancy, how are you? I'm great and trust you and the family are doing well. We are, Nancy. Thank you. Between Ashley's athletics and John's studies at University of California Santa Barbara, we have been plenty busy.

Well, I'm glad to hear it. I'm calling today to tell you the wagons are circling regarding Ashley. In the past week I have received calls from Stanford, the University of Oregon and Washington and the University of Texas and Penn State University. They all are interested in one thing and that is talking to Ashley.

We talked a couple of years ago about this so this is not a surprise. The NCAA member schools have adopted rules to create an equitable recruiting environment that promotes student-athlete well being. The rules define who may recruit, when recruiting may occur and the conditions under which recruiting may be conducted.

The NCAA defines recruiting as any solicitation of prospective student athletes or their parents by an institutional staff member or by a representative of the institution's athletics interest for the purpose of securing a prospective student athlete's enrollment and ultimate participation in the institutions intercollegiate athletics program.

Sarah, there are contact periods, evaluation periods, and both quiet and dead periods.

We are about to enter an open period and you and Jim should expect, as should Ashley, to be contacted very soon by recruiters from the schools I mentioned and I'm sure more.

Early recruiting is becoming more common and in Ashley's case I believe that a number of these schools will be prepared to offer her a full scholarship now with the hope that she will sign a letter of intent and commit to that school.

Sarah, the new rules allow high school juniors to take official visits. Under the old rule, athletes needed to wait until their senior year to take an official visit. All of these schools will offer that opportunity to Ash. The top tier programs all want to start the recruiting process early with the goal to lock down their recruiting classes early. The schools that have contacted me are all top tier swimming schools and there is no question in my mind they want Ash to commit.

Well Nancy, what do you recommend we do from this point on? Well I would begin with a talk with Ash to let her know this is coming. I would also recommend that you all be great listeners, take the campus visits if offered, but do not commit to any of them until you have heard everyone's pitch.

Be particularly observant of the people involved and whether you and particularly Ash is comfortable with them.

I also want you and Ash to know that the US Swim Team coach is well aware of her and her unbelievable abilities. You will not hear from her. She will watch and see which collegiate program she ends up with and then the US coach will grab her from that team if the need occurs.

Sarah and Jim talked to Ash at dinner about the discussion Sarah had had with Coach Nancy. Ash just listened but didn't express any feeling one way or another. She had played her cards very close to the vest and not given either of her parents and idea what schools she might be interested in.

Just as Nancy had suggested, Sarah and Jim began to get calls at home and at the office from the recruiters representing the schools she had outlined. Many scheduled home visits and met with Jim, Sarah and Ashley in the evenings. All wanted Ash to visit their school and Sarah and Jim were able to spread the requests out over the first six months of her junior year.

Ash was very polite and very attentive in all of the meetings but did not reveal her feelings one way or the other either to the recruiting visitors or her parents.

During the summer Ash continued to train and to participate in national swim meets on a monthly basis. It should be noted, that she also continued to win over and over. Her room looked like a medal souvenir shop. Between ribbons, medals, trophies and other forms of recognition, there was enough hardware in her room to decorate her entire High School.

It was late in the summer when Nancy held her next inspiration session. As always her swimmers had no idea who or what would be presented, but all had become accustomed to the sessions making them feel good and ready to take on the world. This inspiration session was set for a Wednesday afternoon at 4 PM.

Ashley attended the session as always and was very surprised to see a uniformed Naval Officer at the front of the room when she arrived.

She could hardly take her eyes off him. He was one of the most attractive, well put together and handsome men she had ever seen. Ashley sat down on the bench with her fellow swimmers until Coach Nancy came into the room and introduced the man at the front of the room.

Good afternoon, Team. I would like to introduce you to Lt. Andrew Freemont. Andy is a United States Navy Seal and is here to present you with a presentation on how swimming helps protect our families and our country from those around the world who may want to harm our country.

Before you arrived, I asked Lt. Freemont if it would be OK to call him Andy and, as I expected, he said sure everyone else does. So if you have questions following the presentation just call him Andy and make sure you introduce yourself at the time you ask your question. OK Andy, they are all yours.

Thanks Nancy and Good Afternoon to all of you. My name is Lieutenant Andrew Freemont, and I am a member of the the the United States Navy and a member of the Navy Seal Team.

The Navy's Sea, Air and Land forces-commonly known as SEALs, are expertly trained to deliver highly specialized, intensely challenging warfare capabilities that are beyond the means of standard military forces.

Our mission includes direct action warfare, special

reconnaissance, counterterrorism, and foreign internal defense. When there's nowhere else to turn, Navy SEAL's achieve the impossible through critical thinking, sheer willpower and absolute dedication to their training, their missions, and their fellow Special operations team members.

You may wonder what in the heck is a Navy Seal Recruiting Officer doing talking to the members of Team Unify Swim Team. Well, as you can tell by our SEAL name, we spend a lot of time in the water. Unlike you, however, we don't have neat, well lit lanes to swim in. In fact there are those who say that some of the places we go to swim should be off limits to the human race.

Ashley and the members of her team all laughed. You also may be wondering why I am talking to a group of you where more than 50% are women. Up until January of 2016 the Navy Seals were made up solely of all men. Women simply were not allowed to serve in combat roles, including special operations forces.

Thank God that is now behind us and women are welcomed members of the SEAL team. There is only one catch. Women do not get any break. They must compete and earn their way on to the team. There are no special favors that their sex can provide, and I should add the training is not for the faint of heart; in fact it is one of the hardest programs every created to pass and complete fully. I will say this, last year, for the first time, two women passed the qualification test but neither was able to complete the program. We know that the first women Seal is out there. We just don't know when or where she will appear.

Today, I want to show you a film that will give you a flavor of what it is like to be a Navy SEAL. Once the film is over I think you will have a much better understanding of what we are all about and why I am standing here in front of a bunch of elite swimmers. Nancy, can we roll the firm?

The recruiting film rolled for 20 minutes. No one in the

room said a word. The film highlighted special operation forces working in the water, on land, and at sea. The challenges shown are beyond what normal human beings could imagine. The vast majority of swimmers present could not imagine a choice like the Navy Seals vs. the United States Olympic Swim Team.

That was with one exception. Ashley said nothing, but she looked at the film and the goals of the program as the ultimate challenge facing any SEAL candidate. She was blown away, and besides the challenge, she could not stop looking at Lt. Andrew Freemont.

After the film was completed, Lt. Freemont described the challenge that would face any potential candidate. He said that the seal program could be accessed either from an enlisted prospect or by attending the US Naval Academy like he did. He also described the challenge and reiterated again that no women had ever accomplished the successful completion of the program.

Andy then went on to say that the average member of the United States Navy's Sea, Air, Land teams (SEALs) spends over a year in a series of formal training environments before being awarded the Special Warfare Operator Naval Rating and the Navy Enlisted Classification Combatant Swimmer or, in the case of commissioned naval officers, the designation 1600 Naval Special Warfare (SEAL) Officer. He said that all Navy SEALs must attend and graduate from their rating's four week "A" School known as Basic Underwater Demolition/ SEAL(BUDS) school, a basic parachutist course and then the 26 week SEAL Qualification Training program.

Andy added that all sailors entering the SEAL training pipeline with a medical rating or those chosen by Naval Special Warfare Command must also attend the 6 month Advanced Medical Training Course and subsequently earn the Naval Special Warfare Medic before joining an operational Team.

He closed by saying that once outside the formal schooling environment, SEALs entering a new Team at the beginning of an operational rotation can expect 18 months of training interspersed with leave and other time off before each 6 month deployment.

Andy opened the discussion for questions. A few of the boys asked questions but none of the girls did so.

After the session was over and everyone was starting to leave Ashley went up to Andy and said, if one wants to move in this direction as an officer what is the best approach to take.

Hi, I'm Andy and who are you? I'm Ashley. Well Ashley, I would recommend that you go the route I did which is to apply to the US Naval Academy as a start. If you are successful with that, then the path will be outlined for you at the academy.

Thanks, Andy, I really enjoyed the program.

CHAPTER 6

SETTING THE PLAN

It was September of her Junior year. Ashley and her parents had spent the last couple of months during the summer visiting schools that were very interested in having her swim for them. To her surprise, two schools also expressed interest in her joining their gymnastic teams. Three schools had already given her, along with her parents, assurances that if Ashley were to pick them that she would be admitted on a full athletic scholarship.

Throughout the process Ash had been a good listener and she was very polite to all she met. She, however, did not reveal to anyone, including her parents, what preference she might have.

It was a Tuesday morning and her appointment was for 10AM. She had made the appointment on her own, and she did not tell anyone that she was going to meet with the college counselor or what the nature of the appointment was.

Good Morning, you must be Ashley Jamison. I am, Mrs. Atherton, and it is very nice to meet you. Ashley, please have a seat and let me know what I can do to be of assistance to you.

Thank you. Would you like some water? No I'm fine, thank you. Well Ashley, I must say that my curiosity is up. I can tell you of all of the students in this school no one has had a brighter spot light on them than you. It seems like every other day I have had another request for your grades, test scores and general background. I'm not sure what you do outside of school hours Ashley, but whatever it is it has caught the eye of every major college recruiter in the United States.

Yes, my parents and I are aware that my athletic abilities have peaked the interest of a number of schools. In fact, I don't think it is a secret to say that i have already been offered a number of athletic scholarships in both swimming and gymnastics.

Well then, with all of that success what can I do to help you?. Well, I would like some advise and direction. As I indicated, I have a number of opportunities in front of me and will need to make a decision in the next two years, but one opportunity I would like to explore has not been presented to me.

Oh really, and what could that be? I would like to know what the process and requirements are to enter the United States Naval Academy.

Well that is a very interesting question and one that I am not often asked. As you know, if you are selected to attend Annapolis and you graduate, you will face a minimum of four years in the regular Navy as an officer.

Yes, I am aware of that obligation. I would like to apply and see if I can make it so I can compare the opportunity at the Naval Academy with the others that have been presented to me.

Well, I have to tell you Ashley, you are one of a kind. In my career thus far, I have never had a student with offers of a full ride facing them ask about a military academy where the end result is military service, possible danger and just to be admitted requires a massive amount of hard work. Obviously you have thought this through, and as such, I would be happy to help guide you down the road with your application.

Let me pull a file for you and that should help us move forward. Thanks Mrs. Atherton. Let me take a look here first.

Well the good news is that you are beginning your Junior

year at Grant and this is the best time to begin the application process. Let's see what this says.

Eligibility

You are eligible to apply for the United States Naval Academy if you meet the following criteria:

- A United States Citizen
- ages 17 to 23
- Unmarried
- Not pregnant and no dependents.
- Have a valid Social Security Number

Well, I fit those categories so far.

It says that the next step is to complete the formal application. I will see if I can get hold of one later today. Have you talked to your Mom and Dad about this?

No, but I had planned to as soon as I met with you. I will talk with them tonight and pick up the formal application from you tomorrow, if that is OK. It's fine with me. I should have it here for you tomorrow morning.

Hi Mom. How was your day Ash? It was great. Is Dad going to be home for dinner? Yes. We are having homemade meatloaf with a dressing that is made with spicy catsup. That sounds great. I think I will see if I can get some of my homework done before dinner. Let me know when you want me at the table.

Ash, dinner is ready. Hi Dad, how was your day?. Not bad and yours? Kind of more of the same. I think my junior year is going to be pretty easy. The classes I have are all the ones I'm interested in, and frankly, I'm not finding any of them very hard.

Mom, this meat loaf is great. The catsup topping is really spicy and I like it a lot.

As dinner was coming to an end Ashley spoke up. I wanted to talk to both of you about something. Let me guess Ash. You have made a decision on which school is going to get you? Not quite Dad. I have made a decision of sorts but it isn't regarding any of the schools we have visited or any of those who have offered us the scholarship to attend. Then what is it? Sarah asked.

Well this is probably going to surprise you both, but I visited with the school counselor today. Her name is Mrs. Atherton and she was very nice. She knew of me, and I have never met her before. Apparently the schools that are interested in me need to go through her to get my records etc and like you she thought I might be coming to her for an opinion on one of those who have indicated an interest in me.

I guess I surprised her just like I am about to surprise you. I have asked her to help me prepare the application to attend the United States Naval Academy.

Jim and Sarah didn't say anything for a moment. They were both in shock. Jim spoke first. Well, as you guessed, this is a real surprise to me and I'm sure to your Mom as well. If you apply to the Naval Academy and accept their appointment, I believe it comes with a minimum obligation of four years duty following graduation. Did you know that? Yes, I have spent some time thinking about this and researching how to go about it.

Ash, I need to ask you something. We have now visited some of the very best educational institutions in the United States and some of the very best swimming programs ever created. Not only have you been offered the opportunity to attend at their expense, but the door is open to you should you decide to swim for the United States and perhaps even go on to the Olympics. If you choose to go the military route you would in all probability forgo some of these opportunities.

I know that Mom, but I have grown up thriving on challenges and I believe that thus far I have been able to meet most obstacles put in front of me. The opportunity to become a Naval Officer and perhaps join one of the most elite fighting teams in the world is a challenge that I think might await me.

Ash, your Mom and I made a decision a long time ago to let

you make your own decisions and, once made, we have done everything we can to support your decisions and help you to be as successful as you can.

Should you choose to go this route you will be entering a world that neither of us know anything about. As you know when we graduated from College there was no war going on and I was free to choose the path I wanted, which was law school and a career as an environmental lawyer.

There is no war going on today but nevertheless the military is not only a challenge but a risky and dangerous venture if you should be stationed in the wrong place in the world. Are you ready to accept those risks if you are selected? Yes Dad. I have thought this through.

There is no guarantee that I can make it into the Academy but it is something I would like to try to do and hope that you and mom will support me as I undertake this venture into the unknown. Well Hon, we love you and will support you as we always have. I assume that this is something you do not want to share with anyone until you know if you have been accepted or not. Yes. I don't want to eliminate any opportunity just because I want to try this avenue. Who knows, I may not make it and if not then I can choose from many of the opportunities that have already been presented.

Ashley thanked her Mom and Dad for understanding, and then asked to be excused and headed to her room to continue to study. Jim and Sarah just looked at each other but didn't say anything. Jim shook his head in disbelief and Sarah just began to pick up the dishes. Neither could believe what they had just heard.

Ashley thought to herself, well I'm sure they are in shock but it didn't go that badly. For sure I am not going to mention anything about the SEALs that will come later if the situation allows, she thought. She competed her studies and fell into bed, quickly to sleep.

The next day she contacted the office to see if she could get a second appointment with Mrs. Atherton. Yes, Ashley, Mrs. Atherton can see you at 2PM. Will that work with your schedule? Yes, I have my study period between 2 and 3 so that will work fine.

At 2PM Ashley arrived at the office and was immediately shown into Mrs. Atherton's office. Hi Ashley, were you able to talk to your parents about the Naval Academy option? Yes Mrs. Atherton. I talked to them about it last night. And how did it go? Well, to tell the truth, I'm not sure. I know both of my parents were planning on me going to a great Division I school in either swimming or gymnastics, with perhaps the opportunity to make the US team in one or the other. This option came right out of the blue, so to speak, and I'm sure that both of them are still a little bit in shock.

Nevertheless, my parents have always been my best supporters and allow me to make my own decisions. So we are good to move forward with the application but as you may imagine we do not want anyone to know about this option. If it doesn't come true then I don't want to risk losing one of the opportunities that have been presented.

Were you able to get a copy of the formal application? I was, and have one for you to take with you and complete. I was also able to better understand the process that is required for entry. Can you give me an overview, Mrs. Atherton?

Yes. Here is what I found. Let's take it in steps.

Step 1 We accomplished yesterday. You are eligible to apply

Step 2 This is the completion of the Preliminary Application. This is what I have for you today. You must complete this to become an official candidate for the class that begins two years from now. Upon completion of your preliminary application, Admissions will review it to determine your competitiveness for receiving a candidate number.

Receipt of a candidate number will then indicate your designation as an Official Candidate for admission. Within your candidate letter, there will be important instructions on how to proceed with completing your official application. You will need the following information to complete the preliminary application.

1. Your Social Security Number
2. Your High School Educational Testing Service (ETS) Code, which I will provide to you.
3. Your High School Class Rank. I will also produce this once you have completed your junior year.
4. Your Congressional State and District
5. Your full Zip code
6. Your SAT, ACT or PSAT scores. Once you have taken the tests I will also provide that information.

So as you can see, this year will be one of completing the testing and class rank that is needed for the formal application. My guess is that we will be ready to send in your formal application at the end of this year. **This is Step 4.**

I have also learned a few things that you should put in the back of your mind.

1. The average GPA of those accepted to the Academy is 3.94
2. The average SAT score is 1410 with 690 in math and 720 in reading
3. The average ACT Score is 31

So, the bar is high. Based on your current GPA these marks are not out of the question, but they are still high and will require that you work very hard to keep your scores in the ball park.

I also learned that although athletic skill is very important it may only weigh in for about 30% of the total. Looks like 70% is based on academics.

It is recommended that once we submit your formal nomination that we move ahead with Step 5.

Step 5 requires that we obtain a nomination from an official source, which normally includes US Representatives or the US Senator that represents your congressional district or state. Finally, I understand the Vice President of the United States must approve the Senator's recommendation. Applying for a nomination is similar to applying for a school. Being personally acquainted with the nominator is not required, but we are encouraged to explore all contacts that could lead to this step recommendation.

They recommend that we submit your letter of application for nominations immediately after you complete your preliminary application.

Many nomination notifications do not go out until early to mid January and the deadline for the USNA application is January 31. The person that nominates you will notify us of your nomination. You do not need to notify the Academy.

I'm also told that Senators and Congressman have their own respective applications which I'm sure we will get when we identify who might be available to help.

Step 6 is very easy and I will handle it. It just requires that we send the Academy a copy of your academic transcripts.

Step 7. Is a full medical examination which I'm told they will schedule for us if we get to that point.

Step 8. This is the easiest step in the process. It is the Candidate Fitness Assessment which I reviewed and you can do with your eyes shut.

Step 9. Is the final interview. This is done with one or two members of the Blue and Gold Group. These are all former graduates or people who are very close to the admission process.

So Ashley, if you choose to move forward with this alternative it will not be easy. Based on everything I have learned about you, I am sure you are up to the challenge, but it won't come easy. If you decide to move ahead as desired, I would talk to your parents and see if they may have contacts to get us going with the nomination process.

Let me know how you are progressing. Thanks, Mrs. Atherton. This is very helpful. I put it down in writing for you, Ashley, so you can take it home to discuss with your parents.

CHAPTER 7

A CHALLENGEING ACADEMIC YEAR

Ashley took the information home that Mrs. Atherton had given her. She asked her Mom and Dad if they could sit down with her after dinner and go over the requirements, which they did.

They had an extensive family discussion but out of it came two items that would prove to be beneficial to Ashley. They decided to enroll her in an SAT prep program and her Dad indicated that he believed through his firm that he could make the formal contacts to get the personal recommendation going from the appropriate State Official.

The year zipped by. Ashley continued with her swimming and gymnastics and continued to win just about every meet she entered. She worked hard on her grades and made sure that for the most part they were A's. A B creped in from time to time but not enough to change her GPA.

She took the prep course for the SAT's and by the time the test was administered she felt she was in good shape to take it.

It so happened that one of the current US Senators from Oregon was a woman by the name of Beverley Ames. Her family owned Ames vineyards in Dundee, Oregon and her family was represented by Jim's law firm. It only took a couple of calls for Jim to get an appointment with her, and the meeting took place in May shortly before the school term ended. Jim thought it would be best if he took Ashley with him and that the Senator would have an opportunity to meet her and hear why she was interested in the Naval Academy. Frankly, Jim was really interested in hearing the answer to that question as well.

Jim briefed Ashley on the date and time for the meeting and set up a lunch in Portland for the three to meet. Ashley told Coach Nancy about the meeting and, unbeknownst to Ashley and her Dad, Coach Nancy had put together a summary of Ashley's major swimming successes and sent it to Senator Ames by mail. She also made it clear in her cover letter that Ashley had already been offered five full scholarships, three in swimming and two in gymnastics, and they were all to what many would say were the best schools in the United States.

Coach Nancy also left her number should the Senator desire any additional information. It wasn't long after she sent the letter to Senator Ames that Nancy received a call from the Senator's office.

Hello, this is Nancy Ages. Nancy, this is John James, and I am one of the assistants to Senator Ames. The Senator would like to speak with you, and I wondered if this might be an acceptable time to have that conversation.

Sure John, no problem. Please hold on for the Senator. Hello Nancy, this is Beverley Ames. I wanted to thank you for your letter regarding Ashley Jamison. I am due to have lunch with Ashley and her Dad next week and thought I would get a little bit more background on her before we have the lunch.

No problem Senator. I'm happy to talk about Ash and answer any questions you may have.

Thanks. Well first, I should say that it is my understanding that she would like to make application to the United States Naval Academy. Based on your letter to me and the success she has had, I guess the real question is why?

I don't really know the answer to that, Senator. Ashley is

one special kid. She is one of the most driven, mature and focused swimmers I have ever had the opportunity to coach. She is just about to finish her junior year in high school, and she has full ride offers to Stanford, UCLA, and the University of Washington in swimming and to Penn State University, and the University of Texas in gymnastics. Most kids I have met would give their right arm just to be considered for admission to one of those schools.

My guess is the Naval Academy presents to her a challenge that she feels would be worth taking on. She loves a challenge and won't back away from it. I don't know in this case if it is the challenge to get in or the challenges that await her after she receives a commission.

Ashley is like a fish in water. Perhaps the Navy and the sea have something to do with it. She just doesn't talk about it but clearly wants to take it on. I know that both she and her parents have not talked to many about her exploring this option as she doesn't want to risk losing the birds in the hand that she currently has.

The other thing I should mention to you Senator is I am aware that about 70% of what the selection boards consider on candidates for the Academy are based on academic performance and perhaps 30% on athletic abilities. All I can say is that if the Naval Academy were to land her, they would be getting one of the best young female athletes in this country. This woman has the potential to represent the United States of America at the highest level of competition, including the Olympics.

Well, thank you, Nancy. This has been a most beneficial phone call. I am due to have lunch with Ashley and her Dad in two days and am now really looking forward to meeting her. I appreciate your time. No problem, Senator. Thanks for calling.

Good Morning, this is Senator Ames office, Jackie speaking. Hi Jackie, my name is Jim Jamison and my daughter Ashley and I are scheduled to have lunch with the Senator the day after tomorrow. Would you please let her know that I have made a reservation at the Byways Cafe for us at 12 noon. The Byways Cafe is located at 1212 NW Glisan. Thanks for calling, Mr. Jamison. I have the lunch down on my calendar and we know the Byways Cafe. She will meet you both there at 12 noon. Thanks very much.

That night at dinner, Jim said to Ashley, Ash, we have our lunch scheduled the day after tomorrow with Senator Ames. I made a reservation for us at the Byways Cafe. Do you know the restaurant? No Dad, never heard of it. Well I hope you like it. It has a good reputation.

I will be home early and pick you up here at 11:15 if that is OK. No problem Dad, I have rearranged my schedule so I'm free that day from 11AM on.

How do you want to handle the conversation at lunch? Well, it's your show. I think we should see how the Senator wants to start the conversation and once that happens you're on your own. This is your interview, so I will be just along for the ride and the one to pay the bill.

Dad, does the Senator know anything about me? I'm not sure but my guess she has done her research and knows more about you than you might imagine. In any event we will see.

Any thoughts on what I should wear? Nope, just be yourself. This is about being you and not someone that you think someone wants you to be. Got it. I'm looking forward to it. Mom, this salmon is delicious. Thanks dear. I coated it with an Asian sauce that has light soy. browns sugar, and sesame oil in it.

I'll second that Sarah, and this Oregon Pinot Gris that you picked to go with it is perfect.

TWO DAYS LATER
12 NOON BYWAYS CAFE

Jim and Ashley were standing outside the Byways Cafe at noon when a black Mercedes pulled up in front and a short, attractive women emerged from the back seat. She said something to the driver and then exited the car.

She saw Jim and Ashley immediately and walked over to them extending her had. Hi, I'm Beverley Ames. You must be Ashley and this must be your Dad, Jim.

Yes, it is a pleasure to meet you Senator, Ashley said. Jim then said, let's go in. Our table is ready.

The table that Jim had reserved was in a back corner of the room where they had more privacy than they would have had, had they been seated in the open area.

As they walked to their table, it was clear they were with someone who was well known. Heads turned and you could hear a low noise of voices that were all saying something like, "That's Senator Ames". They ignored it and went to their table. Once there, their waiter ask them what they would like to drink. Jim and the Senator said Ice Tea please and Ashley said I will just have water.

Ashley at 5'9" tall dwarfed the Senator, but it didn't seem to have any impact on the Senator. It was clear she was used to dealing with people of all shapes and sizes and didn't pay much attention to the physical side of those she met. It was clear she spent most of her time listening to what they had to say.

Well Ashley, this lunch is about you. I'm told that you would like a recommendation to attend the United States Naval Academy. Is that so? Yes, Senator. In order to obtain admission I must have a recommendation from a Government representative, either a congressman or a senator. My Dad was able to set up this lunch through his business contacts, and I am most appreciative of the opportunity to get to meet and speak with you.

Tell me why you want to attend the Naval Academy. In today's world many young people don't want much to do with the military service, and it is my understanding that if you are accepted it requires at a minimum a four year obligation.

Yes, I am well aware of that. To answer your question, I like challenges, and I believe that this opportunity provides a challenge for me both mentally and physically. I am an athlete and have had opportunities presented to me but, in my view, none of them present the challenge that the military does.

I do understand that you have already been offered the opportunity to attend some of the best schools in the United States. Most kids I have met would give their right arm to have the opportunity to attend those schools. I also understand that one of them is Stanford University which, if I'm correct, stands out as one of the best in the United States.

You are correct Senator. I have a number of opportunities that have been presented, some for swimming and others for gymnastics.

None of them, however, require that I meet the standards that the Naval Academy presents.

Just then the waiter came to the table. Can I order you all some lunch? Jim looked at the others and said, have you had time to look at the menu? I'm fine, the Senator said, this is one of my favorite new lunch places in Portland. I would like the Crater Lake Cobb Salad please. I love this salad because it not only has greens, blu cheese, and chicken breast, but the bacon and croutons make it really good.

How about you Ashley? I would like the Mt. Hood chicken salad. It sounds great with the chicken, dried cranberries, and toasted pecans.

And you Sir? Well, I'm not going to eat as healthy as these ladies. I will have the Pendleton Melt, with the BBQ sauce, grilled onions and Tillamook cheddar cheese.

Sounds good. I will be back with your food shortly.

How are you doing academically, Ashley? I have almost a 3.9 accumulative grade point average. I am due to take the SAT's very soon and feel I will do well on them. Mom and Dad have let me take a pre SAT course which I'm sure will be an advantage.

What about outside extra activities?. I don't have any. I don't even participate in any school activities at Grant High School. To be honest, I have swimming four days per week and the other three I am working on Gymnastics. I am now performing at a pretty high level in both and I just don't have time for anything else.

In fact there are many days when I ask if I can just keep up with the schedule that I have set for myself.

Their food arrived and everything looked great. For the next few minutes the talking seemed to give way to eating and everyone was very happy with what they had chosen.

As they got towards the end of the lunch, the Senator said to Ashley, "Ashley, tell me how you get along with others. You are participating in two sports at a high level but they are individual sports rather than team sports. How would you rate your ability to get along with others and work as a team?

Well, one of the things I am very proud of is that at the first of this year I received an award that is unlike any of the others I have received. I swim in a very competitive program called Team Unify and yes, Team Unify is made up of a bunch of men and women who all have their sights on the US Swim Team and the Olympics. However, once per year the members of the team vote for a member that in their eyes is the most supportive of the other members of the team and provides inspiration to all in order to maximize team and individual performance. This year I received that recognition, which I am very proud of.

Well, I see that the time is just moving by too fast and that I must now leave for another appointment. Jim, I want to thank you very much for the nice lunch and Ashley, it has been a real pleasure to get to meet and know you.

I want you both to know that I will write a letter of recommendation for you Ashley and I wish you the best of luck with the admission requirements. I have no doubt that the Academy would be proud to have you as a new member of their team.

I must run now, so thanks again. She stood, shook hands with Jim and Ashley and headed out the restaurant. Her car was waiting outside, and she was obviously off to her next appointment.

Ashley and her Dad sat back down. Well, Dad, how do you think that went? I think you did great Hon. I wouldn't have changed anything you said or how you handled yourself. The fact that she has already told you that she is going to provide you with a recommendation means we accomplished what we wanted to with the lunch. Let's finish up and head home. I'm sure Mom wants to know what went on.

CHAPTER 8

THE PACKAGE IS PRESENTED

Hi Ash, how was your day? Mom, I am totally beat. I'm not sure i even want dinner tonight. I think it is all catching up with me. The last three months have been a killer. Between my practices, regular school, and these placement tests, my head seems to be just swimming in mush.

Well, I understand, but I think that you may get some additional energy from a letter that arrived today. I left it on your dresser in your room. Really, who is it from? The only thing I can tell you is the return address is to Senator Ames' office.

Ashley didn't say another word, she headed for her room and immediately opened the envelop. In the envelop was a copy of the formal letter of recommendation that the Senator had written for her admission to the Naval Academy. Ashley read the letter to herself out loud. The letter was addressed to whom it may concern and it was written on the Senator's personal stationary.

Beverley Ames

UNITED STATE SENATE
WASHINGTON D.C.

To whom it may concern,

My name is Beverley Ames and I am the Senior Senator from the State of Oregon. This letter of recommendation is written for a young woman who resides in our state and desires to attend the United States Naval Academy.

This letter of recommendation is written for Ms. Ashley Morgan Jamison. Ashley is currently a junior at Grant High School in Portland Oregon.

Her transcripts have been enclosed with her application and I am pleased to say that she has maintained a 3.9 grade point average and has recently taken the SAT examination and scored a total of 1480. Her math score was 700 and her reading was 780. From my perspective she has demonstrated the academic commitment needed to successfully complete the Naval Officer Curriculum.

What does not show in her academic performance is what she has accomplished outside of the classroom. Since the age of 3 Ashley has been involved in athletics and has now achieved the highest levels of performance in both Swimming and Gymnastics. In fact I feel it is important that the selection committee be aware that this young woman has received full ride offers from the following schools.

- Stanford University
- the University of California Los Angeles
- The University of Washington
- The University of Oregon

- Penn State University
- The University of Texas

It is important to note that in my experience most young athletes would give their right arm to receive a scholarship from any of these institutions. Three are interested in her for Gymnastics and three want her to swim for them.

I have also been told by her current swimming coach that the United States Swimming team has her at the top of their prospect list.

I mention this to the committee because in my experience it is highly unusual for an Athlete of this caliber to want to forgo the traditional division I athletic program in favor of a position in the United States Navy.

In closing I also want to add that Ashley is not just and individual competitor.

She is a team member in the highest standing with her current swimming program Team Unify and was recently voted the most outstanding team player. This award is presented annually to the swimmer who in the eyes of the other members of the team has done the most to encourage and motivate them to perform the best that they can be.

In closing I cannot remember a candidate that I have recommended that has the overall qualifications that Ms. Jamison possesses. I believe she will make an outstanding Naval Officer and one that the Navy will be most proud of.

Sincerely,
Beverley Ames

Ashley read the letter twice and just smiled. She folded the letter up and put it back in the envelop and walked out to the kitchen. Mom, I want you to read this.

Sarah opened the letter and read it twice. My God Ash, this

is an unbelievable recommendation. You should be so proud of your accomplishment and I can't wait to have your Dad read this when he gets home.

Yep Mom, I'm really pleased and will stop by the office tomorrow to make sure that my complete application is ready to go with the recommendation. I think I will go lay down for a couple of minutes but please grab me when it is time for dinner.

Ash, your Dad is home and dinner is on the table. Ashley woke up to the smell of Garlic French Bread. She was out of bed and to the dinner table in no time. Hey Dad, welcome home. Hi Ash, you seem pretty happy considering I'm used to you barely being able to hold your head up at the dinner table. Yes, I am very happy. Mom do you have the envelop? Yes, here it is. Ashley handed it to her Dad.

What do we have here? Ashley just smiled. Jim opened the envelop and read the recommendation twice. Well young lady you should be darn proud of yourself. When the selection committee reads this they would be out of their minds not to accept you. In fact I will go so far as to say if they for some reason don't accept your application they are real fools. Thanks Dad. Looks like our lunch with the Senator paid off.

Ashley, you may want to drop a personal note to the Senator to thank her for such a nice recommendation. That's a great idea Mom. I will do that in the morning.

Mom, I don't think spaghetti and meat balls ever tasted so good. Dad, would you pass me the hot garlic French bread. Here you go. Eat up, kid.

The next day, Ashley called the office and made an appointment with Mrs. Atherton. The appointment was for 2PM.

Ashley was on time as usual. Hi Mrs. Atherton. Hi Ashley, I bet I know what you are here to see me about. Well, I don't know but I did receive a copy of the recommendation letter that Senator Ames wrote and I wanted to make sure you received it.

I did and I must say it was one of the strongest letters of recommendation I have ever read. I have been assembling your submission package and should have it ready to go out today. I went through the check list again and think we have everything. By the way, congratulations on your SAT result. Those were very high scores and you should be very proud of them.

I also was able to complete your class rank by your academic performance. You rank number 3 in a class of 450 women.

Thanks Mrs. Atherton, that is good to know. What happens next? Well, I should get this package out today registered mail and I don't expect we will hear anything until the late fall.

I'm told sometimes they don't complete their decisions until January of your Senior Year. In your case, I would be surprised if we have to wait that long. My guess is we will hear sometime in the fall. If your application is accepted then we will be notified about a physical and the physical test, which should be no problem. OK Mrs. Atherton, now we wait. If I don't see you have a nice summer off. Thanks Ashley

It was the summer between her junior and senior year in high school. Ashley's schedule didn't change much. She still swam four days per week and worked out with her gymnastic team two and sometimes three days per week. Her accomplishments continued to add up with one victory after another.

Her social life, if there was much of one, was pretty week. She had a few dates here and there but she had no real interest in any of the boys who had asked her out. Most of her dates were generally fun with the exception of one. She was invited out for an evening to go to a movie with one of Grant High School's best athletes. His name was Milt Overmyer. Milt was a good athlete, not great in Ashley's assessment but good enough to be a "big man on campus". The evening went fine until Milt drove to the top of Mt. Tabor and parked the car. He clearly had making out on his mind and Ashley was OK with it to a point. It didn't take long however, before Milt decided to go exploring with his hands. Ashley played along with it for a couple of minutes and then ask him politely to stop. Milt had other ideas which Ashley was not going to put up with.

Ashley simply took his hand by the wrist and clamped down on it. Milt flinched and said, Ashley you're hurting me. Milt, I am going to tell you this just once.

You are a nice guy but your hands do not belong where you are trying to put them. I want you to understand this now because I am only going to say it once. If you don't stop I am going to break your wrist and, in fact, I might break both of them, which I can tell you is not going to be good for your basketball career.

Do you understand? Ashley, I'm not going to put up with this. We are out of here and headed home. He drove Ashley home and once there she simply opened the car door, closed it behind her, and walked directly toward her house. She didn't turn around, look back or say thank you. She had made her point and good old Milt had just been confronted by a women who was capable of tearing his head off and he knew it. It was the last time he would ever talk with her again which was fine with her.

During the summer, the senior recruiters from all of the interested schools continued to contact Ashley and her parents but with no luck. They received the standard and consistent message which was Ashley has not yet made a decision and will probably not do so until early in her Senior year.

In September she began her Senior year at Grant High School. She kept the application to the Naval Academy in the back of her mind, but she didn't let it interrupt her daily routine. She was well known at the school and had a very strong reputation as an elite athlete. She did not tell anyone about her run in over the summer with Milt Overmyer but she was certain he had told some of his friends that his date with her had not gone well. She doubted he had told them that if he continued on the path he was headed that she was going to break both of his wrists, but whatever he told his social pals it was enough that she could tell they all wanted to stay away from her, which was fine with her.

Ashley had never desired to be tops in the social class of high school students. In fact she could have cared about any of that. She was young, strong and focused, and those characteristics had been built over a life time.

She just didn't need to be part of a group or a social structure that others might have thought to be cool. She was her own person and always would be.

Her brother John had just graduated from UC Santa Barbara.

Her parents had suggested that his degree was in sun and surfing but with that they always smiled as John had done well in school, had a great GPA, and had applied for and been accepted to the University of Oregon Law School. John looked to be following in his father's footsteps and if he did so, Ashley knew he would make a great Lawyer.

It was late in November when Ashley received a note from the office that Mrs. Atherton wanted to see her She set up an appointment for 2PM during her free period.

As always, she was on time. The door opened and Mrs. Atherton walked out and extended her hand to her. Hey Ashley, it is great to see you. Please come in.

Ashley did as requested and sat down. Well, I'm sure you want to know what I wanted to see you about. Yes Mrs. Atherton. I don't think I have done anything that would warrant a trip to the office. Far from it my dear. I wanted you to see this, which arrived in the mail today.

Ashley opened the package and as she had hoped it was a letter from the Admissions Department at the Naval Academy indicating that her application had been received, reviewed and that she would be accepted. There were instruction materials on how to go about scheduling a physical and where to send the results. The same was true of the athletic test.

Congratulations Ashley, you have attained another one of your goals. May I ask you this? Now that you have this as another option, what choice do you intend to choose?

Well, tonight I will talk to my parents about it, but I can almost tell you for sure that I want to attend the Naval Academy and look forward to the challenges that it may bring.

Well, I'm not surprised and I wish you all the luck in the world. Thanks for all your help, Mrs. Atherton. I appreciate your efforts on my behalf.

CHAPTER 9

INTRODUCTION TO ANNOPOLIS

Ashley arrived home at the normal 6:30. She had completed her workout at the Y with Team Unify and she was pooped. Hi Mom, what's for dinner? Well tonight we are having filet of Sole. I am making a new dish for you and your Dad. It is called Potato-Crusted Sole with Spicy Ketchup. It is made with baked potato chips which cover the sole after we have applied an egg and flour coating. We do the sole over a very hot pan and it should come out with a very nice brown crust on it.

What is in the spicy catsup? It is pretty simple. It is made with Ketchup, Asian chili sauce, squeezed lime juice and fresh ginger. That sounds delicious Mom. I will grab a quick shower and be ready to go when Dad gets home.

Jim arrived home and shortly thereafter dinner was served. Well, Sarah said, how were your days as she looked at her daughter and husband. Mine was pretty normal. I spent the day in depositions and feel we made some additional progress on protecting our Oregon Coast. These idiots who want to drill off the coast have no concern if they cover Haystack rock with oil residue or not. It really makes me boil.

And how was your day Ash? Well, I would say that it was pretty good. She pulled out the folder that Mrs. Atherton had given her and gave it to her Mom to read first. Sarah just smiled and handed the folder to Jim.

Well Ash, her Dad said. Looks to me like you have attained another goal. Now you have to make a decision. I'm sure you have thought about this day for some time. Have you come to a conclusion on what path you are going to take to college?

Yep, you're right Dad, I have spent a lot of time thinking about this. I have decided that the challenges that the Naval Academy present are the challenges I want to take on as I look to the future. With the two of your support, I will notify them tomorrow of my acceptance.

Hon, as we have always said, you are the boss of your life and career, and if this is the path you choose to take, then Mom and Dad will support you every step of the way. Let us start by saying congratulations. Both Sarah and Jim gave her a big hug.

After dinner, Sarah and Jim retired to the family room. They poured themselves another glass of Oregon Pinot Noir and just stared out at the view in front of the fire. What is this wine Sarah? It is Four Graces Pinot from Dundee. Well it is high on my list. Thanks for pouring it.

Ashley went to her room. She tried to study a bit but was falling asleep so she put her PJ's on and went to bed. She fell asleep immediately with a big smile on her face.

Her Senior year just flew by. She passed her physical and Nancy Ages administered the physical fitness test which Ashley took after a full work out and wasn't even winded by any part of it.

In her final six months at Grant High School only one event stood out as one she would remember. It was her Senior Prom.

Ash had not developed any lasting relationships in high school She had a lot of friends but no boyfriend or, for that matter, no boy who she was remotely interested in.

One day after swimming practice she was sitting around talking to her pals on the team when one of the boys, Marty Freemont, ask her how her final few months at Grant were going. Ash said to him, pretty uneventful. My life right now is a bit boring with workouts, final studies and thoughts of the Naval Academy on my mind.

Are you going to go to your Senior Prom? Haven't thought about it and I guess not as I have no date and no one has asked. Would you mind if I asked you to go? Marty, that is really nice but you don't even go to High School any longer.

Why would a freshman at the University of Portland want to attend a High School Prom? Well, I think it would be fun and if for no other reason we seem to have a lot in common and I would enjoy spending an evening with you. Well then, I accept. Not because I don't have another offer but because I think it would be a fun evening together. Then it is set. When is it? It is at the beginning of May. I think it is May 3rd at the high school. I will get the date and time for sure and give it to you at practice tomorrow. Great. This sounds like fun.

Ashley got the date and time and gave it to Marty at the next practice. Great. Ash, I will plan to pick you up at your house at 7:30 on the 3rd of May. I look forward to a fun night together.

Ash, told her Mom that Marty had invited her to the Grant Senior Prom and she was very happy. Well that means we get to go dress shopping which is something that I rarely get to do with my athlete. This should be fun.

The year progressed and the prom date approached. Ashley and her Mom had made a number of trips to downtown Portland in search of a great dress for the event.

Well Mom, it's Saturday and we are running out of time to find a dress. Maybe today will be the day we find something. I think we will find the perfect dress soon Ashley. You have the perfect body to wear a long tight dress. You mean, I have a swimmer's body and as Coach Nancy says, we have no boobs! Well, that is probably true but I think the swimmers body makes finding the right dress easier than if you were overly top heavy.

They looked most of the day and then at Sac's Fifth Avenue they found one that on the rack looked like it might be the perfect dress. It was an Emerald Color long dress designed for a slim tall body. It had a high neck with an open back and the emerald color had glitter of some sort on it so it seemed to sparkle just hanging on the rack.

Ashley tried it on and it was a fitted gown that really fit. The criss cross high neckline was perfect with the thin over the shoulder straps.

The open back was sexy and the fitted bodice fit her athletic body perfectly. The material was stretch crinkle glitter fabric and fit her as though she was putting on a second skin. It conformed perfectly to what curves she had. The skirt had a small train. Ashley looked at herself in the mirror and the decision was made instantly. Problem solved.

The prom night came quickly. Marty picked her up at 7:30 and was blown away by her perfect looks. He was so used to seeing her in a racing swimming suit that he knew ever curve in her body, but he had never seen her dressed like this. He was blown away and very proud to be her date. The evening went well, the dance was great, they went to a late dinner alone and talked about the future and they ended the evening in front of her home. Ashley moved first and gave him a very long and slow kiss. I want to thank you for a great evening and like we talked at dinner I want to wish you the best of luck as you continue on into the future.

Thanks Ash, I will miss you and wish you the very best as you begin your military career. That ended what was in Ashley's mind a great and memorable night.

Oh, I almost forgot. Are you going to swim for the Naval Academy? Yes, this spring I received a call from the swimming coach at the US Naval Academy. His name is Mike Morgan. To make a long story short, he has been following my swimming for a number of years and was advised by the admissions department of my acceptance. He called to congratulate me and to inquire if I would be willing to swim for the academy. I told him that I would. He sent me a packet of information which

I have been through and believe I will begin working out with the team shortly after arrival. I need to get through the Plebe summer first but then things should settle down a bit.

UNITED STATES NAVAL ACCADAMY

The rest of her senior year passed quickly and before she knew it Ashley was boarding a plane in Portland with her Mom and Dad and heading for Annapolis, Maryland. They would drop her off and listen to a short orientation before leaving her and returning home.

Are you nervous? Her Dad asked her on the plane. Not really Dad. I have been looking forward to this for some time and know it will be a challenge but I'm ready for it. I've been doing some reading about the Academy and it has quite a history. What did you learn? Sara asked her.

Well the place was established in October of 1845. It is the second oldest of the Military academies. It is located on a 338 acre campus that was formally Fort Severn. It is located at the confluence of the Severn River and the Chesapeake Bay. The entire campus is known to insiders as the yard. It is a designated National Historic Landmark and is really designed to develop officers for both the Navy and the Marine Corp. The good news for both of you is that as long as I stay in school it is paid completely by the Government in exchange for an active duty service obligation upon graduation.

I have learned that the first 45 days, which is known as the Plebe Summer is not fun and is tough enough to wash some out of the program. I'm not concerned about that as I feel you have both given me a pretty thick skin.

How about the swimming program? I don't know much about it but it is considered a Division I swimming program so I should have some pretty significant completion. I will let you know more once I get started. Coach Nancy didn't seem to think that the program would be very difficult for me but only time will tell.

What did you pack? I followed the instruction sheet. I packed one simple bag with only recommended items.

They told me to wait until I am settled in and then if there are some things i could use to advise you and have you send them to me later in a care package.

I also read an interesting book on the plebe summer. It has some interesting things to read. The key things I read were the following: Drink a lot of water constantly to avoid dehydration and the onset of immune weakness. Rest whenever possible. They said a sailor's first rule of maintaining stamina for the sake of survival is don't run if you are allowed to walk, don't walk if allowed to ride, don't stand if allowed to sit, don't sit if allowed to lie down.

They also say that now it is heading toward late June and that they recommend that we have water bottles, sunscreen, umbrellas, and comfortable shoes. I guess Annapolis in late June is really hot and humid. I was given a copy of our schedule this weekend. Here is what it says we are going to do.

8 am. Colors Ceremony Tecumseh Court
7-830 am Band Concert outside Alumni Hall
1045 -1245 Picnic Lunch on Hospital Point with family and friends
145 -230 Band Concert Alumni Hall
230 -340 Parents briefing Alumni Hall
6PM Superintendent Welcome aboard and remarks
Oath of Office Ceremony Tecumseh Court followed by l5 minutes of free time to meet family on Stribling Walk

Once that is complete, I'm on my own and will not see you until the Plebe summer has ended. I think it lasts 45 days. I'm told I can make 3 minute phone calls a couple of times over the summer but that will be it.

The flight landed on time. Everything they read was right. It was super hot and very humid. They checked into their hotel and waited until the next day to start their last day together for a while.

The next day, Ashley took her small bag of clothes and she and her parents left the hotel and headed for the Naval Academy. Jim and Sarah left their stuff in the room as they would return after the day's events and fly home to Portland the next day.

It was 7 AM when they arrived. They had no problem parking and with their map headed to the Dry dock restaurant in Dahlgren Hall for breakfast. They were surprised to see the place packed at that early hour. It was clear to all that this Plebe class would be a full one with about 1200 Plebes about to begin their training at the Academy

The day went on as planned. Ashley was separated from her parents for a few hours while she was processed through various stations in Alumni Hall. This was the beginning of the transformation from civilians to fourth class midshipmen. Ashley was cycled through medical examinations, uniform fittings, equipment issue, haircuts and administrative processing. She was also introduced to the first class midshipmen, commissioned officers and senior enlisted personnel who would lead her summer training.

At 6PM they gathered at Tecumseh Court and listened to the Superintendent's welcome aboard and then watched as Ashley and the other Plebes were sworn in, in the Oath of Office Ceremony. The ceremony itself was very moving and both Jim and Sara had tears in their eyes before it was over. They walked with Ashley down to Tribling Walk and there they said their goodbyes.

During the day of Orientation, Ashley that been assigned a company letter which was Charlie (C) company. She had also been assigned a Platoon number and a squad number. There were about 80 midshipman in each company, 40 midshipman in each Platoon and 10 midshipman in each squad.

Ashley was assigned a dorm and was housed with two other women who were entering the Academy. Women were not new to the Naval Academy. In fact there have been women in attendance for more than 70 years. More than 5000 women have graduated and gone on to be highly successful military officers and civilians.

When she got to her room she met her two roommates. Niki Johnson who was from South Carolina and Norma Freed who was from Oklahoma. Ashley was tired and decided to not stay up and talk. There would be plenty of time to do that in the future. She thought that sleep was the best thing to get before her first day of Plebe Summer began so she said goodnight and crawled into her bunk bed. As she fell asleep she thought, ... tomorrow would be a very interesting day.

CHAPTER 10

PLEBE SUMMER BEGINS

Ashley and her roommates were up at 5:30 AM which was their designated wake up time. Ashley used the bathroom and dressed in the clothes she had been given the day before at registration. A uniform was really new to her but it was white so at least it would help with the heat. Norma dressed as well and the two twins headed for the morning formation and then on to breakfast.

During Orientation the day before, Ashley had learned some things that were new, but for the most part she had read about the items discussed. Ashley had read about the Reef Points Book. She was given a copy at orientation and was told that the book would serve as a thorough introduction to the Navy and the Naval Academy. It included the mission history and traditions. Ashley was also told that it was required that she memorize virtually all of the more than 1000 facts that were outlined in the book. The book was not small; it had 225 pages. She and her fellow Plebes were expected to know verbatim the mission, the administrative chain of command, and the first three general orders of Sentry and they were expected to know it by the end of the first week. The book spelled out the following:

MISSION OF THE UNITED STATES NAVAL ACADEMY

The mission of the United States Naval Academy is to develop Midshipmen morally, mentally, and physically and imbue them with the highest ideals of duty, honor and loyalty in order to graduate leaders who are dedicated to a career of Naval service and have potential for future development in mind and character to assume the highest responsibilities of command, citizenship, and government.

PURPOSE OF PLEBE SUMMER

The purpose of Plebe Summer is to lay the foundation of the Academy's four year professional development curriculum. At the conclusion of summer training, each Plebe class shall;

- Be indoctrinated in the traditions of the Naval Service and the Naval Academy
- Understand basic military skills and the meaning behind them
- Appreciate the high standards and obligations inherent in service as a Midshipmen and Naval Officer
- Be dedicated to excellence in a competitive atmosphere that fosters leadership, teamwork, character and a passion for winning.
- Appreciate the importance of mental, oral and physical toughness in all aspects of duty and service
- Be prepared to execute the rigorous academic year routine.

The Plebes were also told at orientation that the Academy can be divided into three equal parts. The first third of the USNMA experience is the six weeks of Plebe Summer. The second third is the Plebe Year, and the remaining third is the rest of your stay at the Naval Academy.

79

All Ashley could think about was OK then, bring on the Plebe year and let's get one third of this over with.

All of the new Plebe's were told that the Plebe summer would be demanding. That they would face a fast paced boot camp style orientation that would culminate after four years of preparation with each of them becoming a commissioned naval officer. They were told that physical and mental demands would be made upon their time and that would be never ending, but that everything they would experience would have a purpose; the development of leadership ability, motivation, moral strength, physical skills and stamina.

They were also told that these items were the attributes that would be found in any outstanding officer in the Navy.

The midshipman were told that as the summer progresses, they would rapidly assimilate basic skills in seamanship, navigation, and signaling.

Infantry drill shooting of 9mm pistols and M-16 rifles, sailing, and handling Yard patrol craft would all be part of the experience. They were also told that they would be exposed to a rigorous physical conditioning program, including calisthenics, running, pull ups, swimming, wrestling, and boxing. Team spirit and the desire to win would be developed along the way with completion in activities ranging from athletics to military dress parades and seamanship drills.

One vary important thing they were told is that they would receive instruction and indoctrination in the Brigade of Midshipman's Honor Concept.

The character development program stresses that each individual has the moral courage and the desire to do the right thing because it is right, not from a fear of punishment.

AND SO IT BEGAN

The six week training began on the first day. There was no time for TV or for that matter any access to TV, movies, the internet or music. Cell phone use was also limited. Ashley was permitted to make only three calls of three minutes each during her entire Plebe Summer.

The pressure and rigor of the summer was carefully designed to help plebes prepare for their first academic year at the Naval Academy and the four years of challenges that would await them.

The summer started to pass very slowly at first, and then it seemed to pick up pace as the routine set in.

Ashley's typical day became somewhat routine. She had always been programmed on a schedule and her typical summer day during the Plebe summer suited her just fine. Her typical schedule looked like this:

530 AM	Reveille
6-730 AM	Physical Education Program (PEP)
740-810	Room clean-up/uniform prep/rate review
810 -845	Morning meal formation/meal
1245- 6PM	Afternoon Training and class work
615 - 7PM	Evening meal formation/meal
7 - 8pm	Evening Training
9-10 pm	Mail call/letter writing, journal entries, study time
10 pm	Each night, before taps/lights out at 10 PM., the plebes sing the Naval Academy Alma Mater Blue and Gold

It was clear to Ashley that Physical Conditioning was a big part of Plebe Summer. She would spend 140 hours of physical education training during the summer including 27 sessions of PEP lasting one and a half hours, five days per week.

She was told that at the end of the summer she must be able to complete the PRT Test which includes a minimum of 20 push up for females, 6 curl ups, and a one and a half mile run in under l0 minutes

These requirements were no problem for Ashley, but her roommate Norma from South Carolina was having some real problems with the physical Conditioning part of the program. Ashley wasn't sure if it was the heat, humidity, or just lack of conditioning, but each week she seemed to get weaker and struggled more.

Finally, one night at dinner, Ashley talked to her on the way over and asked her how she was doing. Norma, what's up. You seem to be so tired and if I'm right you're getting a bit weaker as well. Yes Ash, you're right. I have been thinking a lot about this program and this summer.

I'm fine with the academic portions of the program, but I'm just not cut out for the physical side. In fact I had a talk with my Dad and Mom the other night and told them I would give it one more week, but if I continue to go downhill I'm going to drop out and enroll at Clemson University. I have been accepted there and I really like the school and I am the first to admit, I was not built for this type of physical exercise. Well, if I can help in any way I will. I know Ash, but it is clear, you are built to be an exceptional athlete and it shows. I'm not sure how many or if any of the boys can beat you in any of the athletic tests. Me on the other hand, I think I was born to be a Southern Girl and that may just be what I become.

Sure enough by the end of the next week Norma was gone. When Ashley and Nikki returned to their room after dinner, Norma's stuff had disappeared, and it was clear Norma had decided to bail out.

There was no note but both of them knew the real reason. I tell you, Ash, I understand what Norma was going through. The physical training side was just too much for her. I can deal with that, but I'm getting a bit tired of the rest of the bull shit we have to put up with.

For example I'm tired of being asked, what's up? and having to answer fidelity is up; bayonets are down.

Yesterday I was asked, how long I have been in the Navy, and I had to give the pat answer which was all me blooming life, sir, me mother was a mermaid, me father was King Neptune

Today I got the cow questions. How's the cow?

My answer was Sir, she walks, she talks, she's full of chalk. I have also about had it with my upper-class detailer. I know one thing. I will remember that guy for the rest of my life.

Nikki, I know what you're talking about, but it should get a bit easier each week now that we are in our routine.

Remember it is only 45 days that we have to put up with the Plebe Summer and then things should become a little more normal. Ash, I don't know how you do it. You are super strong and yet you put up with all of this bullshit like it is water coming off a duck's back. In any event, I don't quit and I won't quit but at least I have you to vent to from time to time. Thanks for being a good listener. No problem, Nikki.

It was clear that at the summer progressed it was designed to help plebes prepare for their first academic year and the Academy

Ashley rapidly assimilated basic skills in seamanship, navigation, damage control, sailing, and handling yard patrol craft. She also learned infantry drills and how to shoot 9mm pistols and an M-16.

All of her training was supplemented by a variety of other activities that she liked. They included swimming, martial arts, basic rock climbing, obstacle endurance, and confidence courses.

One day when she was walking back to her dorm, someone had posted a note in the lobby which was entitled **The Plebe.** Here is what it said.

THE PLEBE

Tho' you think you're tough and hard
On the day you hit the yard
You soon find the Navy life's not what you thought it.
First they shave off all your hair
Strip your pride, leave you bare,
and there's a sickness called self-
doubt; you just caught it
so it's a bulkhead not a wall
A companionway not a hall,
And a rack is now what used to be a bed
And Reef Points is your bible.
But it's more'n likely liable
They'll only ask you the parts you haven't read
For its Chop. Chop. Chop
Where's my brasso" Get the mop
Life's a Livn' hell when you're a plebe
They herd you around like sheep

Yet there's lots of time for sleep
If you can figure out how to do it standin'up
No excuse sir' or I'll find out
Your confidence is in full rout
And you feel you're three ranks lower'n a mongrel pup.
Plebe summer's bad but just the start
You can't know they saved the part
That'll make you doubt if you've got
the guts to face four years
Tours, demerits, and getting fried
Test your heart, your soul, your hide
And the closest you get to salt water is your tears
And it's regs, regs, regs
You're a maggot with arms and legs
Life's a living hell when you're a Plebe

Push it up, suck it in
Pop that chest, hide that chin
And no one gives a damn when you feel cruddy.
But miss one little rate;
You'll learn what they mean to hate
And don't expect they care there's no time to study.

Tho'they did their best to break me,
In the end they couldn't make me
Pack it in; I stayed true blue Navy to the core
Now every flamin'Upper Class
Stand aside and let me pass
Cause it's Herndon and there ain't no Plebes no more.
Yes, it's a name to grow to hate
But let me tell you mate,
It takes a hell of a lot of guts to be a Plebe

Ashley read it twice, smiled and thought to herself, there is probably some truth in those words. She turned and headed for her rack. It took her all of one minute to be asleep.

CHAPTER 11

35 DAYS IN AND COUNTING

It was 550 AM, Nikki and Ashley were dressed in their workout clothes and headed for their morning physical exercise workout. It was now referred to only as PEP and was something that most Plebes did not look forward to. It was a standard part of their morning and all geared towards passing the physical education test at the end of the Plebe summer. Plebe summer was 45 days and thus they were at the point where they only had 10 days to go.

Do you know who we have drilling us today Ashley? Yep, I heard yesterday that we have Gunny Sergeant Andy Sanchez. Norma just rolled her eyes. You mean Gunnery Sergeant Andrew Sanchez, otherwise known as the beast.

Yep they are one in the same. Great way to start my day Ash. It won't be so bad. You're getting in really good shape and with only 10 days to go you will be totally ready for that physical fitness test and should pass with flying colors. Thanks Ash, you are always looking at the positive. It helps me a lot. No problem, roommate. I'm glad I'm good for something.

They arrived at the physical fitness area and took their places with their squad within their platoon. Good Morning Plebes, Good Morning Gunny they all answered in unison. I'm sorry you idiots. I think you all need to open your faces and spit some fire. I simply can't hear you. The entire group yelled out louder Good Morning Gunny. Well thank goodness Plebes, for a minute I thought you had lost your voices and your manners. Let's start doing it right the first time. You all seem to have a problem with getting things right even after you have been told. Even Pavlov's dogs could get it right after the second time. What is your problem?

How long have you been in the Navy Plebe's? The entire platoon yelled out at the top of their lungs "All me bloomin'life, sir! Me mother was a mermaid, me father was King Neptune"

I can't hear you the Gunny Sergeant said and once again the platoon yelled back the statement.

That is much better.

Well today Plebes, we are going to take you through some of the basics that you must be ready to pass in l0 days time. You should all be ready for this, so today I want to stretch you out a bit and see how many of you can do double the amount required to pass the test.

The Gunny Sergeant started with pushups, then pull ups, then a run until he had taken the group through the majority of the physical tests they would have to take on. Some were still struggling with making the minimum, some had no problem with the minimum but were unable to double the amount required, but a few were able to handle the double requirement with no problems. Ashley was one of those Plebe's who met all of the challenges presented by the Gunny Sergeant.

While they were in the middle of the pull up tests, a full Lieutenant came up to Gunny Sergeant Sanchez. Hey Gunny, how is it going? Sergeant Sanchez looked up and smiled a big smile. Speaking to him was Lieutenant Roscoe Cook. Lt. Cook was a Navy Seal and had served with Gunny Sanchez overseas on a number of assignments. It is great to see you Lieutenant. What are you doing here at the academy? Well it was time for a transfer and I thought it would be fun to return to the academy, take some graduate classes and handle the

SEAL recruiting assignment. I didn't think I would get it but here I am. I had heard you were here and spending a few hours making sure our new Plebe's were physically able to make it through this place.

Yes Sir. Today is a good day for Plebe destruction and I am doing my best to see that it happens. Once I have completed that, I spend my time building them back up.

It looks to me like you are testing them well. Am I right that they only have about 10 more days to be ready for their physical fitness test. Yes Sir, and I don't want any of them to fail and am bound to see that they do not.

Sergeant, who is the woman Plebe in the second row of this Platoon?

I watched her do the push up and pull up requirements and I don't think there is another Plebe man or women in either this platoon or the other two I have watched today that could match her.

Lieutenant, that is Plebe Ashley Morgan Jamison. She is one hell of an athlete and she has the attitude and temperament to be a first class officer in this man's navy.

She is very quiet and maintains a low profile. By talking to her you would never get the feeling that she is one of the best put together athletes in this entire class.

I don't know all of her background, but I have been told that she is an excellent swimmer and an outstanding gymnast.

In fact, it is my understanding that she had full rides to attend Stanford, UCLA and Washington on swimming scholarships and Penn State University, the University of Texas and the University of Georgia on Gymnastic scholarships.

Well that is really something. Is she going to play athletics for Navy? My understanding is that the swimming coach is counting the hours until he gets to see what she can do in the water. That will happen very shortly after we get through this Plebe Summer.

Well Gunny, it is great to see you. Once again, I think you told me her name was Ashley Jamison. Is that right? Yes Sir. Thanks, so now I'm off to look at some more of our new recruits. Cheers. See you Lieutenant.

As they walked back to their room together Nikki asked Ashley, have you spent any time thinking about the Plebe Parents Weekend?

Yes I have and I have been communicating with my Mom and Dad about the weekend. I also sent them a wish list of the things I think I can use once we finish this Plebe summer experience.

What do you have planned? Well It isn't all finalized yet but the week begins at the end of our sixth week. That is coming up in about two weeks. The visit is for three days. Parents can choose to do a lot of things with the midshipmen, including sailing, attending a dress parade, or sports exhibitions. I plan to take my folks to see the swimming exhibition as I have agreed to swim for the Navy once we are done with this Plebe summer. I also want them to dine in King Hall, and to have the opportunity to meet some faculty and staff members at the academy.

I have been thinking a lot about what I want to study, and I have been talking to them about it. Right now it looks like I want to major in Computer Science. Computers have always come easy to me and I think that will provide me with a solid foundation should I stay in or decide to eventually get out of the Navy.

What about you Nikki, I have not heard you talk much about your parents or your life before Plebe summer. Well Ash, it is an interesting story and too long to tell you during our half hour break. But as you know I am from Oklahoma. My parents and I are members of the Cherokee Nation. As you can imagine my parents have never had much money so the fact that the Navy is paying for all my education is really important to both of them.

I flew out here by myself. We simply didn't have the money for my parents to come with me. I have invited them to come for the Plebe Parents Weekend and I think they are going to try to make it. Neither of them have ever been on a plane in their life so the thought of that plus the travel to get here is almost overwhelming to both of them.

If they come, I am going to take them sailing as neither of them have ever seen a body of water like our Chesapeake Bay. I'm pretty good at it and would feel very comfortable in taking them out.

I also would like them to experience eating in King Hall and, perhaps that would be a great place to have our parents meet each other. That sounds great to me Nikki. Let's plan on it. OK. Time to go to our next event.

It seemed like only a couple of days had passed, but in reality, the end of the Plebe summer was only a couple of days away. It was time for the PRT final test. The test would be administered first thing in the morning. It was timed, and each Plebe was measured individually on their performance. Ashley was not concerned about the test or the result. In fact she spent a lot more time helping Nikki to mentally get ready. She knew she could do it and just wanted to give her the moral support that everyone needs.

The test was administered and Nikki passed with average scores. Ashley on the other hand achieved a level of performance that was almost unheard of. She scored overall at the high outstanding level. She did 100 sit-ups in two minutes, ran I and 1/2 miles in 8 minutes and 45 seconds and did twice as many pushups required of the men. The PRT was scored by averaging the scores of the three key events and Ashley's performance was off the chart. No one really noticed except one man who was observing the Plebes performance. That man was Lieutenant Roscoe Cook. He sat and watched all of the Plebe's performance but only took the time to write down the results of one woman and two men. The one woman was none other than Ashley Morgan Jamison.

Ashley met Nikki after the test, and was very happy to see her with a big smile on her face I take it, from the way you are smiling, that you did what I knew you could do. Yep, I did it Ash, thanks in part to your help and confidence. I can't thank you enough. I don't have to ask you how you did because the rumors have already started. I think you may have beat everyone including the men. No surprise to me, but I'm sure it has a few male Plebe's wondering who the heck you are. Ashley just laughed and they walked back to their room to get ready for the next event.

The Plebe Parents weekend came and went so fast that most plebes couldn't even believe it was over. As planned Ashley's parents, Sarah and Jim, arrived on Thursday. Ashley met them at the airport in uniform and to both of them she looked like she had grown up in just 45 days.

Hugs were had by all and the conversation was nonstop. Her parents got up early on Friday morning and watched the Plebes go through their calisthenics as the sun rose. The Plebes started out running around the field. They passed in waves and Jim and Sara could hear the pounding their feet as they arrived. It was clear that the plebs were incredibly happy to survived the Plebe summer. All the parents were cheering.

They attended a swimming exhibition and were introduced to the varsity swim coach. They had dinner as planned and met Nikki's parents. All in all it was a great weekend and when it was over both Ashley and Nikki sat in their room exhausted but invigorated as well. They were both ready for the next phase.

Both Ashley and Nikki knew that their time as roommates was coming to a close. They had enjoyed being together for the Plebe summer but knew that change was on the horizon.

At the end of Plebe Parent Weekend, they knew that they would be moved to new rooms and issued books, uniforms and computers. That was the case, and both of them were separated and placed with new roommates. Their daily routine also changed considerably. The most noticeable change was that the Plebes were no longer the sole occupants of the Yard. Suddenly there were over 3000 additional upper classmen on campus. They returned which meant new faces and names to memorize.

Having a computer again was a real treasure. They suddenly had instant access to research materials, class notes, the internet and their professor's email addresses.

This gave them instant access to their parents and also they were given a phone number which ran through a switchboard into their room. To Ashley it was not long before her life settled into a pattern of studying, swimming workouts and some free time.

Just before the formal year began, Ashley and her Plebe brothers and sisters, had to take a variety of tests in subjects to see if they had the skill level to test out of certain courses. The tests are called validation tests. Once the tests were completed the Plebes were given their class schedule based on their test scores. Ashley's schedule included six classes It also include a three hour study period as well as time for inspections, formations and drills. Her schedule also included her swimming training which was two full hours every day.

Her formal schedule looked like this

0600 Outside PT and training
0700 Morning formation
700-730 Breakfast
745-1145 Morning Classes
1205 Noon Formation
1205-1330 Lunch and afternoon break
1330-1520 Afternoon Classes
1600-1800 Division I Swimming
1700-1900 Dinner
1930 -2200 Study Time

2200- 2300 Study and Personal time

2300 Taps and lights out.

Once she had been tested and received her schedule she received a call from the Swimming Coach to confirm that she was ready to begin her training. He said he was looking forward to seeing her at the first practice which would occur from 2PM to 4PM at Lejeune Hall beginning on Monday of the first full week of classes.

No rest for the weary. She thought.

CHAPTER 12

ASHLEY HITS THE WATER

It was 3:30 PM on Monday afternoon, Ashley was headed for Lejeune Hall. She was issued her United States Naval Academy swimming suit, and bathing cap. She was told by Mike Morgan, the swimming coach, to be at the pool at 4PM sharp, which by now, she knew meant be their five minutes early.

Lejeune Hall was one of the most impressive athletic facilities at the United States Naval Academy. It also housed the wrestling complex and was named after Lieutenant General John Archer Lejeune, a member of the Naval Academy Class of 1888. Lieutenant General Lejeune, was a Marine Corps officer, and this building was the first building at the academy to be named for a Marine corps officer.

The hall was built in 1982 for $13.5 Million. It is a modern conception building which has regularly placed columns and raised roof area, to compliment the traditional turn of the century French Renaissance style campus. The pool is large, and is 25 meters by 50 miters with an eight foot depth. It has movable bulkheads which enable the team to train at any distances. The pool provides 23, 25 meter short course lanes or 10, 50 meter long course lanes. Deep water, wide lines and the latest gutter technology make the Lejeune Pool one of the fastest competitive facilities in existence.

Ashley arrived early, and was surprised to see a number of women already there and seated in the stands. As she walked in, her new coach, Mike Morgan said, Hi Ashley, welcome to Navy Swimming. Please have a seat in the bleachers.

Ashley said hi and proceeded to take a seat in the stands. Within a few minutes the stand had about 35 women sitting in them. At exactly 4PM Mike Morgan addressed the group.

Good Afternoon Midshipman. My name is Mike Morgan, and I am the Varsity Women's Swimming Coach for the United States Naval Academy. It is important for all of you to know that you are a select group that has been carefully chosen to help the academy carry on its National Reputation in Women's swimming. Some of you will compete at the Varsity level, others at the Junior Varsity level, but I want to reassure you that because you are here today, you are one of the very few who have been selected to carry on our traditions.

You are looking at Lejeune Pool, one of the fastest competitive facilities in existence. The pool underwent a nearly $11 million renovation in the fall of 2012. Included among the list of upgrades to the facility were installed Daktronics, 10mm video board display and a swim scoring system. All the pool filtration, circulation and chlorination systems have been replaced and as you can see, new tile has been laid.

We use this facility for both men and women, and for our diving teams as well, so the schedule is set well in advance and will not be changed.

I encourage you to be on time for your training and to pay close attention to our schedule. We are meeting this afternoon for orientation. Our normal practice will occur 6 days per week, from 4PM to 6PM. When meetings are necessary we will use your study time to gather in the morning. You therefore are reminded, that just because you are a participating division I athlete at the Naval Academy, it does not relieve you of any of your academic obligations. So understand, that when you are in the pool, your other midshipman will be studying. Get use to it and figure out how to make up the study time elsewhere. If you start to fall behind in your studies, come and see me immediately. We may be able to arrange for tutors or additional academic support to keep you up to date.

Our training schedule is not easy and is designed around our competitive schedule. Here is a hand out that I would like each of you to take. The handout will provide you with our schedule for this year.

Ashley, picked up one as the pile was passed around. It was a full schedule and read as follows:

October 5 University of Connecticut
October 6 Louisiana State University
October 19 John Hopkins University
October 20 University of Maryland
Nov 2 The College of William and Mary
Nov 3 Towson University
Nov 16 Bucknell University
Nov 17 University of North Carolina
Dec 1 Army
Dec 2 Penn State University
Jan 12 University of Richmond
Feb 21 Patriot League championship
Feb 22 Patriot League championship
Feb 23 Patriot league championship
Mar 1 NCAA Championship
Mar 20 NCAA Championship

As you can all see, it is a very full schedule and our season lasts for quite a number of months. To participate in this program requires more than excellent swimming skills. You must be focused. You must be an individual performer, and most important, you must be a team player and supportive of every member of our team.

Our practices will begin tomorrow at 4PM. I have asked

members of our current division I team to take you all on an orientation of our facilities, assign you lockers and complete some additional required paperwork. This should take about I hour. I will see you back here at 4PM tomorrow and ready to get in the pool.

Ashley was back the next day and ready to practice at 4PM sharp. The workout was not anything she hadn't seen before, in fact, it was a bit lighter than she had expected. She met a few more of the women who had been recruited and enjoyed most that she met. At the end of practice, Coach Morgan said, that tomorrow at 4PM, he planned to have a 200 meter freestyle race to help him determine the competitive level of all of the team members. He also said that in order to provide some incentive to the women he had invited four of the varsity senior midshipmen men to participate. The women looked at each other with smiles on their faces. Many of them were thinking, I really want to beat those guys, after what we have been through during the plebe summer.

Ashley, however, was not one with a smile on her face. She just didn't care who was in the pool with her. The idea was to beat whoever it was. It just didn't matter to her if they were men or women. She just wanted to do well, and intended to do so. It wasn't about the win, as much as it was doing the best you can, and to defeat whatever obstacles there were that were in the way of attaining your objective.

Her strategy on the 200 meter free had never changed. She learned a long time ago not to try to lead in the beginning.

Stay with the leaders, but don't lead, and don't go out to fast. Use the middle of the race to conserve energy and maintain a constant speed. On the final two laps, go for it, and show the competitors how much you have left in the tank.

That evening Mike Morgan met Cindy Rodrigo at The Galway Bay Irish Restaurant. Mike and Cindy had worked together at the Academy for five years. Cindy was a great coach, and all of the women adored her. She had been a great swimmer at the University of Southern California and was an NCAA champion in the Butterfly. She enjoyed working with Mike and had decided to stay at the Academy even though she was being recruited as a head coach for a number of Division I schools. There was just something about the Academy, the tradition, and the amount of effort it took for the athletes to excel in their sport, while maintaining a full schedule as a midshipman. That is what attracted her and made her want to stay.

They met at the front door for a 7PM dinner. Hey Mike, your all dressed up. Well I don't know about that but if wearing new jeans and a new shirt makes me dressed up, so be it. You look great yourself. Needless to say I don't think that a day goes by that we don't look at each other in Navy coaching sweats.

So what do I owe this invitation to dinner to. Well, I wanted to talk to you about tomorrow, and I wanted to do it in a quiet and pleasant place. The Galway has been here since 1998 and I love it not just for its food but for its lack of televisions and emphasis on quiet conversation.

Sounds good to me. Let's get our table and look at the menu. They settled in a corner table and both looked at the menu. Mike said, I'm going to have what I have every time I come to this place. What's that Mike? I'm having the fish and chips and a cold Coors Light Beer. Sounds good but I think I will go with the corned beef Rubin and join you with the beer.

So, what's on your mind, Mike. Well, as you know, we have the 200 meter free slotting test scheduled for tomorrow. Yes, I was a bit surprised to see you had invited a couple of the guys to swim with the women.

I don't think you have done that before, was there a reason for it? Yes, we have one swimmer in the race tomorrow that you are going to want to watch very closely. If I'm right, we may have our hands on one, if not the best, swimmer, men or women to swim for the United States Navy. Really. Who is that? Her name is Ashley Morgan Jamison.

I think that Ashley is something special, although you would never know it by talking to her. She had full offers to attend Stanford, Washington and UCLA on a swimming scholarship and she had full offers to attend three other schools on a gymnastics scholarship. I just haven't figured out why she picked the Naval Academy. I didn't even think about recruiting her, even though I had been following her since she was five years old. For some reason, she wanted to come to the Academy, and for the life of me I can't figure out why. She breezed through her Plebe summer and scored the highest marks possible on the Physical Fitness Test. Once I learned that she was accepted to the academy, I called her, and asked if she would like to swim for us which she readily agreed to. Swimming however, was not the draw to get here. She has no family ties to the Navy or to the Academy but something triggered her desire to put herself through all of this.

She has had a coach in Portland who I have a great deal of respect for. Her name is Nancy Ages. I know that name. In fact I swam against Nancy in the NCAA's. She was very good.

I know. She has become a good friend and a helpful recruiting source. I talked to Nancy about Ashley, and she told me that she had the potential to be one of the best swimmers in the world. She has no idea what motivated her to come to the Academy, but she has supported her all the way. Ashley has always responded well to women coaches and my feeling is that, in that regard, you could play a very important role in her four years at the academy. She will not want, and I do not want her to have any special treatment, but if I'm right, and we will see tomorrow if this woman is a real nugget that we can fully polish.

Very interesting Mike. Now you have me interested in tomorrow. This Rubin is great. I'm going to have another beer. Please don't tell my boss. No problem there. I'll join you.

Ashley, woke up at 5:30 AM as usual, and dressed for

breakfast. She had a busy schedule this day and would have to run to make sure that she made her swimming practice on time.

She also had a lot of studying to do. It would be a late night of study after everything else was completed. She didn't think much about her swimming practice nor anything about the 200 free test that Coach Morgan had set up. She arrived at the swimming venue on time, changed at her locker and headed to the pool with the other members of her team.

She could tell that some of the girls were really nervous, and a bit on edge. She was sure some were worried about not making the varsity team. Ashley didn't even give that a thought.

Coach Morgan, asked all of the girls to have a seat. He explained that he had set up the 200's in heats and that there would be three heats of 15 swimmers in each heat. As he indicated he had arranged for two of the Varsity Boys to be in each of the women's heats. Ashley received her heat assignment which was in the second heat. What she didn't know was that Coach Morgan had stacked that heat with the very best swimmers he had. All of the women, and both of the men, had very established records some at the Academy, some before arriving as Plebe's. Ashley was placed in lane three and Coach Morgan had put one of the boys in lane one and another in lane four. He did it so she would be able to see where each of the boys was as the race progressed.

Cindy Rodrigo talked to the girls before their heats. She encouraged them to do their best, and that no matter what the result, that they were special and should be honored to be a part of this.

The first heat went out well. The two boys dominated the girls. The time was 1minute 65 seconds which was about 10 seconds off the women's record of 1 minute 55 seconds and almost 20 seconds off the men's record of 1minute 42 seconds. The men and women lined up for the second heat. Ashley took her position on the starting block at lane three.

Cindy watched her closely, and noticed that she didn't

appear to be a bit nervous or concerned about the race. She was just very calm. There were a few people in the stands most of whom were members of the men's swim team.

They had never watched any of their team members swim against the women and most, were high fiveing each other after the first heat win by the guys. They were careful not to celebrate to much, but there was no question that they were happy to win, and felt very relaxed about heat two with their two best men's 200 meter swimmers in the race.

Unbeknownst to anyone in the swimming venue, was the fact, that there was one man in uniform who sat way in the back of the venue by himself. He talked to no one, and was there only to help satisfy a personal curiosity.

No one paid any attention to him, or to his uniform. He was a full Lieutenant which was very common to see on the grounds of the Naval Academy. However, if anyone would have taken the time to look closely, they would have noticed that he wore a Navy Seal Trident Patch on his uniform. Behind lines the Navy Seal's wear no patches, insignias, rank or other symbols. While in the United States the Trident Patch is worn.

Swimmers to your marks. Swimmers ready. Ashley took her position and waited for the gun to go off. It did and she was off.

Out of the blocks she could see the guy in lane one and the guy in lane four. They both started out fast and she could tell that neither of them intended to be beat by a women.

Ashley stayed with them through the first two laps but made a point not to take the lead. As they approached the middle of the race, she eased into her form, and swam fast but totally relaxed. Coach Morgan and Coach Rodrigo both watched with trained eyes, as did the man in uniform in the back of the stands. As they came to the final two laps, it was clear, that there were going to be only three in this race. Two guys and Ashley Morgan Jamison. Ashley made her move with two laps to go and with almost no effort took the lead from the two

Senior boys. Both were struggling to maintain a smooth pace, as both had gone out to fast, and were about to pay the price.

Ashley focused on the last lap, and as it began, she pushed it into high gear and left both of the boys a quarter of a lap behind. The men's swim team in the stands could not believe their eyes. There were no high fives. Both men swam under the ropes and congratulated Ashley, but the guys in the stands said nothing and were in total shock. In the stands one Second Year Midshipman Bryce Alden said to his mate, "That women just kicked our ass and made a mockery of Men's Swimming at the Academy. While I may not be able to do anything about her swimming ability, I can sure try to make her life miserable as a Plebe". Come on Bryce, his friend said, you're really not going to hold a grudge of some sort because she is an exceptional athlete. Bryce responded. I don't like to see us get beat period and especially by a women.

The race was over and Ashley had swam it in 1 minute and 57 seconds which was 2 seconds off the women's record. The Lieutenant in the stands left when the race was over. No one even noticed that he had come and gone.

CHAPTER 13

THE UPS AND DOWNS
OF YEAR ONE

The following morning Mike Morgan met in the coaches staff room with Cindy Rodrigo. Good Morning Cindy, hey Mike. You were right, we have a real athlete on our hands. I couldn't even sleep last night knowing that Ashley came within 2 seconds, even though it was unofficial, of setting a new womens record in the 200 free. Her performance, was beyond anything I have ever seen. I also watched her after she finished and later as she dressed and left the building. It was as if it was no big deal. To me, it looked like she took it all in stride and didn't think much about it.

I told you at dinner that I thought we had a real winner on our hands. Now our goal is to learn how best to deal with it. One thing for sure, there are a bunch of Midshipmen swimmers who are totally pissed off that a freshman Plebe just shredded their entire program before their very eyes.

I'm not sure if it means anything, but I have watched some of the Senior Classmen over the years let their position of power go a bit to their heads and, it wouldn't surprise me if some idiot tries to make Ashley's life a little more difficult than it already is.

Well Mike, I plan to do what you suggested and spend a little more time with Ashley from a coaching perspective. I thought I saw two areas that we can work to improve her performance, and I'm going to talk with her about them, and see if she is receptive to my coaching suggestions. I also plan to call your friend Nancy in Portland, and see if she can give me any more insight into the complexity of one Ms. Ashley Morgan Jamison. Good Idea Cindy. Keep me up to date. Will do.

By the way, what did you see that can be improved? It is a small thing but I think it will make a tenth or two tenth difference in her time.

I noticed that when she is doing her kick turns that she is not bringing her knees up as high as she should to her chest, and also that when she is completing the flip that she has a tendency to rotate her feet a fraction to soon.

They are both minor things but I think they can be improved.

Great observation Cindy. Let me know how receptive she is to your coaching suggestions. Will do. Oh, by the way, please spend some time thinking about what races we should have Ashley training for. My initial thought is she should be a member of the 4X100 relay team, the 100 meter butterfly and the 200 meter free. Please think about that and then when you have time talk to her about what she wants' to train for.

It was the 5:30 wakeup call, and Ashley could hardly believe that it was time to get up and start another day. She had returned to her room and spent the night studying until 11:30 PM. Good Morning Martha. Good Morning Ashley, wow, you stayed up late last night hitting the books. Yep, yesterday was a really full day for me, and we had a swimming trial in the afternoon that took not only time, but lots of my energy. I needed to have time to hit the books and it was one of those days where I simply ran out of time.

Well, today's another day, so we both better get going. Ashley felt lucky, she only had one new roommate which was great for her. Her new roommate was Martha Bridgestone.

Martha was from San Diego, and was the daughter of a Naval Rear Admiral. She had grown up in a military family, and literally had been groomed by her parents to attend the Naval Academy since she started school. Martha was different than Ashley. She was not an athlete. She was certainly capable of completing all of the Navy's physical fitness requirements, but her strength was in her head and she had plenty of brain power.

As they walked to morning formation in uniform, Ashley asked Martha what she had decided to study? Ash, I have decided to major in Political Science, and minor in information technology. I want to go into Naval intelligence and a number of people have told me that these two course studies will help me toward that goal.

That sounds interesting. What about you Ash? Well I'm going to major in Computer Science. Computers have always been of interest to me, and they are going to continue to play an important part in the future, so it should position me to do something should I decide at some point to get out of the Navy. I'm sure that with your information technology minor that we will end up having some classes together which would be fun.

Ash, didn't you tell me you had some kind of swimming trial yesterday? Yes, they use it as a way of determining whether you will swim Varsity or not and what races you might be trained for. How did you do? I think I did fine and will swim Varsity for Navy.

Great, I can't wait to watch you.

Ashley spent the day in class, and when free, she spent the time studying. As usual she had to put up with a bunch of Senior Classman harassments, but she was very use to them and they didn't bother her at all.

She arrived at swimming practice shortly before four and was surprised to have Cindy waiting for her in the locker room. Hey Ashley, I stopped by early to see if I could spend a few minutes with you. Sure coach, what can I do for you. Well, I obviously watched you yesterday and spent the evening thinking about your future races and where you might best fit in. I want to make sure we maximize your individual performance and also help the team. Great. What do you think I should focus on?.

Well, obviously the 200 free is made for you and I would suggest that we keep that in your competitive program.

I also looked at your upper body strength and how you tested out at the end of your Plebe summer. I think, that if you would be willing, that the 100 butterfly could be a great fit for you.

Wow, I have never tried that. That might be really fun. What else? Well without killing you in the process, I think, and I know that Mike would agree, that you should be a member of the 400 meter relay team. That sounds fine to me Cindy. I'm good with all three. Great, I will tell Mike and he will adjust your workouts to focus on the three.

I swam the butterfly in College and at the NCAA's and enjoyed it. I think it will be a great race for you and I look forward to coaching you in the future. Thanks Cindy, I look forward to that as well.

Ashley was slowly getting use to her freshman year at the Naval Academy. There was no question it wasn't easy. Everyone was called Sir or Ma'am. She found herself running through the halls of the dorms, which they called chop. She was given extracurricular training projects that seemed absurd with timelines that were designed to be impossible. She felt like she was continuing to memorize relatively useless information, and then was asked to recite it when requested.

Even with all of the crap she had to put up with, she didn't doubt her decision to attend. She knew that everyone at some point had doubts but not Ashley. She would later describe her first year as challenging and rewarding but the word fun did not fit in when describing it.

One thing she knew for sure was she was learning a lot about herself, and her classmates. With all of the trials and tribulations over the course of the year, she knew that the bonds she was making with her swim mates and classmates would last a life time. The year was designed to help her learn what she was capable of and she knew it was testing her in a variety of ways.

One thing that became an ever present pain in the rear was Alpha Inspections. Alpha inspections are the white glove inspections at the Academy. Ashley learned quickly that when they said white glove inspections they literally meant that. The upperclassmen commanding the inspections would put on white gloves to try to find a single ounce of dirt with their fingertips.

The purpose of the Alpha inspections was not only to force midshipmen to keep clean rooms, but also to reinforce the discipline and attention to detail that is necessary to succeed in the Navy.

Each inspection was graded on a room inspection chit which was designed to show exactly what was being evaluated.

A grade of UNSAT on any of the major items constitutes an overall UNSAT for the inspection,

Each room is judged on the general appearance to include surfaces, walls, overhead blinds, light fixtures etc. The lockers and closets were gone through, as well as the shower, wash basins, and any hardware including computers. You did not dare stuff things in your drawers. Everything had to have a place, and it needed to be neat. Plebes were not permitted to have alcohol their first year but the food in their rooms was all inspected as well.

The Alpha inspections began with the Plebe summer and continued off and on through the first year The inspections were done once per semester, one in the fall, and one in the spring. If the plebes failed an inspection they were scheduled for a second time to be re-inspected. If they passed they were done for the semester.

Ashley learned one trick after she failed her first inspection.

She failed because the inspector said her shower curtain was not properly cleaned, even though she and her roommate had spent over an hour scrubbing it. To solve the problem she simply went to the Mid Store before the inspection and bought a new curtain. She then hung it up right before the inspection. It was simple and it worked.

Alpha inspections taught Ashley how to strip and wax a floor, clean a wide variety of surfaces, and shine bright works. However, probably the most important skill she learned, was how to hide mass amounts of storage in order to give the appearance of a spotless room. She learned that rather than spend the time organizing everything, she just gathered a bunch of stuff up and moved it out of the room on inspection day. Just thinking about those tricks made her smile.

Ashley's academic schedule was finalized and wasn't easy but then again nothing seemed to be easy once she arrive at the Academy. Here is what it looked like for her Fall Semester.

Mathematics.	**SM121 Calculus 1**
Chemistry	**SC151 Modern Chemistry**
English	**HE 111 Rhetoric and introduction to Literature 1**
Government	**FP 130 US Gov't and Constitutional Development**
Cyber Security	**SI 110 Introduction to cyber Security**

Ashley had math for 4 hours per week, Chemistry three hours per week, English three hours per week, Government three hours per week and Cyber Security 2 hours per week.

When you added all of these up plus her Division I Swimming program it was easy to see that she was maxed out on her time and needed to be super organized in order to fit everything in.

Even thought she knew what she wanted to major in, she did not need to make a selection of a major until the end of her plebe year. She would then begin formal course work in her major in the second year at the Academy.

Ashley was also provided her second semester schedule which was no easier than her first semester one. It looked like this.

Mathematics.   **Calculus 2**
chemistry   **Basic Chinese language**
English   **Literature 11**
Naval History
Leadership.

CHAPTER 14

THE ALPHA INSPECTION

It was the beginning of November. The leaves had turned and the fall chill had turned to bitter cold. The first four swim meets were over. The first was the University of Connecticut, the second was Louisiana State, the third was John Hopkins and the one that was just finished was the University of Maryland.

Cindy had spent a lot of time with Ashley perfecting her turn, and working to keep her feet straight. She found Ashley to be totally open, and very receptive to her coaching.

Ashley's athletic ability coupled with Cindy's coaching had paid off in significant results from the very beginning. Ashley had followed Cindy's recommendation, and was competing in the 100 meter butterfly, the 200 meter free style and the 400 meter relay. She remained undefeated in both the butterfly and the 200 free style. Her relay team was not as successful. They had not won yet, but had come close in most races. Ashley was not bothered by the result, although she was not use to loosing, this was a team event and she did her best to swim fast as a team member. She also encouraged her team mates to do the same. Without a doubt, she was becoming one of, if not the most popular women, on the Navy team.

Her reputation was now known. The Navy women's team was beginning to draw crowds of men and women the likes of which they had not seen before.

It was a Tuesday Morning, Ashley and Martha had stayed up late and gotten up early. They dressed and headed for their morning formation, and then went on to breakfast together. Today was an important day, in that they had been advised they would undergo their Alpha Inspection after breakfast. After breakfast they were told to return to their room, and wait for the upper class inspectors to arrive with their white gloves in hand.

Both were a bit nervous. They had been through a number of inspections before, and usually passed with little or no problems, but this inspection was the semester Alpha Inspection. If they passed they would not have to undergo another one until the Spring. So it mattered and they both wanted to do well.

Bryce Allen had spent a lot of time and research on how he was going to make Ashley's life miserable for beating the socks off the best men's swimmers in the 200 trial. He knew that he was taking a big risk, and as such, his plan needed to be fool proof. He was well aware of the no alcohol mandate for first year Plebes, and he knew that it was an offence that could not only result in disciplinary action but potentially could get a plebe kicked out of the academy. He was fine with either but the later would be his preference.

He was also well aware of midshipman's code of honor and that if anyone knew that he was the one behind this action, they would be bound to let their superiors know. As a result, he had waited for a couple of months since the swimming trial occurred, and he had said nothing to anyone as he developed his plan. He didn't know Ashley or her roommate Martha, but it didn't matter to him anyway. His focus was totally on Ashley and how to make her pay for making the men's team look so bad.

Bryce had researched and purchased a maintenance workers uniform, and had learned what Ashley's and Martha's schedule was, so he knew exactly when their room would be empty. He was also able to get a copy made of the master pass key that would allow access to their room.

He was well aware of the inspection schedule, and waited

until the morning of the inspection to make his move. After formation, and while the other midshipman were having breakfast, he slipped on the maintenance uniform in his room. He put on his black puma running shoes and the ball cap that the workers wore with their uniform. He pulled the ball cap all of the way down so his face would not show. He then exited the room, and headed for the women's section of the dorm.

There were no people present as everyone was at breakfast. He used the pass key, and slipped quietly into the room. He went directly to Ashley's desk and opened the bottom drawer.

He then removed a half empty bottle of beer from his pocket, and put it in the back corner of the bottom right had desk drawer. He was out of the room within a minute, back to his own room, and back in uniform within five minutes. Mission accomplished.

Ashley and Martha finished breakfast and headed back to their room to get ready for the inspection. The room looked good. so they both inspected each other uniform to make sure that everything was perfect. Satisfied, they took their positions at attention outside of their room. Within 2 minutes, two lst class midshipman arrived to complete the inspection. One was a man and the other a women. The Senior Classmen were all business as they began their inspection of Ashley and Martha's uniforms. Both girls stood at attention, and did not say anything. Once the inspectors were finished they opened the door to the room and entered. Once the inspectors were in the room, Ashley and Martha said in unison "Sirs, request permission to come aboard for the Alpha Inspection." Permission was granted, and the two girls stepped into their room

The Female upper classman went to work with white gloves on their closets while the male inspector checked out the shower, the shower curtain, and the floors. The last item to undergo the inspection were the two girls desks.

Martha was asked to step forward while the female inspector

went through her desk. She checked each drawer and looked to make sure that all was in proper order which it was.

The male inspector then called Ashley to step forward which she did. He began with the desk drawer and then went through all of the drawers on the left side of the desk and started on the right side. The last drawer he looked at was the bottom right had drawer. Suddenly he stopped and looked at Ashley.

Plebe Jamison is this yours? He said, as he pulled the half empty beer bottle out from the bottom drawer. Ashley and Martha just looked at each other with total shock on their faces.

No Sir, that bottle of beer is not mine, and I have no idea how it got in my desk Sir. Well Plebe Jamison, I must inform you, that having a liquor bottle in your room is against all regulations. This could be grounds for your dismissal from the academy. This Alpha inspection is over, and as a result of this finding you both have not passed the inspection. Plebe Jamison, you will be reported to the Division Commander this morning and it will be up to him to decide what your fate will be. Is that clearly understood? Yes Sir.

You will receive a message this morning when you are to meet with him and the panel of Upperclassman to determine your fate.

Ashley did not show any emotion even though she was boiling in side. Who would do such a thing to her and why? She had no idea, but if she ever found out, she would personally deal with it.

Once the inspectors left, Martha just looked at her and said, "How and Why would someone do that to you? I just can't believe it. You have not had a drink of anything since I met you, and based on your athletic ability, I would venture to say that you have never had, or perhaps only once or twice, drank a beer. This is one of the cruelest tricks I have ever heard of.

I am so sorry Martha, we failed the inspection after so much work, and will have to do it all over again because someone decided to single me out. Ash, I could care about their stupid inspection, what I care about is you, and making sure that this does not hurt your record or, in the worst instance, be grounds for your dismissal from the academy.

Thanks Martha. They took the bottle away, if there were finger prints on it, I hope they don't screw them up.

Later that morning Ashley received a message that she should report to the Administrative Building at 5PM sharp to discuss the inspection findings.

Ashley took the note and crumpled it up in her right hand. It was the only emotion she had shown, but there was no question she was mad as hell and would not go down without a fight.

At 4PM she arrived at swimming practice. She didn't say much to anyone but she also didn't put her suit on. Cindy saw her and noticed a change in Ashley's otherwise positive behavior. Hey Ash, Cindy said, "Is something wrong? I see that you're not getting changed for practice? Hi Coach, yes something is wrong, and I can't practice today. What's wrong?

Well today was my roommates and my Alpha inspection. Everything was perfect until the inspector got to my bottom right hand desk drawer and pulled out a half empty bottle of beer. He did what? He pulled out a half empty bottle of beer from my right hand desk drawer.

I have been asked to attend an administrative hearing regarding the inspectors find this afternoon at 5PM. I don't believe this Ash, you are a superb athlete and a by the book midshipman, how in the hell would a bottle of warm beer ever get in your desk drawer?

I can't figure it out and neither can my roommate Martha. We were up super late last night getting ready for the inspection. We double checked everything in our room I went through her desk and she went through mine. Everything was perfect. We went to bed. We were up at 5:30 AM for formation and then went to breakfast. The room was locked when we left, and we came back early to give it one more check before the inspectors showed up.

Well, I've seen a lot of rotten tricks played on Plebe's over the past five years but I have never seen anything that could result in disciplinary action. This certainly meets that criteria, and it looks to me like someone set you up for this. It is as dirty of a trick, if that is what it was, that I have seen.

I'm totally pissed off about it, and if I am, I can't imagine what is going on inside of you. Ash, I want to talk to Coach Morgan about this. It is very strange, and I know he is going to be totally irritated by it. For now, just plan on going to your Administrative hearing at 5PM, and we will see what transpires after that. Don't worry Ash, someone is going to pay for this, and it is not going to be you. I will talk to you soon.

Cindy found Mike in the Coaches room. Hey Cindy, what's up. Well more than I want to tell you. What is it? I just talked to Ashley, she will not be at practice this afternoon. Why is something wrong with her? No, other than she is totally pissed off, but not showing it as usual. What happened? Well I don't know yet, but this morning Ashley and her roommate had their Alpha inspection, the inspection all went well until the midshipman doing the inspection pulled a half empty beer bottle out from her bottom desk drawer. What, are you kidding me?

No Mike, we both know Ashley and we both know that she is about as straight shooter as this Academy has ever seen. She and her roommate Martha are beside their selves, and have no idea how this could have happened. Obviously, someone planted this alcohol knowing that is totally against Plebe rules and, because she is under age, it is also a violation of both state and federal law.

Wow, I have heard of some dirty Plebe tricks in my time, but I have never heard of anything this vicious. This could get her not just on probation but kicked out. When is she scheduled for the administrative hearing? Ashley told me it is scheduled for 5PM today in the Administrative Building. Well, Cindy you run the practice today, I'm going to an administrative hearing to find out what is going on. I'll talk to you when I return. OK Mike, let me know what happens will you? Sure and I can also tell you that we will get to the bottom of this, if it takes the next couple of months to do it.

The rumor mill was quick to pick up on the failed Alpha Inspection and the rumors were not all together accurate.

Word travels fast at the academy, and it so happened that Lieutenant Roscoe Cook heard about the incident right away. He couldn't believe it when he was told that it was Ashley Jamison's room, and was totally blown away when he learned it was a half bottle of beer in her bottom desk drawer.

He made two quick phone calls and cancelled his afternoon activities so he could sit in the back of the administrative room and listen to the charge and rebuttal of the failed Alpha Inspection.

At exactly 5PM Ashley was sitting outside the disciplinary room in the Administrative building. The door to the room opened at 5PM and she was asked to come in. Sitting at the front of the room was a panel of three lst class midshipman. To their sides were two Navy Jag Officers. Ashley was asked to stand before the group. She could not see behind her but there were a few people sitting in the room including her coach and Lieutenant Cook.

Plebe Jamison, Yes Sir. You have been brought before this administrative disciplinary panel as a result of a failed Alpha inspection that was conducted this morning in your room. We are told, that on inspection, a half of a bottle of beer was found in your bottom right hand desk drawer. Is that correct Plebe Jamison? Yes Sir, that is correct. Was that bottle of beer yours? No Sir, I have never seen that bottle before it was removed from my desk. Did you consume any beer at any time in your room or on the grounds of the US Naval Academy. No Sir, I did not.

You do realize that the Navy has a very strict policy on

Alcohol and drug abuse and, a violation of that policy, will not be tolerated and can be grounds for disciplinary action up to and including dismissal from the academy. Yes Sir, I have read the policy. Do you also understand that you are not of legal age to drink and if caught doing that, that is a violation of both State and Federal law. Yes Sir, I understand that.

Do you also understand that midshipman are to be held accountable for failure to adhere to our policy and that irresponsible use of alcohol is inconsistent with the mission of the Naval Academy and will not be tolerated. Yes Sir, I understand that.

What do you have to say to this panel Plebe Jamison? Well Sir, If I may speak, I would like to tell the members of the panel that I am an athlete that is proud to compete for and represent the Navy. I am not a drinker. I do not know how that bottle of beer arrived in my desk. My roommate Martha and I prepared for inspection the night before, we double checked everything in our room and we only left the room for a brief time this morning for formation and breakfast. We returned to our room early to do one last check before the Alpha Inspection began. We were both in total shock when the inspector removed that bottle from my desk. I don't know whose or if there were finger prints on it but I can assure all of you that they were not mine or my roommates.

I have thought a lot about this since it occurred this morning, and I have no idea who would do such a thing to me or for that matter why. To my knowledge I have no enemy's here at the academy, have not been in any trouble or caused trouble for anyone. I am at a complete loss to understand this.

I can only say that whoever did this is a pretty sick person. My hope is, that at some point, we find out who did this and why. Then I hope that that person, or persons, has to come before this panel and explain why they would focus such hate on me.

With that Ashley stepped back and remained at attention.

She showed no emotion and stood there ready to take whatever punishment was deemed to be necessary.

Thank you Plebe Jamison. The panel will take under advisement what you have said and will let you know within three days of our findings. You are dismissed.

Ashley left the room. The others remained. When she was gone, the lead panel member asked those left in attendance if anyone had anything that should be shared with the panel before they took this case under advisement.

Mike Morgan raised his hand. Yes Sir, please step forward. Mike did so and said "my name is Michael Morgan and I am the varsity swim coach for the Naval Academy.

Ashley Jamison is a member of our women's swim team, and is an outstanding athlete. In fact she may be one of, if not the best athlete, we have ever had in the program. She is also a "to the letter"," by the book" woman and one who knows the rules and follows them to the letter. While I don't know what happened here, I can tell you that about two months ago we had a placement race to determine the skill level of our swimmers before we began the season.

I knew in advance that Ashley was a very talented swimmer, and I thought it would be interesting to increase her competition a bit, so the men's coach and I agreed to have a few of his team members swim in the trial with the women. I then placed Ashley in a trial group that had two of the best Senior Male Swimmers at the academy in it.

To make a long story short. Ashley blew both of them out of the water beating them in the 200 year freestyle by almost 1/2 a lap each. I know that this was a source of embarrassment to the men's program, and I have no idea if it had anything to do with this, but I do know that the competition can be fierce. Perhaps there was some grudge or carry over that resulted from that race. We have had no other contact with the Men's program since that time and the two swimmers who she beat congratulated her and seemed fine with the result.

So I will leave you with this final thought, you just had a Plebe in front of you that in my estimation is destined for big things in whatever she chooses to do. I would hate for a dirty trick like this to in any way hinder her positive progress. Thank you for the opportunity to speak.

CHAPTER 15

CATCH ME IF YOU CAN

The disciplinary hearing ended with the presentation made by Mike Morgan. Lieutenant Roscoe Cook left as soon as the hearing ended, and headed back to his office. He immediately dialed a number that he knew by heart. Good Afternoon, Security, this is Captain Kyle Obermeyer. Hey Kyle it's Roscoe. Hey Lieutenant, what's up? Don't tell me you are cancelling our workout together? No Kyle, we are still on for our normal 10AM session tomorrow. Then what can I do for you kind sir?

This morning we had an incident occur during one of our Plebe's inspections that doesn't make any sense to me. What happened? I haven't heard anything. It occurred during an Alpha inspection when one of the Senior Inspectors found a half of a bottle of beer in one of the female plebes desks. That is really weird. Alpha inspections are known in advance and all of the plebes really prepare for them.

What can i do to help? I would like to look at the security film of the hall that room 207 is located on. I only need to look at the half hour between 8AM and 830 AM this morning. That shouldn't be a problem. I can pull up the security tape right away and if you want, your free to look at it when you want. Thanks Kyle. I should be by in about 30 minutes.

Roscoe arrived in the Security Department within 20 minutes. Hi Kyle, he said.

I've got the type pulled up for you, I'm afraid there isn't a lot to look at. It looks like it was taken during morning formation and Breakfast so there are almost no people in the film. I guess there are a couple of exceptions where maintenance guys are working as usual but I didn't see anything else.

Thanks Kyle, where do you want me to look at it. Just here in my office. I will pull it up for you. The tape begins at 755 and ends at 825.

That should do it. Roscoe sat down and began to look at the film. As Kyle had told him, there wasn't a lot to look at, however, at 8:11 AM a maintenance worker in uniform appeared down the hall and then walked toward room 207. Roscoe watched as the worker stopped at room 207 and then used a pass key to enter. The maintenance worker was in the room for less than one minute and then reappeared, locked the door behind him, and headed back down the hall. Roscoe watched the rest of the film and saw only one additional maintenance worker who was down the hall. That worker entered another room and then exited in the same manner as the one that Roscoe had watched.

He reran the film again and paid very close attention to the worker. It looked like it was a he rather than a she, but it was hard to tell because the baseball hat had been pulled way down so it almost covered the workers face. The uniform was standard, and the shoes were standard running shoes that were all black. Not much to see that would help identify the person that entered the room.

It took three times until Roscoe finally noticed something that he had totally missed before. On the back of one shoe was a very small but identifiable mark. It was a small Puma which identified the maker of the shoe.

He took one more look at the film and then stopped. He now knew almost for certain that the person who entered the room at 811 was the same person who left the beer bottle surprise for Ashley. He also knew that that person owned a pair of black puma running shoes and that the right shoe had the small puma figure on the back of the shoe.

He got up and thanked Kyle for the opportunity to look at the film. Did it help? Kyle asked. Not sure, but it may have given me a lead that I want to follow up on.

Let me know if I can be of any help, in any event I will see you tomorrow for our 10AM workout. I will see you there and hope that this time you can keep up with me. They both laughed and Roscoe headed out.

Now the next step was to figure out what to do with the information he had gained. A plan developed in his mind. He did not want to get involved but he had a vested interest to make sure that Ashley was cleared of these charges.

By the time he got back to the office he knew what he would do and he would take Kyle up on his offer to help. He called Kyle back and said, hey Pal there is something that you can do to help me with my Plebe mystery.

No problem, how can I help?

Well, I would like you to call Mike Morgan, he is the Varsity Coach of the Navy's women's swimming team. Mike has a real vested interest to see that one of his swimmers is not put out of commission by this event. What I would like to have you do, is to tell him that you are Head of Yard Security and were advised of the strange beer bottle that showed up during the Alpha inspection this morning.

Tell him, you reviewed the dorm security tape to see if it had anything on it, and tell him that it showed that a maintenance worker did entered the Plebe's room at 8:11 AM this morning. This was during the time when the Plebe's were at breakfast. Tell him, the film does not allow us to tell if the maintenance worker is a man or a women, but it appears from the persons manner it is highly probable that it is a man.

Tell him that the only thing that gives us some help with identity was the fact that the maintenance worker had on a pair of black running shoes, and that the right shoe has a very small puma logo on the back of it.

Tell him you were advised of his talk before the disciplinary board this morning, and that he may want to check with the Men's swimming coach to see if any of his swimmers has a pair of black shoes that match this description.

I don't want to get involved Kyle, and want to stay out of this so keep my name out of it. Just handle it like it is a normal security follow up. Then lets' see what the coaches come up with.

Great idea Roscoe. I will make the call in a couple of minutes. I will look at the type one more time so I can see for myself what you saw. I'll let you know how it goes in the morning.

Kyle re-ran the tape twice and saw exactly what Roscoe had told him. He then picked up the phone and called Mike Morgan's Office. Hello, this is Mike Morgan. Hey Mike, my name is Kyle Obermeyer and I am head of Security here at the yard.

Hi Kyle, what can I do for you. Well, I wanted you to know that I was briefed today on the inspection incident that involved one of your swimmers Ashley Jamison. I decided to look at the security tapes of Ashley's floor during the time she and her roommate were at breakfast, and we were able to see that someone entered her room at 8:11 AM yesterday morning. It appears the person was a maintenance worker. They have on the maintenance workers uniform, and had a pass key to make the entry. We could not tell if it was a man or a women. I called our maintenance staff and they indicated that they did have one person on the floor during that time but that person did not enter room 207. We could not tell if the person was a man or a women, but it appears from the way they are walking that it is a man. The person had on the standard uniform, and hat, but it was pulled way down so we could not see their face.

I'm calling you because I understand that you talked to the disciplinary board this morning on Ashley's behalf, and you mentioned the possibility of perhaps some jealously between the men's team and the women's. I bring this up because who ever entered the room had on a pair of black running shoes, and the right shoe had a very small puma logo on it. I thought you might want to mention it to the men's coach and perhaps they can be on the lookout for a pair of those shoes in their locker room. Thanks very much Kyle. This information is very helpful, and I will follow up on your suggestion tonight.

I would like to see if we can get this figured out before Ashley hears back from the group in three days. No problem Mike, just let me know if I can be of any further help.

Good Evening, this is Brad Johnson may I help you. Hey Brad it's Mike. Hi Mike, good to hear from you. Your women's team seems to be having a very good season thus far. I have been watching Ashley Jamison, and if I'm right, she hasn't lost a race this season. Your right and it is Ashley that I am calling you about.

What's up Mike? Well this morning some of the Plebes had their Alpha inspection. Ashley and her roommate were two of those Plebes. They did just fine until the inspector got to the bottom right hand drawer of Ashley's desk, and removed a half full bottle of warm beer. Your kidding me. That's not only a major violation of the Academy rules, but in her case, because of her age it is against both Federal and State Law. That is all true, and this afternoon, she was called before the disciplinary board. They made sure she understood the rule, and everything else that goes with the violation.

Mike, I just can't believe it. She is one hell of an athlete, and a violation of that sort could get her kicked out of the Academy. i know and that's why I'm calling.

I got a call from Kyle Obermeyer who is head of Security this afternoon. Kyle went through the security film of Ashley's floor from just before 8 AM this morning until about 8:30 AM. During that time, Ashley and her roommate were at formation and breakfast. They returned to their room before 8:30 AM to finish their inspection preparations.

The film showed that at 8:11 AM, a maintenance person entered the girls room. We think it was a man but no one knows for sure because whoever it was had their hat pulled down over their face. The person was in the room for less than 1 minute and then exited and left down the hall.

Kyle checked with the maintenance staff and they did have one person on the floor during that time, but that person was at the other end of the hall, and did not go near Ashley's room.

So we know now that someone went into that room, and we believe that that person planted the beer bottle in Ashley's drawer.

Man, I have heard of a lot of plebe tricks, but this is way beyond a trick, and if i may say so, seems like a viscous act designed to take out revenge for some reason or another.

Your thinking is the same as mine, and the only thing I can think about was my placement 200 meter event before the season started. If you will recall, we put Ashley in a heat with two of your best swimmers and the end result was she blew them away.

Yep, I do remember that, but those two guys are great midshipman, and both were extremely complimentary of Ashley's abilities. In fact I know that both of them have followed her progress, and I think they may have also attended one or two of your meets just to watch her.

Brad, I don't think either of those guys have done anything but I do think someone else who watched that placement race that day, may have not liked a women beating two of the top men. I have no idea if I'm right, but we do have one small clue. Whoever entered that room this morning had on a pair of black running shoes. The right shoe has a small black puma logo on it. I would appreciate it if you would keep your eye out in your locker room, and if you happen to see a pair of shoes that fit that bill, please let me know.

I don't want either of us to be involved in this, so if the shoes appear, we will turn it over to Kyle and his security staff to make the appropriate inquires.

I'll do it Mike, I feel very bad for Ashley and hope we have some luck identifying this guy.

In fact, I will make it a point to be in the locker room tomorrow as the team members arrive to change for practice. Who knows, maybe we will get lucky. Hope your season continues to be great. Thanks Brad, I appreciate your keeping your eye out.

CHAPTER 16

MISSSION ACCOMPLISHED

It was 10:15 AM and Roscoe and Kyle were standing under the pull up bar at the Gym. OK, who goes first today Roscoe? I think it's your turn Kyle, so have at it.

Kyle Obermeyer was 34 years old and a former military policeman. He was in great shape, and stayed that way in part due to his job as head of security for the yard and in part because that was a part of his makeup. He had met Roscoe in the gym shortly after Roscoe had been assigned the Naval Seal Recruiting position at the Academy. They were about the same age and both were in perfect shape.

They had become good friends, but both were competitive and their workouts together provided them the chance to earn bragging rights for a couple of days between workouts. Kyle jumped up and grabbed the high bar and began his pull up routine. His goal was always to hit 20. Some days he exceeded his goal and other days he fell short. Today was a good day, and as he approached the 20 number, he felt good enough to squeeze out 6 more. He dropped off the bar and said Mr. Seal you are up with a smile on his face.

Roscoe loved the challenge and easily pulled the first 20. Once there it got tougher, but he knew all he need to make was seven more. He did it and dropped down and said two words to Kyle. Gotch Ya.

As they moved over to the weight room, Roscoe asked Kyle if he was able to get hold of Mike Morgan regarding the Plebe Harassment issue they had discussed. Kyle briefed him on his conversation with Mike, and told Roscoe that he had made the suggestion to Mike that he talk to the Men's Coach about his concern and the black running shoe issue. Mike immediately called the Men's Coach Brad Johnson, and explained the situation to him, and his interest in the black running shoes with the white puma on the back of the right shoe.

Brad was helpful and said he would keep his eye out.

So, now Roscoe, we wait, but I did decide that if I don't hear anything back today or tomorrow morning that I am going to contact the disciplinary panel and let them know what we found on the tape.

I think they need to know that someone went into that room while those girls were at formation and breakfast. The panel needs to know that fact before they come back to Plebe Jamison with a finding.

Thanks Kyle, I think that will be most helpful. While it isn't total proof it does confirm the fact that someone went in to their room that was not authorized to do so and they did so just prior to the inspection taking place.

I also told Mike that I would be more than happy to handle any additional investigation should our mystery shoes show up on someone. Great Kyle. I'm sure that the coaches are relived that if something does come up that it will not be up to them to deal with the issue.

At 4PM Mike held the normal women's practice. Ashley was there and went about her business like nothing had happened the day before. At 2PM Brad Johnson wandered into the men's locker room and made small talk with some of his varsity swimmers as they were getting changed. They had the pool from 2 to 4

It didn't take him long to spot a pair of black running shoes with a small white puma on the back. He almost said something, but then decided against it. He spent a little more time looking at the shoes and saw that they belonged to a second year midshipman by the name of Bryce Allen. Allen was a Junior varsity swimmer, so Brad did not know him well. He did know that he had a reputation as someone who was very competitive and didn't like losing. Brad left the locker room and conducted the practice until it was over at 4PM.

At 4PM he made a call to Kyle Obermeyer at the security office. Hey Kyle, this is Brad Johnson. I am the Men's Varsity Swimming Coach here at the Academy.

My pal, Mike Morgan, gave me your name and also gave me a brief assignment to determine if I had a swimmer in my program who had a pair of black running shoes with a small white puma emblem on the back of the right shoe.

Well, I had the opportunity to be in the locker room this afternoon when the guys were changing for our work out, and as luck would have it, I spotted a pair of black running shoes with a while puma on the back of the right shoe.

They belong to a second year midshipman whose name is Bryce Allen. I don't know much about Mr. Allen as he swims on our junior varsity team but I have heard that he is very competitive and doesn't take well to loosing. Mike told me to let you know if I found anything out and that you would take it from there. Thanks Coach, I will be in touch with Mr. Allen in the morning and we will see what we can find out.

Kyle made a couple of phone calls and eventually contacted the Company Commander that was in charge of Midshipmen Allen's company. Kyle explained to the company commander that he wanted to speak to midshipman Allen regarding a security matter and he would like him excused from the morning formation and to report directly to the security office. The Company Commander agreed and said he would advise Midshipman Allen in the morning. He said he would direct him to the office around 8:15 AM.

Kyle then called Roscoe and briefed him on the finding and

told him that he would question the kid in the morning. Kyle indicated that he would report the result to the disciplinary panel. He also told Roscoe that if Midshipman Allen had entered the girls room without authorization that that act, in and of itself, would be a major violation of Naval Policy, and the grounds for immediate administrative termination from the Academy. In addition he let Roscoe know that he had talked to a couple of other people that had shed some real light on the whole thing.

All Roscoe said was "What a stupid kid". Thanks Kyle, I'll be interested to hear what you learn.

The next morning at formation, the company commander asked Midshipman second class Allen to come forward. He then told him that he was dismissed from the formation, and was to proceed directly to the Yard Security Office. He was told to ask for the Head of Security Mr. Obermeyer.

Bryce's antenna went up immediately. All he could think about was did they find out? and if so how?. He had not mentioned a word to anyone and it had been more than two months since the placement race had occurred.

In any event, he knew that it was unusual to be called to the security office, and so, by the time he arrived he was very nervous.

He entered the office and was greeted by a women at the front desk. She was obviously a civilian dressed in civilian attire. Good morning Mam, my name is Midshipman Bryce Allen and I have been requested to meet with the Yard Security Director Mr. Obermeyer. Just a minute Midshipman Allen, I will tell Mr. Obermeyer that you are here.

A few minutes later, Kyle Obermeyer appeared and proceeded to walk over to Midshipman Allen. Midshipman Allen I presume. Yes Sir. Good Morning. My name is Kyle Obermeyer and I am the Security Director for the Yard. Kyle extended his hand and Midshipman Allen shook it and said it is nice to meet you sir.

Please come into my office. Midshipman Allen followed Kyle

into his office and remained standing. Kyle sat behind his desk and said, please have a seat. I'm sure you are wondering why you are here this morning Midshipman Allen, so I want you to know right away that I have some important questions to ask you, and I expect to get truthful answers to all of them. Do you understand? Yes Sir.

Well, let's start with an easy one. Do you own a pair of black running shoes with a small white logo on the right shoes heal? Yes Sir, I do. Good, now let me ask you this.

Did you attend breakfast after formation yesterday morning? No Sir, I did not feel like eating and returned to my room after formation.

Midshipman, have you ever been in or on the second floor of the Women's section of the dorm? Bryce paused for a brief moment and then said no Sir. Are you sure of that Midshipman Allen? Yes Sir, I don't ever recall being on the women's dorm room floor.

Well, that is very interesting because most Midshipman have excellent memories, and to meet one that doesn't is a bit surprising to me. Let me show you a brief video tape Midshipman Allen. Kyle flipped the computer screen around from facing him on the desk to facing Midshipman Allen. Now, let me show you a video. Allen just watched in silence.

Does the person in that video look familiar to you Midshipman Allen? No sir. Take a look at the shoes that person has on. Are those your shoes Midshipman Allen? They look like the pair I own, but I don't know if those shoes are mine Sir, maybe someone took them from my room and wore them without my permission.

Let me ask you a couple of more questions Midshipman Allen. Did you attend a women's swim trial that occurred over two months ago, before the competitive swim season began?

I don't recall Sir. Well let me refresh your memory. You did attend that event with another junior varsity swimmer whose name is Peter Flemming. Midshipman Flemming told me last night that you were with him and that you were frustrated that one of the women swimmers beat the best two Varsity Men's swimmers in that placement trial. Now do you remember?

Now that you mention it, I do remember that, I attended that meet but what does that have to do with me here this morning?

Well Midshipman Allen, I think it has a lot to do with you, and if I am correct then you are about to face a number of various charges.

Let's go back to video for a minute. I want you to watch what the maintenance worker in that video does. Bryce watched as the worker entered into the room and was back out and headed down the hall within a minute. I am going to ask you one more time Midshipman Allen. Is that maintenance worker in uniform you? No Sir.

OK then, can you explain to me how your roommate Midshipman Adderly observed a Yard Maintenance Uniform wadded up in the bottom of your closet yesterday morning? He saw it when he returned from breakfast.

No Sir, I can't explain that. Midshipman Allen, I want you to know that this security office is about to file a formal charge against you for stealing and duplicating a master maintenance dorm key, breaking and entering into a women's midshipman dorm room and for planting a half full beer bottle in one of the women's desk drawers with the knowledge that the women in question was about to undergo the Alpha Inspection. You knew that the bottle of beer would be grounds for failing the inspection, and could be grounds for much worse.

It is our contention that the women who you targeted for this action was none other than the women who beat the two varsity swimmers in that trial two months ago.

It is also our belief, that for some weird reason, you held a grudge against this women and hoped that by taking the actions you did that this woman would be disciplined and perhaps dismissed from the Academy for a violation of the Plebe Alcohol policy.

What do you have to say Midshipmen Allen? Bryce just looked down at his hands that were in his lap. They were both shaking.

I guess I would like to know what happens from here? Once you file the complaint, what happens? Well, the charges that we are intending to bring against you are criminal and the filing will be made with the Maryland Police Department. They could carry with them some jail time if you are convicted. At a minimum, you will be dismissed from the Academy, and your parents will be notified.

I'm not sure why you did such a stupid thing, but even though you have not admitted it, I think it is pretty clear you did it. I do have one thing that you may want to consider before I turn this over to the police.

What is that Mr. Obermeyer? Well, if you admit that you did this, and agree to be administratively discharged from the academy, then I would be willing to not file the complaint with the police department, If that happens you would not be put through the formal arrest and trial procedures.

My findings would be made to the base commander, and in most of these incidences the commander follows my recommendation. If this were to happen, it will happen quickly and you will be out of here and on your way home tomorrow night.

It sounds to me like I don't have much of a choice. I did it and I'm sorry I did it and put Ashley Jamison through the failed inspection and disciplinary hearing. I don't even know her and I have never met her, but I let my temper get the best of me and this time I will really pay a price. Will I have to face her and formally apologize for my actions? No, we have nothing to gain by that. You will simply sign a confession statement this morning and we will have a ruling from the base commander shortly thereafter. If we get the ruling today, you will be gone this evening. If we get the ruling tomorrow,

you will be gone by noon tomorrow.

Needless to say son, you have really screwed up, and are about to pay a big price for your actions. May I tell my parents. Sure, I don't care who does it but I want them to know what you did and why you are being dismissed from the Academy.

I will want you to show them a copy of your signed confession and will ask that a signed copy of it be returned to my office by them once they have seen it.

OK Mr. Obermeyer, I am prepared to sign the statement and will insure that my parents see it and return a signed copy to you.

OK then let's get it prepared and signed. Once we have that done, I will ask that you return to your room, and wait to hear from me later today.

The statement was prepared in detail and Bryce signed it. Once that was done, Kyle called the Senior Midshipman on the disciplinary panel and let him know what had transpired.

Thanks Mr. Obermeyer, no one on our panel wanted to discipline Ashley for anything, but without additional evidence we were at a loss to know what to do. This helps us a lot. We are scheduled to call her back to give her our finding later today so this will make it easy. We will find that she did nothing wrong, that the issue has been resolved, and appropriate action taken and that the Alpha inspection for she and her roommates room will be marked as completed satisfactorily.

Ashley got word before practice that she needed to appear once again before the Disciplinary Panel at 5PM. She let Cindy know, but had no idea what would happen next. Mike talked to Cindy and once again was present at the hearing.

At 5PM Ashley was asked to enter the room and stand before the panel. Midshipman Jamison, you have been asked to appear before this panel this afternoon to receive notification of the findings, and actions we intend to take, regarding the incident involving the open beer container located in your room.

Ashley said nothing she just looked straight ahead at the

panel members. It is our finding that in this case you did nothing wrong.

It is our opinion that you had nothing to do with the open beer bottle found in your room and as such, all charges considered have been totally dropped.

It is this panels further finding that you and your roommate completed satisfactorily the Alpha inspection, and thus, you will receive a passing grade on that. Do you have any questions? No Sir. Then you are dismissed. Ashley turned and left the room. Mike sat in the back of the room and just smiled. He knew that he now owed the men's varsity coach both drinks and a dinner.

Ashley walked slowly back to her room. It was though she was in a daze. She just couldn't believe what had just happened and she had no idea what had transpired.

Something must have gone on behind the scenes but no one had told her anything.

Roscoe got back to his office and called his pal Kyle Obermeyer. Good Evening, Obermeyer speaking. Hey Kyle, it's Roscoe. Hi Pal, what's up. I just wanted to thank you for your effort on behalf of Ashley Jamison. I attended the administrative hearing this afternoon and all charges were dropped and she and her roommate were given a passing grade on their inspection so all is now well.

Did you get to the bottom of why the kid did it. Yep, he was just really stupid and very competitive. He didn't even know Ashley or her roommate

He just wanted to get even for the trouncing the men took in that swim race two months ago. It is amazing to me how hard someone has to work to get in and through this place and to have it all thrown out the window with on e stupid act is almost beyond me. Oh well, all's well that ends well. Are we on for our workout tomorrow morning. Yep, I will see you there. Thanks again.

CHAPTER 17

AND THE BEAT GOES ON

Bryce Allen sat in his midshipman dorm room. It was now 2PM and this was the worst day of his life. He just got off the phone with his Dad, and had explained to him that he would be leaving the Naval Academy, and returning home either late today or tomorrow. He explained to his father what he had done, and why, and admitted that it was the dumbest thing he had ever done. His Dad was very disappointed, but knew what the consequences of his son's actions could have been, and was only glad that the Security Staff had given Bryce an alternative that did not involve the local police.

Bryce had called his Dad, as he just didn't have the stomach to call his Mom. She was so proud that he had been selected to attend the Naval Academy, and had told all of her friends about how her "outstanding" son had been selected. He would leave it to his Dad to break the news to her.

As he sat there, he had a tear develop in his eye, and was lamenting his situation when the phone rang. He picked up and said, Good Afternoon this is Midshipman Bryce Allen speaking. Midshipman Allen, this is Kyle Obermeyer. Yes Mr. Obermeyer. I just heard back from the Academy Commandant, and he confirmed what we discussed. Effective today you will be administratively discharged from the Naval Academy. The paperwork is being sent to my office and should be here in an hour. You should plan to drop by, and sign the necessary forms on your way out of the yard.

You are to leave all of your Navy issued clothes and equipment in your room, and pack your civilian clothes for departure. Once that is completed, you should plan to stop by my office on your way off campus. Have you contacted your family yet? Yes Sir, I have talked with my father and he is aware of all of the details that we discussed. He is also prepared to sign the form we discussed, and will do so when I return. Thank you Midshipman Allen.

Do you have any additional questions? Just one Sir. Should I leave a note for my roommate? No, that will not be necessary. We will make sure he is informed of the fact that you have decided to leave the Academy. No more will be said. We intend to move forward as though this event did not happen.

OK. Thanks Mr. Obermeyer.

Bryce did as he was instructed. When his stuff was packed and his Navy issued clothes and equipment were placed neatly in the closet, he headed out the door with his suitcase.

He had called the airport and confirmed that there was a flight leaving at 7PM that evening for Atlanta and he planned to be on it. The sooner he put this mess behind him the better.

He arrived at the Security Office, signed the appropriate papers and caught a cab to the airport. What a miserable day it had been.

Ashley arrived back to her room at about 530PM. Your back so soon Martha said. Is everything OK?

Yes, everything is fine, but this whole incident is just one big puzzlement. Why? What happened at the disciplinary hearing? Actually, nothing. I was called in. I stood at attention, the lead panel officer looked at me and said that all charges against me had been dropped, that my record would not reflect any of this, and that our room had been given a passing grade for the Alpha Inspection.

I was then dismissed. What? You have got to be kidding me

Ash. This whole thing makes no sense to me. It doesn't make any sense to me either Martha, but I have decided to forget it ever happened, and just get back to normal. Probably a good idea Ash, but it still is a big mystery to me.

It is to me too Martha, but I have been told in the past that the Military has a way of making things disappear when they want, and perhaps this was one of those things. In any event let's go to lunch.

I have practice at 4PM, and I don't want to miss it. These stupid hearings have cost me to miss two of them, and we have another meet coming up in two weeks. I'm all for lunch Ash, let's go.

Ashley made practice at 4:00 PM, and didn't miss another practice from then on. In November they had dual meets with the College of William and Mary, Towson University, Becknell University and the University of North Carolina.

Ashley continued to participate in the three events she had agreed to. The 200 freestyle was her favorite. The 100 meter butterfly was real hard work, but she felt it was a good test of her upper body strength. The relay team experience was the one team event she could participate in and enjoy with her team mates.

She continued to go undefeated in the 200 freestyle event and finally lost a butterfly race to a women from the University of North Carolina. She swam well, but just couldn't stay with the women who had specialized in the butterfly race since she was little. Cindy met with Ashley after the race loss to make sure she was OK with it, and would learn from it. She knew how competitive Ashley was and, she didn't want her to get down after her first individual loss of the year.

Hey Ash, how did you feel about that butterfly? Cindy asked. Well Coach, I really don't like to lose, but I knew going in that the girl I would face specialized in that race, and has since she was 3 or 4 years old. I'm OK with the loss but will look forward to another chance to race her at the Patriot League

Championships in the spring. Good Ash, I thought you swam well, and saw a couple of things we can work on that should help you get the edge you want. Thanks Coach.

Ash returned to her room after the North Carolina race. Martha was there and said Hey Ash, have you thought anything about Thanksgiving?

Not really, other than it will be the first break that we have had since day 1. I would really like to fly home, and see my Mom and Dad and my brother, but I'm not sure there is going to be enough time.

We only have a couple of days off, plus the weekend and my coaches want to continue with optional swimming practices over the holiday.

We have Army on the race calendar in early December, and I know that is a match that they really want to win. What are you going to do Martha? My folks want me to come home to San Diego, but like you, it is a long way for a very short turn around. I'm thinking that for me, Christmas will be a much better holiday to go home than Thanksgiving. I know a lot of the west coast midshipman are choosing to stay here for Thanksgiving, since they are watching expenses, and will be going home for Christmas instead. I have checked into the options available if we stay here, and there are a few that are of interest. What did you find out Martha?

Well I'm told that a number of midshipman are going to spend the day with their sponsor family or go home locally with a friend who lives closer to the Academy.

Personally, I don't know anyone who lives close and have no invitations. My host family has invited me for Thanksgiving dinner, and if I stay around, I will take them up on that.

I have been given that option as well, and if I stay, I plan to train, rest, and go to dinner at their home. I haven't made a final decision and I know my folks will be disappointed if I don't come home, but I think they will understand particularly with the Army dual meet coming up right after the holiday.

Well Ash, let me know what you decide. It might be nice to have a couple of days together here to rest and catch up. I agree Martha, and will let you know after I talk to my coaches.

Hi Mom, Hi Ash how are you doing? I'm fine but will be glad when this Plebe year is finished. There are times when it tests all of the patience you have. I understand Honey. What brings you to call today?

Well, I had a good talk with my coaches yesterday about Thanksgiving. We have our big swimming meet with Army set for December 1st and as a result they are going to have practices during the Thanksgiving Holiday. I checked the schedule, and we only have a couple of days off for that holiday, so I think I will stay here, use the time to train, rest, and study, and look forward to the Christmas Holiday when we have some real time off.

Well that is disappointing news, we were so looking forward to having you home. What will you do for Thanksgiving Dinner? I have been invited by my host family to have it with them, so I think that is what I will do. My roommate Martha is not going back to San Diego for Thanksgiving either. She just doesn't think that there will be enough time to enjoy it before she is on a plane and headed back here.

What do you think your Christmas Holiday will look like Ash? Well, all I can say is, Hooray for Christmas. I'm told that we have a lot of time off. I think it will amount to several weeks. So I plan to spend the entire time at home. It will give me time to catch up with friends, see Coach Nancy, and spend some time with you and Dad.

I will plan to work out with team Unify while I'm home, so I don't think it will have any impact on me. We also have what's call MAC flights available to us for $10.00. They are flights that a military member can use from any military airport.

That sounds like a great benefit, but I can tell you that it is not one you will need for Christmas. Your father has already said that he is flying you first class to Portland International Airport, and he is ready to make the reservations when you give me the dates. Thanks Mom, that will be really something to look forward to.

Dad and I have been reading about your swimming, and it looks like they are pretty happy to have you swimming for the Navy. Yes, I have had a good go at the 200 yard free and so far I'm unbeaten. The 100 meter butterfly is another thing.

I'm really working at it, but I got beat by a girl from the University of North Carolina the other day, and I didn't like it. I think I am just going to have to pick up the pace and work harder. Ash, hard work is your middle name so I have no doubt that you will improve and I already feel sorry for that girl if you meet her in the Patriot Championships in the spring. Thanks Mom, but your just talking like a Mom is supposed to.

How is school? So far no real problem. I have to declare a major after this year and I want to talk to you and Dad about it when I'm home for Christmas. Right now it looks like computer science, but who knows. I will go over the alternatives with you when I'm home.

Well, I've got to go, my time limit on the phone is now over. Love you Mom, I'll talk to you soon. Bye Ash.

Ashley let Martha know that evening that she had decided to stay on the yard for Thanksgiving, and told her that she had discussed it with her Mom and Coaches.

Martha had decided to do the same so the two of them would have some time to be together without the rigors of the Plebe schedule.

The weekend came fast and on Sunday Morning Ashley awoke early went for her morning run and then stopped off at the gym. She wanted to work out on the high bar, more to see if she could still do it, than to prove anything to anyone. She felt the upper body workout would be good for her, and maybe help her with her butterfly performance..

When she got to the gym she could see that there were

two men working out in the Gymnastics room. One was on the parallel bars, and the other was working on the rings. They were obviously gymnasts as both had very well developed and strong upper bodies.

Ash did some warm up exercises and then moved over to the high bar.

Both of the boys looked at her with surprised looks. They simply were not use to seeing a girl in the gymnastics room. There were two reasons for that. Number one was that the Academy did not have a women's gymnastics team. and number two the equipment in the gymnastics room was so specialized that few knew how to use it.

Ashley looked at the boys and said, hey guys, would you do me a favor and spot me on the high bar. I want to do a few rotations and a dismount, and I don't want to end up on my head. Both boys just looked at each other and with great doubt they said sure and moved to positions on either side of the high bar.

One of the boys, helped Ashley as she jumped up and grabbed a hold of the bar. Once up she was feeling good, and soon was able to swing her body back and forth and then with one smooth motion she was over the top of the bar with a 360 rotation. She did it four times in a row and then did a single summersault dismount and landing it perfectly.

The two boys were dumbfounded. All Ashley said was thanks guys, and she headed out the door and back to her room.

Did you just see what I saw one of the guys said to the other. I don't believe it, but I know I saw it. Wait tell we tell the coach. He may want to integrate our team. They both laughed and went back to their workout.

CHAPTER 18

HOME FOR THE HOLIDAY'S

It was Monday afternoon. Ashley was at swimming practice, and today she was going to work with Cindy on the butterfly. She was bound and determined to get better at that race and today was the new beginning.

Across campus at Macdonough Hall the men's gymnastics team was getting prepared for their daily workout. This year the Navy would host the All Academy Gymnastics Championships, and for the first time in a long time, the Navy was the defending champions.

The all academy Championship would be the third time that all three Academies went at each other in a joint meet. The last time, the event was held on the West Point Campus, and the mids were able to beat the Black Knights, but it was not an easy win. The Navy was faced with a 3.65 point deficit with just two events left, the parallel bars and the high bar, the Navy Gymnastics Team put its head down and earned a dramatic .55 point come from behind victory over the Army Black knights. It provided bragging rights for some time for both the coaches and the athletes and you could tell from the intensity of the practices that the coaches definitely wanted to repeat, especially since it would be held in their YARD.

One of the hero's of that event was Ryan Joshua. Ryan was one of the leaders of the men's team and specialized in the high bar. He put on a great performance and with the help of his team mates, pulled off a great upset. It was the high bar performance that put the team over the top. Today at practice Ryan and his best friend Travis Michaels were standing under the high bar about ready to begin their routine practice. Just as they were about to mount the bar their coach, Tim Worthy, came up to them and said, "you guys ready to go, we need another great performance out of both of you?" Yep coach, I think we are both ready but before we get started today, we want to tell you a quick story about this bar.

OK shoot. Well, Ryan said, we were working out Sunday morning in here when a woman midshipman came in to the gym. She had obviously been out for a run and then came in here to do some stretching etc.

Travis and I thought nothing of it until she finished her stretching and came over to the high bar. Obviously, we are not use to seeing a women work out with, or even come near, any of our gymnastic equipment. So we were super surprised when she asked if we would mind spotting her while she worked out on the high bar. We looked at each other and then said, sure no problem. We helped her mount the high bar, and then took our spotting positions. She was obviously comfortable with the equipment and got her body swinging right away. It didn't take her but a moment to get moving and then she did four perfect 360's and a summersault front dismount. To emphasis the fact she knew what she was doing, she stuck the landing.

After her perfect dismount, she looked at us, said thanks guys, and left the gym. I'm telling you coach, I don't think we have anyone on our team that could pull of that routine as perfect as she did. Wow guys sounds like this might be the time to integrate the Men's gymnastics team. They all laughed and went back to work.

That night after practice, the coach told his assistant Marty Bleak the story. Marty thought for a moment and then said, "I bet I know who that was? Who? and how would you know? Tim asked.

Well, you may not be aware of this, but we have a Plebe who is swimming for Navy on the women's team that is really good. In fact, I think she is currently undefeated in the 200 meter free, and is breaking records almost each time she goes out.

Her name is Ashley Morgan Jamison. Ashley grew up in Portland Oregon and swam for Team Unify. I know this because Team Unify is one of the teams in the United States that my girlfriend scouts for the major schools in the Patriot League.

Team unify is one of those teams that produces the quality of swimmers that can make it to the United States Team.

The academy generally does not recruit from Team Unify as admission here requires a lot more than gifted athletic ability, and besides that it comes with a military obligation following graduation. Not all athletes aspire to that.

In any event, for some reason that no one knows, Ashley decided she wanted to apply to the Naval Academy and was accepted. Mike Morgan almost fell off his chair when he heard she was going to come to school here, and he couldn't wait to get her participating on the Navy Women's' Team.

To make this already too long story come to an end, I am told that Ashley had five full time offers to attend Division I schools on scholarship. Three were for swimming and two were for gymnastics.

One of the schools that offered her a gymnastic scholarship was Penn State University which is a member of our conference. My girl friend has seen Ashley both in the pool and on the high bar, and she told me that she is super special. So, if I'm right, we have a swimmer, swimming for the Academy, who is also an outstanding gymnast. My guess is that that person is Ashley Jamison. Mystery solved. Well I'll be dammed. Both Travis and Ryan said they had never seen anything like it, They said that what she did in front of them on Sunday morning they didn't think anyone on our team could do. I think I may attend the next swimming meet just to see this woman in action. My guess you will be wowed by her.

Thanksgiving came and went and was pretty uneventful. Ashley and Martha actually went to a movie, had a couple of dinners out together, studied and slept. They both went to their respective sponsors house for Thanksgiving dinner, and both enjoyed the company and the break from Plebe life.

It was December 1st and Army was in the YARD for their swimming match with Navy.

Army vs. Navy anything got everyone's juices flowing and, given the great start the Navy Women's team had had this season, the stands were filled to the brim.

Ashley was scheduled to swim in her three races. The 100 butterfly would be first, followed by the 200 meter freestyle and then the final race of the event would be the dual relay. Ashley was scheduled to swim in the third position of the relay.

When it was time for the Butterfly, Ashley approached her lane and looked up in the stands. They were packed, and while she had swam in front of some large crowds before, she was sure that she had never swam in front of a crowd this large.

She took her position on the starting block, assumed the ready position and was set to go when the gun went off. She had been working on her upper body strength and could tell halfway into the first lap that the training was paying off. She was stronger and more in control of her butterfly strokes. By the end of the first lap she had a lead on the field, and by the end of the race, when her hand touched the wall she could hear a huge roar from the crowd. She looked up at the clock and saw what the commotion was about. She had just set a new Patriot Conference record, and she did it in the butterfly.

The results of her 200 meter freestyle were just as impressive. While she didn't break the woman's record, she was inching closer, and was only I full second off. The relay was anti climatic but Navy did squeeze out a victory and the Army team left the YARD with their heads down.

There were some people in the stands that were very interested in Ashley, but all for different reasons. Roscoe brought Kyle to let him see the real Ashley Jamison in action, and Marty Bleak brought Tim, Ryan and Travis. When Ashley came out to take her position for the Butterfly Marty looked at Ryan and Travis.

Is that the women who you met on the high bar in the gym?

I'll be damned. It is her. What is her name? Ryan asked.

Ashley Morgan Jamison and I'm sure you will hear that name over and over again for the next few years at this Academy.

It was two weeks before Christmas. Their first semester at the Academy was completed and all of the Plebes were anxious to get out and everyone wanted to know what kind of grades they got. Plebes could access their grades from home, but they had to have an account set up prior to leaving for Christmas leave. All of the midshipmen were given ample notice and instructions before leaving for break. Only midshipmen who had set up a remote account could access their grades. All other had to wait until they got back to the Academy to see their results. Ashley and Martha had both set up remote accounts and neither was worried about their grades. Ashley knew Martha would do well and she felt good that her grades, while not at the very top of the class, would be fine.

There was lots of talk by both men and women Plebes during the weeks leading up to Christmas about how they were going to deal with past relationships once they got home. After the first semester, many of the high school relationships just went by the wayside, and Christmas was usually the time when prior attachments failed.

Most attachments did not last through the Plebe year. It just seemed that by Christmas many girlfriends/boy friend's had readjusted to a world without their sweetheart. Plebes had discovered a whole new world that outsiders just couldn't understand. There was often stress, and emotional breakups at this time of the year.

Ashley was just very happy that she had no one to break up with. She felt for Martha who she knew had a boyfriend at home, and that this would be the end of that relationship.

Ashley gave Martha a hug and headed for the airport. She was dressed in civilian clothes, and frankly felt a little strange not to be in uniform.

She had a United Flight to Portland. It was a round trip first class ticket that her Dad had sent her with a note that said, we can't wait to see you have a good flight.

Ashley had never flown first class in her life so it was a new experience. Everyone around her was drinking free drinks but she had no interest, She just ordered a diet coke. She was so tired, she missed half of the flight because she was asleep. She woke up when the pilot came on and said Ladies and Gentleman, this is the Captain speaking. We are beginning our final approach into Portland International Airport We should be on the ground in about 15 minutes. The weather in Portland is pretty standard for Portland. It is 60 degrees and a light rain is falling. The good news is everything I am looking down on is green except that big white mountain we are about to fly over. For those of you on the right side of the plane you will shortly see Mt. Hood, which is eleven thousand five hundred feet high.

Ashley realized that because she was in first class she would be exiting the plane first. She only had her one carryon bag so she was ready to go when the door opened. She walked off the plane and through the airport. Once she had exited the secure part of the airport she saw them. Her Dad and Mom were there with open arms and, even her brother John was there to greet her.

Hugs were had by all. The night seemed to be one of constant questions and conversation. Before she knew it, it was 11:00 PM and she was totally beat. She headed for her own room, and fell into bed, as though the last six months had just been a dream.

Ashley woke up at 330 AM. At first she didn't even know where she was, and then it all became clear. Her body was telling her to get up for formation, but that was just not going to happen today nor for the next couple of weeks.

She had a big smile on her face as she fell immediately back to sleep.

She finally got up at 9:30 AM and headed out to the kitchen. Hey sleepy head, welcome home. Can I make you some breakfast? Wow, that would be great Mom. How does two eggs over easy with ham, toast, orange slices, and coffee sound. No problem with that Mom. I'll go clean up a bit and be back in a couple of minutes.

Well what do you have planned for today? Sarah asked her. I am going down to the Y to see Coach Nancy and schedule some time to work out with the team. I have also made a time to see Mrs. Atherton at Grant tomorrow. I just wanted to drop by and thank you for her help and to give her some feedback on what the Plebe experience is all about. That sounds like a good plan.

What time will you be home tonight? I plan to be home by 6PM for dinner, if that is OK. Sure, no problem. I'm sure your Dad will have about 100 more questions for you at dinner. I'm thinking that Mexican might be good tonight? Does that sound good to you. Sure I'm up for anything. OK, I'll try to surprise you.

Ashley was dressed, and out the door by 11:00 AM. She caught Max and headed downtown. Her first stop was going to be "Killer Burger". Killer Burger was located at 510 SW 3rd avenue right downtown. It was on the corner of 3rd and Washington and Ashley knew exactly what she wanted.

She walked in and ordered at the counter. I would like to have the 1/3 lb Peanut Butter, pickle and Bacon Burger. Yes Mam, that comes with fry's how would you like it done. Medium

Please. What would you like to drink? Diet Coke Please. Here is your number your burger will be up shortly.

Ashley took a seat in the booth and her mouth started to water.

She finished her burger and headed over to the Y. She was sure that she had just had the best meal of her life. It tasted just like she remembered and she vowed to make sure she would return at least one more time before she headed back to the YARD.

Coach Nancy was waiting for her and hugs were had by all. Team Unify would start their practice at 3:30 PM so Ashley had some time to catch up with her. She didn't have to fill her in on much, because Coach Nancy had kept up with Ashley's progress and record performances.

How do you like the Butterfly Ash? Getting use to it. Last time out against Army it went well. I have been working a lot more on my upper body strength, and that seems to be making a difference. I got beat in the race by a girl from North Carolina but I think I will have the opportunity to meet her again in the spring and I am looking forward to the challenge.

Your performance in the 200 continues to amaze me. Do you realize how close you are getting to a world record? Yes, I guess so. Well girl, I can't wait for you to break it, because I know you're going to do it. I don't know when it will happen, but I sure wish I could be there to see it when it does.

Are you going to train while your home? Yep, that is one of the reasons I wanted to see you. Would it be OK if I worked out with the team while I'm home. My coaches would like it if I did. It would be fine. Cindy already called me. She and I go back pretty far. Do you want to do it from 4 to 6 like normal. That would be great. OK then we are all set. It's great to have you home Ash. I will look forward to seeing you in the pool tomorrow afternoon. Thanks Coach. I'll be here.

CHAPTER 19

BACK TO THE YARD

The Christmas Holiday went by so fast Ashley could hardly believe it. She managed to workout with Team Unify three days per week, and she had a great Christmas with her family. As a plebe, Ashley had little need for traditional Christmas gifts, so her parents thought long and hard about what to get her that would be really appreciated.

They knew that Ashley had a lot to deal with in her second semester at the YARD. Not only would her studies be difficult, but her swimming schedule would culminate with the Patriot Championships and perhaps the NCAA finals after that.

So all of their research indicated that the one thing that meant the most to Plebes during their second semester was spring break.

Some would want to return home, but the vast majority of plebes and midshipman for that matter, used that break as a way to get out of town and go to someplace warm and inviting.

The Caribbean and Florida were at the top of most lists. Jim and Sarah learned that some plebes planned months in advance to take a trip to some new and exotic place. They learned that midshipman's military status gave them special room rates and discounts in theme parks, and hotels, and that often they could get discounts at restaurants and movie theaters.

So after their research was completed, they decided on the perfect gift. Under the tree with her name on it was an envelope. In the envelop were two round trip pre-paid tickets to anywhere that United Airlines fly's.

The note simply said, "Merry Christmas" Enjoy your spring break with a friend. Love You. Mom and Dad.

Needless to say it was a gift that Ashley loved and it started her thinking about spring break months in advance.

Before she left Portland, she made one last trip to Killer Burger and had the 1/3 lb Peanut Butter, pickle and Bacon Burger. She savored every bite, as she knew, there would be nothing like it on any meal menu she would have over the next six months.

Before she left home, she confirmed with her folks her swimming schedule. They had indicated that they would like to come to the Patriot League Championships, and they wanted to confirm time and place. They knew that Ashley would have little, if any, social time during the event, but they had become real swimming race fans over the years and to some extent found themselves living vicariously through Ashley's numerous athletic performances.

The flight back was uneventful, and before she knew it, life was back into the same groove it was before Christmas. Martha was back as well and, as she had indicated prior to going home, her previous love life was over. As it turns out, it wasn't just a one way street, her boyfriend had also come to the conclusion that the long distance relationship was just not going to work, so they parted good friends.

Ashley's swimming schedule continued with one dual meet in January. It was with the University of Richmond. She raced in her three events and won both of the individual races by a wide margin, and her relay team won as well. She continued to work on the butterfly and her upper body strength. Before she knew it, the Patriot league Championship were right around the corner. They were being held at the end of February at Bucknell's, Kinney Natatorium in Lewisburg, Pennsylvania.

The Championships were to begin on Wednesday Feb 20th, and conclude on Saturday Feb 23rd. Preliminaries were slated for 10AM on Thursday, Friday, and Saturday, with the finals scheduled for 6pm each day.

Ashley was scheduled to swim the 200 free on Thursday and the 100 Butterfly on Friday. The relay team would swim on Saturday, the final day.

There were three heats in each race. The top three swimmers in each heat moved to the final that evening.

Over the years Navy had finished in the middle of the pack most years. The quality of swimmers at the other division one schools were just a cut above the swimmers that the Navy was able to recruit. This year, however, the Navy coaches were very optimistic. They knew that they had one swimmer who was a cut above everyone else.

The coaches worked with the swimmers on an individual basis leading up to the Championships. They wanted to perfect performance where possible. The workouts were no more strenuous than normal, but they were more focused. In the 200 Cindy continued to work with Ashley on perfecting her turns, and in the Butterfly, more attention was paid to building her upper body strength.

Jim and Sarah scheduled their trip to Lewisburg so they would arrive on Tuesday evening and fly back to Portland on Sunday morning. Jim scheduled the flights and was surprised to learn that they could fly directly to Lewisburg from Portland International. It was a flight that took about 4 hours, but was direct so they were happy.

Neither had ever been to Lewisburg, so they were both looking forward to both the swimming, as well as a tour of the Bucknell campus and downtown Lewisburg.

Sara spent some time researching the town of Lewisburg. She learned that Lewisburg is a hub of cultural and economic vitality in Central Pennsylvania's Susquehanna River Valley. She was aware of Bucknell University, but didn't know much about it, so the University itself would be interesting to learn about as well.

She learned that the town off Lewisburg is what historians have classified as a Pennsylvania Town, which means it has a distinct town layout, developed in Colonial Pennsylvania

The classic form, which Lewisburg followed, had a main street with a town square in the center, usually with a courthouse.

The streets in the typical colonial Pennsylvania town are numbered in one direction, and named after trees in the other. In the case of Lewisburg, the streets parallel to the main street were all named after saints.

Sarah learned that the town itself is quite historic with buildings dating back to around 1780. The town has an extensive Historic District, which is notable, because each of its neighborhoods have their own character, and all of them have survived into the 21st century, intact.

It didn't take Sara long to figure out what she and Jim would do between Ashley's races. They were both Oregon kids and had spent their lives in the Northwest. Pennsylvania would be a new experience for both of them, and they looked forward to it.

Sarah booked a room at the Lewisburg Hotel, which was right in the heart of the historical district.

Ashley had sent them the Patriot Championship Schedule so they knew that she would swim on Thursday, Friday and then compete in the relay on Saturday.

Ashley, told them that the men's team and the women's team would take a bus from the Academy to Louisburg. The distance was about 172 miles, so it would be a little over a three hour ride. She also told them where the team would be staying, and how to get hold of her.

Jim arranged for their flight to arrive on Tuesday evening and he figured out how to get from their hotel to the Bucknell pool. Their travel arrangements worked out well and they arrived in time for an early check in and dinner in the historic district. They knew they would not see Ashley until Wednesday so they were not in a rush to do much of anything.

They walked around the historic district after dinner and then went to bed early. The next day they were up early explored Lewisburg. They talked to Ashley on Wednesday night but would not be able to see her until Thursday. Ashley had told them that she would be in the second qualifying heat on Thursday, and that it was expected to begin at about 10AM.

Jim and Sarah were in the stands before the first heat was called to the starting blocks. They knew that the women's world record was around 142, so based on that they could judge how the competition would stack up against Ashley. The swimmers were called to their marks and they were off. The first heat's winner in the 200 free clocked in at 150.56. Ashley had broken 150 on a routine basis, so they weren't to worried about the winner of heat one.

When the second heat was called to their marks, Jim and Sarah saw Ashley for the first time since Christmas. She didn't look much different, but both of them could see the extra definition in her upper body. She was still tall and thin, and built like an Olympic swimmer, but it was clear that the muscles in her arms and shoulders had continued to develop as she worked to improve her performance in the 100 meter butterfly.

Heat two was off with the sound of the gun, and as was her practice, Ashley stayed with the leaders through the first lap. She then increased her pace and did the next two laps with almost identical times. As the last lap began she did a perfect kick turn and turned on the speed. She won her heat by almost one half of a lap. Her time was 145.0.

The third heat was faster than heat one with the winner in at 148.35. Ashley was able to see her parents briefly after the preliminary heats, but her coaches wanted her well rested for the final that evening so she spent most of her day either watching other members of her team or resting in her room.

The final for the women's 200 meter free style was made up

of the first three finishers in each of the three heats. The woman who had won the third heat was from Bucknell University so she had quite a large crowd following, and rooting for her.

The swimmers were called to their marks and the gun went off. Ashley was in lane four and the winner of the third heat was in lane one. Ashley could see her as they finished lap one and two and noticed that she picked up the pace going into lap three. Ashley stayed with her but then as she began the final lap she increased her speed and beat the woman by 2.5 Seconds. Her time in the final was a new meet record at 141.5. She was getting close to the NCAA record which was 139.1, and she knew in the back of her mind that it was within reach. The crowd had roared during the first three laps but then went silent as Ashley kicked it into gear. She knew immediately that the time she had achieved qualified her for the NCAA Championships.

Her coaches were thrilled with her performance. The next day she was able to see her parents briefly. She had a great conversation with them but left them after a brief conversation to be with her team. Sarah and Jim then did the tour of Lewisburg that Sarah had planned to do in advance.

On Friday morning the competitors were given their heat and lane assignments for the 100 meter butterfly. Ashley would be swimming in heat one, lane three. Her completion from the University of North Carolina was Heather Greenstone. Heather had beat Ashley in the butterfly in their dual meet, and she was sure to be tough completion in the Patriot Championships. Heather was scheduled to swim in heat three and she drew lane three as well.

The women's NCAA record for the 100 meter Butterfly was 49.43. Ashley's best time was 51.0. Heather had clocked in at 50.5 in one of the races earlier in the year.

The preliminary heats were held on time. Ashley went off on schedule and she swam to an easy victory in her heat. Her time was 51.5.

Heather also won her heat with some ease. Her time was 51.0. Not a personal best but faster than Ashley.

Jim and Sarah rarely got nervous before one of Ashley's races primarily because she almost always won.

This final would be a little different, and would push her to her limit. The race was non-stop, go all out and give it everything you have. The strategy in the 100 meter butterfly was give it all you can from beginning to end.

Lane assignments were drawn and Ashley felt lucky. She had drawn lane three, and Heather would be in lane one. This gave Ashley the opportunity to see exactly where her competition was.

The swimmers were called to their marks and the gun went off. Everyone was in the water and giving it everything they had. Ashley knew that she had improved her upper body strength since the last time she swam against Heather, and she was bound and determine that all of the work she had put in would pay off.

She stayed with Heather through the first lap and then made a great turn and jumped out a tiny bit in front. Once she had the lead it was give it everything you have got kid. She did so and touched just in front of Heather. Her time was a personal best of 50.43. Heather was clocked in 50.56. They congratulated each other. E xternally Ashley made no big deal of the win, however, inside she was glowing like a hot fire cracker.

Jim and Sarah watched the relay race on Saturday morning but it was clear that Navy was not going to make the finals. They were, however, thrilled with Ashley's performance as was every member of the Navy team. The headlines in the Midshipman news would make sure everyone in the YARD knew that they had once special competitor in the making.

Ashley said goodbye to her parents after the relay race. Sarah had a few more things she wanted to see before they left Lewisburg, so they spent the rest of the day being tourists. They returned to Portland the next day feeling really good about how their daughter had done. It was funny though, on the way home, Jim said to Sarah, you know hon, I still haven't figured out why Ash chose the Naval Academy. Someday I'm sure she will tell us, but I'm still kind of baffled by her decision. I know what you mean dear but what's done is done. You might as well make plans for our next event because Ashley will be competing in the NCAA championships in March.

Do you know where they are? I think they are in Texas, but I will check when we get home.

CHAPTER 20

NCAA CHAMPIONSHIP AND BEYOND

Ashley's times in the Patriot Championship both met the A standard. The A standard time for women in the 200 freestyle was 143.17, and the A standard for the 100 meter butterfly was 51.03. Ashley won the butterfly with a time of 50.43 and the 200 freestyle, with a time of 141.5.

There are two standards in NCAA swimming. The A standard and the B standard. If enough people qualify in the A standard then no one who hits the B standard will qualify. If there is not enough of a pool to fill the A standard, then the best B standard times were allowed to compete.

By the time Ashley and her team had arrived back at the YARD the word was out that the Women's team had made their best showing at the Patriot Championships in years, and the star performance was put in by a Plebe by the name of Ashley Jameson. The Midshipman newspaper had the headline, "We have a rock star in our midst" The story went on to describe Ashley and her swimming success, not only in the Patriot Conference, but in the Championships as well. It also noted that Ashley's times qualified her for the A standard setting in the NCAA Championships that would be held in Texas at the end of March.

This was no small feat. No women swimmer in the history of the Academy had ever qualified for the A Standard in Women's swimming. In fact only three women from the Naval Academy had ever made it to the NCAA finals.

Her athletic success, however, did not provide a cushion or free pass when it came time to Plebe life and academics. Both were first in every regard at the Naval Academy and there would be no exceptions.

Roscoe read the newspaper article with interest, however, there was no surprise contained in the article.

He had been watching Ashley since her Plebe summer began, and nothing surprised him about her accomplishments any more.

It was the Monday morning after they had returned from Lewisburg, and the Patriot Championships. Mike Morgan was sitting in his office when there was a knock on the door. Come In, he said.

His assistant coach Cindy Rodrigo entered and said," Hey Coach you wanted to see me" Yep, thanks for coming Cindy. First I wanted to tell you how much I appreciated you coaching Ashley and the results of your work were obviously evident with the Patriot Championship. Thanks Mike, I was very proud of her, and she executed the turn moves we had worked on so well, I couldn't have been prouder.

Second, Mike said, you are aware that she has now qualified in both her races for the NCAA Championships in March in Texas. She qualified at the A level with her times, so she will be an automatic seed in both races. This will be the first time that we will have ever had a women in a Navy swim suit competing at this level.

Yes, I'm well aware of that. Well, what you aren't aware of is, I want you to be the coach who accompanies her to the NCAA Championships. Wow Mike, that is very nice of you, but you're the head coach and this opportunity just doesn't come along real often here at the Academy. I know that Cindy, but you have worked well with her, and I want the two of you to be the team that represents us, and the United States Navy, at the NCAA's. So plan your schedule accordingly and let Ashley know that you will be going with her.

I will do so Mike, and thanks very much for this opportunity. I know that Ashley will do well, and represent the Academy in such a way to put us on the map with women's swimming.

Cindy left the office with a huge smile on her face.

She was not only pleased with what Mike had said to her, but that he had the confidence in her to take his swimming star to another level.

The month past very quickly. Ashley worked hard both in the pool and in the gym. She was bound and determined to do well, and was pleased that Cindy would be her coach for the event.

Back home, Jim and Sarah planned their trip to Dallas, as did Coach Nancy. Coach Nancy had followed Ashley for years and she was not going to let the event pass without being there to cheer her on.

The NCAA Swimming and Diving Championships were scheduled to be held at the Lee and Joe Jamail Texas Swimming Center. It was the 7th time that the University of Texas had hosted the championships but it was the first time that the University of Texas hosted both men's and women's championships in the same year.

The Texas Swimming Center had hosted numerous national, collegiate, club, and high school aquatics meets, since it opened 40 years ago. Among the special events it had hosed were the US Olympic Diving Trials, the AIAW National Championships, and the US Olympic Swimming Trails.

The women's events would be scheduled over a three day period at the end of March. Ashley and Cindy planned to arrive one day early to look the place over and obtain Ashley's seeding information for both races. At the NCAA Championships the 200 meter freestyle would be held on Wednesday with the 100 meter butterfly to follow on Friday Morning. Ashley would have Thursday to rest and regroup.

Her Mom and Dad let her know what their plans were, and they hoped that she would have a little time on Thursday to see them, but they would understand if that didn't work out.

They also let her know that Coach Nancy would be coming, so Ashley would have a couple of people in the stands yelling for her. When her Mom told her, it just made her smile. The thought of her Mom, Dad and Coach Nancy yelling at the top of their lungs for her from the stands was almost two much to envision.

The time passed quickly, and all of a sudden Ashley found herself sitting with her coach on a plane flight to Dallas Texas.

On arrival, they went directly from the Airport to the swim center, where they checked in. They received their lodging information and schedule. They read through the information, and learned there would be one heat in both the 200 freestyle and the 100 butterfly. All of the women in the 200 had met the A standard, and about 50% of the women in the butterfly had met it. The remaining participants were the best times of the B qualifier. As she expected her friend from North Carolina was once again to compete against her in the Butterfly.

On the day of the 200, Cindy met with Ashley in the morning and went through their strategy one last time. It was etched in Ashley's brain, but as the coach, Cindy wanted to make sure that they planned everything for this once in a lifetime opportunity.

Ashley did not see her parents until she was called to the starting blocks for the 200. She looked up and saw both of them along with her brother John, and sitting next to John was coach Nancy. This was the audience she wanted and would prove to them how their lifetime support had paid off. Once again from inside her came a level of determination seldom possessed by others.

Ashley had drawn lane two which did not give her much of

a view of the total field. All of the swimmers in the race were excellent, and all had posted times high enough to make the cut so she knew this would not be an easy race.

Her strategy would be to go out hard, but not full blast, assess where she was in the pack in lap two, and then begin to pick up the pace in lap three with the final burst for home in lap four. She was not nervous at all. If anything, she had a quiet confidence about her that kept her very focused.

Swimmers to your mark, set and the gun went off. Ashley was off the blocks in perfect form. She kept a faster pace than normal on lap one and made the perfect kick turn that she and Cindy had worked on. She could hear the crowd yelling as she went into lap two but had limited visibility to see where everyone was. She was well ahead of those she could see but the volume of yelling told her that a couple of swimmers out in lanes seven and eight were moving well through the water. At the turn heading into the third lap she got a glimpse of a swimmer in lane 7 who appeared to be ahead of her. She picked up the pace with the goal of being even with her as they made the final turn. She made that kick turn perfectly and then put the pedal to the metal. She touched first and the light above her went on positing a time of 140.0. She just smiled and was congratulated by the swimmers on both sides of her. She had won by 3 tenths of a second. She was now an NCAA Champion.

As she left the pool to head for the locker room Cindy was there to meet her with a big hug and a great smile. You did it Ash, I am so proud of you. She just smiled and said thanks. She looked up in the stands and there was her family all giving her a thumbs up with giant smiles on their faces.

She was able to meet her family and Coach Nancy for breakfast the next morning. They were all very proud of her, and were jumping for joy over her time. While it wasn't a world record it definitely was a time to be proud of and it would go into the record books. No one really talked about her next race.

They knew she was already thinking about it and didn't need to be reminded that it was yet to come in the morning.

She left them after breakfast and headed back to her room to rest. She planned to meet with Cindy in the afternoon and go over their strategy for the next morning.

That afternoon she met with Cindy and went through all of the women's qualifying times, and their lane assignments. She was very lucky to draw lane three. Her main competition it seemed would again be Heather Greenstone from the University of North Carolina. Ashley was the only person all season that Heather had lost to, and Ashley was sure that she would be going all out for the win. The best news that Ashley got was that Heather would be in lane 5 so she would be easy to watch.

Friday morning came quickly, and before long, the swimmers were being called to take their marks. Heather had smiled and said Hi to Ashley, but that was the extent of the warm greeting. She was all business and knew exactly what she had come here to do.

The strategy that Cindy and Ashley worked out was simple. Go all out the entire way and make one perfect kick turn prior to the final lap.

The swimmers were called to their marks, set, and the gun went off. Heather was off to a very quick start and Ashley knew immediately that she had no room to plan a new approach. She simply had to use all of the upper body strength she had gained, and put it all into use as she made the final turn. Her turn was perfect, and she could see once again that like the Patriot final, her turn gave her a slight edge. That was all she needed to pour it on home. Ashley touched first with Heather right behind her. Ashley's time was 50 flat and Heathers was 50.3. They congratulated each other but inside Ashley was glowing. She had just swam her personal best and was now a two event NCAA Champion.

Her family and Coach Nancy were jumping up and down

and thrilled as was Coach Cindy. Cindy was on the phone to Mike after the time was posted. Hey Mike, guess what? You have a two event NCAA Champion on your team.

Should be a good next three years. Mike was over the top with pride, and could not wait to congratulate Ashley on her great success.

Cindy and Ashley returned to the YARD and the Midshipman Newspaper carried Ashley's story on the front page. The swimming season was officially over, but the rest of the first year was still in front of Ashley and it was not going to be easy.

She worked out a training schedule with Mike and Cindy but planned to spend more time in the gym than she did during the swimming training season.

Spring Break was on the minds of all of the Midshipman and Ashley was no different. She had told Martha about the gift she received from her parents for Christmas, and had invited Martha to use the other ticket to join her in Florida. They were going to Disney World and both were really looking forward to it.

CHAPTER 21

THE END OF PLEBE YEAR

Spring Break was behind her, and Ashley could now begin to see the end of a long Plebe year. She and Martha had a blast at Disney World. They stayed at the Disney's Caribbean Beach Resort. The hotel was designed to transport guests to a relaxing paradise that captures the essence of 5 distinct islands; Barbados, Jamaica, Martinique, Trinidad and Aruba. There were fun things to do, beaches to lay on, hammocks for resting, and transportation to get to wherever they wanted to go.

To both girls, their hotel provided an island escape, without actually going to the Caribbean Islands. The resort offered them everything they wanted, and it was all in one place. Neither of the girls expressed any desire to find guys to have a great time with. Martha had ended her relationship with her boyfriend in San Diego and Ashley was just too focused on her athletics to care about male relationships at the moment. So they took the time to sight see and to rest. It all worked out well, and both felt the spring break time was great. When they returned, Martha took the time to write a brief thank you note to Ashley's parents. The prepaid plane ticket made the break even better.

They returned to the YARD feeling totally relaxed, and ready to take on the rest of the semester. They had two things that they both faced. One was more of a team event, and the other allowed the individual to shine.

The team event was simply known as Herndon. It involved all of the Plebes, and was known as the Plebe Recognition Ceremony. The Plebe class works together to accomplish the goal of retrieving a white plebe Dixie cup hat from atop the Herndon monument, and replacing the hat with an upperclassmen's hat. It is a tradition that has endured at the Naval Academy for many years.

In essence, when a cannon blast occurs, the Plebe class of more than 1000 charges the 21 foot gray monument that has been covered by the upperclassman with more than 200 pounds of lard. The goal of the event is for a Plebe to climb the lard covered monument, make the hat exchange, and do it in record time.

To understand the tradition, and emotion of the climb, it is important to have some background on the tradition. Commander William Lewis Herndon lived from 1813 to 1857. During his life, he was a renowned Naval Officer who insisted on discipline, teamwork and courage. He was in command of the Naval forces in Central America and lost his life when returning to the United States by ship. His ship was hit by a huge hurricane off of Cape Hatteras, and the Commander and all of his crew were killed..

The Naval Academy tradition of climbing Herndon never had a specific date documented to its origin but it has always been associated with the Plebes ending their first year, and moving up to the upperclassmen status. In fact, the term ""Tain't no mo' plebes," was a rally cry for many Plebes over the years. The Herndon ceremony starts off with a canon blast at precisely 2p.m. This is the signal that starts the Plebe class dash to the stature. At first sight, Herndon looks much taller than it actually is, perhaps due to the hundreds of pounds of lard slathered on by the upperclass. The class tries to remove the fatty, white goo with their hands, shirts and bodies, and then sets in place their strategy for climbing to the top. Lots of different strategies have been used. Some successful, some not so successful.

Ashley and Martha, as well as the 10 other female Plebes, left the planning up to the male plebes. The strategy developed by their class was not very well defined, but basically boiled down to this, "we are going to build a human pyramid and have the lightest Plebe in our class climb it, and do the hat transfer". Each Plebe was given a row and position. Ashley was strong and given a third row assignment.

That meant she would be on all fours on top of some male midshipmen who were in row two. It also meant she would have a row on top of her. Martha was not as strong, and was in the row on top of Ashley. A rehearsal was planned in advance, and the person selected to climb the human pyramid was a woman plebe who weighed 98 lbs.

Tradition states that the plebe who reaches the top will rise to the rank of admiral first.

The rehearsal went well. Times had been recorded for years. The fastest time was one minute 30 seconds, which was completed in the spring of 1969. the longest was recorded by the class of 1998. Their time was four hours five minutes and 17 seconds.

All Ashley cared about was not being last. When the event time came, her class was respectable. The woman plebe scampered up the human pyramid and made the hat exchange in 1 hour 10 minutes. The thing that took the class the longest, was getting all of the rows of bodies in place with people balanced on top of each other.

The entire exercise of climbing Herndon served as a test for young Midshipmen, reminding them of the values of teamwork, courage, and discipline, that are instilled throughout the year.

Ashley had continued to work out in the gym not just to continue to improve her upper body strength but also because the last event of the Plebe year was coming up. It Is called Sea Trials.

Sea Trials is an exciting, exhausting, exhilarating, capstone to the Plebe year. Sea Trials begin at 4am and go straight through 9pm. There are four phases which occur at four different locations.

The plebes rotate into a new phase every four hours so they all get to participate in each event.

Approximately 40 Plebes per company get divided into two platoons, each consisting of two squads. Each company has four squads of about 10 plebes per squad. Every phase of Sea Trials incorporates different aspects of leadership and utilizes various challenges based on simulated situations that exist in the fleet.

The obstacle course, covers the entire Naval Academy grounds, and the Naval Station complex.

It offers challenging scenarios in various settings, to include, several water obstacles. The course also involves tests of physical endurance, basic seamanship and problem solving exercises, fostering teamwork, and demonstrating a plebe's knowledge of the academy. The daylong, action oriented event is modeled after the Marine Corps 54 hour crucible It requires plebes to use skills they have learned during their first year at the Naval Academy.

Sea Trials involve both tasks that must be achieved in a group, and others that are totally designed to focus on the individual participant.

The Sea Trials bring out lots of spectators, including some parents, who are close enough geographically to the Academy to be able to watch the event. There was one spectator in the crowd who had a clip board, and was making notes on a couple of Plebes. One of the Plebes on his list to watch was Ashley Morgan Jamison.

Lieutenant Roscoe Cook was thinking ahead by three years. He had already completed his recruiting work from this year's graduating class, and had a good handle on the junior class possible recruits. However, the Navy SEALS were still an all male force, and Roscoe just didn't see much in the pipeline that could change that. That is with one exception. He had never seen a woman quite like Ashley Morgan Jamison. She at this early stage seemed to have the basic skill base and mental toughness to be a future candidate.

He was anxious to watch her compete against the men in the Sea Trials and knew that she would do well. He just didn't know how well she would do.

Roscoe invited Gunnery Sergeant Andy Sanchez to join him. The gunny was a real proven SEAL who had served with Roscoe on a number of SEAL operations before assuming his position at the academy. Roscoe knew he was tough as nails, and really valued his opinion.

Hey Gunny, glad you could join me today. Hi Lieutenant, Thanks for asking me. Sea Trials are always fun for me to watch. Do you have your sights on any particular plebes today? Yes, three men and one woman.

Let me guess, the woman is Plebe Ashley Morgan Jamison. You got that right Gunny. Lieutenant, I can tell you this, based on everything I know, and have observed, about this woman is that she is as close to SEAL material as any of the men or women I have seen in some time.

So far Gunny, my gut tells me the same thing. I have watched her since her arrival, and not only have been impressed but she is now the only women NCAA swimming champion produced by the Academy, and she did it in two events. Pretty special I would say.

I have divided the events into two groupings today. The ones that require group participation and those that require individual participation. I plan to spend my time watching the individual participation events as that is where I will be able to see the talent and persistence we need in our recruits. Here is what I have divided.

GROUP EVENTS

- **AMMUNITION CARY** - An ammunition box has to be carried by a group of Plebes across Lejeune Pool and back without getting it wet.
- **HOT WIRED-** Plebes have to answer questions in a smoke filled tent to save their comrades. Task must be successfully completed before a bomb goes off.
- **UNDERWATER ASSEMBLY-** At the bottom of the pool are placed pieces of an object that must be assembled by the team.
- **POW CAMP-** Plebes go through POW camp and have to try to escape

INDIVIDUAL EVENTS

- **ROPE SWING PULL-** Plebes have to swing across pool on suspended ropes and then pull themselves up to the top of the rope.
- **ENDURANCE COURSE-** A long journey through swamp, mud, trees, underbrush and through the mud pit.
- **OBSTACLE COURSE-** Plebes go through a series of rope climbs and other obstacles to test their endurance. This is a very hard individual exercise.
- **LOW CRAWL RESCUE-**The Plebes crawl under a barbed wire in mud while being hosed. Then they enter a plastic tunnel full of mud
- **BRIDGE AT DONG HA-** Plebes must rope crawl across a river and then climb a herndon replica.
- **COMBAT TUNNEL-**Plebes go under barbed wire in a low crawl trying to save a comrade.

Well Lieutenant, these should give Ashley a good test, but I will be surprised if she doesn't do well with all of them. Me too Gunny. I have been watching her over the past five months, and she has been working on her upper body strength. My guess is the rope climbing part of all of this is going to be no problem.

As you know, however, there is a lot of planning and organizing to accommodate the whole plebe class. The day is dangerous and I hope they all make it without injury. It will be interesting to see if the upperclassmen have invented any new and interesting twists for each task at hand.

Ashley and Martha left there room and joined the Squads that they had been assigned to. They were in different Squads and thus would not see each other until the day was finished. They both hoped that the end of the day would find them both filthy, and happy, with their results. They wished each other luck and the day began just as planned at exactly 4AM.

Ashley's squad was made up of all men. She was the only women, but she did not see that as a problem. For that matter, neither did the men. It was the end of the first Plebe year and everyone knew of Ashley's accomplishments in swimming, and some also knew about her workouts in the gym. There was no question that no exceptions would be made for her because of her sex and that was just fine with her.

The day began with a mixture of tasks. The first was the group ammunition carry. Her squad did well. They did not finish the task first but they were respectable and in the middle of the pack. This event was followed by the Rope Swing Pull.

The rope swing pull suited Ashley just fine. It was across water and required upper body strength. To no one's surprise, she led her squad in this exercise. She swung across the pool easily on the suspended ropes, and then pulled herself up to the top of the rope and wasn't even breathing hard.

The gunny looked at Lt. Cook and just said," one down and more yet to come". Roscoe turned and looked at him, smiled and said nothing.

Her squad handled the underwater assembly and the pow camp exercises well. Again they were not the leaders of the pack but they were very respectable and everyone felt good about the results they achieved.

When it came time for the Endurance Course, and the Obstacle Course, Ashley kicked it into high gear.

She was first in her squad in both, and beat the second place Plebe in her squad by a sizeable margin. There was no question that she was in better shape than all of the men, but it was also clear that she had a drive and initiative that was unmatched in her squad.

When the day ended, her squad was tired, happy, and covered with mud. All gave hugs to each other and most of the squad congratulated Ashley on her individual effort. She had beaten every male in her squad in every individual contest, and she had recorded times that put her in the top 10% of her entire Plebe class.

When the day was finally over she met Martha in their room. Martha looked like a happy half drowned rat. Ashley, you look a lot better than I do, but I made it.

I knew you would, let's grab a shower and then I want to go to bed. They both stayed in the shower for a long time. Went back to their room and were both sound asleep as soon as the lights went off. It had been one heck of a Sea Trial Day.

Both Lieutenant Cook, and Gunny Sanchez, stayed until the Plebes had finished their Sea Trials, and then they headed back to their respective quarters. Roscoe had taken a lot of notes, and all of them were positive regarding Plebe Ashley Jamison. Well Gunny what did you think? I think that we both know now that we have the potential of helping to sponsor the first woman to ever wear a SEAL insignia.

We obviously have a long way to go, and a few years before she would face the test, but I know now that the foundation is there for the making of a great SEAL officer. I agree with you Gunny. Have a good rest of your evening.

CHAPTER 22

MIDSHIPMAN THIRD CLASS SUMMER

The summer was just about to begin for Ashley. The summer between her Plebe year and third class year would be full, but did include a three week leave for summer vacation at home.

Ashley and Martha received their orders just before the Plebe year was over. Both were going on a midshipman cruise, but both were going to have very different experiences. The good news was they were both going to be based out of San Diego which was Martha's home town, and a great West Coast location.

The Navy uses the summer between year one and year two to orient the midshipman to both Navy ships, and submarines, around the world. Ashley was scheduled to be part of the crew of a Navy Submarine based out of San Diego, California. She would become part of the crew for three weeks, take part in drills, gunnery exercises, and learn to stand watch underway. It was a midshipman's orientation to real Navy life. The goal of the summer was to orient the midshipman, and potential officers, to learn, and appreciate the talents, responsibilities, and perspectives, of enlisted men and women. There is an old Navy saying that says the "Chiefs run the Navy" and there is some truth to that.

Following her Navy cruise, Ashley would take leave, and fly from San Diego to her home in Portland. She was looking forward to her cruise, but had never been more thrilled to go home, than she was for this three week leave.

They sat in their room and studied their orders. Both were to report to their ships one week after the Plebe year ended. Martha was to report to the USS Paul Hamilton DDG 60. The Paul Hamilton, is an Arleigh Burke class destroyer that was named after Paul Hamilton who was the third Secretary of the Navy. the Hamilton was commissioned in Charleston South Carolina and then was transferred to Pearl Harbor Hawaii.

From Pearl Harbor she was transferred to San Diego and is now home ported there. The Hamilton is 505 ft in length, and has a beam of 66 feet. It carries 33 commissioned officers, 38 chief petty officers, and an enlisted crew of 210.

Ashley opened her orders and read through the material provided. She was being assigned to Attack Submarine USS Annapolis, which was home ported in San Diego.

She read through the material and learned that the USS Annapolis is a Los Angeles class fast attack submarine. It was moved, from Groton, Connecticut, to San Diego. The ship was assigned to Commander, Submarine Squadron 11.

Ashley didn't know anything about submarines, and had no idea how she ended up on one on her first midshipman cruise. Like most other Plebes, she assumed she would end up on a Destroyer (Tin Can), or a Guided Missile Destroyer like Martha.

She read on, and learned that The Annapolis had quite a history. She was deployed on her first mission in November of 1993 to the North Atlantic. During that deployment she was awarded the Submarine Group Two Silver Anchor Award for enlisted retention.

She was deployed again in January of 1994, to the North Atlantic, where she made her first visit to Bergen, Norway. There the crew had an opportunity to attend a few of the 1994 Winter Olympic events, including the Men's gold Medal hockey match. During that deployment, the boat and crew, earned the Navy Arctic Service Ribbon. Following an in port refit, Annapolis participated in a six month pre deployment workup with the USS Dwight D. Eisenhower, and followed that with a six month Mediterranean Deployment with the Eisenhower Battle Group.

During her Mediterranean deployment, the ship earned her first Sea Service Ribbon, the Navy Expeditionary Medal, and the Meritorious Unit Commendation.

She did not deploy again until 1997, when she returned again to the Mediterranean with the George Washington Battle Group Annapolis entered Portsmouth Navy Yard for an extended overhaul in April of 2003.

Ashley read that the sub was a Los Angeles class submarine. It was 6000 tons, and was 362 feet long, and 33 feet wide. The one thing that Ashley focused on was the crew size. There were 12 officers, and 115 men. It would be a great opportunity to get to know, and learn, from a few people rather than being a midshipman lost in a sea of officers and crew.

She also learned that Annapolis was one of five Los Angeles class subs home based in San Diego.

After reading the orientation materials, Ashley was really looking forward to her midshipman cruise. Who would have thought that it would be on a fast attack submarine.

Their Plebe year finally ended. It had been full of highs, and lows, for both Martha and Ashley, but they had made it, and both had done well. Ashley's athletic accomplishments had made her one of, if not the most well known, Plebes in her class. Martha had one goal at the beginning of the year and that was to make it through, get decent respectable grades, and make her military family proud. She had accomplished her goals.

They both caught the same flight to San Diego. Their plan was to spend the first three nights with Martha's family and then report to their respective ships on the fourth day.

Both were technically on duty, and thus both wore their midshipman whites while travelling. They were greeted at the San Diego Airport by Martha's parents, who greeted them both as though they were long lost sisters. Ashley had never met either of them, so the warm greeting was very welcomed. They knew a lot about Ashley from Martha, and also were well aware that Ashley had been a strong supporter of Martha when it came to the physical side of her Plebe year.

Martha had not talked about her family much during the year, but Ashley knew that she was close to her parents and was an only child. It was obvious that they had missed her a great deal, but it was equally obvious that they were extremely proud of her accomplishments.

They both grabbed their Navy issued bags, which were full, due to the fact that both were going on three weeks leave following their midshipman cruise. They had their civilian clothes packed as well as their military gear in their bags.

Martha's parents were John and Mary Bridgestone. John Bridgestone, was Navy Rear Admiral John Bridgestone, and he was still on active duty so he was in uniform.

As they walked out of the Airport they made quite a sight. A Navy Rear Admiral and his wife, followed by two Naval Academy midshipman. All of the military folks were in uniform.

To Ashley's surprise there was a car waiting for them. It was a Naval Car with a driver. The driver was an enlisted man in uniform, and he assisted both Ashley and Martha with their bags and then drove the family home.

Martha had not talked a lot about her family or home. She had only said that she had spent a lot of time on the beach while growing up. The driver headed up the coast to a small, and very prestigious town, by the name of La Jolla. The driver left highway 5 and turned west on Torrey Pines Road and then onto La Jolla shores Drive. They shortly arrived on Prospect

Street, and then pulled up in front of what looked to Ashley like an ocean front mansion.

Ashley just watched, she didn't say anything, but Martha knew by looking at her that Ashley was pretty impressed with the home she was looking at.

Welcome home Martha her mom said.

Your room is ready and we put Ashley down the hall in the guest room. Her Dad thanked the driver, and told him what time to be back in the morning.

Ashley and Martha grabbed their bags, and headed into the house. It was a huge home but what was more impressive to Ashley was the view. Ashley knew that this was a very special place to live but she had no idea how special and expensive La jolla was.

Hey Mom, Martha said, how much time do we have before dinner. I'd say, based on what we have planned, that you have about 2 hours. That's great. I want to show Ashley around town and that will give us just enough time.

Ash, let me show you your room, and then we will change into some casual clothes. I've got just enough time to show you around our little town before dinner.

They changed and were out the door in no time. Ash, let me tell you a little bit about our town. It is a very special place, and I feel very privileged to live her. It is a town that for many, is a landmark that is a must see for visitors. It has lots of boutique hotels, and as you can see. the beach is right at your finger tips. Wow Martha, the color of the water is really something.

As you can see, we are not far from San Diego, and in fact, La Jolla is part of San Diego. There is another special town to the north that is called Del Mar.

The name of our town comes from the Spanish word La Jolla, which means the Jewel. The name sure fits the location, Ashley said.

We only have to walk about three blocks and we are in town.

As you will see our town is totally walkable in fact driving in it is discouraged.

They walked to town and then by all of the small shops and restaurants. After they finished Martha took them to a stairway that led to the beach. Once on the beach they took their shoes off, and walked back home on the warm sand. Ashley could only think, "Wow this is one special place."

They were back well within the two hours and joined Martha's mom in the kitchen. What's for dinner Mom? Well, since we don't often see you for dinner these days we are going to have something that you like. Take a guess. Well based on the smell, my guess is we are going to have Cornish Game Hens that are stuffed. Good Guess Martha. I am also going to serve it with cranberry sauce and baked zucchini chips.

Boy does that sound good, Ashley said.

OK ladies, I should have everything ready in about 30 minutes go enjoy yourselves for the time remaining. I think your Dad is in the den he would probably love to talk to you both about your midshipman cruise assignments.

We will go find him Mom. Hey Dad, Mom told us we might find you here. Hey kid, welcome home. Have a seat please. Ashley, it is finally nice to meet you, we have heard so much about you, and of your athletic accomplishments. Thank you Sir. It was a difficult but rewarding year.

Martha tells me that for the most part you showed the male version of midshipmen that the other sex can prove to be very powerful competition. My guess is, that was good for the Academy, and the Navy overall.

Where are you two off to on your midshipman cruises? Well Dad, I am going to check in with the USS Paul Hamilton DDG 60 and Ashley is going to spend her time underwater on the USS Annapolis.

I know both of those ships and their Captains. You both should have a great experience. I think that your cruises are about three weeks. Am I right? Yes Sir. We both have the three week cruise, and then are scheduled for three weeks of leave, before we report back to the yard to begin our second year.

When do you both have to check in? We were given one week from the end of our semester.

So after today we have three days then we must check in. What are you planning to do for the next few days Martha?

I'm going to show Ashley what I do best. Let me guess, her Father said, you're going to the beach.

You got that one right Dad. I'm going to teach Ashley what is like to live here, and show her how to deal with the stress of it all. Her Dad just laughed.

Well, how about I offer you both a ride into the base in a couple of days when you're ready to go? That sounds great Dad. Thanks.

Martha's Mom called them into dinner. Dinner was great and both were totally stuffed when they left the table. Neither had room for desert. They both had coffee, and then spent the rest of the evening talking with Martha's parents about their first year.

By 9PM they were totally beat and went up stairs to bed. Both slept very soundly and they were up early for breakfast. It wasn't long after that, that the bathing suits came out, and the beach bag was packed for a day of stress relief.

After three days of being beach bums they dressed in uniform and headed for the San Diego Naval Base with her Dad. It had been a very welcomed rest. Now the next challenge would begin.

CHAPTER 23

USS ANNAPOLIS SSN 760

Admiral Bridgestone's driver let Ashley out first at the entrance of the pier that the USS Annapolis was tied up to. Ashley gave Martha a big hug, and thanked Admiral Bridgestone for his hospitality and ride. She grabbed her Navy issued bag and wished Martha good luck. As she began to walk, she looked back over her shoulder and said to Martha "Have a good time and I'll see you back in the YARD in a couple of months."

She walked down the pier, and arrived at the gang plank that led from the pier on board the ship. The watch officer was on duty and he returned her salute. Midshipman Third Class Ashley Jamison reporting for duty Sir. Welcome aboard Midshipman Jamison, we have been expecting you. Please remain here and I will let the Executive Officer know that you have arrived. Thank you Sir.

A few minutes later the XO arrived to greet Ashley. Good Morning Midshipman Jamison, I'm Lieutenant Commander Mark Michaels, welcome aboard. Thank you Sir.

I have asked Lieutenant Masters to join us, and to show you to your quarters. In fact, you will be bunking with Lieutenant Masters. She should be with us in a few minutes. In the meantime I can tell you that we will have a briefing at 0200 to orient you and your counterparts to our ship and your schedule for the next three weeks. You are one of three midshipman that will be with us for this cruise. The others are both men, but they are not from the Naval Academy. They are both ROTC students at Oregon State University. As I remember, you are from Oregon, so I'm sure you are familiar with OSU. Yes Sir, I know Oregon State well. In fact my brother, and both of my parents, went to OSU's rival school The University of Oregon.

Before the conversation went further they were joined by Lieutenant Masters. Hi Ashley, I'm Julie Masters, welcome aboard.

I've heard a lot about you and look forward to getting to know you over the next few weeks on your midshipman cruise. Thank you Sir. Please call me Julie. We are probably more informal around here than we should be, but it seems to work, and we have a great time working together on the Annapolis.

Come on, I'll show you where you're going to bunk for this trip. Did the XO tell you that you are scheduled for an orientation meeting at 0200. Yes Julie, he did. Great, please follow me.

Lieutenant Masters took Ashley below to her quarters. It was the first time Ashley had ever been in a submarine and she was immediately aware of how tight the quarters were below deck.

Ashley have you ever been on a submarine before? No. This is the first time I have ever even been close to one. Well, it will take you a bit of time to get use to it. As you may be aware there are 12 officers on this ship and 125 sailors. I am the only woman officer and like you, I am a graduate of the Naval Academy. My guess is, that is why the Captain linked us together.

By the way congratulations on completing your Plebe year. Thanks, it was a heck of a year and I am very glad it is behind me.

Yes, I remember it as well. In fact that year is something that will stay with you for the rest of your life. What did you decide to major in? I'm going to major in computer science for no other reason than the subject interests me, and I seem to have a easy time of it.

I think it is a wise choice. Computers are everything today. I majored in nuclear Engineering and I'm sure that is one reason that I ended up on a nuclear submarine instead of a surface war ship.

Well here we are, welcome to officer quarters. We are a bit lucky as we have our own room.

The guys bunk three to a room and as such they don't have much space.

You get the top bunk, so I hope you're in shape to climb the ladder once a day. Julie then started to laugh. I'm only kidding Ashley, I'm well aware of your athletic abilities. You have made a lot of people at the Naval Academy proud. Thanks Julie, it was a good year athletically for me.

It doesn't take much time to tour you through our room. As you can see, we have two bunks, a single desk, and this wonderful small sink and mirror. You get three drawers the others are full of my stuff.

There are no other female officers on board, but as I understand it there are now more than 100 female officers serving on submarines. We do have female sailors. My understanding is that the Navy assigns female sailors to ships that have female officers, and as such, I have an additional role to fill as a role model and mentor to the female sailors. So far it has not been an issue. We have about 20 women sailors on the Annapolis.

I have got to leave for about a half hour. Use the time to unpack your stuff. I will be back, and then we will tour the sub together.

Julie took off and, as she was told, Ashley used the time to unpack her stuff.

By the time Julie returned Ashley was unpacked and ready to take the tour. When they finished it was time for lunch.

As they walked toward the ward room Julie asked Ashley,

"Ashley what are your first impressions of the Annapolis?" Well, it is longer than I thought it would be at over 300 feet, but 33 feet in width doesn't seem to be very wide. Do people begin to get a little crazy in such a small space after you have been down for a couple of weeks? Sometimes it can be a problem but everyone seems to get use to it. How long does it stay underwater?

I don't exactly know how long it can stay under water, but since I have been on it, the longest has been two months.

They arrived in the ward room, and Julie introduced Ashley to the six other officers who were present.

She also introduced herself and Ashley to the two midshipman that would be on the cruise with them from Oregon State University. Both of midshipman were majoring in engineering, and both were very happy to be aboard a nuclear sub. Their names were Fred Roberts and Hans Ledbetter.

The ward room was comprised of some built in shelves that also had a flat screen TV above them. There were two tables that would hold 8 officers. The tables were stand alone, but were designed to go together if they needed to hold the full complement of Officers.

Just as they were about to sit down, the Captain entered the Ward Room. He was a full Commander and walked directly over to the midshipman. Good Day and Welcome Aboard. You must be Ashley Jamison? Am I right? Yes Sir. And you Gentleman must be Fred and Hans but you're going to have to help me out with who is who. Fred said, I'm Fred Roberts sir. Hans then introduced himself as well. It is a pleasure to meet all of you. My name is Jim Freemont and I am the Captain of The Annapolis. We look forward to having you aboard, and have an interesting three weeks planned for you.

Please have a seat. Lunch will be served in a few moments. Lunch was served, and during lunch the Captain asked each of the midshipman about their backgrounds. He seemed to know a lot about Ashley already but not as much from the other two ROTC students.

The Captain went on to explain that at 0200 Lieutenant Commander Mark Michaels would brief them on what they had in store for them during the next three weeks.

At 0200, Ashley joined Fred Roberts and Hans Ledbetter in the Ward room. It was just the three of them and Lt. Commander Michaels.

Well Good Afternoon. Are all of you settled in to your quarters. The three replied Yes Sir in unison. Great. For the next hour or so, I want to give you a bit of an orientation to what you can expect on your 21 day Midshipman Cruise.

I also want to give you some information on the ship, your schedules, and then will open it up to answer any questions you might have. To begin with, this cruise will serve as a starting point through which you can become familiar with the role of junior officers on board a nuclear submarine. The effort you exert to learn about the duties and responsibilities of junior officers will be directly reflected in how instructive and rewarding your summer cruise will be.

Our ship and this cruise, is all designed to help you understand the Submarine side of the US Navy. Obviously, you may or you may not, be assigned to a Submarine when you become and Ensign and receive your first set of orders, but the fact that you are here now is an indication that someone feels that you would make a good submarine Naval Officer. During our cruise you are encouraged to learn as much as possible about the qualification process required of all Submarine Officers. If you desire to qualify at a particular watch station, see the Senior Watch Officer for watchbill assignment. Recognize that final watchstation qualification will be difficult during a 21 day cruise and that the total submarine qualification process can take up to a year and a half to complete. You are encouraged to use and work on the personnel qualification standard (PQS) for each watch station you are assigned. The PQS are designed to help you focus and enhance your learning about each area of the submarine.

Each of you have been assigned a Junior Officer. It is the Officer you are bunking with. Use this opportunity to talk to the junior officers aboard about their experiences.

They are in the position, in which you will find yourselves, after you graduate and are commissioned. Remember, the more you can learn now, the easier it will be when you receive your commission, and first ship assignment.

As your Junior Officer may have already told you, we are a bit informal on the submarine. As such, you should feel free to call the junior officers by name. You can call me XO, and you should always call the Captain **Captain.**

I am going to hand out to you now your Midshipman's submarine cruise guide book. As you will see it is divided into sections. The sections are as follows:

1. **BASIC SUBMARINE KNOWLEDGE**
2. **ENGINE ROOM KNOWLEDGE**
3. **OPERATIONS KNOWLEDGE**
4. **STRATEGIC WEAPONS**
5. **TOPSIDE AND SAIL**
6. **SHIPBOARD SAFETY PRECAUTIONS**

As you will see, there is a lot to learn about each of these subjects. Your guide will help you to focus on each area that I mentioned, and guide you through the key elements of knowledge that you should know by the time we complete our 21 days together.

As to your cruise. We will be sailing out to the Hawaiian Islands, and in fact, will have two days of shore leave when we reach Pearl Harbor on the island of Oahu. If you have not visited Oahu, you will really enjoy the island, and have enough free time to see what you need to see.

We will also use our 21 day cruise to assist a few Navy Seals with their underwater training requirements. If you are not familiar with this branch of the Navy, I can only tell you that you will be very impressed with those men who are going through training.

Each Navy Seal must complete what they call BUD'S training. This is Basic Underwater Demolition Training. I think the total BUD's training takes about 24 weeks and we are only a small part of it but the SEALS assigned to us will be with us for some of the 21 days we are at sea.

Once the XO mentioned the Navy Seals training Ashley sat just a bit higher in her chair and paid close attention. The opportunity to see them in action would be something that she almost couldn't wait for.

The XO then went on to tell them that when assigned to a Watch station that their watches would be a full three hours in length.

He also told them to memorize the Captains standing Orders, which were listed in their guidebooks.

The XO then told each of the midshipman that they would be assigned to a category based on the weeks of the cruise and that their assignments were listed in the training manual which was personalized for them.

Ashley opened her manual and noted that her assignments were as follows:

Week 1 Operations knowledge
Week 2 Engine Room Knowledge
Week 3 Strategic Weapons
Week 4 Topside and Sail

Her book noted that she would study the shipboard safety precautions, and the basic submarine knowledge throughout the cruise. Neither would have a specific assignment.

Once he had finished the XO asked if any of them had any questions. They did not, so he dismissed them, and encouraged them to use the time before dinner to begin to study the Basic Submarine knowledge section, and to tour the ship. He explained that they would get underway at 0800 in the morning.

Later that afternoon, six Navy Seals came aboard carrying what looked like major military fighting equipment. Ashley watched them come aboard, and based on their size, it was easy to see that they were all in exceptional physical condition.

Ashley thought to herself that watching them train was going to be a real experience, and one that she did not want to miss a minute of.

CHAPTER 24

UNDERWAY SHIFT COLORS

That night, after dinner, Julie asked Ashley if she knew how she had been assigned to a Nuclear Submarine for her midshipman cruise. I have no idea Julie, my orders came and here I am. My roommate at the Academy was assigned to a DDG. The one she was assigned to is based out of here. She specifically requested a DDG, and her Dad is an Admiral stationed here, so I wasn't surprised when she got it.

I did not put a specific ship preference in or a geographic location. I just wanted to see what would come up, and see what I would be assigned. So my assignment to a Nuclear Submarine is a bit of a mystery. I am not majoring in engineering like you did. I assume most people who put in for a Nuclear Submarine assignments have an engineering background, but I really have no idea if that is true or not. In any event, I'm looking forward to the experience, and am happy I was given this assignment.

Your right Ash. It is a bit strange, but I'm very happy you are here. Tomorrow we get underway and you will begin your first Watch Assignment.

What Ashley or Julie was completely unaware of, was a Navy Seal Lieutenant by the name of Roscoe Cook, assigned to the US Naval Academy, happened to know that Navy Seal Qualification training would be occurring on the USS Annapolis SSN 760 while the ship was also conducting a midshipman cruise. Lt. Cook made sure that Ashley Jamison was assigned to the USS Annapolis for her midshipman cruise. He was a very good recruiter who worked behind the scenes, and he didn't want to miss an opportunity to have Ashley see Navy Seals in action. He had no idea if Ashley would be interested in becoming a Navy Seal, but he did not want to miss an opportunity to peak her interest. In any event, Roscoe made sure that Ashley would never know how her assignment was determined.

At 0800 Ashley, along with Fred Roberts and Hans Ledbetter, were asked to join the Captain topside to watch as the crew prepared the submarine to get underway. The Captain explained the order in which the ropes would be released, and that the submarine would be powered as they left the pier by its diesel engines.

As soon as the ropes to the pier were released the submarine began to sway as it headed out toward the open ocean. The Captain explained that submarines are not very stable on the surface of the water. The reason being, they have a round hull, rather than a deep keel, like most surface warships have. The deep keel, like those on Destroyers help keep the boat stable.

Ashley had never been sea sick in her life, but she certainly could feel the sway of the boat as it headed out the harbor.

The Captain explained that as soon as the boat was out of the harbor and in deep enough water, that he would begin the submerge process.

It was not long after they cleared the harbor that the Captain gave the order to Clear the Bridge. At that point, everyone topside went below decks. The Captain was the last one off the bridge, and he closed the bridge hatch behind him and headed for the control room. The control room sits just below the Submarines Fin and it is the space from which all commands are given.

In the control room the diving officer then gave the order to stop the engines and switch to battery power. The diesel engines were shut down, and in the maneuvering room, the electricians took the motors off generator power, and put them on battery power. At the same time the diving officer set the speed at all ahead two thirds.

Ashley was amazed at how precise the process went, and in a very strict order. She mentioned it to the Captain and the Captain told her that all submarines follow a carefully rehearsed procedure in order to get under water.

The procedures are carefully followed even in the direst emergency situations, because each step is essential, and skipping a step can and has sunk a boat and killed everyone in it.

The Diving Officer then gave the order to close the main induction air intake pipe. It was located at the rear of the conning tower. It must be closed before diving or the engine rooms will fill with water. Once that procedure was completed the time came to even the pressure in the boat.

The main induction pipe is normally the last hull opening to be sealed. Once this has been done, the hull opening indicator board will show all green lights, which confirm that the seal has occurred successfully. To confirm this, air pressure is released into the hull, if the pressure holds it indicates that all openings are sealed.

From that point, the Ballast tank vents were opened, which allowed the tanks to fill with water. As soon as there is pressure in the boat, the negative tank is flooded to increase diving speed.

The Captain then explained that the Diving Officer would now adjust the bow and stern planes. These planes project out to the sides of the boat, and are used to fly the boat through the water. By varying the angle on these planes the boat may be made to rise, fall, or remain at the same depth as it moves forward. Since the boat is normally trimmed to be slightly positively buoyant the planes are used to hold it down. The Captain explained that this is a safety factor. If all power is lost it is normally preferable to slowly rise to the surface and not to sink.

The Diving Officer than gave the order to rig out the bow planes and adjust the stern planes. The planes were kept folded up against the superstructure to prevent damage while surfaced. These planes were then changed, and set on full dive. The stern planes were used to control the boat's angle while diving.

Next the Diving Officer insured all vents were closed. When the boat reached 45 feet in depth he reduced speed to 2/3rds full.

It was easy to tell that the boat was diving but after a point Ashley could tell that it was starting to level off. The Captain explained to the Midshipman that this would occur when they had reached I5 feet short of their desired depth. Once that was achieved, the Diving Officer ordered that the flooded negative tank be blown to restore neutral buoyancy.

None of the Midshipman had any idea what this meant. The Captain explained that this process was designed to make sure that the ship remained undetected. He noted that this tank was never blown completely dry at sea in order to avoid sending air bubbles to the surface.

Once the flood valve was closed the excess air pressure was vented into the hull.

Finally the submarine reached its desired depth and the boat leveled off. At that point the diving officer reduced the speed to 1/3 speed. Vents were cycled, and the diving officer made the necessary adjustments to the trim. When he was sure that everything was correct, and in order, he turned to the Captain and informed him that the process was successfully completed.

That afternoon, Ashley stood her first watch in the control center. It was a three hour watch which began at 1300 right after lunch. She was relieved from watch at 1700 and headed back to her stateroom for a rest before dinner.

That evening she sat next to the Captain at dinner. Ashley, I have heard from a number of my friends that you made a lot of people proud at the Naval Academy this year. Thank you Sir. That is nice to hear. On hearing that comment the two midshipman from Oregon State perked up and strained to hear what was coming next. What had Ashley done?

You know Ashley, I went to the Academy for four long years, and during that time we never did much of anything in any sport. We just couldn't draw the athletic talent away from the Division I schools.

My experience was that there just weren't that many super athletes' that wanted to spend the next four years of their life in the United States Navy. So along comes Ashley Jamison, and suddenly, the Naval Academy has a National Champion in two swimming events. Well done Ash. So my curiosity was peaked when I learned about your performance, if you don't mind me asking "Why did you choose the Naval Academy over the number of schools that were willing to give you a full ride in not one, but two sports?

Well Sir, that is a question that many people have asked me, including my parents. The answer is, I like a challenge and the Academy provides me with both the Athletic challenge and the Academic challenge. I might add, that now having finished my Plebe year, there are a lot of challenges that I had no idea I would face that are neither athletic or academic.

The Captain started to laugh as did Julie and a couple of other officers who were academy graduates. You're right Ash, the Plebe year is certainly not for everyone. I'm sure you are glad it is behind you. Yes Sir, that is an understatement.

They finished dinner, and Ashley and the other midshipmen retired to their rooms to study. They had a lot to memorize and it needed to get done. At 2100 she was totally beat and headed for bed. She would go on watch again in the control room beginning at 0900.

They had been at sea for about five days when the Captain

advised the three midshipman that the six Navy SEALs on board would begin their lockout training the next morning. I would like the three of you to watch how the SEALs approach their training. They are the most disciplined fighting force I have ever seen, and a lot can be learned from just watching them go through their drills.

The Captain then explained what the Seals would do.

He said that under normal war, or combat conditions, that the submarine could carry a full platoon of SEALs. A platoon is made up of 14 men.

The practice session in the morning would demonstrate how the SEALs get off the ship when the ship is submerged. The Captain went on to explain that the ship contains a lockout trunk. The Navy SEALs enter the lockout trunk, and then water is added to the trunk until the outer sea pressure is matched. Once the pressure in, and outside the ship match, the hatch will open and the SEALs can swim out of a fully filled chamber. Once they are out of the chamber they will swim up to the sub's tower, which the Captain explained, is the portion that sticks up vertically. Once there, they will take the gear they need from another compartment called the special forces operation box. In the box are all the weapons they need, and some additional equipment.

The Captain said that normally the submarine would be a couple of thousand yards from the beach where the SEALs would conduct their operation and they would swim in with all their gear. He went on to say, that since they were out in the middle of the ocean and no land operation would be conducted that the SEALs would remove portable life rafts from the operation box, and then inflate them, board them with their gear in tow.

Once that is complete, the SEALs will reverse the entire procedure and reenter the submarine.

The Captain went on to say that the weather topside is clear, and the seas calm. When the seas are rough this is a difficult exercise.

Ashley, and the other two midshipman, didn't say anything but there was a difference in how they were thinking. The two guys from Oregon State were thinking these Navy SEALs are crazy, while Ashley was thinking this sounds like one fun adventure. Different strokes for different folks.

The Captain told them that the exercise would commence at 0900 and that the midshipman should be at the lockout trunk prior to 0900.

At 0845 the three midshipman were standing by the lockout trunk when the Captain entered. Good Morning Midshipman. In a few minutes our Navy SEAL guests will begin their training exercise. Please observe how they handle themselves, and the discipline with which they go about their tasks.

A few minutes later the six seals entered the lockout chamber room. They were all dressed in diving gear, but did not have packs or weapons other than knives strapped to their legs. They each entered the chamber and then checked to see that all of the air in their tanks was operating normally. The Captain explained that their packs and weapons were stored above, and they would retrieve them prior to inflating the life rafts.

Once they were all in the chamber the senior enlisted man signaled to the Captain that they were ready to have the chamber sealed and filled with water.

Ashley just watched in amazement, the other two boys started to sweat just with the thought of how claustrophobic the entire exercise was.

It took a full hour and 15 minutes for the SEALs to complete the exercise. The Captain took the midshipmen up to the control room and allowed them to look through the periscope to see what the men looked like in the life raft.

Ashley could not believe how much gear and weapons they carried. She knew she was a strong swimmer but wow carrying all that equipment could present a real challenge. But then again, challenge was Ashley Jamison's middle name.

CHAPTER 25

HAWAII CALLS

Just before the end of the second week the Captain told Ashley, Fred, and Hans, at dinner that the ship planned to enter Peal Harbor in Hawaii in two days time. He indicated that the three midshipman would be granted an overnight leave in Honolulu. They would have the choice to spend a night in the city or return to the ship which ever they desired. Ashley had been to Hawaii before but neither of the boys had.

The Captain also told them that they would soon be near Necker Island Hawaii. Necker Island is a small island in the Northwestern Hawaiian Islands. The island is rocky with steep sides and has very little soil. The Island has few signs of long term human habitation, however it does contain 33 stone shrines and some stone artifacts. We are going to move our submarine in close enough to the island so it will be within swimming distance for our Navy Seals.

Tonight they will begin another training mission. This will involve a night compass dive, which is part of their combat swimmer training. They will leave the ship at night while we are under water. Get their full gear on and then using only their night compasses make their way to the island. They must then locate one of the stone shrines on the island, photograph it and then return to the ship. This will all occur at night. We will maintain our position off shore but will not surface.

Fred then said to the Captain. I'm sure glad I was able to see the SEALs in action Captain. It has done one thing for me. What's that Fred? the Captain asked. It has convinced me that I don't want to be a Navy SEAL. The thought of leaving our sub at night, and swimming in open water when you can't see anything, just gives me the creeps. I hear you Fred. What do you think Hans and Ashley. I think I'm with Fred, Hans said. It must take a special will to be a SEAL and it doesn't look like it is something that everyone would want to take on. Ashley did not respond until the Captain asked her again.

What about you Ashley? Well Captain, I've spent most of my life in the water, and watching these guys work as they do, looks like it would be a real challenge. They certainly have earned my respect.

Well the good news for you three is you do not have to get up to watch any of this training. It will all be done in the dark so your off the hook.

The SEALs began their training at 2100. They were back on board at 0400. Their training was a success.

The next morning the USS Annapolis arrived in Pearl Harbor. The three Midshipman were assigned to act as assistant topside supervisors while mooring. This involved conducting a walkthrough of topside identifying all important items, explaining the name, and location of all lines, and discussing line handling safety procedures.

At noon they were released to enjoy two days in sunny Hawaii. Has and Fred had not been to Hawaii before, so they were off as soon as released. They planned to spend the night in Honolulu. They were both 21 years old so a few beers were on their minds. Ashley was about to turn 20. She had been to the Hawaiian Islands a couple of times. She planned to spend the time at Peal Harbor, reading about the history, and learning about the Japanese attack during World War 2. She planned to stay on the sub and study the first night, and then hop on an on and off bus the next day to have a guided tour of Honolulu and the surrounding area.

After her tour of Pearl Harbor, she was returning to the ship when she noticed that the six SEALs had packed their gear and were leaving the ship. Ashley said to them, Hey you guys leaving so soon? One of them smiled and said Yes Ash, we enjoyed our cruise ship to Hawaii. Now that we have had all of the tropical drinks we can stand and enjoyed the cruise ship food for two weeks it's about time for us to move to our next event.

We now get to spend a couple of delightful weeks doing Land Warfare training.

We get to practice the fine art of live fire immediate action drills, It is all great fun as long as you like firing and maneuvering at night using pop flares, smoke grenades in conditions that are less then easy to see in. Just another day at the office. Have a great rest of your cruise Ash. They waived and walked down the pier together.

Ashley spent the night on the submarine reading the material that was required. The next morning she was up early and off to Honolulu. She caught a cab to downtown, and then went to the hop on and hop off desk at the Sheraton Hotel. She bought a ticket for the Oahu Circle Island Tour. It was 104.77 and would take 6 full hours.

She was picked up at the hotel with a small group of other tourists. She wore civilian clothes, so she blended in with everyone else.

The first stop was to see Diamond Head crater which was an extinct volcano. Ashley had seen Diamond Head before, but she had never been up to the extinct Volcano. The guide then talked to the group about the landmark's cultural significance, before heading on to Hanauma Bay. The next stop was at Halona Blowhole where all of the group had an opportunity to see the whales migrating. Next up was a visit to a macadamia nut farm, and to lean about how the nuts are cultivated. Form the farm it was off to Kualoa Ranch, which is one of the most beautiful locations on the island of Oahu. From the ranch you could see Kualoa Beach, and the views were incredible.

Lunch was available from the Kahuku Shrimp truck, which was a very authentic Hawaiian plate lunch. After the shrimp truck it was off to Sunset Beach and the rural surf town of Haleiwa.

The tour concluded with a tour of the Dole Pineapple Plantation. Shortly thereafter, the van dropped her off at the Sheraton Hotel where her journey began.

She grabbed a cab from there and headed back to the Submarine. She was back on board and in uniform in time for the officers dinner in the Ward Room.

The next two weeks were packed with things to learn and be tested on. She spent a lot of time with Julie, and was most appreciative of her help. She was able to identify all of the ship's compartment and the major spaces in each. She learned the names, and uses, of all the IC circuits and the correct pronunciation for all letters and numbers in the IC manual. She demonstrated the correct use of the sound powered phone, and correctly donned an EAB (emergency Air Breathing apparatus) and an OBA (onboard air compressor).

Her biggest challenge was the week spent in the Engine room. She knew little about engineering, and thus it was a challenge for her. She was able to diagram the primary coolant system, and was able to observe the actions for a SCRAM (system configuration, reconfiguration automation model) and FRSU (fixed radio subscriber unit). She was also able to observe an all ahead flank cavitate from maneuvering and a steam generator blowdown.

She successfully traced the power generation steam cycle including; finding and explaining the use of the main engine turbines and reduction gears. She also learned and successfully explained the condensers, condensate pumps, and fee pumps.

The engine room was a big challenge for her with no

engineering knowledge but Ashley was a quick study and she impressed every officer that she interfaced with.

Her last week was spent in the control room. She was able to learn to change depth, speed and course and she was able to demonstrate that she knew how to operate the planes and rudder in emergency.

She spent ample time with the periscope and she stood a watch as a helmsman under instruction, and as a plainsman under instruction.

Last she stood one watch as Chief of the Watch under instruction and she performed a pump from tank to tank with the trim pump.

With two nights to go before they returned to San Diego Julie sat with Ashley in her stateroom. Ash, I have to tell you that you have been one great roommate for the last three weeks. I am most impressed with what you have learned, and demonstrated, and I know that my fellow officers feel the same. Thanks Julie, that is really nice to hear.

It is also pretty clear to me that you are one driven woman, and very little phases you. When faced with a challenge you would be someone I would definitely want on my team.

Thanks for all your support Julie. You have been a very good mentor for me, and I really appreciate the time you have spent with me. I wasn't sure how I would deal with all of the engineering jargon but I surprised myself. It took me some additional study but I got through it and was proud of it.

I think that one of the things that I enjoyed the most was having the opportunity to see the SEALs in action. Those guys are really something.

Yep, your right. If I'm correct, no woman has ever made it through training. I think a couple tried last year but they washed out. It will happen someday, but it is going to take someone very special to break that glass ceiling.

Tomorrow night Ash, we have the Captain's dinner. This will be your last night on our ship.

The Captain always asks the midshipman what they liked best about the cruise and what they liked least about the cruise. You might want to think about that because I know he will ask the question. Thanks Julie, I will be ready with an answer.

The next evening they joined the other officers in the wardroom for dinner. The Captain sat at one end of the table and the XO sat at the other. The Captain arranged for all three midshipman to sit next to him. As Julie predicted, he asked the midshipman what they enjoyed the most about the cruise and what they liked least about the cruise.

Fred responded first. Well Captain, first off the entire cruise was great. I learned more than I thought possible, and feel like I earned some respect from some of the crew along the way. I guess, if the truth be known, I would have to say that I liked the two days off in Honolulu the best, but I'm sure that is not what you really wanted to know. Everyone laughed. Fred then said, I enjoyed my week in the engineering department the best. I have been taking engineering at Oregon State for the past three years and it was really fun to see how some of the stuff I learned is really put to use. I think the thing that was hardest, and I'm still getting use to is the lack of sleep. Watches that start at 0300 and last until breakfast are something that takes getting use to. Again everyone laughed.

What about you Hans? Well Captain, I enjoyed my time in the control room the most. It was where everything seems to be happening. Something was always going on day or night. It was action central and I loved it. As to what I liked the least. Well that is an easy one. I can't imagine being a Navy SEAL, and doing that night dive. My mind just couldn't get over the thought of bumping into something big in the dark in the middle of the ocean. I don't think I slept for two nights after watching that. Those guys were crazy and they all had more guts than I could ever have.

Yes Hans, your right. It takes a special breed of person to be able to do what they do for a living but I can tell you from my own experience, we are very lucky to have them on our side.

OK Ash, you're up. What did you like the most and the least about our time together?

Well Captain there are two things that I really enjoyed. The first and probably the most important was the challenge of doing what we were asked to do with absolutely no knowledge of submarines and no engineering background. I think I have memorized more acronyms during the past three weeks than I have in all the years of my life put together. Everyone laughed. The second thing I really enjoyed was watching the SEALs in action. I have spent a lot of my life in the water, and watching them, just brought a whole new meaning to the term let's go for a swim. Everyone laughed again.

As to what I liked least. Well the week I spent in the engine room was enough to make me not want to be an Engineering Officer on any kind of ship. I don't think I was made to spend my time around grease and engines.

I should also add, that I have really enjoyed the people on your ship. Julie has been super to me and I have enjoyed interfacing with all of the Officers and enlisted men. It is clear to me that you have a skilled, well trained crew and that they welcomed us in every way they could.

Thanks Ash, that is good to hear.

Well you all are about to complete your midshipman cruise. We have enjoyed having you, and wish you the best as you continue your quest to graduate and become Officers in the United States Navy. We wish you both good luck and God speed as you leave us tomorrow. One last thing, Ash we will all be watching your progress in the pool. Make the Navy proud again kid. Thanks everyone, that concludes our final dinner. Cheers.

CHAPTER 26

HOME AT LAST

It was a bright sunny day in San Diego. Ashley said goodbye to Julie, and thanked her again for all the support. She was dressed in uniform and was headed to the San Diego Airport to fly to Portland. Her three week leave was about to begin.

She had not thought much about the leave until about one week ago when it hit home. Three weeks off she thought. I can't wait. She caught a cab to the airport and boarded her Southwest flight to Portland.

The plane left on time with a scheduled arrival in Portland at 1130 AM. She had let her Mom and Dad know when she was due to arrive, and she was sure that they would both be there to meet her. She had not seen either of them since her NCAA Championship in Texas.

As the plane touched down, Ash felt really excited and a little bit nervous. She had no idea why, but she knew it was really good to be home again.

She had checked her bag, so she went directly to baggage claim to retrieve it. Then she exited the security area, and right away, she saw her Mom, Dad and Brother waiting for her. They were all smiling and so happy to see her. Hugs were had by all, I and then they all headed for the parking garage across from the main terminal.

It took only 20 minutes to get home from the Airport. During the drive they all had questions about her cruise, and what life was like on a submarine. She told them everything including the fact that the Navy SEAL's had been aboard going through tests.

Sarah made an Italian dinner for them all. It was handmade ravioli, hot French bread, bread and white bean salad, and Italian gelato for desert.

After dinner it was one question after another until it was 1030 PM. Ashley was beat, and said she was heading for her room to sleep. She told her Mom, not to wake her for breakfast, as she was determined to sleep in.

Ashley slept like a baby and she didn't wake up until 1030. She walked out to the kitchen and said Good Morning to her Mom. Hey Sleepy Head, welcome home. I trust you slept well. Like a baby Mom. Do you still have coffee. Yes, let me pour you a cup. Do you want breakfast? That would be great. How about two eggs over easy and toast? I can handle that order.

What's your plan for your home leave. I really don't have any plan other than I need to get back in the pool, and I want to work out with the gymnastic gang. I have not swam or worked out, in over a month and I need to be in shape by the time I get back to the YARD.

I plan to call Coach Nancy and see if I can schedule regular workouts with team unify. I'm sure that isn't going to be a problem. Has the coaching staff at Gymnastics changed or are they the same? I don't know Ash, you may want to stop by there and see what's going on. Good idea Mom, I will do that today.

Ashley, dressed in her civilian clothes and headed out. No need to think about lunch for me Mom, I'm heading downtown to see Coach Nancy, and i will try to stop by the gymnastics place on my way home. I'll be home for dinner.

Ashley took the Max down town. She thought about having lunch at Killer Burger, but decided against it since she hadn't been working out. She went directly to the Y, but she stopped at the Mexican food truck on her way, and ordered two chicken soft taco's.

The girl at the front desk of the Y recognized her immediately, and welcomed her back. Ashley asked if Coach Nancy was around.

She was, and within two minutes, she was out and giving Ashley one big bear hug. It is so great to see you Ash. I was so proud of you at the NCAA Championships. I'm sure the Naval Academy was pretty happy with the results of your effort. Yes they were, they haven't had many NCAA champions at the Academy, so they were pretty proud.

How long are you home for? I'm here for three weeks, and would like to see if I can work out with Team Unify during that time. Sure, we would love to have you back. I'm sure that everyone will be really excited. They have all been following your progress. Great. If it will work for you, I would like to swim every other day. I need to get back in the gym on the off day to keep my upper body strength up. No problem. If you're ready we can start tomorrow. What is a good time for you. I would like to be in the pool at 10AM and workout for two hours. Will that work for you? Sure but most of the team won't be in the pool until 3PM. They still go to school. Oh I forgot. Let's make it 3 to 5 so I can work out with them. Great, I'm sure they will be excited.

Why don't you come by tomorrow at 2 PM. I would like to catch up on your life and what it's been like at the Academy. I will do that. I'll see you tomorrow at 2PM.

Ash took Max and got off near her old gymnastics gym on Sandy boulevard. When she walked in, a class was in session. The girls looked to be about 10 years old. Her old coach Tom Timmons was teaching and saw her come in. He immediately told the class to take a break, and came over to give her a hug. Hey Ashley, it is great to see you. How are things at the Academy? They are going well Coach. I heard all about your swimming success. Congratulations. What brings you back to this place. Well, I was wondering if I might use the weight room, and some of the equipment, while I'm home. I need to keep working on my upper body strength and I thought this might be a great place to work out. Sure, the place is yours. Use it when you want to. Even when we have classes going the weight room is empty and all yours. Thanks Coach.

I'm going to try to come by every other day beginning the day after tomorrow. Great. It will be fun having you around again. See you soon Ash. He then returned to his class, and got the girls all moving again.

Hi Mom, what's for dinner. Well, I'm going to try something new tonight. I'm going to make Thai Beef Salad. That sounds great. Is Dad home? No not yet but I expect him anytime. How was your day? It was successful. I am going to start working out with team unify tomorrow, from 3 to 5, in the afternoon and then, I am going to work out at the gym on the opposite day. I talked to Coach Timmons and he welcomed me back with open arms and said I can use the place whenever I want.

Sounds like a great plan. I hope you also schedule some time for rest but I'm not overly optimistic that you will do so. Just then, Jim walked in the door. He gave both Sarah and Ashley a kiss and headed for the bathroom to clean up. What's for dinner Hon. I'm trying something new. We are going to have Thai Beef Salad. I cooked the steak this afternoon and have had it marinating all afternoon. Sounds great. What do we have in mind for wine. Tonight it is a cold Pinot Gris. I think it will go well with it. I have one picked out from Dundee. It should be good.

Dinner was great. After dinner, Ashley did the dishes, then joined her parents by the fire. Hey Ash, tell me what you have to face academically when you go back for your 3rd class year.

Well I have two fronts to deal with. On the pure Navy side, we are required to take three courses, which include navigation, naval engineering, ethics, and moral reasoning.

As you know, I decided to major in computer science, which is the study of the theory and application of computational algorithms, and information processing in computer systems.

Ash, I'm not sure I know what you just said. Well Dad,

let me put it this way. A computer science major provides a foundation in computer architecture, systems programming, data structures, and networks. Upper level courses include computer algorithms, software engineering and programming languages. Examples of elective courses are artificial intelligence, robotics and computer graphics complete the major. Basically, the computer science program at the Naval Academy supports advanced study in computer graphics and visualization, cryptography, artificial intelligence, and robotics.

Next year, I will have to start the upper level courses, which make things more complicated. I'm actually looking forward to it. The course work seems easy for me, so I know I can handle it, while I continue to swim for the Academy.

Ash, her Dad asked. I'm curious about something. How did you end up on a midshipman cruise on a Nuclear Submarine? Good Question Dad. I have no idea. Most midshipman that are assigned to Nuclear Submarines are engineers. It is a very sought after assignment, and many midshipman have pointed their entire efforts toward the Nuclear workforce. I didn't even specify a type of ship, or a geographic location.

I talked to Julie, who was the Lieutenant that I roomed with on the submarine. Julie went to the Academy as well, and she couldn't figure it out. In any event I'm really happy I got it. I had a great time and was very challenged by all of the stuff I had to deal with. I know the Captain was pleased with my performance as well, so that is all that really matters.

What do you see in the future for your Computer science major? Well, upper class computer science majors can participate in summer internships with the National Security Agency, the Defense information Systems Agency, or the naval research labs. Some midshipman get the chance to participate in a Service Academy Cyber Defense Exercise.

Once you graduate from the academy the graduates have the opportunity for assignments in the highly competitive information professional or information warfare career field options. IP officers harness technology, information and knowledge, to ensure battle space dominance. They also conduct offensive cyber warfare operations.

I picked the major because I'm interested in it, and find it easy, but also because I wanted a major that I could use if I decide to get out of the service after my obligation is completed.

Sounds like a good strategy to me Ash. Just don't ask me to help you with any of your homework. Me neither Sarah said.

The next day Ashley slept in again, and was ready to swim with Team Unify at 3PM. She arrived at the Y at 2PM to meet with Coach Nancy.

OK Ash, what was the first year like? Well Coach, to be honest, it was difficult. It began with what they call Plebe summer, which is basically two months of harassment. During that time you are strengthened both physically and mentally. Needless to say, I will never have a messy room again.

Plebe summer ends with the return to the YARD by upper classmen. There are two parts to the year. There is the formal inspections, dress parades and other formal Navy stuff, and there is the academic. Nothing is easy, and there are a number of Plebes who drop out. Some, including one of my roommates, gave it up before the Plebe summer was over.

I was lucky, thanks to you and team unify, because I got to participate in the Division I swimming program for the Academy. This provided me with a diversion from the constant formality of everything else that goes on. As you know, I had good success with swimming. It has provided me with lots of opportunity to meet others, and be recognized among the over 1000 Plebes.

I like both of my coaches and I know that you know both of them. They have a tough job. They are asked to compete against a lot of Division I schools that have the opportunity to recruit top swimmers from all over the country. However most recruits have no desire to spend four years in the Navy following their college career. I think they were both very happy, when they learned that I had decided to go to the academy. I think for them that they both felt that finally there was a light at the end of their tunnel. It has worked out well for them, and personally for me.

I'm looking forward to this next year, and I want to repeat as an NCAA Champion. I have set that as a goal for myself.

You will do it Ash, I have no doubt.

What about your summer cruise on a Nuclear Powered Submarine/ Well it was pretty interesting. My Dad asked me last night how in the heck I ended up on a Nuclear Powered Sub. The answer is I have no idea. It was a challenge, as I don't have an engineering background, and most midshipman who are assigned are engineers, and have had that as a goal assignment since before they entered the academy. I managed to get through it, and did well. One of the interesting aspects of it, and you won't remember this, but you had a Navy SEAL come for one of our motivational sessions when I was a sophomore in high school. I got to see the Navy SEALs in action on the submarine. They were assigned to the sub for some underwater training. Wow, were they impressive, and some would say crazy. In one exercise they exited the submarine underwater at night. Using a compass they swam to an island, reached their target, and then returned to the sub all the while working in pitch dark land and water. It was really something to see.

Sounds like that was a real challenge. OK, time to get your suit on and show off for Team Unify. They were so excited to learn that you are going to be around for the next three weeks.

It wasn't long before Ashley was locked in her routine. She had swim training one day followed by work in the gym the next. She even managed to work some on the high bar and parallel bars, and found that she still had a little talent in that area.

The three weeks went fast, and yes, in the last week she made two trips to Killer Burger to have their special.

CHAPTER 27

BACK TO THE YARD

Her three weeks had gone by so fast she couldn't believe it. As she sat on her plane heading for Maryland she tried to reflect on all that had gone on during the past year. It had been a year to remember, but now it was back to the grind.

She kept thinking about the 1000 new Plebes who were about to complete their Plebe summer and she was just thankful that that part of the Academy experience was over.

She arrived by cab at the gates of the YARD. Paid her driver, and walked in through the gates with her bag in hand. She was dressed in her civilian clothes, but they would soon be packed away, and the uniform would again take priority.

She headed for her dorm room. She was happy that she didn't have to change rooms, or roommates, like she did after her Plebe summer. When she got to her room Martha was already there and unpacked. Hey Ash, great to see you, she said, as she gave her a great big hug.

So I want to hear all about the last two months. It was really interesting Martha, and I will tell you all about it over dinner. Let me get this stuff unpacked and we can walk over to dinner and catch up.

Dinner was great, and their conversation went until 2100 when they both looked at each other and said, "To be continued tomorrow" They said good night, and both of them were asleep within five minutes.

They had a couple of days before classes were to begin. Ashley used the time to confirm her academic schedule, and to meet with her swimming coaches Mike Morgan and Cindy Rodrigo.

Once she had her schedule all sorted out, it was clear that free time was going to be at a premium.

Over her three weeks at home she had decided on three goals that she wanted to achieve in her second year. They were as follows:

1. Do well academically. No need to be at the top of the class, but definitely be in the top 1/3.
2. Repeat as NCAA Champion in the 200 freestyle and 100 Butterfly
3. Learn more about the SEAL recruitment process, and the requirements that would be facing her in the future.

Her fall class schedule shaped up to look like this:

- Calculus 111
- General Physics
- Premodern World
- Chinese and Asian Language
- Ethics and Moral Reasoning
- NCAA Swimming.

When she met with Mike and Cindy, they both felt that she should continue to work on her upper body strength, so she carved out two hours each Sunday morning for a five mile run and work in the Gym. The rest of Sunday would be spent resting and studying. All she could think was, "So much for a social life"

Ashley fell into a routine, and even with all of the tight

schedule, she felt she had it under control. and was comfortable that she could achieve her objectives.

It was a fall Sunday morning after a run when she went to the Gym to begin her workout. The gym was almost empty, as it was most Sunday mornings, but there were two guys working out on the high bar. She recognized them as the two guys that had spotted her during one of her workouts Plebe year. She said hi to them, as she passed them by, and headed for the weight room.

About l5 minutes later the two guys entered the weight room. Excuse me but are you Ashley Jamison? Yes, that's me. I'm Ryan Joshua and this is my best friend Travis Michaels, We are members of the Navy Gymnastics Team. Hi, it is nice to meet you.

Actually, we met you once before when you asked us to spot you on a high bar routine that involved four revolutions and a perfect dismount. Oh yes, I remember now. We wanted you to know, that we have about half of our Men's team that would love to even come close to what you did that day. Most of them can only dream about being that good. Thanks Guys, that is nice to hear.

We have also followed your swimming achievements and congratulate you on your two NCAA championships. That accomplishment made a lot of folks at the Academy very proud.

You guys are both upperclassmen. Are you in your third or final year here? We are both first class midshipman. This will be our final year, and we can only say that it is the best year so far. We are a long way from the memories of our Plebe year. That was something neither of us every want to repeat. I hear you.

Well, we will let you get back to your workout. It was nice to meet you, and again congratulations on all of your athletic success. Thanks Ryan, it was nice to meet you and Travis as well.

Ashley finished her workout, but continued to think about Ryan and Travis. They both seemed like nice guys perhaps she would get to know them better as the Sunday mornings went on.

At the next swimming practice, Mike handed out the meet schedule. It was very similar to the year before. It was the middle of September, and their first meet was scheduled for October 10th. It was with Louisiana State University. That was then followed by a regular schedule that took them through October and November. Ashley noticed that the big match against Army was scheduled in early December.

She also looked at where the University of North Carolina fell on the schedule. It was not until the middle of November, then there was the break for Thanksgiving, before the return to the YARD to face Army. The Patriot League championships were scheduled for February, with the NCAA finals up again in March.

The schedule was a good one. The only concern she had was the women from North Carolina who had challenged her in both the meet match and the NCAA's. However, that problem was solved at the next practice when Cindy told her that her competitor from North Carolina graduated and was now swimming in the US Team program.

It was soon the end of October, and there was frost on the pumpkin. Halloween was just around the corner, and she had already swam in four meet competitions. LSU was first, followed by the University of Connecticut, John Hopkins, and the University of Maryland. So far Ashley had won every race, and in most instances by a significant margin. Her upper body strength continued to develop, and her butterfly technique continued to improve.

It was the Sunday before Halloween and she had just completed her five mile run and was headed for the gym. As she entered the gym she noticed there was one other guy working out and she recognized him right away. Hey Ryan, how is it going? Hi Ashley. It has been a good season so far. Our gymnastics team has pretty much split the schedule with half victories and half defeats. For me personally, it has been a great season, and I will be sorry to see it come to an end in a couple of months.

I have been reading about your swim team success, and from what I can tell, you are having another great season. Thanks Ryan. It has been good, and I really enjoy the break from all the Navy stuff we have to do.

Are you just starting your workout or are you about to finish? I'm just starting Ashley. How would you like to work out together? I could use a spotter and some pointers, and I'm sure that you are capable of doing both.

That sounds great. I have never had the opportunity to work out with anyone in this gym, and think that would be fun and a great idea. I'm still focused on my upper body strength, so your workout on the high bar and parallel bars, would be fun, and if I might say it, it would be a real blast from the past. Ryan, do you guys work on the rings as well? Yep, that is a strength event that I really need practice on. Well then let's get at it. You do what you need to do. I will spot you and then I will try to copy what you did. Sounds like a plan.

They worked out for two full hours and when finished they were both beat. Great workout Ashley. Thanks for joining me. It made the entire thing fun, instead of work. I feel the same way Ryan. Look forward to doing it again in the near future.

The weeks past, and so did her progress, both academically and athletically. Ashley found that since she had chosen Computer Science as her major that she spent a significant amount of time in labs working with computers, servers, routers, switches, and other computer equipment. She enjoyed the work and was slowly learning how programming languages are structured. She also, was slowly beginning to understand, what her major would mean to her when she became an upper classman in her junior year. She learned that she would have a lot of independent study, and might have the opportunity to participated in an internship with the National Security Agency.

She had at this point no idea what the future would hold, but she was sure that choosing this major would provide her with a variety of career opportunities if she did not stay in the Navy.

She began to team up with Ryan on Sunday mornings and found that the workout was good for her and that she was starting to look forward to Sunday mornings more than most other things. Their workouts together were a challenge. They were both very competitive which made the tests of each other even more fun.

One Sunday morning, when they entered to the gym, there were two older guys working out.

Both of them were in exceptional physical condition, and both were having a friendly competition. Ashley and Ryan began their workout which soon caught the attention of the two guys. Hey Roscoe, check out this guy on the high bar. Ryan finished his routine and then did a perfect dismount. Pretty good, if I don't say so myself, Ashley said to him. OK, it's your turn to shine. Ryan helped Ashley jump up to reach the high bar and quickly began her swing into a full 360 rotation. She completed four perfect circles and then did a front summersault dismount and stuck the landing. Way to go Ash. That was amazing.

Roscoe looked at Kyle, and said what did you think of that? Amazing. It would be fun to see if either you, or I, could even swing to a handstand on that high bar. Those two kids did it like it was nothing. Roscoe said to Kyle, do you know who those kids are? No clue. Well the guy is Ryan Joshua. He is the number 1 member of the Navy Varsity gymnastic Team, and the girl with him, is Ashley Jamison, who is the reigning NCAA swimming champion in the 200 meter freestyle and the 100 meter butterfly.

Is Ashley the same midshipman that we were involved with behind the scenes when the kid tried to get her kicked out of the academy. Yes she is one and the same.

If she is a swimmer, what is she doing working out with a gymnastics star. My guess is that she is working on her upper body strength. She was an excellent gymnast before she came to the academy, and I'm sure this training to her is like water off a ducks back. Wow, with both swimming and gymnastics training she must be on your radar screen. Yep, Kyle. You got that right.

They continued to watch as they both worked on the rings, and took the iron cross position. Ashley finally gave up when she started laughing. She could only hold herself up in that position for a limited period of time, but she was improving. It was one more thing that Roscoe logged in his notebook.

No question he was looking at someone who had the basic potential to become the first woman Seal ever.

It was shortly before Thanksgiving. Ryan and Ashley had finished their workout and were packing up their things. Ash, what are you going to do for Thanksgiving? I'm not going home again this year to the disappointment of my parents. I'm going to have Thanksgiving with my sponsorship parents like I did last year. I talked to my coaches about it, and they would prefer that I stick around and train. We have our match with Army coming up in early December and I'm sure they want me to do well. Oh heck, if the truth be known, I want to destroy those girls. Ryan started to laugh. Well, based on what I have seen of your training, I for one would not want to be in competition against you. Thanks Ryan. That is nice to hear. What about you? I'm going home to be with my Mom and Dad and my sister. This will be my last Thanksgiving before I start a real job with the Navy so I'm not sure when I will have the next opportunity to celebrate Thanksgiving with them again. I will be back right afterward, as I need to practice as well.

Hey Ash, I've been meaning to ask you something but I'm not sure how. What is it you want to know? Well, I have never talked to you about your social life and I wondered if you have a boy friend, or are seeing someone on a regular basis? Why do you ask Ryan? Well, to be honest I have really grown to like and respect you, and I wanted to know if you might want to go to the Army Navy Football game with me in the middle of December. I think this year it is being played in Philadelphia so it would be a full day or two event.

That is so nice of you. No, I do not have a boyfriend, and I am not seeing anyone on a regular basis. My life is made up of the YARD, school and athletics. I haven't had time for anything else. I don't know what the academy policy is regarding midshipmen dating, but if it is allowed, I would love to go together.

I think it would be great fun to watch some other Navy Athletes work, while I sit in the stands eating a hot dog. Ryan laughed. Never thought of it that way Ash, but I know what you mean. So we have a confirmed date for the Army Navy Game. They left the gym and headed back to their respective dorms. Ashley walked the entire way with a big smile on her face.

CHAPTER 28

ARMY VS NAVY

Ashley spent Thanksgiving with her sponsor parents. It was a very nice, low profile afternoon, and a welcome change from the hectic life she had been experiencing. Her training was intense, and seemed to increase the closer that she got to December I. December Ist the Navy Midshipman Varsity Women's Swim team was due to meet Army. The meet was at Navy and there was a lot of talk about it.

The Army Navy rivalry began in 1890 when the Navy football team was challenged by the newly formed Army football team. The squads faced off on "The Plain," at West Point, on November 29, 1890. The Naval Academy had been playing organized football since 1887, and they came out on top of the newly established Army squad. Ever since, through the many years, there have been intense cheers, unforgettable plays, and climactic moments. The Army Navy rivalry has been etched into the minds of countless fans and followers. This was exactly the case with all of the Army Navy athletic teams.

The Navy Women's Swim Team had been undefeated in dual matches thus far this year, in part due to an unbelievable showing by Ashley Jamison. Ashley was only a third class midshipman, but she was the unanimous choice of all team members to be their captain. Ashley was the only member of the Navy team to have won every race she entered during the year. She had trained hard, built her upper body strength, and was killing her competition in every meet.

The Army Navy rivalry was not lost on the midshipman. The entire YARD was interested in what the women were doing. The Army Navy Football game was coming up later in the month so there was a competitive tension in the air.

On the morning of December 1st Ashley, was up at the normal 530 AM time. She and Martha attended to their morning drill activities and then it was breakfast and on to class.

At noon, Ashley headed over to Lejeune Pool. The joint meet with Army was set to begin at 2PM.

She arrived and headed for the locker room. As she walked by the entrance to the Lejeune Pool facility, she was surprised to see that there were already midshipman lined up to get a seat in the stands for the meet. This was unusual. Usually there were some people in the stands, many of whom were parents, or friends of the competitors, but it was rare to see the stands even 1/3 full.

Once in the locker room, she put her sweats on and did her warm up stretching exercises. Cindy, her coach, stopped by, and ask her how she felt. Ash replied I feel fine and am really looking forward to this meet. Me too, Cindy replied. Based on what I saw before I came in here, we are going to have a pretty energetic crowd out there. The stands are already filled and there is still a line of people wanting to get in.

Great. We deserve a crowd. You got that right Ash. Best of luck girl. Keep that winning streak moving forward. I'll give it my best coach. Cheers.

At 2PM the meet began. The Navy Swim Team entered the pool area, and the crowd went wild. Ashley had never heard a crowd so loud at a swimming meet. Even at the NCAA's there was nothing like this. It was immediately clear, what the Army, Navy rivalry was all about, and in Ashley's mind, there was no way she was going to let these fans go home without something to be proud of.

Ashley's first race was the 200 meter freestyle. Her best time in the event was still the 141.5 she swam at the NCAA Championships the year before. She had come close to that mark in a couple of her dual meets, but still had not topped it.

The 200 free was the third event of the meet. The swimmers were called to their marks. Ashley was in lane 3 which was good because the strongest Army swimmer in the 200 free was in lane 5 and Ashley could see her and where she was throughout the event. Swimmers were called to their marks, and the gun sounded. The Army swimmer was off to a fast start.

Ashley thought to herself, she is going out to fast but I'm not going to take any chances so she stayed with her during the first two laps. The pace was faster than Ashley liked, but she was bound and determined to not lose to anyone let alone someone from Army.

As they made the turn for the third lap, Ash could tell that the girls pace was catching up to her. She started to slow a bit. Ashley felt great and said to herself, "now is the time, let's go for it" and she did. She finished the 200 in 140.5 which was a new meet and individual record for the Navy. When she exited the pool after the race, she could hear the crowd. They were going crazy, and yelling Ashley, Ashley, Ashley at the top of their voices.

The crowd was all it took to keep Ash completely pumped up. Her butterfly race was scheduled as the seventh event, so she had some time to rest in the locker room before she was called to the starting blocks. Her best time in the butterfly was still 50.43 which she did at the NCAA Championships, but with all of the work that she had put in on her upper body, she knew, that she was capable of beating that time.

When the time came for the race to begin, she was surprised to again hear the crowd calling her name. This was all new to her, but it seemed to be one great way to motivate her. She took the lead in the butterfly from the start and powered it home in the second lap. Her time was 50.25. Another meet and individual record had been broken.

Her final event of the day was the 4 bye 100 relay. Ashley swam the third leg easily and Navy went on to win the dual meet going away.

It had been one great day for Ashley, her team, and the Naval Academy.

As the crowd filed out, there were two guys who had beaming smiles on their faces. One guy was a full Lieutenant in the US Navy by the name of Roscoe Cook, and the other was a first class midshipman by the name of Ryan Joshua.

The following Sunday, Ryan and Ashley had finished their workout. As they began to pack up their stuff, and head back to their rooms Ryan said, Hey Ash, I have confirmed our plans for our date to the Army Navy Game. I got the tickets yesterday. I'm not sure they are the best seats, but they should be good enough.

Here is what I arranged. I booked us into separate rooms at the Wyndham Philadelphia. It is downtown in the historic district, and a short subway trip to the stadium. It is within walking distance to the Prep Rally, which will be held on the Friday afternoon before the game. The Prep Rally, is at Liberty place, which is close to our hotel. On game day, we have been invited to a tailgate party that is being hosted by a bunch of my first class pals, and then it is on to the game.

We can take Amtrak from here to Philly and Home. I think, if we leave early on Friday morning, we will be in time for the rally, and then we can take the train back after the game. So we will only have to stay the one night. Does that sound OK to you? Sounds perfect Ryan, I'm really looking forward to it. Just let me know what I owe you. You don't owe me anything Ash. Remember this is an official date and I'm the one that asked you. OK Ryan, this is going to be real fun.

After she got back to her room, Ashley realized that she was really looking forward to her date with Ryan. She also realized she didn't know anything about the Army Navy rivalry. So the next day she walked over to the library during her study time and grabbed a small paperback that gave the history of the Army Navy Rivalry.

The brief summary stated the following. The rivalry kicked off 128 years ago when a Army cadet named Dennis Mahan Michie accepted a challenge from the Naval Academy to play an organized football game. Over the history of the event there have been I0 times when it was not played. The game was canceled once in 1909, when army canceled its entire schedule after the death of Cadet Eugene Byrne in the game against Harvard. Twice during World War 1, on orders from the War Department, the game was not played. That was in 1917 and 1918.

Then it was cancelled again in 1928 and 1929, when the academies could not agree on player eligibility standards.

Ashley read that the longest, and perhaps most telling interruption, occurred between 1894 and 1898 when an incident occurred between a Real Admiral and a Brigadier General that nearly led to a duel after the 1893 victory. Ashley also learned that in 1899 Philadelphia was chosen as a neutral locale to host the Army Navy Game, and it has done so since that time.

Mid December came very quickly and so did their trip to Philadelphia. It was a great weekend. Their train trip worked perfect both ways. The Rally and Tail Gate Party were great, and best of all, Navy won the game 21 to 14.

They arrived back at the YARD late on Saturday night and headed for their respective dorms. Before they split off, Ashley said to Ryan. This was one great weekend and I appreciate everything you did to make it happen. I'm not sure what I can give you in return but I know one thing I want to give you more than anything. With that she turned and gave him a very long and slow kiss on the lips. She then said, thanks for everything, turned and headed to her room.

Martha was there when she opened the door, and wanted to know everything about the weekend. They stayed up and talked until 130 in the morning.

The Christmas Holiday Leave began. It was a three week leave and Ashley was excited to be home for the Holiday's. She had been in contact with Coach Nancy, and had arranged to workout with Team Unify every other day during the holiday leave. When she returned, she would have three additional swim meets before the Patriot Games began, and she was bound and determined to win each of them. She was having a great season and was determined to end it successfully.

Her Christmas Holiday was great. She spent more time with her Mom than she had in years, and helped get the house in shape for Christmas. There was just something about being home for the Holiday's that made them very special.

She talked to her brother who was in his final year of law school, and trying to determine what he wanted to do next.

It was clear to Ash, that John would be a great lawyer, and that he would stay in Oregon like her Dad had done.

She didn't say anything to her parents or brother about her thoughts on the Navy Seals, nor did she mention anything about Ryan Joshua. She just wasn't sure about how either of those subjects would turn out, so she felt that at this point, it was best to keep them to herself.

Ashley wasn't surprised, but she was very happy with her Christmas present which was the same one she received the year before. Two roundtrip tickets first class to anywhere she wanted to go that United Airlines flew. Spring break here we come, she thought.

She only made one trip to Killer Burger but she thought about making more than one trip but decided that it really didn't fit with her training schedule. So on the last day after training at the Y, she headed over to 3rd avenue and ordered the Peanut Butter Pickle Bacon Burger. It came with bacon, peanut butter sauce, house sauce, mayo grilled onion and pickles. What a treat, but one she couldn't tell any of her coaches about.

She was back in the YARD in time for New Years and back in her routine both academic and athletic. Her last three swim meets were with the University of Richmond, Penn State University, and the University of North Carolina. All of the meets went well, and Ashley won all of her races. She was glad that the woman from North Carolina had graduated and she was also happy for her, when she learned, that she had made the United States Swim Team.

The Patriot league Championships were held in February and as expected Ashley ended her season with wins. It was an undefeated year for her but she still faced the challenge of the NCAA Championships in March.

She had not matched the times she recorded in the Army dual meet, so she set a goal to beat both of them in the NCAA finals. Time went by quickly, and before she knew it, she was on a plane with her coach Cindy Rodrigo to Dallas, Texas to swim in the NCAA Championship.

Ashley's parents and Coach Nancy planned to attend again, so she set her schedule up so she could see them all for breakfast on her day off.

Cindy had worked with her individually on perfecting her turns in both events, and it was clear to her, that the work that Ashley had put in at the gym was paying big dividends in her butterfly performances.

The competition was strong again this year, more so in the 200 freestyle than in the 100 butterfly, but that just made Ashley want the win more. As usual, she rarely expressed any kind of emotion, or nerves. She was one of the calmest competitors that Cindy had ever been around.

She drew good lane assignments. In the 200 she drew lane five and Cindy told her that the woman in lane 7 was the one to watch out for. In the butterfly she drew lane 2 but was not concerned about tracking anyone. Her performance in both races was over the top and she set personal bests in both races on her way to defending her NCAA Championship. She swam the 200 in a flat 140, and the butterfly in a flat 50. Both were outstanding times, but neither broke the NCAA records. That would have to wait for another year.

The news was out before she and Cindy arrived back at the YARD, and the headlines in the local papers were amazing. Ashley paid little attention to any of them, and focused only on Spring Break.

CHAPTER 29

A VERY IMPORTANT MEETING

Spring Break was a blast. Ash used her extra ticket to take Martha with her again. This time they headed for the Bahamas', and specifically to the city of Freeport, on Grand Bahamas Island.

Ashley researched where to stay, and what to do, and then she booked a reservation for she, and Martha, at the Rosewood Baha Mar, Luxury Bahamas Resort. The hotel was new and offered a onetime special entitled the ultimate girlfriends getaway. Both Martha and Ashley had turned 21 years old, and both were looking for a quiet restful way to end their second year at the YARD.

The ultimate girlfriends getaway included, a luxurious suite with a bubbles, and a blowout session, where they could enjoy a bottle of champagne, while enjoying a very relaxing session at the spa. It included an afternoon tea and a gift card, along with a $250 spa credit. Breakfast was included, as was the round trip airport transfer. Ashley thought it would be perfect, and it was. They laughed, read, laid in the sun, swam in the robin egg blue water and ate and drank more than they should of. It was a grand spring break, and when they returned to the YARD they were ready to finish their second year.

Ashley had one more thing to accomplish. She wanted to meet with the Navy SEAL Recruiter. She didn't know him, but she knew where the SEAL office was, and she needed to understand the next steps if she decided to go that route, and try to become the first woman SEAL ever.

She looked up the information and learned that the SEAL recruiter was a full Lieutenant, by the name of Roscoe Cook. She called the SEAL office, and made an appointment to meet with him.

It was early on a Monday morning when Roscoe arrived at his office.

As he always did, he checked his calendar to see what his assistant had booked him into for the week, and one thing just jumped out at him. On his calendar for Tuesday afternoon at 2 PM was an appointment with a midshipman by the name of Ashley Jamison. Roscoe just smiled, sat back and poured himself a cup of coffee.

At 2PM the next day, Roscoe was sitting in his office. His assistant buzzed him and let him know that his 2PM appointment was here.

Roscoe got up from his desk, and opened the door to greet Ashley. Midshipman Jamison, Hi. I'm Roscoe Cook. Please come into my office.

Thank you Sir, Ashley said.

Please have a seat, and let me know what I can do for you. Thank you Sir. Well Sir, my name is Ashley Jamison and I am about to complete my second year at the Academy. I wanted to take this opportunity to learn more about what it takes to become a Navy Seal, and I thought the best place to begin with would be to start with you Sir.

Well Ashley, you have come to the right place, but I have to tell you at the outset that the road to becoming a Navy SEAL is not an easy road and in fact, as you may be aware, no woman has ever made it. Two tried last year but neither of them made it past the first month.

What interests you about the possibility of becoming a SEAL? Well Sir. Let's start with the fact that I like a challenge and I know that to become a SEAL would be a real challenge. Second, I am an athlete, and have spent years in the water.

I must tell you Ashley, that I read the papers here, and your name has been plastered all over them for the last couple of years. Congratulations on repeating as a NCAA swimming champion. You have made many people very proud of you, and your association with the Navy. I'm sorry I interrupted you, please continue.

Thank you Sir. Third, I am very goal oriented, and I think if I set the goal to become a Navy SEAL that I can be the first woman to do so.

Well those are very good reasons, and all are critical if you want to successfully become a SEAL. Where did you spend your midshipman cruise last summer? I was assigned to the Nuclear Submarine, Annapolis, based out of San Diego California.

Oh, the Annapolis. If I recall, a SEAL team was assigned to do some training during that cruise. Am I correct? Yes Sir. There were six SEALs assigned, and they conducted a number of different drills, including a night swim.

What did you think about it? I thought it was really cool, and I loved the challenge that was put before them. What summer cruise have you been assigned this year? I have not put in any preferences at this point. I didn't put any in last year, and I think a lot of folks were surprised when I was assigned to the Submarine.

Let me look at your record for a second Ashley. Roscoe pulled some information up on the computer and said. Well, it says here that you were very impressive and the marks that were given to you by the Captain were very high. Once again it looks like congratulations are in order.

Let me ask you another question. How have you done with your marksmanship training? I have done well Sir, both with automatic and small arms fire. I am not at the top of the class but I am in the top third of all midshipman. How do you feel about the possibility of having to kill someone? I really have never thought about it Sir. But if I had to do it, and it needed to be done, then I would do it.

Well Ashley, it looks to me like you have the potential to become a Navy SEAL. The challenge will be harder than anything you have ever faced in your life. To begin that challenge, I would recommend that you be assigned to CORTRAMID for your third class summer training.

What is CORTRAMID Ashley asked. Well, this is a summer that consists of training in all of the specialized areas of the Navy. The summer is divided between surface, submarine, aviation and Marine Corps Orientation. The Marine Corp training will tell you if you still want to go the Navy Seal route, and it will provide you the competition you desire.

What do you think about that option?. I think it would be great and a real challenge. What would be my next challenge during my 2nd Class year.

Well, if you still want to pursue the SEAL route, after the summer of CORTRAMID, then the next step for you would be to take the SEAL screener test in fall of your third year. What is the SEAL screener test? Ashley asked.

Well, it is a 36 hour physical event that both Academy and ROTC midshipman participate in. It has a number of components to it, but the key elements are a swim, pushups, sit ups pull ups and a mile and a half run in combat boots. Each is timed and there is a minimum threshold that must be attained on all to move ahead. The midshipman are judged on their performance, and those that are at the top are designated as potential SEAL candidates.

I know you must be in great shape Ashley, but the SEAL screener is a real test. Here is a list of the minimum passing requirements.

- SWIM - 500 yards in 8 minutes and 15 seconds.
- PUSHUPS - 85 in two minutes.

- PULL UPS - 15
- SIT-UPS - 85 in two minutes.
- RUN - 1.5 miles with boots on in 8 minutes and 25 seconds.

That will give you some idea about the minimum levels. Remember if you meet all of the minimums that is only the start, and most who do, don't go on to become SEAL's,

Well Thank you Sir. This has been most interesting to me. I would appreciate the assistance in getting me assigned to CORTRAMID. I'm happy to help with that step Ashley. Please check back in with me after you have completed your summer training and leave, and let me know if you still are interested in taking the SEAL screener in the fall. Will do Sir.

After Ashley left his office, Roscoe just sat behind his desk and smiled. He knew exactly what Ashley was thinking when she looked at the minimum physical requirements and that was, "I can do this in my sleep". The entire question with her would be, does she have the mental toughness to deal with the rest of the stuff.

That night, Martha asked her how her day was. Ashley said it was very interesting. She did not tell her about the SEAL discussion with Lt. Cook, but she did tell her that she had put a preference in to attend CORTRAMID training during the summer. Martha had no idea what that was so Ashley explained it to her. It was a program to help you decide what branch of the Navy you may want to go into. Martha was interested, but she was a surface Navy girl, and her mind was made up. She had requested a destroyer for her 3rd class midshipman cruise.

Two weeks went by and Martha and Ashley's orders arrived on the same day. Martha received orders to the USS Higgins DDG 76, which was based in San Diego and Ashley received orders to attend Career Orientation and Training West for Midshipmen (CORTRAMID). Ashley's training was also based in San Diego.

She read in her orders that CORTRAMID is a four week summer event that is designed to provide insight into the various Navy commands. She read that her training would begin in June and last the entire month. She was assigned to group 1.

Both Martha and Ashley were happy with their assignments. They were also happy that they would be able to fly to San Diego together, and spend a few days at Martha's house before their training began.

It was early on a Sunday morning. Ashley had finished her run and met Ryan at the Gym. Their Sunday morning workouts continued even after their athletic seasons were completed. They were not a couple but they had become really close friends since their date to the Army Navy Game.

Hey Ash, Ryan said. I got my orders for my first real job this week. I am going to flight school in Florida beginning in three weeks. Congratulations big guy. I know how badly you wanted this and I'm really happy for you.

Thanks Ash, where are you going to spend the summer? Well I'm going to CORTRAMID training in San Diego. I'm told it will provide me with an overview of what the Navy and Marines do on land, sea, and air. I think it will help me decide where I want to end up. I've heard about that training Ash, and everything I have heard about it is good. Based on what I know it is not easy to get into the program, so you should be proud you were selected.

Yeh, I'm looking forward to it. Have you got time for coffee when we finish. Sure. Let's do it. They finished their workout, and walked over to the coffee shop together. They sat down and just looked at each other. Ryan, I want you to know something before you leave for a real job. What's that Ash?

Well, I just wanted to tell you that I have really loved our time together for the past six months, and I am going to miss the heck out of you. I feel the same way Ash, but as you know, and we have talked about it before, the career path we have chosen just doesn't lend itself to long term relationships at this point.

Who knows what the future will bring, but for now it is important to stay focused on our own individual goals. Your right, but I didn't want you to get out of here without me telling you.

I really appreciate that Ash. You are a very special person to me, and I won't forget our time together. Which reminds me, we still have one more Sunday together can you make it. Yep. Same place same time.

They finished their coffee and left together. Ashley was sad as she walked back to her dorm, but she knew that Ryan was totally right, and a relationship was not in the cards for either of them at this time. They had one more Sunday together and then who knows where the wind would blow them.

The next three weeks flew by. Ashley said goodbye to Ryan and made sure that he wouldn't forget her by giving him the longest and best kiss she had ever given anyone in her life. It worked and he said, Ash, I'm never going to forget you. With that the good bye was over and she hopped a plane to San Diego with Martha. It had been one heck of a year, and she was looking forward to the training, and to her three weeks of leave following it.

CHAPTER 30

AND THE BEAT GOES ON

Martha's Dad and Mom picked them up at the San Diego Airport. Both Ashley, and Martha, were in uniform, as was Martha's father. So as the group left the airport it was quite a procession, and as they approached the Admiral's waiting driver, a number of people stopped to look at them.

The girls had two great beach filled days in La Jolla, before they reported to their respective assignments, at the San Diego Naval Facility. The weather was great, and they both managed to get some time in the sun, which was rare for both of them.

Ashley's CORTRAMID schedule was for four weeks. The training was designed for each midshipman to see what it was like working onboard a ship, a submarine, in a plane and with a Marine unit.

Ashley reported in as ordered. She soon learned that she was not alone. There were 500 Midshipman, from all over the country, going through the same training. She was placed in group one. There were four groups. Each had a different rotation. Ashley's schedule had her going to aviation training first. That training would be followed by a surface ship experience. Week three was with a submarine unit and her final week would be spent at Camp Pendleton where she would go through Marine training.

Her first week was interesting. She was sent to, and toured, the Marine Corps air Naval Station at North Island, in San Diego. This was where the Navy and Marine Corps pilots and crews underwent their training. Ashley was given the opportunity to participate in a simulator for Marine Corps helicopters, and the MV-22 Osprey tilt rotor helicopter based at Miramar. She also rode in an MG60 Navy helicopter, and a turboprop military training aircraft, located at the Naval Air Station, North Island.

During her second week she was able to visit and ride both on a destroyer and an amphibious assault vessel. She also participated in trainers, that were designed to experience firefighting, and damage control, on Surface Ships.

Week three was the easiest of the three. She attended submarine officer week at the Naval Base, and was given hands on training with two trainers at the submarine learning center. There she experienced all of the things she did in her first summer including how to turn, dive and drive a submarine. the ship's controls were configured as a nuclear submarine ship control room, which she had experienced for real, so the training was easy and she impressed those in her class with her knowledge. Last, she was able to take a brief cruise on an Ohio class, ballistic missile, submarine.

It was the final week that she enjoyed the most. She spent the week at Camp Pendleton. There she observed marine operating and supply units in action, and got a firsthand look at the jobs that the Marine Corp offered.

She watched armored tracked vehicles conduct live fire fight exercises and she was offered the opportunity to learn how to shoot some of the weapons used by Marines. She also spent an overnight stay at the Marine Infantry Immersion Trainer. The trainer was set up to look like a foreign town, with buildings and markets. She learned how difficult it was to search streets, and markets, with snipers waiting on every corner. The experience was lasting with virtual reality enemies everywhere. She also got a good feel of what it must be like to deal with live snipers, and how to guard against Improvised Explosive Devices.

She was surprised to find herself drawn to the Marine exposure rather than the pure Navy exposure, and she made up her mind that if she did not make it as a SEAL she would become a Marine Officer.

Once the training was completed, she caught a flight from San Diego to Portland, and was once again greeted by her Mom and Dad on arrival. During her summer she did not forget about the Navy SEAL physical screening test that she would face in the fall.

She told herself that she needed to continue with her workouts and to focus on those areas that would be critical in the test.

Her parents were full of questions about the experience that she had gone through, and they wanted to know her thoughts about it. The next day, she contacted Coach Nancy, and arranged a schedule for her pool workouts with team unify. She also stopped by the gym, and confirmed that she would have access to it during her time at home.

It was on the third night home, that she made the decision to let her parents in on what she was thinking about. At dinner she said, Mom and Dad I wanted to let you know what I have been thinking about, and about a goal that I have set for myself. Her Dad looked at her and said, Well Ash, we are anxious to learn. Mom and I have had many evening discussions wondering what your focus was going to be and we are both interested to learn what's on your mind.

Well, it has taken me some time to determine the route I would like to go, and the more I learn about it, the more difficult it may be to achieve my goal. I will say this, that if I do not achieve my goal, I have decided that I want to be a Marine Officer leading troupes.

Both Jim and Sarah were surprised but didn't say anything. OK Jim said, so what is your mystery goal? Well, I want to be a Navy SEAL. Both Jim and Sarah were completely silent. Then Jim said, Ash, I don't know much about the SEAL's, but I do know that they are one of, if not the most advanced military units we have in the United States. I don't even think that they have ever had a woman make the grade.

Dad, you are smarter than you think.

You're right. The SEAL's are the most advanced fighting force we have in this country and no woman has ever made it through the basic tests that are required to achieve the status.

There is no difference between men and women. They must take and pass the same tests, and it doesn't matter if you are an officer or an enlisted man, you must pass the same exact training.

I have been thinking about this goal for a long time now. Last summer when I watched those SEAL's training on the submarine I knew that that's what I want to do. I met before the year ended with the SEAL recruiter at the YARD, and he was the one that encouraged me to take the training I just completed. I'm sure he wanted to see what I would think about the marine training as that is a part of what the SEAL's are all about.

When I get back to begin my third year at the Academy, I plan to take the Navy SEAL physical screening test. What's that? Sarah said.

I'm not all together sure, but I know it is a series of timed physical tests that have minimum thresholds. If you don't pass them all your out. It is that simple. I do know that the tests include swimming, push-ups, pull- ups, sit- ups and a 1.5 mile run in combat boots. I'm sure that there is a lot of psychological aspects to it as well. The SEAL's who conduct the training, specialize in getting into the heads and under the skin's of those that want to make the grade. I'm sure that being a woman in that world will also add some extra measure of difficulty.

But guess what? What Ash? her Dad said. They have never met anyone like Ashley Jamison, and once they do, they are not going to forget me. Both Jim and Sarah started laughing.

Ash, you have never failed to amaze us since you were three years old, and if this is what you want, and you set your mind on getting it, I feel sorry for anyone who wants to stand in your way. Mom and I are with you all the way. Thanks you guys. I love both of you to death, and have never doubted your total support. It means a lot to me.

Ashley went to bed that night feeling great. She also planned to tell Coach Nancy what she had decided, and how, without knowing it, Coach Nancy had something to do with her decision.

Her time at home was very restful although she worked out every day and focused a great deal on her upper body and arm strength. She knew that both would be necessary to pass the SEAL physical screening test.

She worked out with Team Unify, and continued to focus on both the butterfly, and the 200 freestyle. For the first time Coach Nancy mentioned that if she had another great year and another repeat at the NCAA championships that it was very possible that she would be contacted by US Swimming. The Olympics were coming in about a year and a half, and Coach Nancy indicated that she wouldn't be surprised at all, if those focusing on that event, were already watching Ashley closely.

Ashley had not thought at all about the possibility of representing the United States in the Olympic games, Her total focus was on the SEAL screening test at the moment.

She returned to the YARD to begin her third year. She met with Coach Mike and Coach Cindy, and they all agreed that her goal with NAVY swimming should be to repeat as both the Patriot League Champion and as a three time NCAA champion. She would stay focused on her two events.

After two weeks, she was back in the routine and made a second appointment to meet with Lt. Cook. She wanted to fill him in on her decisions and how the summer training went.

She also wanted to get more information on the Navy Seal Physical Screening Test, and when it was scheduled for. She made the Appointment for 10AM.

Good Morning, I am Midshipman 2nd class Jamison to see

Lt. Cook. Yes Ms. Jamison he is expecting you. Let me tell him you are here. Thank you.

The door to Roscoe Cooks office opened and he walked out and extended a hand to Ashley. Hi Ashley, great to see you again. I'm anxious to learn how your summer went. Please come in to my office.

Thank you Sir. Well, tell me all about it. How was your summer training. Well Sir, it was all very interesting, but it did one thing and that was to help me understand where I want my focus to be. And what may I ask is your focus?

Well Sir, I have firmly decided that Naval Special Warfare and Operations is my first choice, and if I am unable for some reason to make it as a SEAL, then I want to be a Marine Officer. I just felt that the week I spent with the Marines was a week filled with excitement and action, and it just further emphasized the challenges that that career option will have.

I want to take the Navy SEAL Physical Screening Test, and will need to know when it is scheduled so I can work my academic and athletic schedule around it.

Do you feel you are in good enough shape to pass it now? Yes Sir, I am in good shape, and have worked hard on my upper body strength, so I believe, that while it will be a challenge, I'm up for it. How does the process work from this point?

Well the Navy SEAL Scout Team identifies the potential SEAL candidates and signs them up to take the PST. I am a member of that team, and I plan to recommend that you be one of the midshipmen designated as a potential SEAL candidate. The test will tell us who of the candidates appear to be best able to advance to BUDs training. BUDs training, would begin after your graduation. It is a 24 week school, known as basic underwater demolition/SEAL school, it also includes a basic parachutist course, and then a 26 week SEAL Qualification program.

In your case, I would recommend that you take the PST this year in the fall, and take it again next year in the fall as well. By taking it twice, and successfully passing it twice, you will increase your chances of being successful with BUDs. You would begin BUDS after you graduate, and based on what you have told me, you would be going through BUDs as a 2nd Lieutenant in the Marine Corp.

The PST test is designed to test your overall readiness to participate in the rigorous Naval Special Warfare Operations pipeline. It is important to remember that if you make it to BUDs, that everyone there will have passed the PST, and yet only 50 percent of those that start will successfully finish.

The only advice that I will give you regarding the PST is, you must successfully pass all of the tests with at least the minimum score. Each event is timed, and so is the amount of time you have between each event. So as an example if you are in the push up event and doing well, don't kill yourself by substantially exceeding the minimum because after a brief rest you will be on to the pull ups. Do you understand what I am saying. Yes Sir, pace is very important.

When we last talked you mentioned that you are very goal oriented. What are your established goals for this year?

Well here they are.

1. Successfully complete all academic requirements and stay in the top third of my class.
2. Defend my Patriot League Championships in the 100 meter butterfly and the 200 meter freestyle.
3. Pass the PST with marks that will keep me in the top 1/3 of all who take the test.
4. Repeat as NCAA Champion in the two swimming events.

Well Ash, if you accomplish all that you have on your plate, I will say, you will have had one very successful year at the Academy. I will advise you when the PST will be schedule and what you will need to wear to participate in it.

I wish you the best of luck. Thank you Sir. I will do my best.

CHAPTER 31

NAVY SEAL PHYSICAL SCREENING TEST

It was the middle of September when Ashley received word from Lt. Cook that the PST would be conducted over the weekend of September22nd. The test would begin on Saturday morning, and would conclude on Sunday. It would be a 36 hour test of physical strength and endurance.

Once she received notification, she asked to see Coach Mike and Cindy. She met with them, and explained that she had decided to try to become a Navy SEAL, and to do so, she would need to first past the Navy SEAL physical screening test. Her competitive athletic schedule did not begin until October 5th, so the timing of the test worked out well. Mike and Cindy listened closely as Ashley explained why she had made the decisions she had. Neither of them was surprised, and both of them thought she had a real chance of making it. They both were familiar with the difficulty required to become a SEAL, and both were well aware that no woman had ever made it before.

As near as they could tell, her decisions would not interrupt her swimming competitions, and both were happy about that. They both wished her well, and then got back to the business of practice.

September 22nd came quickly. Ashley was told to dress in

her military fatigues, a white tee shirt, and her military boots. She was told to bring her bathing suit as well, and that was it.

She was told to meet at the pool. The swim would be the first event. She arrived 15 minutes early which was her standard way of making sure she was on time. She was surprised to see a group of about 20 midshipmen gathering but it was clear they were all men. She was the only woman in the group.

Within 10 minutes of her arrival, a group of three men walked over to the group assembled. They were all dressed alike, and they were led by a monster of a SEAL.

Each wore UDT swim trunks, the Standard Blue and Gold tee shirt emblazoned with UDT/SEAL Instructor on his breast and shiny jungle boots. From the looks of each of them, they were not young men that you would feel comfortable taking home to Mom and Dad on your first date.

The midshipman were told to line up at attention. The three men then walked the line looking at each of the potential prospects. Each SEAL instructor took time to inspect each midshipman. Some had to endure comments that were not exactly professional in their nature. In fact, Ashley was sure she heard a few words that she had never heard before, as they described some of the physical characteristics of the candidates that they stood in front of.

When they got to Ashley, the big guy stopped and looked her up and down. As she expected his eyes stopped on her breasts, before moving down the rest of her body. Well, well, well. What do we have here? Looks like a body type that I'm not use to seeing. What is your name Midshipman. Midshipman 2nd class Ashley Jamison Sir. So Ms. Jamison you seem to stand out from the other jerks I see in this line up. Do you think you will be able to keep up with any of them? Yes Sir, I can Sir. Well that is yet to be seen midshipman. Time will tell.

He finished his inspection and addressed the group. When I release you, you have 10 minutes to get your swimming trunks on and get back here in line. Your first event will be a 500 yard swim which you can either use a breast stroke or a side stroke on. You will have 12 minutes and 30 seconds to pass this event. If you don't pass, your sorry ass is out of here. Do you all understand? The group all said in unison Yes Sir. OK then, you are dismissed.

They were all back in line within the l0 minutes, and they were divided up into 3 groups of 8. There were eight lanes in the pool and each was assigned a lane. Ashley was in group 2. The first group went off and right away it was clear that some of the body builder types had not spent much time in the water.

When it was over the SEAL instructor dismissed 4 of the first group. You four have failed. So get your sorry asses out of my sight. Group 2 line up.

On your marks, set, go. Ashley was off. She used the side stroke because she knew it would be faster and require less energy. She knifed through the water like a shark. There was no one in her group even close to her at the half way mark. She finished the swim in under 10 minutes. 5 in her group did not qualify and were dismissed.

Group three then went. Four passed four failed. Ashley again noted that the big muscled guys were very strong but not good swimmers, and they were the first to struggle.

No one said anything to her about her time or performance, even though no one came remotely close to her time.

She knew that the next two events would be difficult, and that she needed to pace herself to make sure that she didn't wear herself out. First, it would be the pushups, with a minimum required of 42, in a two minute time frame. Then there would be a very brief rest and the pull ups would begin. The only good news about the pull ups was there was no time limit but the minimum was 6 from a dead hang.

After the first event it was down to 11 midshipman out of the 24 that began. The midshipman remaining were given 10 minutes after the swim to get in their boots and long pants before continuing the test.

It was clear to Ash, that most of the successful midshipman that passed the swim were zapped of their strength, and most felt like a limp noodle getting out of the pool. Unlike them she felt refreshed.

The pushups were next, and they needed to be done in perfect form. This meant that elbows must break a 90 degree with your shoulders, and you could only rest in the up position for 2 seconds before continuing.

Do as many as you can in 2 minutes, Lady and Gentleman, the instructor barked.

The midshipman sat in a line with the three instructors each watching three at a time. Ashley was on the end of the line and had the big SEAL watching her very closely. She was sure he couldn't wait to see her fail, but he just didn't have any idea what he was dealing with.

She began with a steady pace making sure each was done correctly. She passed the 50 mark with 30 seconds to go and continued on to 70 before she quit. She was not surprised to find that only two of the midshipman failed with the pushups.

She had expected the pull ups to be next but she was wrong. The group was given two minutes to rest before they began the sit ups. They needed to be done perfect as well, which meant that a instructor would hold the candidates feet down. The candidate then crossed their arms on their chest, and they were told that their hands can never leave your chest. Hands losing contact with the chest means disqualification.

Ashley had 2 minutes to do as many sit-ups as she could. She did not pause but maintained a sold pace and did 70. The minimum required was 50.

Pull ups followed shortly thereafter. 3 more midshipman failed to make the pushup/ sit up combination and suddenly the group was cut down to 7.

Ashley knew her arms were tired, but she also knew that the minimum pull up requirement was 6 from a dead hang and she was sure she could do it with no time limit.

Once again the big guy was her instructor. He kept a rotten smile on his face with each event. She could tell he just couldn't wait for her to fail but it proved to be just additional motivation.

The pull up section did not last long. She did 9 and quit. She was tired, but she had satisfied the strength requirements, and did not let the instructor intimidate her in any way. She said very little and just went about her business. The run would be next and she knew she was in shape for that.

The pull up section eliminated another 2, so it was down to 6 when they began the run.

When each midshipman was dismissed, the Instructor made sure they knew that they had failed and were not cut out to be SEAL's. Ashley felt sorry for each of them. They were totally humiliated by the instructors, and weren't just dismissed they were told they were kicked out and to get the hell away from those who had not failed. It was brutal, and the rest of the experience didn't get any easier.

They were given a 10 minute rest after the pull ups before the run was scheduled to begin. The course that had been set up was 1.5 miles long. They had a 11 minute and 30 second minimum requirement and they needed to do it with their boots on. On your marks, get set, go. The remaining 6 ran together. No one tried to get out front and show off. They were all tired but they had all made it this far and they all wanted each other to make it all the way. Ashley thought the guy who was the strongest runner led the pace and had his watch timed to make sure that they would not fall behind and miss the minimum. It was clear, he had a strategy for the group and that was to exceed the minimum, but not set any records in the process. The strategy paid off and all six of them came in with times that were around the 1030 minute mark. There was relief in all of their faces when they finished the run.

The three instructors were loud, constantly in the faces of the six remaining midshipman, and made it a point not to compliment any one on anything. The rest of the time was spent in formations, obstacle courses and other types of military exercises she had been doing during her entire time at the YARD.

When the test was over, the big instructor had them stand in line at attention. He looked at each of them one last time and said "Congratulations. You have passed the PST and will now be placed in our SEAL pipeline. For those of you who will be graduating, you will receive notice if you are selected to go on to BUD/S training after graduation. For those of you who are not going to graduate for another year, I encourage you to sign up next year to go through this one more time. It will increase your chances of being selected to attend BUD/S. Once again congratulations to each of you and good luck.

As they were dismissed the Big SEAL came over to Ashley and said only this. "You my dear are one hell of a woman" Well done.

He was not the only one who was proud of what she had done. Lt Cook and Gunny Sanchez watched the entire thing and neither was surprised. Base on her times and performance Ashley was number 2 overall in the group.

She was totally beat when she returned to her room. Martha was there but she could tell Ashley needed to rest. Ashley put her head down on her pillow and slept for the next 7 hours.

The following week it was back into the normal routine. Her class schedule was more interesting, both with the military and the academic subjects. Her second semester schedule required that she take five courses which included strategy and tactics, naval engineering, weapons, naval electricity and electronics, and a leadership course. The leadership course focused on the dynamic interactions between leaders and those they lead. Besides her swimming, she had about 13 hours in the fall and spring of infantry drills and dress parades.

Her work toward her degree in Computer Science continued. The Computer Science Department continued to focus on being the leading edge of research and technology.

The department was home to 10 PHD professors and 5 military faculty. In her third year she now had a range of electives to choose from as well as access to the research facility. She continued with her language study in Chinese. She wasn't really sure why she chose that language, but once again, it was probably because it was very difficult and a real challenge to her. She had no idea what she would do with it, but only time would tell.

Ashley's dual meet swim schedule was set to begin in two weeks. In October she had four dual meets which included the University of Connecticut, Louisiana State University, John Hopkins University and the University of Maryland.

She was ready for the year to begin, and was happy that she had the PST behind her. She made a note to make an appointment with Lieutenant Cook before the Christmas break. She wanted to talk to him about next steps and also about her final summer of training.

She also met with Coach Mike and Cindy to talk about this year's goals and areas that she should work on. They were all in agreement, this would be the year that she not only made it to the NCAA championships and won, but that she set the goal to break both the records for the 100 meter butterfly and the 200 meter freestyle.

CHAPTER 32

THIRD YEAR GOAL PROGRESS

Ashley had no real trouble with her first four dual meet races. She won them all with respectable times, but not the times she was shooting for. The NCAA record in the 200 Freestyle was set by Misty Franklin, from the University of California, in 2015, and it had held up since that time. Her time was 139.10. Ashley's best time in her first four dual meets was 141.0.

Her performance in the butterfly was behind her goal as well. The NCAA record in the 100 meter butterfly was set in 2016 by Kelsi Worrel, from the University of Louisville. It was 49.43. Ashley's best time this year was 51.0

She met with Coach Mike and Cindy, to try to figure out how she could shave some time off her current meet times. All three of them knew that the butterfly is considered the most difficult stroke to master and that if it's swum with improper form, the stroke is extremely tiring and inefficiently slow. To help her improve, they videotaped her, and then went through a detailed evaluation of her stroke together.

They analyzed the key elements of Ashley's Butterfly beginning with her timing. They knew that timing is the most important part of the stroke, and that every other component is an extension of the stroke's timing. Her timing was perfect.

They then evaluated "the Catch" which is moving the body forward to push water back. Her Fingers were pointing down, with palms facing back. They could see no problems with the Catch.

They evaluated the Press, which occurred when Ashley would drive her body forward with her chin and chest down. They made sure that her chin was not tucked or diving down. This was all being done properly.

It was when they evaluated her kick that they saw an area where improvement could be made.

They wanted two kicks, equal in power. They noticed that on her second kick, at the exit, that her knees did not fully bend to set it up and as such she was not getting the full power of the second kick. The underwater dolphin kick was a major component of swimming butterfly, and this they felt was where the improvement could be made.

They evaluated her breathing, because they all knew that breathing too high or at the wrong time would kill a good stroke. The key was to stay low and breathe forward. Her breathing was perfect.

Last, they evaluated her hand entry, which should be at shoulder width or just wider. The palms are downward facing and the thumbs should come in first, or at the same time, as the rest of the fingers. They also wanted to make sure that she didn't create a lot of splash with her hand entry, when entering the water. This was not an area of concern.

So Cindy went to work on perfecting her second kick and after a number of practices both she and Ashley felt that improvement was being made.

They then focused on the freestyle. They did it in the same detailed manner as they had the butterfly. They videotaped Ashley and her freestyle stroke, and then they broke it down. They looked at her head position, to make sure it was in line with the rest of her body, and that she was looking down at the bottom of the pool. No problem there.

They then looked at her buoy in the water, to make sure

that she maintained a good balance and that her body was horizontal and her legs not dropping. It looked fine to all of them

They checked her breathing to make sure that she was not lifting her head forward before turning sideways to breathe. If she did it would cause her hips and legs to drop. They saw no problem there at all.

They made sure she was rolling her body from side to side over the stroke cycle and not swimming flat. This would enable her to activate the larger back muscles in addition to the shoulder muscles, which gave her additional strength to her arm stroke. No problem here.

They checked her breathing to make sure she was breathing out continuously in the water with her face down.

They found a slight problem with her elbow position. A high elbow position allows the swimmer to hold a vertical forearm for a longer period of time. To do this successfully, a swimmer needs to bend the elbow and bring the forearm into a vertical position as quickly as possible during the underwater phase of the arm stroke. This was an area where they thought Ashley could improve. By holding her forearm vertically, it would increase her grip on the water and improve her overall propulsion.

They then evaluated her two beat kick, and the turn that that had worked on before. Both looked good.

So Cindy began to work with Ashley on the elbow issue and sure enough her propulsion began to improve.

It was the little things that make a difference Cindy had told her, and sure enough by November they were seeing improved times. She went undefeated including the early match against Army and her over all times in both events dropped.

She swam her best time of the year in both events against Army. Her butterfly time dropped to 50.5 and her freestyle time dropped to 140.5.

Before she left for Christmas break she scheduled another meeting with Lt. Cook. She had not talked with him since before the PST, and she wanted to make sure that she didn't miss any steps along the way to becoming a SEAL.

It was one week before Christmas leave, and her appointment was again scheduled for 10AM in the morning. Good Morning, I am midshipman 2nd class Ashley Jamison to see Lt. Cook for my 10AM appointment. Oh Hi Ashley, it is nice to see you again. I will tell Lt. Cook that you are here. I know he is interested to talk with you. Thank you. Please have a seat. He will be with you shortly.

His door opened and Lt. Cook came out and shook hands with Ashley. Hey Ashley it is great to see you again. Please come in. Thank you Sir.

Well, what can I do for you? Well Sir, I just want to make sure that I stay the correct course regarding my desire to be a SEAL. I'm not sure what my summer program should be, but I do know that I will take the PST again in the fall of my final year.

I looked at your performance in the PST this fall. You did an outstanding job. If I'm correct, I believe that you achieved the second highest score overall and that put you in the SEAL pipeline. I'm glad you are going to take the PST again in the fall. I'm sure you will do well in that one as well, and I know if you do, it will increase your chances of being selected as a candidate for SEAL training.

As to the summer, you have a couple of options. You could take another Marine training assignment if you want, or you could do something for yourself that could benefit you in the future. What would that be Sir.

Well, I know that you are studying Chinese and I know that China is one part of the world that we watch all of the time. Being fluent in that language could be of great value to you, and our country, if you become a Navy SEAL. I am told that the Academy now supports summer travel and language study abroad for midshipmen. My recommendation would be for you to check into it, and if it works out take your last midshipman summer and spend it in China learning the language. Of course you would have to stay in shape, but I think that is built into your head and would happen whether I said anything or not.

Oh by the way, I wanted you to know that you made quite an impression on the SEAL trainers. I don't think any of them had ever seen a woman, or for that matter most men, perform like you did in the PST. Congratulations. Thank you Sir.

I appreciate the suggestion and I will plan to look into that option as soon as I return from Christmas leave.

Before you leave Ash, tell me how you are doing with your swimming. So far, so good Sir. I am still undefeated this year and plan to keep it that way. My coaches have spent a lot of individual time with me and we have made a couple of changes that seem to be improving my times. My plan is to continue to improve and then do well at the Patriot Championships and the NCAA's.

Well best of luck to you Ash, keep up the good work.

Ashley and Martha said goodbye and each headed for the West Coast. Ashley to Portland and Martha to San Diego. Both were looking forward to spending Christmas with their families and both knew that they would only have one more opportunity, after this, before they were active in the real Navy and who knows where they would spend Christmas in the future.

Ashley was dressed in uniform when she arrived at Portland International. Jim and Sarah were there waiting for her and big hugs were had by all.

The Holidays were great as usual. Ashley spent hours with her Mom, shopping and decorating the house. She also made time to swim every other day with Team unify, and work in the gym on her off days. She talked to Coach Nancy about the two things her coaches felt would improve her performance in the butterfly and freestyle. Nancy spent time with her on both while she was at home training.

It was at dinner one evening when Jim ask Ashley what her plans for the summer were. Well Dad, I'm still trying to finalize what I'm going to be doing. Before I left the YARD I met with Lt. Cook who is the Navy SEAL recruiter on campus.

He has been very helpful to me in guiding me down a path that maximizes my chances of making the program. He suggested something to me shortly before I left for home that has peaked my interest. As you know, for the last two years I have been taking Chinese and actually find it challenging and fun. To my surprise, Lt. Cook told me that the academy now offers a six week university summer session in China. The program is managed by the Languages and Cultures Department, and provides midshipmen who have completed at least two years of a foreign language, with opportunities to gain first hand knowledge of foreign people, their cultures and their world views, through total language immersion.

Lt. Cook felt that if I make it to become a SEAL, that the Chinese language could be a real benefit, not only for me, but to the country as well. I've even learned, that in some cases, it can involve receiving foreign language proficiency pay.

Since I did so well on my PST test, he seemed to feel that this training could be far more beneficial than another stint with the Marines.

Wow, Ash, that sounds great. If it works out let us know. Mom and I have always wanted to visit China, and to do it and have a chance to see you, even for a dinner, would be a great trip highlight.

This Lt. Cook seems to be a real help in guiding you down the path you want to pursue. Sounds like he really knows what he is talking about.

Last year, when you were home for the holiday's, you told us about your friend Ryan and the great time you had with him at the Army Navy game. What happened to him?

Ryan is a great guy and he graduated and is now an Ensign and was selected for flight school.

He wants to be a Navy Fighter Pilot I don't hear from him often but I know he is in Florida and I know the path that he has chosen is not easy. He is bright and smart and I know he will do well.

Of all the guys I have met during the last few years, he is clearly the one that I have enjoyed the most. I was sad when he left but we talked about it and it was pretty clear to both of us that the careers we have chosen are not ones that allow for lasting relationships at this juncture. I hope our paths will cross again sometime in the future but who knows.

Mom, as usual dinner was great. Is John going to be with us for Christmas dinner? Yes and so is Coach Nancy. She didn't have any place to go so we thought we would host a real Holiday party. Sounds great. What are you going to serve.

Well I was going to surprise you all but I gave up on that Idea. I am going to host a Dungeness Crab Feed. As you know Christmas is in the heart of crab season so why not.

We are going to have Dungeness Crab, Caesar Salad, Garlic French Bread, lots of wine and then some sort of desert if there is any room left. I'm putting your Dad in charge of the wine and you my dear can help me with the salad and French bread.

This sounds like a feast fit for a king! It should be a great evening.

Christmas worked out great and, as in past years, Ashley's present were two airplane tickets to anywhere she wanted to go in the United States or its territories. It was only a few days later that Ashley was back on the plane and headed for the YARD to begin the second semester of her third year.

Her first priority was to firm up a spot in the summer study abroad program.

CHAPTER 33

A HETIC SCHEDULE OF GOALS

Ashley returned to the YARD after the Christmas holiday and spent the first couple of nights catching up with Martha. Both of them had had a great time with their respective families and both were looking forward to finishing their third year at the Academy.

Ashley was back into her routine and was looking forward to the Patriot League Championships. She had two more dual meets before the Championships. They were both in January with Penn State being the first and The University of Richmond being the last. The Patriot League Championships were held in early February.

As she had planned she made an appointment with the Languages and Cultures Department. She knew the department well, as she had minored in Chinese and had already completed two and a half years of the language. She wanted to check into a summer emersion program that she could participate in and was hoping for either the four or six week program in China.

She learned that because of her academic performance that she would be eligible to participate in the six week program. The program was conducted in association with Peking University. The University is a major research university located in Beijing, China and a member of the elite C9 League of Chinese Universities.

Next on her list of things to do was to meet again with Lt. Cook and make sure that her path to becoming a Navy Seal was clear to her.

Good Morning, I am Midshipman Ashley Jamison here for my 10 AM appointment with Lt. Cook. Hey Ashley, nice to see you again. Lt. Cook is expecting you. I will tell him that you are here. Thank you.

Roscoe opened his office door and extended his hand to Ashley. Hey Ash, nice to see you again. Please come in.

What can I do for you today? Well Sir, I wanted to tell you where I'm at now that I am in my final semester of my third year. First on the academic side, I have met with the Languages and Cultures Department and based on my academic performance and the fact that I have taken almost three years of Chinese they have agreed to allow me to attend the six week emersion course in Beijing China beginning on July 15th. Normally this would not be available to me because I am not majoring in the language.

When I return to the YARD to begin my senior year, It is my understanding I must then designate which branch of the Navy I intend to pursue. As I have discussed with you, I want to pursue the 1600 Special Warfare Operations SEAL Officer designation. I plan to take the PST for the second time in the fall as you suggested. My goal will be to exceed the marks I got on the first PST. My understanding is that I must be selected to try for the Special Warfare Operations Officer classification but I don't know how that works.

If I am unable for any reason to not be selected I plan to designate the Marines as my next choice.

On the athletic side, I have completed my swim season and continue to remain undefeated in my two events. I will compete in the Patriot Games Championships in two weeks and if I do well then I will have the opportunity to once again participate in the NCAA Championships.

I have talked with my coaches about those competitions

and we have set goals for each event. I'm making progress toward those goals each time I swim.

So that's where I'm at at this point. Do you have any additional recommendations for me? No Ash. I am glad that you plan to take the PST again.

Your performance on the first test was great and if you can better those marks on you second try I can guarantee you that you will receive my recommendation on the 1600 designation.

I'm really pleased about the language school. If you are able to get through the next PST and BUDs after you graduate, it will be a very valuable skill to have and I know the SEAL team leaders will be most interested in you.

Thank you Sir. I will not disappoint you on my PST performance. I'm sure that will be a fact Ash. Thank you Sir. I will leave now. I appreciate your input as always.

No problem Ash, that's what I'm here for. Oh by the way, best of luck with the championships and the NCAA's. Go Navy. Yes Sir.

Two weeks went by very fast. Ashley met with her coaches one last time before the Patriot Championships. They were all disappointed to learn that both of Ashley's events would be held on Friday. As in the year before the games were being hosted by Bucknell University and the swimming and diving competitions would be held in the Kinney Natatorium.

The relay team would compete on Thursday but with both of her events booked on the same day it would be a real test of her physical endurance. No one had high expectations for the relay team but all were pleasantly surprised when the team made it to the finals and took 2nd overall.

Ashley's first race on Friday morning was the 100 meter butterfly. Her best time this year was 51.0 which was more than one and a half second off the NCAA record. She went out strong and kept the pace up throughout both laps. She won easily and posted her best time of the year which was 50.5. She had room to improve but felt that she was making good progress and should be ready by the time the NCAA's came round next month.

The 200 freestyle was held later in the afternoon and while she had some time to rest, she could tell that doing both races in the same day and trying to achieve personal bests in both was going to be difficult. She used the same strategy that she always did. She went out keeping pace with the leaders and stayed that way for the first two laps. On lap three she picked up the pace and she finished strong. She won for the third year in a row but she was disappointed with her time. Her best time of the year was 141 which she equaled.

Cindy and Mike were happy with her achievements but Ash was disappointed she didn't make a personal best in the 200. She would improve by the time the NCAA championships came about.

What Ashley didn't know and what both Mike and Cindy knew is that her times at the Patriot Games were well within the times needed to qualify for the US Swim Team. The Olympic Games were going to be held during the summer right after her graduation from the academy.

Both Mike and Cindy believed that if she finished in the 1st or 2nd in one or both events next year that she would in all probability be asked to take a spot on the US Swimming Team. Neither of her coaches ever brought the subject up. Ashley had been and continued to be a real winner and neither of them wanted to create an expectation that may or may not be possible.

The NCAA swimming and diving Championships were held at the University of California Los Angles. UCLA had not held them before so the venue was new to most of the swimmers. Ashley had visited the campus, so she knew it but she had never competed there. Her Mom and Dad along with Coach Nancy made the trip down from Portland. It was much easier to fly there than it was to Texas but once they landed it took them almost as long to drive up Interstatel 5 from the airport as it did to fly down from Portland.

Ashley made the trip out with her coach Cindy.

They were happy that she had the butterfly on the first day of competition then she had a day of rest which was then followed by the freestyle on Friday.

She performed as expected she won the butterfly with a personal best of 50.3 and she accomplished another one of her goals by winning the 200 freestyle in a personal best of 140.0. Neither time was an NCAA record but she was getting closer to it and set the goal to make it happen during her final year at the YARD.

She was back at the YARD and was greeted by headlines in every newspaper in Maryland. **Midshipman wins again, is now a three time NCAA Champion.** She was clearly a subject of attention for the next three weeks. She didn't like the attention and spent as much time as she could out of the spot light.

Next up was spring break. She and Martha talked about where they wanted to go and both agreed it would be a year for cold beer and sunshine. They used the week to once again head south. This time to Porto Rico.

They made reservations at the San Juan Marriott Resort and Stellaris Casino. The hotel was waterfront right on the beach, located in the Condado District which was high end and had its own casino attached.

They booked a Cabana Lanais room with pool access. It had 2 double beds a great patio with direct access to the pool. It was $500.00 per night or $250 per person. They decided that they would stay for five nights.

The weather was great, the hotel was perfect. They had the beers they wanted and even found some time to gamble in the Casino. It was another great spring break. When they returned to the YARD, they were well rested and each of them had a mild tan.

The year ended quickly. It was hard to believe that they had finished their third year and next yeat would be the final one.

Her orders came in shortly before the school year ended. She was to report to the Director of the Languages and Cultures Department at Peking University in Beijing China. She was to report on June 15 to begin a 6 week emersion program in the Chinese language and Culture.

She would be provided a dormitory room on the campus. Following completion of her program she was granted a three week leave of absence and then was ordered to return to the YARD at the end of August to begin her final year.

Coach Mike arranged for her to have access to the pool and the gym while on campus at Peking University so that was one less thing she had to think about. Coach Cindy put together a personal training program for her. Since she had already taken the PST she knew what to expect and what to focus on in the gym.

She briefed her parents on the program and the dates she would attend and they arranged to take a trip to China during her stay and would plan to spend some time with her in Beijing.

Peking University was established on July 3 1898. The school was known as the Imperial University of Peking and is consistently ranked as one of the very best academic institutions in China.

The campus of Peking University is located in northwest Beijing, in Haidian district, near the Summer Palace. The area is traditionally where many of Beijing's most renowned gardens and palaces were built.

Ashley researched both the history of the institution and the campus itself. The campus was beautiful. It has a beautiful stone bridge inside the Peking West Gate and a lake called Weiming Lake that occupies the central part of the campus.

Ashley knew that the academic challenge of total Chinese immersion would be difficult but then again that is what she liked and she felt she was up for the challenge. It would be a very interesting way to spend the summer and she planned to make the most of it.

There were no military flights headed to China so she was told to book her transportation on her own and that the military would reimburse her for it.

She booked a United Flight to Portland with a stopover for three days and then a direct flight from Portland International to Beijing.

She caught a cab to the main campus and then walked to the building that housed the language and culture department. There she reported in for duty. She was given instructions on her class schedule and how to find her room.

She checked in to her room. It was about as basic as it could have been. There was one double bed with a night stand and lamp on it. In the corner there was a small desk with a reading light on it and in the other corner there was a overstuffed chair that faced a small television set that was mounted on the wall. The good news was, she had her own bathroom and shower and thus avoided parading down the hall when nature called.

She settled in. Her classes did not begin until the following day so she had a day to orient herself to her surroundings and that is exactly what she did.

CHAPTER 34

CHINA SUMMER

That first night, Ashley spent time looking at the map of the campus and reviewing her schedule. She had a very full schedule during the week, and then on weekends, she had time off but lots of studying to do. During the week she had Chinese writing classes three hours each Monday, Wednesday and Friday. Tuesday and Thursday she had Chinese speaking classes for three hours in the morning. Two days per week on Tuesday's and Thursday's she had what were described as field trips. Each was designed to help her learn about the culture and traditions of the country. All of her instructors were Chinese.

Monday, Wednesday and Friday afternoons were left to study the lessons of the week. To her surprise she learned that she would be assigned to a Chinese student for the six week period. The student was to be available to her for ongoing discussions in Chinese, and where possible to introduce her to the modern day culture of Beijing.

On the first day of class she met her student assistant. Her name was Ming Lee. She was 22 years old and was born and raised in Beijing. Ming spoke perfect English but she was only allowed to use it if necessary. She was young, cute, single, and fun to be around. Ash liked her immediately.

She arranged her workout schedule, which included both

weekend mornings and afternoons on Tuesday and Thursday, after her field trip was over.

She also made a list of the things she wanted to see before the six weeks were over, and after she checked the list with Ming, she sent it on to her parents to make sure they had it all covered on their tour.

Her list included the following.

1. Get to know Beijing. Visit the City Wall, Tiananmen Square and the Forbidden City.
2. Tour the Royal Palace and the Temple of Heaven.
3. Explore the Great Wall
4. Travel to Xi'an to see the Terracotta Warriors.
5. Travel down the Yangtze River and see the great Dam that was built
6. Tour Shanghai and see the Yuyuan Garden
7. Tour Guilin and see Elephant Trunk Hill
8. Learn how to make Chinese dumplings
9. Travel to Xian to taste the best Chinese dumplings
10. Go to a Chinese Disco in Shanghai after dark

She sent the list to her parents but left number 10 off of the list she provided to them. She just couldn't picture Jim and Sarah at a shanghai Disco after dark and she wasn't sure she wanted them to know she intended to do it. It was not long before Ashley was in a routine. Her classes were intense but working with Ming after class, particularly in speaking Chinese, was a real help. Ming also arranged for afternoon day trips to absorb the culture.

She showed her high rise buildings, that had no water or elevators, and she told her that some rooms contained 6 family members with no indoor plumbing. She took her to a Chinese home. She wanted to show Ashley how many Chinese homes were designed with Feng Shui. Feng Shui is an ancient system based upon the observations of heavenly time and earthly space. A Feng Shui house is always spick and span which allows positive energy to flow in. It is brightly lit to avoid dark and dreary space.

About half way into her 6 weeks of immersion her folks arrived in Beijing.

They stayed for three nights, and Ashley and Ming, hosted them to something new each night. Ashley was able to take two day trips with them. The first was to explore the Great Wall and the second was to visit the Terracotta Warriors. Both were of great interest. The Terracotta Warriors were at the town of Xian, which is also where the most famous dumplings in China are made. Ming arranged for them all to have dinner at the famous De Fa Chang Restaurant on Bell Tower Square. The meal was unbelievable and it crossed off another goal on Ashley's list. After their three days together Jim and Sarah continued on with their trip.

With two weeks to go, Ashley and Ming, flew to Shanghai. They only had time to stay one night but they made the most of it, and crossed off the list the night club after dark. They had a great time and danced until 2AM. They were back on the plane to Beijing the next morning, and back to class that afternoon.

Ashley's Chinese abilities continued to develop, both her writing skill, and her verbal skill. There was no question that she felt very comfortable with the language and was incredibly thankful that Ming had been assigned to her.

She managed her time well, and made sure that she continued with her swimming workouts. She stayed focused on those things in the gym, that would help her with the PST, when she took it on her return.

She completed her six week course and passed with no problem. Saying goodbye to Ming, was almost like saying goodbye to a sister. She had spent so much time with her, both day and night, that she was very sad on the day she had to say goodbye to her, and head back to the United States.

Ashley had three weeks of leave coming which she intended

to take, and stay at home in Portland, so she flew directly from Beijing to Portland. Her parents were there to meet her and the entire talk all evening was about China. Her parents had had a great trip and wanted to know if Ashley had done everything on her list. She had completed her list.

Her routine at home fell into the same one she had done each time she was home. It was back in the pool with Team Unify, and to the gym on her off days. She continued to work on her upper body strength, and by the time she was ready to go back to the YARD, she felt like she was in the best shape of her life.

Ashley was back to the yard by the end of August and had her schedule set. She would take the Navy Seal Physical Screening Test in September. Her swimming schedule would start in October, and go through February. If she was again successful she would have the NCAA finals in early March. After that it would be graduation and if all went well, she would start BUDs training with the SEALs following graduation. She would graduate as a 2nd Lieutenant in the Marine Corp but would carry the special operations designation for as long as she could remain with the SEAL training. If all went well, she would pass all of the BUD's training, and would become a Navy SEAL Officer. The first woman to do so. That was the plan anyway.

The PST was scheduled over a weekend in the middle of September. She had been through the drill before so she had an advantage over the 30 other midshipmen who were trying to pass the PST for the first time.

Once again she arrived at the swimming facility in her military fatigues, and a white tee shirt. The swim would be the first event which was the same as the last time. This time Ashley was in group 1 and she was assigned lane 2. Her plan was the same as before. She wanted to go out strong and finish well and she wanted to beat her time from before. She was on her mark and ready to go when the gun went off. She eased through the water, making very strong and powerful side strokes, and after the first lap she was well ahead of the other 7 people in her group. She finished the swim in 9 minutes and 10 seconds which was easily first in her group and way under the Competitive repetitions time of 10 minutes.

Like the first time she took it, only four in her group passed. Once again the guys with the big muscle groups failed to qualify.

When the swim was completed, Ashley's time of 9 minutes and 10 seconds was the fastest of all, and was 50 seconds better than the competitive repetition time. The swim eliminated 10 of the 30 midshipman.

The SEAL instructors were tough, and made sure that each midshipman who failed knew that they had failed and simply were not cut out to be a SEAL. Ashley had heard the banter before, but didn't let any of it bother her. She simply came to do her best and not worry about the other stuff going on.

The pushups were next and then with a two minute rest they were followed by the pull-ups. This was a different order than the first time she took the test.

Like she did the first time, she knew that these two tests were the toughest to do on time, with good form, and still left to be ready for the rest.. She finished the first 50 pushups with 30 seconds to spare and went on to complete 75 before she stopped. She stopped on purpose, so she would have the strength to handle the pull ups. She was stronger than she was the first time she took the test and completed 10 pull ups with ease. In both cases, she exceeded her marks from the prior year. At the end of the push-up pull up tests, there were only 12 midshipman remaining. Everyone else had failed and were sent on their way.

The run followed the pushups and pull ups and like before, the 12 remaining midshipman started out together with their combat boots on. After the 10 minute break they began the run. It was I.5 miles long and they needed to complete it at a minimum of 11 minutes and 30 seconds. Ashley knew that the last time she completed the run her group stayed together and finished in about 10minutes and 45 seconds. She wanted to beat this time but was careful not to go out to fast. She watched her watch and when it came to the last half mile she picked up the pace and stayed with the top three runners. She finished in 10 minutes and 30 seconds.

The sit ups were last but they were no problem. There were three who failed to meet the minimum run requirements and they were sent home. Of the 9 who passed all of the tests Ashley ranked number 2 overall which was just fine with her. Little did she know, that watching from the sidelines, was Lieutenant Cook and Gunny Sanchez. Both had huge smiles on their faces, and the expectation that Ashley Jamison was on her way to becoming the first woman to receive the Navy SEAL classification.

Later, the lead SEAL instructor came up to Roscoe and Gunny Sanchez. They all knew each other. The lead instructor looked at the two of them and said, looks like you are grooming someone who can achieve the impossible. We sure hope so. Gunny Sanchez said.

The instructor said, I tried everything I could to get inside her head but I didn't get to first base. It is like nothing bothers her. That women is something else and, I for one, want her to make it. So do we Roscoe said. So do we.

Roscoe left word that he would like to see Ashley sometime during the next two weeks when her schedule permitted. She made the appointment and arrived at his office in time for her 930 AM appointment.

Oh Hi Ashley, his assistant said. Great to see you and I heard that you really did well on the PST. Thank you. That is nice to hear. Lt. Cook is expecting you I will tell him that your here.

Roscoe opened his office door and extended his had to Ashley. Well Ash, please come in and thanks for coming. Yes Sir.

First, let me tell you that I went over the results of your second PST, and like you said, you did not disappoint. You took second overall and bettered each of your marks from the first time you took it. Congratulations. As I told you I plan to recommend that you carry the special operations designation and following graduation you will be assigned to BUD's training.

Thank you Sir, hearing that is a welcome relief. How did you do with your language training in China. Well Sir, I had a great time, and learned a lot. I feel that I can read, write and speak the Chinese language well and look forward to my last year of it this year. I'm glad to hear that Ash because I think it is going to be important to you, if you are able to complete the BIUD's training.

From this point on, you will not need me, but when you are in your last semester I will want you to touch base with me to talk about the BUD's program and specifically the things I want to coach you on before you have to deal with it.

Thank you Sir. I will make sure I see you. Best of luck to you with your swimming. It would be nice to say we have a four time NCAA Champion in our midst. I will do my best Sir.

CHAPTER 35

THE FINAL PUSH

With her second PST behind her and the special operations designation in place Ashley set her sights on two things. First she wanted to graduate in the top third of her class, and second, she wanted to repeat as a four time NCAA Champion. Her coaches wanted her to break the NCAA record in one, or both, of her events but that goal was not hers. She simply wanted to win. If a personal best, and a NCAA record came with it, then so be it.

Her academic schedule was not easy but since it contained courses that she was interested in, it did not present a difficult problem for her. Her course schedule was as follows:

- Principles of ship performance
- Advanced Chinese
- Law for the junior officer
- Junior Officer practicum
- Advanced principles of Information Technology
- Advanced programming
- Basic Artificial Intelligence

On the athletic front, the goal she set with Coach Mike and Cindy was to win the Patriot Games Championship, and repeat as a four time champion, at the NCAA swimming meet. She set her training schedule up like she had for the past two years. She swam with the team during the week and spent every Sunday morning on the track and in the gym. She knew that her SEAL goal would be the most challenging thing she had ever taken on, and she was bound and determined to be ready for BUD's when it happened.

Her swimming meet schedule was similar to the past three years, with the exception that, the Patriot Championships would be held in early February at the University of North Carolina.

She also learned that the NCAA Championships would be held at the University of North Carolina as well.

The Koury Natatorium was the home of the Carolina swimming, and diving programs. It opened in 1986, and had gone through a number of significant remodels since. The intent has been to insure that it is one of the most modern aquatic facilities in the nation. Ashley swam in the facility her 3rd class year and she liked it a lot. To be able to have both the Patriot Championships and the NCAA Championships, in the same facility one moth apart, was a real advantage.

One thing that Ashley really liked about the facility was the lighting. Koury Natatorium has one of the most advanced lighting systems of any swimming facility in the United States. The light reflected down through the water of the pool which made it very easy to see what your competition was up to,

The season had progressed very quickly, and it was already November. Ashley had remained undefeated in both the 100 butterfly and the 200 freestyle. She had her sights focused on Army, and that match would come up in early December, before the Army Navy Football Game.

She and Martha decided that they would make a weekend of the Army Navy Game, and that would include the pre-function the day before, the tail gate the day of, the game itself and some sightseeing the day after. It would be there last Army Navy game for some time, and they were bound and determined to make the best of it.

The Army Swim Team would be in the YARD, and the meet was scheduled for December 1 and 2. As was her habit, Ashley showed up over two hours early. She was super surprised to see that the line to get in had already formed, and the place was going to be packed.

By this time, there wasn't a midshipman on campus that had not heard about Ashley and her swimming success, and the word was out that she had nailed the PST not once but twice, and she was going to try to become a Navy Seal.

She was never sure which was more important to her classmates, her swimming success, or her Navy Seal designation. One thing was for sure, she had made a significant impact on the Naval Academy, and on her classmates.

Her first race was the 200 freestyle. She didn't tell Coach Mike or Coach Cindy, but she had it in her mind, that she was going to go for at least a personal best and if possible for a record. This was the time to do it, while she was home at the YARD and in front of a full house of her fellow midshipman.

When she was introduced and took her position in lane three, the crowd went crazy, and they started yelling Ashley, Ashley, Ashley, For Ashley who never wanted a spot light on her it was a little bit embarrassing.

Swimmers to your marks, get set and the gun went off. Cindy noticed it first. She had a stop watch on Ash and for the first time Ashley went out faster than the pack. This had never been her strategy before and Cindy couldn't figure out what was going on. At the half way mark Ashley was ahead of her competition by almost a quarter of a lap and then, to Cindy's surprise, she picked up the pace. She won the 200 in a personal best time of 139.60 which was a new meet record. It still didn't beat the NCAA record but she was getting very close. To her surprise when she got out of the water, she received a standing ovation from the entire crowd. She just smiled and walked back to the locker room. She had one more race and she was going to go for it as well.

When it was time for the Butterfly she took her position in lane 7, and once again, the crowd started yelling Ashley, Ashley, Ashley. This time she couldn't hold back a very small smile that most people couldn't see. In between races, she told Cindy that her strategy was going to be to go all out and try for a record. Cindy was on board with it and all she said was "You go Girl". The 100 meter butterfly is an all out, go for it, race. Ashley's best time was 50.3 which she achieved in the NCAA finals the year before. She went for it and the result was a 50.1. New meet record and new personal best for her.

Once again she had managed to achieve another goal which impressed everyone watching, including a Lieutenant by the name of Roscoe Cook. Next up was the Army Navy game in Philadelphia.

Ashley and Martha made reservations to stay in Old Town in the Wyndham Hotel. It was the same hotel she had stayed in when she attended the game with Ryan.

They planned to attend the pre-game rally on Friday, and then go to a prefunction before the game on Saturday. Sunday would be a shopping day for both of them, and then it would be back to the YARD by train on Monday Morning.

The weekend was cold and clear with no snow. Just prior to the commencement of the game, a Navy helicopter flew above the Army cadet section and dropped thousands of ping pong balls from the sky on the Army cadets.

Both Ashley and Martha hoped for a win because, the winning team, along with its fellow students, celebrate a tradition known as a night of liberty, where the winning side is given a night following the football game free of homework and various other midshipman responsibilities

Navy won the game and they both enjoyed the night off.

When she returned to the YARD she received a surprise email from her Chinese Pal Ming Lee. Ming told her that she had been invited to attend a meeting at the University of Portland over the Christmas holidays, and wanted to find out if Ashley was going to be around.

Ashley was thrilled with the news, and called home that evening. She wanted to know if it would be OK for Ming to stay with them, and celebrate Christmas with the family. Sarah was thrilled with the idea and couldn't wait to have both of the girls home for Christmas. Ashley got right back to Ming, with the invitation to spend the holiday's with her family. Ming jumped at the opportunity and the date was set.

Ming would fly into Portland on the 22nd of December. Her meetings were set up for the 27th and 28th of December. She would then fly home in time for New Years which worked perfectly with Ashley's schedule.

Ashley was totally excited for the Holiday and to spend time with her friend. She planned to meet her at the airport and then spend the next few days giving her a first class tour of Portland. She arrived home on December 20th and was met by her Mom and Dad as usual. The dinner conversation that evening was all about Ming's visit, with a little break, to talk about Ashley's performance against Army.

Mom, I know this may be a little late, but could we do another crab feed for Christmas Eve dinner. Last year was so much fun, that it deserves to be repeated. Ash, for once in my life I am one step ahead of you. We are going to do a total repeat and Coach Nancy is going to join us again. What a great Christmas this is going to be.

Your Dad and I thought about the dinner and how we wanted to handle the gift giving. We thought, since we have guests this year, that we would do a goofy Gift Exchange. What's that Mom?

Well it works like this. We tell all of those spending Christmas eve with us to go out and find a wild, crazy or goofy gift. The gift cannot cost more than $25.00.

Then everyone must wrap their goofy gift and put it under the tree. After dinner we will then play the game. We will put numbers in a hat that equal the number of gifts under the tree and the people playing. Everyone will draw a number and the order is set beginning with the person who got number I. Number 1 then goes under the tree and chooses a gift. Once they chose a gift, they open the gift, so everyone can see. The person with number 2 then is up. They can do one of two things. They can pick another gift from under the tree, or they can steal the gift, that was chosen by the number I player. If a steal occurs then number I picks another gift and opens it and it is number 3's turn to either pick a gift or steal from number 1 or 2.

The game goes on until all of the gifts are open. A gift can only be stolen three times. The third time it is stolen it is retired and the person with it gets to keep it.

That sounds like it will be really fun. So with John home, that will mean there will be six of us playing. Should be a very fun evening.

Two days later Ming arrived at Portland International. Ashley was there to meet her, and once Ming had picked up her bags the two of them could not stop talking. On purpose most of the talking was done in Chinese.

At home after dinner, Ashley and Ming sat in front of the fire looking out at Portland. What a beautiful city you have Ash. The view from your house is amazing. I know. I am very lucky that my parents found this place when they did.

So what have you planned for us to do, and see, while we have this short time together.

Well, I want you to see some of the highlights our town has to offer. So I am going to try to pack as much as I can into the two full days we have to tour together. I know you have always been interested in trees, landscaping and flowers so I am working some of that into our program. Here is what I hope to show you.

- The Portland Japanese Garden - Here they created a traditional Japanese garden, that was first presented to the city, when we became the sister city of Sapporo

Japan. It is one of the most visited spots in the city and gets over 300,000 visitors per year.

- The Portland Rose Garden - Portland is known for its roses, and this garden is the oldest rose testing program in the United States. It opened in 1917. The garden is one of 24 official testing sites for the all America Rose Selections association, which provides its seal of approval on all new rose varieties.

- The Hoyt Arboretum- It is a museum of living trees that was established in 1928. It has 190 acres in Washington Park and hosts nearly 10,000 individual trees and shrubs.

- The Pittock Mansion- Henry Pittock arrived in Portland in the late 1850's. The town was then just a muddy village. He worked his way up from being a typesetter at the weekly newspaper to becoming the Oregonian's owner and publisher. He and his wife built their home in 1914. It is where he raised his 8 children. It is well worth the visit.

- The Grotto - The Grotto is a world acclaimed Catholic shrine and botanical garden. It attracts over 200,000 people each year. It is an outdoor shrine that is unique in that it is set on top of a 110 foot cliff.

- Downtown Tour- I have to get my workout in late in the afternoon so following it I plan to give you a downtown tour followed by dinner at a great place in the Pearl District.

- On our second day, I want to drive you up the Columbia River Gorge, to see Multnomah Falls. I wish we had time to go up to Mt. Hood but we won't so my hope is we get a clear day and you can see it.

Mom has a great crab dinner planned for Christmas eve, followed by a really fun gift exchange, which I will fill you in on and help you find a perfect gift to take. Christmas day we will get to rest. Then we have the 26th to see anything we missed, before you start your meetings, and I head back to the YARD.

Their time together was great. Christmas dinner was perfect and so was the Goofy Gift Exchange. The Highlight for Ashley was the gift her brother John got stuck with. He got a pair of slippers that had dust mops on the bottom of each slipper so he could dust his apartment while walking around the house. It was the first gift he opened and no one wanted to trade for it so he was stuck with it.

Ashley said goodbye to Ming and dropped her off at the University of Portland for her meetings. Ashley got a flight back to Maryland the next day and she was back in the YARD for New Years. It had been a great vacation.

CHAPTER 36

THE END IS IN SIGHT

Ashley and Martha went out to dinner on New Year's Eve. They wanted a quiet time together, and they wanted to catch up on the Christmas Holiday. The time spent by both with their families was as good, as always, but they both wondered where they would be when the next Christmas comes around. Ashley told Martha all about Ming, and her Portland sightseeing effort, and she told her about John ending up with the "Mop Slippers" on Christmas Eve.

With only six months to go until graduation and commission, both could finally see the light at the end of the tunnel. The four years had gone by fast, but now it was almost over for both of them. They both felt really comfortable with their academic schedules, and neither of them, felt that the final six months would be that difficult.

Ashley continued to swim and went undefeated in her last two swim meets before the Patriot Championships. She looked forward to the Championships at Koury Natatorium, and was focused on making it four for four. She knew that the Carolina athletic department had purchased new starting blocks, and invested in significant improvements to the timing system. She was sure that it was done in part because the NCAA Championships would be held in the same facility a month after the Patriot Championships. She was very happy that she would be able to get a start on the new blocks, before the NCAA's were held.

The Koury Natatorium was now in its 27th season of use, and had gained a reputation as one of the finest pools in the nation. From the sound of it, Ashley was sure, that everything they had done would only enhance its reputation.

The Patriot Swimming Championships went on schedule in February and as she had planned Ashley repeated as a Champion in both the 100 meter butterfly and the 200 meter freestyle.

She did not beat her personal best, which she had set in the Army dual meet, but she produced a strong performance in both events and took first, without much push, from the competition.

Following the Patriot Championships, and unbeknownst to Ashley, the US Olympic Swim Team Coach, Hector Montoya contacted Coach Mike to talk about Ashley. He made it clear that the US Team had been following Ashley for the four years she had been at the Academy, and that they would want to talk with her if she continued to perform well at the NCAA Championships.

The Olympic Games were scheduled to be held in Tokyo Japan in July, and the US Coach wanted to understand how she might participate, given her graduation in May and her commission in the Marine Corp. To have a midshipman qualify for the US Team, and participate in the Olympic Games was something totally new to the coaching staff, and they all wanted to understand how it could work.

Coach Mike and Coach Cindy could not answer Hector's questions. They had never faced the possible situation before. Both knew that Ashley had chosen the Marine Corp as her first option, and that she would graduate as a 2nd Lieutenant in the Marine Corp. Both also knew, that she had earned the SEAL team candidate designation, but neither had any understanding how that would work after graduation.

Coach Mike said he would get back to Coach Montoya once he talked to those that would have the answer within the Academy. His first call was to Lieutenant Roscoe Cook, at the Navy SEAL recruiting office.

The phone rang in Roscoe's office and he answered it on the second ring. Lt. Cook may I help you? Lieutenant Cook, this is Mike Morgan. I am the Coach of the Naval Academy Varsity Women's swim team, and I was wondering if I might schedule an hour visit with you in the near future.

Sure Mike, I very well know who you are, and also have followed the progress of one of your super stars for the past four years. Well, we both know your referring to Ashley Jamison, and in fact that is the person I want to talk to you about. Is Ashley in any kind of trouble Mike? No, not at all, but what I need to talk to you about is confidential.

How about tomorrow morning at 9AM. That would be great, I will meet you at your office. Great. See you then Mike.

The next morning Coach Mike met with Lt. Cook. Good Morning Mike, please come into my office. Thank you Lieutenant. Please call me Roscoe.

What can I do for you? Well, this is confidential, so it needs to be kept on a need to know basis. I can definitely do that Mike. What's up?

Well, as you are aware, Ashley Jamison has had one heck of an impact on the Naval Academy's swim program over the last four years. She just finished her forth Patriot Games Championship, and finished first once again in her two events.

She is getting ready for the NCAA's, which will be held next month, in North Carolina. If she is successful there, she will become the only person in the history of the Naval Academy to have been crowed an NCAA Champion four years in a row.

I have followed her career at the Academy, and if her physical condition has anything to do with her chances at the NCAA's, then I don't believe she can be stopped.

Well, that is why I am here. Yesterday morning I got a

call from the United States Swim Coach. His name is Hector Montoya. He, and the rest of the US Swim Team staff, have been following Ashley for the past four years, and needless to say they are very impressed. As you may be aware, this summer the Olympic Games will be held in Tokyo, Japan. They are scheduled for July.

Coach Montoya told me that, if Ashley repeats again as an NCAA Champion, in one, or both of her events, that they would like to tap her for a spot on the US Olympic Team representing the United States. We have never had anyone from the Naval Academy in this possible situation.

As you know, Ashley selected the Marine Corp as her option, but based on her PST results, she also carries the Navy Seal Training designation. The question that I need to pose to you, is as follows: If Ashley repeats as an NCAA Champion which I believe she will do, she will then graduate and be commissioned in May. As I understand it, based on her designation, she will receive orders, in all probability, to begin BUD's training in San Diego. My question to you is how can she participate in the Olympic Games representing the Navy and the United States and still maintain her commitment to the SEAL training?

Well Mike, you have asked me a very interesting question, that I'm not sure I know the answer to. I know what my gut tells me, and that is let this women represent the Navy, and the United States at the Olympic Games, and then get on with life after it.

My guess is, it will take an exception from Navy SEAL command, but I can't think of any reason why they would want to stand in the way. This is a win win for everyone, including the Navy, and the people of the United States.

I tell you what. I will contact the Navy SEAL command confidentially and see what they recommend. I will get back to you right away with our strategy. Does Ashley know anything about this? No, my assistant Cindy and I decided not to tell her.

She is so focused on the NCAA's that we don't want anything else to disrupt her.

Good, then if she doesn't repeat that means the problem would go away and somebody else would receive the honor. That's right Roscoe. Good, I'm glad that she doesn't know.

By the way Roscoe, just out of curiosity, what is BUD's training? It is a long story and not an easy one to tell or for people to accomplish. BUD's training is a 24 week A school, known as Basic Underwater Demolition/SEAL school.

It includes a basic parachutist course, and then is followed by a 26 week SEAL qualification Training program. There is a lot more to this training that meets the eye, and in fact, even though women are now allowed to try if selected, no women has ever achieved the SEAL certification, and the two who tried last year didn't make it more than a couple of weeks.

It took Roscoe a week to work his way through the military bureaucracy, but he was finally able to reach the decision maker at Navy SEAL training headquarters. It took a lot more discussion than Roscoe thought necessary. SEAL command was having a real problem making an exception to of all things a women. After a lot of discussion they finally took Roscoe's word that Ashley Jamison was worth the wait.

It was decided, that if Ashley was asked, the Navy would grant her temporary orders to train with the United States Olympic Swim Team, and participate in the Olympic games. Following that participation, she would receive orders to begin BUD's training on August lst.

Roscoe called Mike and told him what the decision was, he decided to leave out the part about having to convince a bunch of macho men that they were about to have to deal with a woman SEAL. This he was absolutely sure of. Once again Lt. Roscoe Cook had Ashley Jamison's back, and she didn't even know it.

The NCAA swimming and diving championships went on as scheduled in early March. Ashley's first race was the 200 freestyle and it was held on the first day of competition. She then had a day to rest followed by the butterfly.

Her parents, and Coach Nancy, made the trip from Portland to North Carolina for the event, and they were there to witness a bit of American History.

Ashley not only won both events, but she set a new NCAA record in the 200 free and achieved a personal best in the butterfly. Her parents were thrilled, all of her coaches were thrilled, and the entire US Naval Academy was over the top with excitement.

The Academy had just produced a four time NCAA swimming champion not just in one event but in two. Her times were amazing. The record for the 200 freestyle that was set by Missy Franklin at 139.10 fell. Ashley swam it in 139.0. Her time in the butterfly while not a record, was exceptional at 50 flat. The record was 49.43.

She and Cindy travelled back to the yard together and were greeted by headlines in every local paper that all said the same thing.

ACADEMY MIDSHIPMAN DOES
THE IMPOSSIBLE
FOUR TIMES NCAA CHAMPION
YOU GO GIRL

Back on campus, Mike and the rest of the women's team planned a celebration dinner for Ashley, which was to be held on the Monday following her return. On Sunday evening Ashley received word that Coach Mike and Coach Cindy wanted to meet with her for an hour before the event was to begin. She was told to report to Mike's office which she did on time.

To her surprise Mike and Cindy were not the only ones present in Mikes office when she arrived. There in uniform was

Lt. Cook and another man wearing a US Swim Team Sweat Suit.

Hi Ash, please come in. I believe you know Lt. Cook. Yes I do, great to see you Sir, and in this corner is someone I want you to meet.

His name is Hector Montoya. Hector is the Coach of the United States Swim Team. Nice to meet you Sir. Ash, we asked you to join us for a few minutes before the celebration begins. Hector wants to ask you something, and Lt. Cook is here to support what he wants.

Thanks Mike. Ashley, we have followed your swimming career at the Naval Academy for the past four years, and are well aware of the amazing accomplishments you have achieved. Thank you Sir. I am here, to present to you, a formal letter from the US Swim Team asking you if you would be willing to represent the United States of America, in the Olympic Games, that are set to begin in July.

Wow, thank you Sir but, I have a couple of issues that might stand in the way of my participation. First, I will graduate in May and will be commissioned an Officer in the United States Marine Corp. Second with my commission will come orders to do something or go somewhere. As Lt. Cook knows, I have worked hard to gain a potential Navy SEAL training designation, and if that holds, I will be assigned to BUD's training following graduation.

Ashley, let me speak for the SEAL Command and the United States Navy. We have reviewed the situation presented, and as you know, you are quite the exception to most things we have experienced. If you would like, the Navy will issue you temporary orders upon graduation to train with the United States Swim Team, and participate in the Olympic Games. Following the games, you will be issued orders to begin BUD's training in August.

Wow, thank you Sir. With that having been said, then I would like to formally accept Mr. Montoya's invitation and become a member of the United States Swim Team. Everyone in the room just clapped. Coach Cindy then said, you have a bunch of girls waiting to throw a party for you. Let's go. Cheers everybody and Ashley followed Cindy out to the pool deck.

CHAPTER 37

GRADUATION AND COMMISSION

It was early April, and even though the swim team season had ended, Ashley continued to work with Coach Cindy on a daily basis. She planned to do so until graduation, and then would fly to Santa Clara California, where she would begin her training with the United States Swim team, in preparation for the Olympics.

She did not forget that Lt. Cook had asked to see her prior to graduation, so she made an appointment to see him at his office.

She arrived on time for her appointment, and was greeted warmly by Lt. Cook's assistant. Ashley, I will let him know that you are here. He is looking forward to talking with you. By the way, congratulations on your NCAA titles. That my dear was one hell of a performance, and I can guarantee you that every member of the Academy staff stood a little taller when word reached us of your accomplishments.

Good Morning Ashley, Lt. Cook said as he opened the door to his office. Please come in. Thank you Sir. You requested that I meet with you prior to graduation, and that is the reason for my visit this morning.

Thanks Ash, I did want to speak with you. We have now established that of the 1100 midshipman that will graduate next month 225 will be commissioned as Marine 2nd Lieutenants and the other 875 will be commissioned as Ensigns in the United States Navy. Of the 225 Marines, 27 will carry the Navy SEAL designation of which you will be one.

If past history is any indication of the future, then I expect that of the 27, who will go through BUD's, less than 10 will go on to enter SEAL training following BUD's.

As you are aware, you are the only woman who qualified to earn the SEAL designation, and no woman has ever come close to making it through the BUD's training.

I have watched you for four years, and I am convinced that if any woman can do it, you will be the one. Thank you Sir.

Now having said that, I want to give you some information on the BUD's training program that may help you weather the storm, so to speak.

You will start BUD's following the Olympic games in July. While I expect that you will perform very well at the Olympics, no matter what the outcome, no one that will be dealing with you at BUD's will give a rats ass how you performed. BUD's is a 24 week "A" School known as Basic Underwater Demolition school. It also includes a basic parachutist course, and then that is followed by a 26 week SEAL Qualification Training Program.

Everyone that enters the SEAL training pipeline must also attend a 6 month Advanced Medical Training course and subsequently earn the Naval Special Warfare Medic classification before joining an operational Team. The point of this is, for you to finally reach SEAL status, you are going to have to go through a lot of both physical and mental tests.

During your 24 week training challenge your mental and physical stamina will be challenged every day and you will also learn to be a leader. During BUD's you will have many timed physical condition tests, with the time requirements becoming more demanding each week. BUD's consists of a three week orientation, followed by three phases, covering physical conditioning (seven weeks), combat diving (seven weeks) and land warfare (seven weeks), respectively. Officer and enlisted personnel go through the same training program. During BUD's, no one is going to give a hoot about your being an officer. It probably won't even come up. The training is all about your stamina, leadership, and ability to work as a team member.

You are going to have an extra burden placed on you because you are a woman. While I would like to think that won't matter, it in all reality, will matter.

The SEAL trainers are going to do everything in their power to make you fail. So this is the first piece of advice I want to give you. **CONTINUE TO BE HUMBEL AND DON'T EVER FLAUNT AN ACHIEVMENT.** I have watched you for the past four years, and have seen you have many opportunities to flaunt your achievements. You never have, and I doubt you ever will. By being humble, doing your best, and maintaining a low profile, you will have the best chance to succeed.

Your physical conditioning phase will consist of physical conditioning, water competency, teamwork, and mental tenacity. Physical conditioning will consist of running, swimming and calisthenics, and will grow harder, and harder, as the weeks progress. You will participate in weekly four mile timed runs in boots, and timed obstacle courses, swim distances up to two miles wearing fins in the ocean, and learn small boat seamanship.

The first two weeks of basic conditioning will prepare you for the third week. This week is known as Hell Week. During Hell Week, you will participate in five and a half days of continuous training. You will sleep at most a few hours during the entire week. You will have to run more than 200 miles, and your physical training will continue for more than 20 hours per day. The remaining four weeks involve the acquisition of various methods of conducting hydrographic surveys and creating a hydrographic chart.

Because of its particularly challenging requirements, many candidates begin questioning their decision to come to BUD's during the first phase, As a result many drop out. Dropping out is called DOR. The tradition of DOR consists of dropping one's helmet liner next to a pole. A brass ship's bell is attached to the pole and it must be rung three times to indicate a candidate has given up. I can guarantee you that you are going to hear this bell ring almost every day.

During Phase 2, which is the Combat Diving phase, you will learn to be a competent basic combat swimmer. Your physical training will continue but it will become even more intensive.

You will concentrate on dive physics, underwater skills, and combat SCUBA. You will learn two types of SCUBA: open circuit and closed circuit. You will also learn basic dive medicine, and medical skills training will be provided. Emphasis will be placed on long distance underwater dives, with the goal of teaching you how to use swimming, and diving techniques, as a means of transportation from your launch point to your combat objective. This is the skill that separates SEALs from all other US special operations forces. By the end of the second phase, you will be very comfortable in the water, and will have the ability to perform in stressful and uncomfortable environments.

I believe that phase two will suit you well, and if you make it that far I believe that you will sail through the entire phase. This phase will weed a lot of people out. Many candidates never get comfortable in and under the water. So many will not survive phase two.

The last phase is your Land Warfare Training. It will teach you how to handle basic weapons, demolitions, land navigation, patrolling, rappelling, marksmanship and small unit tactics. During this phase, you will be taught to gather, and process, information that will complete an overall mission. There is more classroom work in phase three. You will focus on map, compass, land navigation, and basic weapons skills.

The final 3 and a half weeks of training you will go offshore about 60 miles from Coronado to San Clemente Island. On the island you will practice the skills you have learned. The days will become longer and more work intensive. I think that this is the hardest part of the training. At least is was for me. Training is conducted seven days a week with minimal sleep all while handling live explosives and ammunition. Interaction with instructors is also never ending, and the punishments are at their harshest level. By the end of the third phase you will have to complete a timed 2 mile ocean swim with fins in 75 minutes and a 4 mile timed run with your boots on in 30 minutes. Once this is done you will have to complete a l4 mile run.

The point I want to make here has to do with the interaction with the instructors. They are going to be on your ass from day one and they will be relentless.

Once again the key is not to let it get to you. Just stay focused and within yourself. Remember **BEING ANGRY WILL ONLY HURT, NOT HELP YOU. YOUR INSTRUCTORS ARE TAUGHT TO FEED ON IT.**

Well Ash, that is the overview that I wanted you to have. Do you have any questions? No Sir. I appreciate the task ahead, and believe I will be up to it. I want to take this opportunity to thank you for all you have done for me, and I will do my very best to make sure that you don't regret going to bat for me.

Oh Ash, one last thing before you leave. Bring home a medal for the United States of America and for the Navy. Yes Sir, I intend to. They shook hands and Ashley left thinking totally about the challenge that she had ahead of her.

It was May and graduation day came sooner than they could imagine. Ashley was dressed in her formal Marine uniform with white pants and Dark Black jacket and Martha was dressed in her formal Navy Uniform in her dress whites. Both of their families had arrived, and were enjoying all of the activities that had been set up.

Graduation would consist of a formal ceremony, after which, 1100 Marine and Navy Midshipman would be commissioned as officers in the United States Navy.

It was graduation day, and the sun was out and the sky was

a perfect blue. It was spring and thus not yet too hot or humid. All of the graduating midshipman were seated in front of a large stage, and all were dressed in their formal attire. There were over 30,000 people gathered to watch the ceremony.

The ceremony began at 10 AM sharp. It began with a formal statement of welcome from the Superintendant of the Academy, who also introduced the guests on stage including the President of the United States. Everyone was greeted to a 21 gun salute, and the fantastic Blue Angles did a fly over.

The National anthem was sung by a midshipman, and the invocation was given. The President gave a very warm and interesting address which laid out the challenge that each of the, soon to be, officers would face in the future. More than once, the terms, fight to the end, and lead, fight, win, were used. The Undersecretary of the Navy then spoke and he was followed by a Marine General who administered the oath to the 225 Marine Midshipman. Ashley along with the other Marine Midshipman stood, raised their right hands, and accepted the oath, by saying I do. With that they accepted their commissions as 2nd Lieutenants in the United States Marine Corp

The Marine General was followed by the Chief of Naval Operations who administered the oath to the remaining 875 midshipman. They would be commissioned as Ensigns in the United States Navy. They were asked to stand and given the oath, after which, they all said I do in unison.

Once that was done, each midshipman was called up to the stage to receive their diplomas, and official officer hardware. As each midshipman's name was called, their family and friends were asked to stand in appreciation.

Jim, Sarah, Coach Nancy and John all stood when Ashley's name was called. It was a thrill for them. One they would never forget.

After the last midshipman was introduced, the class was again asked to be seated.

The president of the next year's class then was introduced

and asked to speak to the new 1100 officers. He said that on behalf of the classes that are next to come we want to give three cheers to this year's class. With that he said Hip, Hip, Hooray, which was repeated three times by all of the midshipmen in attendance that would graduate in the next three years.

He was then followed by the President of the current graduating class who asked the newly commissioned officers to return the cheer to those yet to graduate. A loud Hip, Hip, Hooray, was then given by all of the new graduates.

Anchors Away was then played, and all of the new officers through their hats in the air. It was a ceremony and a day to remember for everyone.

Ashley met with her family after the ceremony, and then left with them to have dinner outside the yard. Ashley had made Jim and Sarah proud over and over throughout her life but never had they felt like they did on the day of graduation. It had been a dream come true for them. Not only did they have an NCAA Swimming champion as a part of their family, but they now had a Marine Officer.

At dinner Ashley told them what her plans were. She had received orders to report to Santa Clara to begin training with the United States Swim Team, and she would attend the Olympic Games which were to be held in Tokyo Japan in July. Following that she was to report to San Diego to begin BUD's.

Ashley would stay one more day in the YARD in order to say goodbye to Coach Mike and Cindy, and to a number of her friends on the Navy swim team. Jim, Sarah and the gang headed back to Portland the next morning.

CHAPTER 38

THE OLYMPIC GAMES

TOKYO JAPAN

Ashley caught a flight to San Francisco. She was in uniform, because she was now a 2nd Lieutenant in the United States Marine Corp, and she was not on leave. She was to report to the Coach of the United States Swim Team, located in Santa Clara, California. Santa Clara, was not far from the San Francisco International Airport so Ashley grabbed an Uber car and off they went. It took about 45 minutes, with traffic, to reach Santa Clara. The United States Swim Team was training in The George F Haines International Swim Center. The Center is the site of many international swim meets, and a home for world class and Olympic swimmers, divers and synchronized swimmers. Ashley was dropped off at the swim center, and quickly located Coach Hector Montoya's office.

Ashley went into the Swim Team Office, and surprised the receptionist who was not use to seeing a 2nd Lieutenant in the Marine Corp standing in front of her. She looked up and said, May I help you Sir, I'm sorry, I mean Mam. Ashley just smiled and said, My name is Ashley Jamison, and I am here to meet with Coach Hector Montoya. Oh yes Ms. Jamison, we have been expecting you. Let me tell Coach Montoya that you are here. Thank you Mam.

The door opened and Coach Montoya stepped out. Great to see you again Ashley. We have been expecting you, and have your orientation materials all sorted out. Thanks Coach. I bet your tired from all the ceremony and commissioning that you have been through in the past month, but I hope not too tired, to give us a great lift at the summer games.

No Sir, I'm not tired. I am looking forward to the opportunity to compete, and will give it my best. Great, that's what I like to hear Ash.

Please come into my office and we can go over the schedule, housing and meals. Just leave your bag out here, it will be fine. Thank you Sir. Please have a seat.

First, congratulations on your performance at the NCAA's, and on making the United States Swim Team. Thank you Sir. You have qualified in two events, and it is those two events you will swim. You will not have to swim the relay, as we have established the best sprint team we can put together to handle that task. So it will be the 200 meter freestyle and the 100 meter butterfly.

Your competition in both events will come from outside the United States, and based on the international times that have been posted, you will be tested in both events. From everything I have learned about you, you are a real competitor, and have managed to go undefeated in both events during your entire four years at the Academy. Your competition knows all about you, and will be gunning for you at the Olympic Games. My goal will be to maintain your undefeated record.

I also understand from my meetings at the Academy, that you are to report to San Diego following the games to begin BUD's training, which I understand is the qualification training, that can lead to becoming a Navy SEAL.

Yes Sir that is correct.

I also have been briefed, somewhat, on what that training entails, and understand that you must have some time to continue to develop your abilities other than swim training with us. Yes Sir, BUD's training is not easy, and it will require extra work on my part to ensure that I am ready to go after the Games conclude.

Well Ash, I can't help you with what you should train in, but I can tell you that I plan to give you two hours each morning to workout outside the pool. So your pool training will begin at 10 AM and will conclude at 4PM six days a week.

Thank you Sir, that will be very helpful. I know what lies ahead with BUD's, so I know what I will need to do each day before I begin to swim with the team. The extra time will be very helpful to me. There has never been a woman yet who qualified as a SEAL, and in fact, no women has ever made it past the second week of BUD's, so I have my work cut out for me.

Ash, here is your orientation package. As you will see, you will be living here on campus in a dorm room. You will have a roommate who is already here, and has been training with the team for a couple of weeks. Her name is Monica Franklin. Monica is a sprinter and she will swim the 100 freestyle and anchor our relay team. She is a junior at UCLA, so she is one year younger than you are.

I talked to Lt. Cook about your uniform. He said that he felt it would be best if you dressed in civilian clothes while you are with the swim team, and then, of course, back into uniform to report for your next assignment in San Diego.

Great, that makes it real easy for me.

Before I let you go, and get settled in, I want to tell you a little bit about this facility. The training facility has a number of pools which have been turned over to our team for exclusive use over the next month and a half. There are two training pools. One training pool is 75 feet x42 feet. The racing pool is 75 feetx50 meters. There is also a Diving Well, which will be in used by the members of our diving team.

When we are not here training, the George F. Haines International Swim Center is home to the Santa Clara Swim Club which is one of the most premier swim clubs in Northern

California The center, is considered internationally, to be one of the best centers in the United States. It was founded by the guy whose name it carries. George is considered by many to be one of the best swim coaches in American history.

Because the facility is a swim club, it has a lot of different members. We have agreed that our practices are open for public viewing, from 2PM to 4PM, each day. Based on our experience so far, the stands are packed for each practice.

As far as our team goes, we are a real team. We are just made up of a lot of super performers but we do everything as a team, which includes eating, training, and some socializing.

Oh, that brings me to the socializing talk, that I am forced to give to everyone. During the next month and a half no dating is allowed, and it is lights out at 10 PM every night.

Ashley just laughed. Right now Coach the dating thing is only a dream, and on my priority list it is at the bottom. To have the ability to go to bed at 10 PM is a gift from God, and I for one will make sure that rule is never broken.

Coach Montoya just laughed. I kind of expected that answer given what you have been through.

Well, that is enough of my lecture. You have tomorrow off as it is Sunday. Training will begin on Monday for you at 10AM. Your swim gear and sweat stuff is all in your room, and has been sized to fit you. Monica will brief you on what to wear and when. Coach Montoya extended his hand and said, welcome to the United States Swim Team.

My assistant will take you to your room. Thanks Coach.

Ashley, this is Jennie Summers, my assistant. Jennie, would you please take Ashley to her room. Yes Coach. Ash, follow me.

The swim facility had strong relationship with Santa Clara University. With school out for the summer the team was housed in the University Dormitory and utilized food services provided by the University.

Well here we are Ash. Jennie knocked on the door of room 605 and a voice said Come in. The door opened and a tall women opened the door and extended her hand. You must be Ashley. Hi I'm Monica, welcome to room 605, your home for the next month and a half. Hi Monica, great to meet you.

Come on in. Your bed is the one on the left and your drawers are right next to the bed. They brought your US Team cloths and they are stacked on the end of your bed.

The closet is over there, it isn't very big but it does allow you to hang some things up. I'm not sure if that means your uniform or not.

I will be fine. Coach Montoya told me that they worked it out with the Marines, as such I will be uniform free until after the Olympic Games are over.

Great. Coach told me that you would help me to understand what I'm supposed to wear and when.

No problem. It is pretty simple really. Most of the time we wear the US Team Shirts and shorts under the US Team Sweats. Your suit is also in the pile. As you can imagine ours are all the same. By the way, most of the women on our team, have followed you, and your swimming career, over the past four years. Some of them have met you and all of them admire the fact that you have been an NCAA Champion in not one but two events for four years in a row. Those of us who swim, know that that is not easy thing to accomplish. So way to go girl. Thanks Monica.

Ashley, I know that you have a slightly different training schedule than the rest of us because of your Marine Corp obligations but that is all I know.

Yes, Coach Montoya told me that I have until 10 AM each morning to work out on my own and then I must report to the swim venue for my daily workout which I understand goes until 4PM. Yep that sounds right and we go six days a week with Sunday's off.

If you don't mind telling me what kind of workout do you have to do before you hit the pool. Well after the Olympics I have orders to attend what's called BUD's. BUD's is Basic

Underwater Demolition School. This is the first training step in trying to become a Navy SEAL.

I thought SEAL's were all men Ashley. Monica, call me Ash, everyone else does. You are right, all Navy SEAL's are men. Women are allowed but no one has ever qualified. It is very difficult training. So the answer to your question is I will be working out to make sure I am in shape to pass the BUD's test.

That means I will be doing a lot of upper body training and a lot of running in combat boots. My plan will be to be up and out of here by 6AM and finish my morning training by 830.

Then I will get something to eat and clean up in time to begin my swim training at 10 AM. On Sundays I will not get up that early but I will still have to train.

Wow, that is an amazing schedule. I'll let you be for a bit, but I will be back in about an hour, and then if you want, I will show you around this place. We have the rest of today, and tomorrow, to get you oriented.

Thanks Monica that would be great.

Monica was back in an hour and they spent the rest of the day together, After her workout on Sunday morning, they spent the rest of that day together as well.

The following day Ashley began her training which consisted of a three mile run in her boots followed by an hour in the gym working out with weights. She finished her workout by working with the climbing rope.

She began swimming with the US Team and she was happy to have the same coach as Monica. Her days were very full, and by 10PM, she was ready for bed and had no trouble sleeping.

Meanwhile, in Japan, the Olympic Flag arrived from Rio De Janeiro, Brazil, and completed its tour by visiting all of Tokyo's cities, towns, wards and villages, before heading out across the rest of the country. Over the course of the tour, more than 80,000 people joined welcoming ceremonies, hosted in each of Japan's 47 prefectures. After the ceremonies, the flags toured each prefecture for one month, giving even more members of the public an opportunity to interact with them. In addition, Tokyo organized local events at elementary and junior high schools across the country. The Flag tour successfully created a sense of unity across the country by communicating the Olympic ideals.

The US Swim Team completed its training in Santa Clara and boarded a private Jet for the trip to Tokyo.

Jim, Sarah, John, and coach Nancy, boarded a plane at Portland International Airport and headed to Tokyo to watch Ashley and her team compete for the highest honor in her sport.

Ashley felt good about her training, and also she felt that she had prepared properly for her BUD's experience. By the end of the month she was running 10 full miles with her boots on, and her upper body was in the strongest shape it had ever been.

Her swimming training had gone well, and she had been advised that her competition in each of her events would come from outside the United States. The current world record holder in the 200 meter free style is Federica Pedlegrini from Italy at 153.0. And the current record holder in the 100 meter butterfly is Sarah Sjostrom from Sweden. Her time is 55.48. Both women would be in the field and both times were better than Ashley's best.

Ashley however, was not concerned, in fact, she was more focused on BUD's than the Olympics which was a good thing. She didn't ever get nervous. She felt very confident, and she was very relaxed and ready for the challenge. The 200 free would be the first race and it would be followed by the 100 butterfly two days later.

All of the US Athletes had been briefed on the Olympics. They learned that the ancient games were held in Greece from 776 BC to 393 AD and many of the traditions set in the original games were repeated in the modern day games The opening ceremony, the closing ceremony, and the medal presentations, were all examples of that.

The ceremonies have evolved over the centuries, but the original concepts have remained intact. They begin and end the games. They are still today, designed to showcase the artistic expression of the host nation.

Ashley was there to walk with her team in the Parade of Nations, in which she marched into the stadium with the rest of the United States Team. The uniforms were red white and blue. The red being a cowboy hat that celebrated the United States wild west. It was a very proud moment for Ashley, and she could not believe how it made her feel to walk in with the rest of the athletes in the US delegation.

After all of the nations entered, the President of the Organizing Committee made a brief speech. He was followed by the International Olympic Committee Chairman, who introduced the host country head of state who opened the games. It was a night to remember.

Ashley was able to see her Mom, Dad, Brother and Coach Nancy, before her first race. They all wished her well and all could see that she was not nervous but rather very confident.

The day soon came when she was called to the starting platform for the 200 meter freestyle. It was strange for her to hear in her introduction that she was introduced as Lieutenant 2nd Class Ashley Morgan Jamison from the United States Marine Corp.

She had drawn lane 2 which was great because Federica Pedlegrini had drawn lane five. So Ashley could see her every move. Her strategy was simple. This was her last official 200 meter swim race, and she was going to give it everything she had. She planned to stay with Federica for the first two laps and then would give it all she had in a sprint to the finish.

Her strategy was perfect. She stayed with Frederica for the first two laps and then reached down into herself, and went all out for the final two laps. She beat the world record holder by two tenths of a second. Her time was 152.8. A new world record and a gold medal for the United States.

As she stood on the gold medal platform and received her medal she had a tear in her eye, as she realized she had achieved the ultimate goal in her sport.

She put her hand over her heart as the United States National Anthem was played. What she couldn't see were 2000 midshipman at the Naval Academy standing and clapping.

Next up was the 100 meter butterfly. She decided to just give it 100% from the beginning of the Butterfly to the end. She was in lane one and could not see Sarah Sjostrom who was in lane 7. The swimmers were called to their marks and the gun went off. She gave it everything she had but it wasn't enough. For the first time she would have to settle for second place. Sarah Sjostrom was just a fraction of a second better. She set a new world record at 55.40. Ashley finished with a personal best of 55.45. She received a silver medal and was very proud as she stood on the winners stand and received her medal.

Ashley stayed for the closing ceremony, and then said goodbye to her team mates and her family, and caught a flight from Tokyo to San Diego. She slept the entire flight.

CHAPTER 39

NOW IT BEGINS BUD'S

Ashley arrived in San Diego after her long flight from Tokyo. She was not tired, as she managed to sleep, most of the way. She grabbed an uber car and headed to the Navy SEAL training center, located at the Naval Amphibious Base. in Coronado, California. The base sits right across the bay from San Diego, California, and is situated on the silver strand between San Diego bay and the Pacific Ocean. On arrival, she was directed to the Basic Underwater Demolition/SEAL Training School.

She found the administration buildings, and checked in. A Marine Gunny Sergeant with the Navy Seal insignia on his shirt, was behind the counter. He was in uniform, and his last name James, was embroidered on his shirt. Ashley handed him her orders and said, Lieutenant Second Class Ashley Jamison reporting for duty. The sergeant looked up from the book he was reading, and was surprised to see a woman standing in front of him dressed in a Marine Lieutenants uniform.

The sergeant didn't say anything initially, he simply read her orders, and then said. Relax Lieutenant. From this point on you will be addressed as Jamison. Your military rank has no further meaning, until BUD's has been completed. I probably don't have to tell you, that you will be the only woman going through, and no woman has ever made it before. Yes Sergeant, I am aware of that fact.

Good, then you know where you stand, before you begin. You have a long uphill battle ahead. I wish you the best of luck. Here is your orientation package to BUD's. As you may be aware, BUD's is divided into three, 7 week sessions, followed by a three week test of your overall skills. You first phase will be physical conditioning which will begin tomorrow morning at 0700. You will be housed in the same dormitory as the men, but you will have a separate room, and your own bathroom. If you make it through the first phase, you will begin the second phase which is titled combat diving, and if you make it through that phase you will begin the last phase which is land warfare.

Your dormitory room is in that building behind you, and you are in room 102. All of the information you need regarding what to wear, and when, including when you will be able to eat and sleep, is in the package.

As you may be aware, Officers and Enlisted men train side by side. Since December of 2015, women have been eligible to enter the SEAL training pipeline, provided they can meet the same acceptance guidelines as men. You have obviously met our selection guidelines. As such, with your acceptance, you will undergo the same training regimen as do the men. I will note, that as of November of 2018, only two women have entered the training pipeline but they dropped out during the first week of BUD's.

I encourage you to read the orientation materials thoroughly, because missing any event, or being late for any part of the training, is unacceptable, and will be grounds for dismissal from BUD's. Am I clear Jamison. Yes Sergeant, you are very clear. Then off you go and good luck.

Ashley headed for her dorm room, unpacked, and began to read the orientation materials. She read where dinner was served, and made the decision to make it but to not eat much, in light of the task she had ahead of her in the morning.

That night, Sergeant James was at dinner with four of the

SEAL instructors. Hey Sarg, I hear we had a chick check in today. Yes Sir, a Second Lt. from the YARD.

My guess is she won't make it through the first week. One trainer said to the others. If history is any indicator, then you're probably right Pal, the Sergeant responded. It will be interesting to see how she does tomorrow and then we will have some indication of what we may have on our hands.

At 0700 Ashley was in place on the training grounds. She was dressed in combat fatigues, a white tee shirt and combat boots. She looked like everyone else except she had a chest that looked a lot different than the others.

Attention lady and gentleman the lead trainer said, my name is Sergeant Reichardt and before this is over you are going to hate me, and my name.

My purpose, is to push you harder than you have ever been tested. Some of you may make it through BUD's, but most of you won't. Some of you, will probably drop out before this day is over. When you have had enough, and no longer can gut out the training, just take off your Helmut, set it next to that bell over there and ring the bell three times. If that happens to you, then head for your room, pack your gear, and go to check in where Sergeant James will issue you your new orders. Is that clear?

Yes Sir the group said in unison. I can't hear you. Yes Sir the group said louder.

The next step the group was divided into 16 man platoons. Ashley was grouped with all men who all looked to be in good shape. They all looked at her, but did not take the time to introduce themselves. That would come later.

You have been divided into Platoons. This is your team. You will be tested individually and as a team. We plan to test your physical skills, your mental skills, and watch how you work as a team.

I'm going to say this only once but you need to know it. Today, we have a woman who is beginning the BUD's training. Women are allowed to test themselves just like men, but in order to succeed, she will be required to do everything the men do. Just keep that in mind. We do not play favorites or give favors. The fact remains, that while we hope you make it, our job is to try our best to make you fail. Is that understood? Yes Sir the group yelled in unison.

OK then, BUD's will now commence. Ashley's platoon was directed to the obstacle course where a trainer was waiting for them. Each person was tested individually. To begin the course, you crawled through the mud, and then had to flip tires, and maneuver yourself over logs. There were mud pits to low crawl through and a rope that was required to climb. There were tires that they had to go through, and a wall to get up and a barrel to walk across. The obstacle course took half the day and everyone including Ashley was super tired when it was over. As a reward, the platoon was asked to run to the lake, lock arms, and get in the water.

They were assigned to lift a boat and some seriously long and heavy logs. The logs had to be held over their heads for 40 seconds and the lifts were repeated until all of the trainees thought their arms were going to drop off. And this was all done while standing in the water up to their waste.

Ashley was prepared for harassment, but not for the amount that the trainers dealt out. At least, she could see, that she wasn't the only one. Every time a trainee was slowing down or was having trouble the trainers were all over their asses. She particularly noticed it on the rope climb, where a few of the guys just couldn't do it covered in mud and with their boots on.

The day ended after 830 PM with a timed run in combat boots. Five guys put their helmets by the bell and each of them rang it. The one women did not.

By the time Ashley got to her room it was 930. She had had a small dinner but just wanted to get a shower and get to bed. Day one of BUD's was over.

That night over dinner, the BUD's instructors talked about the first day. We went easy on them today Sergeant Reichardt said. Yeh, but it still took its toll. I think we had five guys hang it up, and ring the bell. Well tomorrows another day and it will be a much longer one for them. Sergeant James then spoke up, How'd the chick do?

Reichardt responded, Well she surprised me a bit. She managed the obstacle course with the best of them, and really showed little emotion. We verbally climbed all over her ass, and to her credit, it didn't seem to bother her. To be honest she made most of the guys look second class on the rope climb. The girl has a very strong upper body. But it is only the beginning. We will see how she does once she is submerged in the water.

The next day began with 10 laps around the training grounds with one steep uphill and one slow uphill. Once that was complete 6 more laps were required and 30 pushups, 50 sit ups and 50 air squats.

Just when they thought they were done, they were directed over to the heavy punching bags and were required to do left punches, right punches and kicks. That was followed with 2 more laps, I5 pushups,50 sit ups and 50 air squats. The day finished with a half of an hour of jumping jacks. When day two was over, there were 4 more helmets on the ground and the bell had been rung four times.

So the week moved forward and each day was more strenuous. Ashley was tested in so many ways, that she couldn't believe it. The obstacle course was difficult for her but she never let on to anyone. Carrying the giant navy seal boat with 4 people on heads, shoulders and arms, was a real test of her upper body strength. She knew that her team was concerned about her ability to lift that much weight, but no one said anything to her and she made sure that her corner of the boat never drooped below her shoulder. She was formed into different marching techniques and her team had to put together a Navy SEAL Zodiac boat. The day came after her team was assigned to clean the mess hall where she, and everyone else, had their heads shaved.

Ashley didn't mind it at all, it just saved her time in the morning, and every extra minute of sleep was worth its weight in gold.

Ashley was still holding her own through the second week but every day marked the end of BUD's training for at least two of the trainees. It was also in the second week when one of the trainees fell from one of the features of the obstacle course and broke his leg.

The day, the team had to lock arms and walk across the pond, was a day she wouldn't forget. They crawled through the mud and rocks with 5 different mud pits, and rock filled river crossings during the event. Running was a part of every day. You didn't walk in BUD's you ran. You ran everywhere from the lake to the obstacle course and vise versa.

Sergeant James was having a beer with sergeant Reichardt after the training session had been completed. How is Jamison doing he asked Reichardt. Well Pal, to be honest, she has taken everything we have thrown at her.

I thought we might get her with the drowning test. I thought we might spook her when we tied her hands behind her back and tied her ankles together and then had her do three laps in the pool, but I was blown away when she was first in her team to complete the test.

You do know about her background, don't you, Reichardt? No, I know she is from the YARD but that is about it. You are dealing with a four time NCAA swimming champion, and a gold medalist in the Olympic games that just occurred in Tokyo. You watch, if she makes it through hell week next week, she will move to the second phase which will have her underwater a lot. I think she will be more comfortable in that phase than just about any of the other trainees.

No wonder the underwater didn't bother her. I'll be damned. Oh yes, and you probably have wondered about her upper body strength. Remember you told me about her performance on the rope climb. Yeh, I remember. Well she took a silver medal in the Olympics in the butterfly. Guess where the upper body strength comes from. I'll be damned.

Good Morning Sergeant James, this is your old SEAL buddy Sergeant Sanchez. Hey Juan it is great to hear your voice. To what honor do I owe this pleasure.

Great to talk to you too, Pal.

So how are things in the YARD? Are you still working with Lieutenant Roscoe Cook. Yep, our team is still together and doing well. I still remember you two guys at BUD's. I don't think I have ever seen two guys work so hard to beat each other.

Yes, we have had a lot of laughs about that over the years. We have also completed some pretty hairy operations together. While we have a great difference in rank we are still as close as brothers.

OK, so what's up, why the call? Well we were both curious to see how Lieutenant Ashley Jamison is doing in BUD's. Ah yes, Jamison. Well I can tell you this, we have not been able to break her, and we are now through week two. She has Hell Week next so we will all be watching to see what transpires.

Sergeant Reichart has done his best to get in her face, and challenge her. She doesn't bite and shows no emotion. She just takes it and moves on. So far I would say she is one tough woman.

To give you some idea, she is always first up the rope, and when we put her in the water very few guys can stay with her. We put her through the drowning exercise, she was first in her platoon.

So, the answer is, she is still here, and from what I can gather is going to make it through to Hell Week.

Great. Both Roscoe and I believe she has the inner makings of a SEAL and we are interested in following her progress. Thanks for the information Pal, it is great to talk to you. No problem, give my best to Lieutenant Cook. Will do.

The rest of the second week was more of the same with less sleep.

It was in week three that they had stealth navy seal boat training, and crawled out of the lake through mud. There were pugil stick battles on the boat in the middle of the pond. Ashley was knocked into the water a couple of times by some big guys, but she was also successful in knocking a couple of guys in on her own. The running continued and a lot of concealed low crawling through the field. There was also a push up competition which Ashley did not win but she finished in the top third of her platoon. The push up completion was for both amount and time and you had to do a push up every l0 seconds, then 5 seconds and finally three seconds. Each day finished with work on the bag punching and kicking.

Each night was shorter and each day everyone was more beat than the day before.

When the third week was over 40 of the beginning 100 had dropped out. Five were from Ashley's platoon. After the third week, Ashley knew from her own experience, why the motto of the SEAL's was **"The only easy day was yesterday"**

Tomorrow Hell Week would begin. She couldn't even think about it as she put her head on the pillow for a full night sleep of three hours.

CHAPTER 40

HELL WEEK

HELL WEEK IS THE DEFINING EVENT OF BUD'S TRAINING. IT IS HELD EARLY ON IN THE 3RD WEEK OF THE FIRST PHASE BEFORE THE NAVY MAKES AN EXPENSIVE INVESTMENT IN SEAL OPERATIONAL TRAINING. HELL WEEK CONSISTS OF FIVE AND ONE HALF DAYS OF COLD, WET, BRUTALLY DIFFICULT, OPERATIONAL TRAINING, ON FEWER HOURS OF SLEEP THAT YOU COULD COUNT ON ONE HAND.

Ashley had read, and heard, a lot of stories about Hell Week. She knew, that over the course of the five and one half days, she would run more than 200 miles, and do physical training more than 20 hours every day. In total, she had been told that she would sleep only a few hours per day, but most of the time it would be less. Ashley knew that completion of Hell Week would define those candidates who have the commitment, and dedication, required of a SEAL. It would be the ultimate test of a person's will

Ashley had been told that the hardest part of Hell Week, was the sleep deprivation, that everyone would experience. It hits people in all kinds of ways. Yawning, moodiness, fatigue, irritability, difficulty learning new concepts, forgetfulness, inability to concentrate, lack of motivation, clumsiness, and increased appetite. These were all typical. All of the symptoms could get in the way of getting through hell week.

Ashley had also learned some of the tricks to deal with lack of sleep, and she intended to use them all. The number one thing, she was determined to do, was to stay focused. This was something she had practiced since childhood, and it was something she could do well. Stay organized, and avoid doing more than necessary. Look out for yourself first and others second.

Lack of sleep can make one impatient, and lead to stress. Ashley knew this, and also knew that she did not need to be the best at anything. Just finish within your limits, and let the performance speak for itself.

This is where her head was, when she lined up with her platoon at 5AM to begin Hell Week. It was pitch dark, and there were guns going off, and explosions everywhere. It was the start of a very difficult week.

Sergeant Reichardt, said Good Morning Lady and Gentleman. In unison the group responded Good Morning Sir. Louder Please. Good Morning Sir, they yelled at the top of their voice. Good, it is a fine morning for a run. Let's get this started with a 10 mile run. Platoons ready, commence your run.

The run was timed as usual and each trainee was expected to improve their time every time they ran. Ashley set her sights on being in the top third. She set a pace that she could manage, and she stayed focused.

The run was completed, and immediately her platoon was sent to the log lift, and they carried the log for a full mile.

That was followed with the normal timed pushups, sit ups, and air squats. The day ended with regular, and stealth, boat tactics. When the first day was done it was 22 hours long. There were only two hours allowed for sleep, and the next day began. When the first day was completed, there were 10 more helmets on the ground, and the bell had sounded 10 more times.

The class began with 100. By the time Hell Week began the group was down to 50. After day one that group now numbered 40, with Ashley Jamison being one of the 40.

Day 2 was the hardest day of her life. In fact, it is the day that she came the closest to giving up, something she had never done on anything before in her life. It was a hot day, and it was boat lift time.

Ashley was in position 2, which is toward the middle of the boat and the hardest to handle, if the boat starts to sag.

It requires all the strength one can muster and it is critical to keep your head and chin up, during the entire lift. At one point, Ashley thought her arms were going to drop off, and she felt her head and chin beginning to droop. All signs that failure was looking her straight in the face.

Somehow, she heard a voice inside her head, that said, "Ashley look up" "Ashley look up" and she did. That action brought her head up and her chin back to the proper position. When that event was completed successfully, she knew that she had just dogged a bullet headed directly for her.

That afternoon, and into the dark of the night, she was underwater almost the entire time. She was not bothered by it, but there were real tests. One being that she was attacked underwater by two guys, the second guy tied her air hose in a knot. She needed to untangle the mess while holding her breath. If she ran out of she would flunk the test and not pass. She handled it.

By the end of the second day, the group was down to 35. The bell had rung 5 more times. Day 2 finished after 21 hours, which meant that since the Hell Week began, Ashley had less than five hours of sleep in total.

Day three was hostage day. There were numerous tests, which required that the platoon work as a team, to free a hostage and then escape without being captured. One exercise was done in the woods, a second was done by clearing buildings, and the third was done in the water.

Normal was now a 10 mile run, and it was required every day. Times needed to improve, or you risked being eliminated by the staff.

Ashley was well aware of her times, and stayed completely focused while making sure to stay in the top third, but never trying to finish first in anything.

After the 10 miles, it was into the Zodiac Navy SEAL boats, and 20 laps around the lake were required. The platoon was now functioning as a team, at a very high level, and Ashley felt that she could feel her own confidence growing and that of her fellow team members as well. To their credit, not one person ever mentioned anything about Ashley being a woman. She thought, that some secretly, were waiting for her to fail, but with each passing day the doubters were beginning to believe that this woman deserves to be here.

Every day, the candidates were in the water. However, on day four, they were in the water for a full 23 hours. The day began with life rafts moving out in the ocean, over the incoming waves, it continued with rope crossings over water, and finished with night water training in full gear, with weapons exploding all over the place.

Ashley and her fellow SEAL trainees were covered in mud, and sand, from start to finish, and just when she thought day four was about to end, it was off on a 10 mile night run. Ashley had paced herself, and stayed focused. She expressed little emotion, but with about one lap to go on the night run she noticed that one of her platoon members was starting to weave and looked like he was going to pass out.

He was in front of Ashley when he fell down. Ashley looked at her watch, and saw that she had a little extra time to finish, and still show improvement, so she reached down, grabbed the guy by the arms and lifted him into a walking position. OK Pal, let's get your ass in gear she said, and with that, she dragged him over the finish line. She finished with a time improvement and little did she know that Sergeant Reichardt saw the entire thing.

While he didn't say anything, it stayed with him. By God that is a SEAL in the making he thought.

As the end of the day, the guy she helped finish walked up to her and said, Ash, I wouldn't have made it without you. Thanks. She smiled and said my pleasure solider.

Day 5 was totally exhausting. The lack of sleep was catching up with all of them. In fact, most, including Ashley, felt like they were walking around in a daze. The day was spent in, on, or around water. It started out with the six man life boat drills, out through the surf then back to the beach. Empty the boat of water, and then hoist it up over your head, for a head carry in the wet sand. The day never seemed to end and, in fact, it almost didn't, because when it was over it had lasted for 23 hours. With only one hour of sleep and less than 4 hours of sleep total for the entire five days it was a huge test of will, endurance, focus and plain old guts.

The Navy SEAL teams trace their history back to the first group of volunteers selected from the Naval Construction Battalions in the Spring of 1943. Their mission was clearing obstacles from beaches chosen for amphibious landings, thus, the first formal training of the Naval Combat Demolition Units began. The Naval Combat Demolition Units distinguished themselves at Utah, and Omaha beaches, in Normandy and in Southern France. It was obvious to Ashley, that history set the stage for the massive amount of training both in the water and on the sandy beaches.

The first SEAL teams were commissioned to conduct unconventional warfare, counter guerilla warfare, and clandestine operations, in maritime and riverine environments. Every exercise during Hell Week was related to those founding principles.

The training during Hell Week had been continuous. In Ashley's case she had less than 5 hours of sleep. She knew sleep deprivation was all part of the test, and that that was all part of the mission.

She was told that her class was lucky. They got a few hours of sleep over the normal amount.

The week was designed as the ultimate test of one's physical and mental motivation, and it proved to Ashley that the human body could do ten times the amount of work the average man or women thinks possible.

Her strategy of being cool headed, focused with perseverance, in everything she tried, proved to be the right strategy.

Being a team member, and being able to carry your weight, alongside men was also critical to success.

By the end of the fifth day there were only 25 SEAL candidates remaining. 75 of the original 100 had dropped out. Ashley wasn't at all sure what phase two would bring, but she was sure that whatever the challenge she was ready for it after Hell Week ended.

Hell Week finally ended. Ashley and the remaining members of her platoon were bonded completely. Each, had enormous respect for each other, and each had learned that you can be individually strong, but you can't always achieve your objective by yourself.

The final three weeks of phase one was devoted to teaching various methods of conducting hydrographic surveys, and how to conduct a hydrographic chart.

During her first phase Ashley was able to accomplish the following:

- 50 meter underwater swim
- Drown proofing test
- Basic lifesaving test
- 1/2 mile pool swim without fins
- 3/4 mile pool swim without fins
- 1 mile pool swim without fins in 60 minutes
- 1 mile bay swim without fins 70 minutes
- 1 mile bay swim with fins in 50 minutes
- 1.5 mile ocean swim with fins in 75 minute
- 2 mile ocean swim with fins in 95 minutes

- 4 mile timed run in 32 minutes
- Completion of the Obstacle Course in l5 minutes.

So the last three weeks continued, with lots of physical exercise both in and out of the water, but it was supplemented with classroom time, devoted to acquiring an understanding of hydrographic and nautical cartographic methods.

It was a bit of welcomed relief after Hell Week, and the course work was interesting. She had had some basic courses on the subject at the YARD so she welcomed the academic challenge. The academic work really focused on the science of measurement, that affects maritime navigation and construction, with an emphasis on soundings, shorelines, tides, current and how to map them.

Phase I was over and now it was on to Phase 2.

CHAPTER 41

YOU HAD BETTER LIKE WATER

Ashley was exhausted from the first seven weeks of training. She had never run so much in her life, and actually doubted that if you added all of the running that she had done in her life, added together, it would not come close to the amount she had run in the past seven weeks. Add to the fact, that all of the running had been in combat boots. That, coupled with absolutely no sleep, had taken its toll on her.

She had lost some weight, so she focused on building her carbohydrate load with every meal. She knew, that having completed the first phase, that she had proved to the instructor staff, that she was motivated to continue more in depth training. In addition, she knew that phase 2 was the diving phase.

She had been told, that during phase 2, her physical training would continue but the times were lowered for the four mile runs, two mile swims and obstacle course. She actually found herself looking forward to the water phase. That is where she really felt at home.

There is a very old phrase that referred to a fish out of water. It can be traced all the way back to Chaucer, where the metaphor was used in the prologue of the Canterbury Tales, "A monk, when he is cloisterless is like to a fish that is waterless"

It obviously means, that someone who is in a situation that they are unsuited for, is like a fish out of water. Well, Ashley was as close to being a fish as a human being could be, and she was sure that in phase 2, that trait was going to come in handy.

Phase 2, was an additional 8 weeks, during which, she would be trained as a combat swimmer. The physical training would get tougher, because most of it was done in the water. SCUBA diving in long underwater dives, and special techniques would be taught, in order to set the Navy SEAL apart from other forces.

The platoon lined up, but instead of 100 candidates set into platoons of 12, there were now two platoons. Good Morning Lady and Gentleman, Sergeant Reichardt said. I am sure that you are all well rested and ready to begin the second phase of your training. Am I right? Yes Sir, the 25 recruits said in unison. I can't hear you. Yes Sir, they yelled at the top of their voices.

That's better. Over the next eight weeks we intend to introduce you to combat swimming. In this phase you will learn underwater skills, such as planting explosives on ships, and navigating underwater using a compass. You will also have to familiarize yourself with the LAR V Draeger Rebreather system, since that is what you will be mainly using during your time in the water. I can tell you this. If you are not comfortable in the water and under water then you are going to have some trouble ahead.

So let's begin this morning with a nice four mile run. Platoons ready, begin your run.

When the run was completed, it was back to the sit ups, and pushups. Once that was completed they changed into their swimming suits and jumped in the Pacific Ocean for a two mile swim without fins on. All of that was before lunch.

After lunch, it was to the classroom to learn about open circuit scuba, and closed circuit scuba.

The instructor began the lecture by describing a self contained breathing apparatus or SCUBA. He noted that the device is worn to provide breathable air in a hostile environment. When it is not used underwater, it is sometimes called an industrial breathing set. The term self contained, differentiates SCUBA from other apparatus connected to a remote supply by a long hose. He made it clear, that for all of this portion of BUD's, SCUBA would be defined as underwater use only.

The instructor explained that SCUBA has three main components; a high pressure tank (2200 psi to 4500 psi); a pressure regulator, and an inhalation connection, which was the mouthpiece or face mask. All of it was mounted on a frame to be worn.

There are open circuit systems that are breathing sets that are filled with filtered, compressed air, the same air we breathe normally. The compressed air passes through a regulator, is inhaled by the user then exhaled out of the system, quickly depleting the supply of air. Most modern SCUBA's are open circuit.

The closed circuit SCUBA, filters, supplements, and recirculates, exhaled gas. It is used when a longer duration supply of breathing gas is needed.

The LAR V Draeger Rebreather is the main system used by the SEALS. It is designated as the MK 25, and is a closed circuit SCUBA device. It runs on 100% oxygen. All expelled breath is recycled into the closed circuit, where it is filtered for carbon dioxide. The result is a complete elimination of expelled bubbles, which makes the Draeger ideal for clandestine amphibious operations. It has a maximum depth of 70 feet. The units relatively small size and front worn configuration, makes it suitable for shallow water operations. The instructor made sure that the candidates knew this would become one of their best friends.

The first day of the second phase, ended with a two hour practice session with a Draeger rebreather, and that was followed by another four mile timed run.

Ashley had no problem with the rebreather. She was totally comfortable in the water, and had practiced with one at the YARD. She did notice, however, that a few of the remaining candidates struggled a bit when under water, particularly when under for more than one hour.

Sure enough, after the first underwater ocean swim with the rebreather on, two more helmets were set on the ground and two more bells rang.

Each day was spent in the water. Either the lake, pool, or ocean. Hours were spent swimming. Some days with fins, some days without fins. Practice sessions with the closed circuit gear on and practices sessions with the open circuit gear on were now an everyday occurrence. The pace of physical fitness just kept accelerating with long runs scheduled every day.

In the beginning, the water work was all done during the day, in week three of the eight weeks, the training shifted to night dives, long night swims and tactical strategies underwater using a compass to guide one to the target.

Night swimming and diving in the ocean is not for everyone. In fact, just under the water, when it is pitch dark, can be a bit frightening. None of it bothered Ashley. The instructors could see that she was in her element, and nothing they put in front of her was going to bother her. In many ways, she was stoic. She simply became a person who could endure pain, and hardship, without showing her feelings or complaining to anyone.

Sergeant Reichardt watched her with interest. He had never met, or served with, a person that had her mental toughness

Once day in class, one of the candidates finally asked the instructor the question that had been on the minds of all of the candidates since they began phase two. What about sharks? Have SEAL's been attacked by Sharks?

The instructor looked at the guy and said to tell you the truth the answer is yes but it is a very rare occurrence. To be totally honest, I know what you have yet to face in your training, and I can tell you, that the last thing on your minds is going to be worrying about a shark. I can tell you, based on my experience, that there will be times when you will wish a shark would attack someone other than you of course, as it would stop the painful swim or dive evolution you are participating in. Has it ever happened? Sure it has, but I can't tell you when the last one happened.

It is very rare. For the most part they are not interested in you, and frankly you're going to be so busy you won't have time to be interested in them.

The academic work continued on a regular basis. They were taught Dive Physics, Dive Medicine, and Emergency Procedures.

The most difficult task for almost all of the candidates was held in the combat training tank. Here each candidate had to deal with what was known as Shark Attacks. In essence after most of your air was gone a SEAL instructor would dive down and attack the candidate. In the process they messed with your equipment and tied your air hoses in knots. The task was simple. Hold your breath, and untangle the mess they created. Do it underwater. If you run out of air because you can't untangle the mess, and then surface, you are out of the program.

Ashley was totally calm during her shark attack and successfully untangled the mess and then surfaced when the instructor said OK. Two more candidates failed to make the cut on that exercise alone. Each candidate knew what tests they must pass, in order to move on to phase 3. They had to complete a 2 mile swim with fins on in 80 minutes, a four mile run with boots on in 31 minutes, and a 3.5 mile and 5.5 mile swim both of which are timed.

Ashley worked hard at being a good team member. She made a point to try to be one of the guys, although that was never going to happen. She knew that everyone of the candidates was watching her performance, as were the SEAL instructors.

The number of candidates was now down to 21 out of the 100 that began. Phase 2 continued to go well for her, and when it came time to be tested in the 2 mile swim there was not contest. Ashley just paced herself, and kept her eye on her watch. She finished as she had planned in the top third of the group. After all of the running during phase 1, the run test at four miles was not difficult. The long swims were difficult for everyone. A 3.5 mile swim and a 5.5 mile swim is a long way and requires a lot of focus and stamina. Ashley had both.

She paced herself, and made sure, that in both tests, she did not go out to fast. She varied her strokes to avoid becoming too tired.

When the long swim tests were over, there was some relief among the 21 candidates. They could see the light at the end of the tunnel in phase two, and they were ready to get out of the water and back to doing something on land.

Ashley had wondered about harassment and weather she would be exposed to any of it. As it turns out, the general harassment that was given out was given out equally to all the candidates. There was no sexual harassment. Frankly, sleep deprivation reduces the sex drive to about zero and everyone was so tired all of the time that the thought of sex was simply not in the mind set of anyone.

Over the course of the eight weeks the candidates conducted over 25 day and night, compass dives They began with the basics and progressed to full mission profile combat swimmer, conducting submerged ship attacks against enemy vessels.

Night dives sere not for the faint of heart. The water was cold and dark, you had to navigate where you were going by using a compass and the targets of your attack were never easy, which required on the spot thinking and planning.

During the last week of Phase 2 sergeant James got a call from Juan Sanchez. Hey Pal, I wanted to check in to see how Ashley Jamison is doing Is she sill an active participant?

Hey Juan, great to hear your voice. Hope you and Lieutenant Cook are well. We are doing well, and are sizing up our next potential SEAL candidates and guess what? Lieutenant Cook is no longer a Lieutenant he has been promoted to Lieutenant Commander.

Please give him my congratulations. So what is there to know about Jamison? Let's start with the fact that she is still here and holding her own. Our class of 100 is now down to 21. We are in the final week of stage 2, and it is pretty clear to all of us, that when there is water around she is in her element.

Frankly Juan, the woman does not get rattled. Sergeant Reichardt and his trainers, have done everything they can to harasses her, just like the other candidates. Jamison just doesn't let it get to her.

She is very focused, and it is clear she intends to complete the BUD's course. I can tell you this, I think she is going to do it, and I don't think much of anything we can throw at her is going to deter her from her goal. Reichardt also told me, that on one of the timed runs during phase 1, some guy fell in front of her exhausted, and it was clear he would not make the timed limit, but Jamison figured she could help him up and get herself and him over the finish line before the time expired and she did it.

The guy ultimately put his Helmut down and rang the bell but he, and all of the other candidates, saw what Jamison did and no one has forgotten it.

Well this is good news for both the Lieutenant Commander and myself. We are betting on the fact that Jamison will become the first woman to complete BUD's, and we sure hope it happens for the Navy and for the SEAL's. Thanks for the input Pal, I will touch base with you later when she is in the Land Warfare Training Phase.

CHAPTER 42

WELCOME TO LAND WARFARE

Hi Mom, Ash, it is so good to hear from you. Your Dad and I have been pretty worried since we haven't heard from you since you started BUD's. That was almost 15 weeks ago. I know, I'm sorry I haven't been in touch, but I can only tell you that there has not been time to call. I know it sounds silly, but it is true, and in time I will fill you in with all of the details.

I finished the second of phase of BUD's today. It was the diving phase and I have literally spent the last 8 weeks in the water or underwater, both in the ocean and in a lake, or a swimming pool. Needless to say, I have been tested in every way, but I passed phase one and two, and now move on to the next seven week segment, which is phase three, Land Warfare Training.

I don't have time to go into what I have been through, but I can tell you and Dad, it has been the biggest challenge I have ever faced. We began with 99 pretty fit men, and me, and today we are left with 20 men and me. I am focused, and I am going to make it. However, I have to tell you, it has tested me in ways I never thought possible.

I have 9 weeks in this phase, and then move on to additional training. I will call you guys when I finish. I miss you all, give John my love, and I will talk to you in 9 weeks. Love you Ash. Goodbye.

Ashley, got off the phone with a tear in her eye. She missed her family and was getting tired of being the only woman on her planet. She now was ready to move to the third phase, land warfare. The demolitions, reconnaissance, and land warfare phase was nine weeks in length. Physical training would continue to become more strenuous, as the run distances would increase.

She also knew that all of the tests would be timed, and there would be minimum passing times for the swims, obstacle course, and runs. The third phase would concentrate on teaching, navigation, small unit tactics, patrolling techniques, rappelling, infantry tactics, and military explosives.

Everyone had talked about the difficulty of the final four weeks of phase 3. It was during this time, that candidates would spend their time on San Clemente island. There they would apply the techniques acquired throughout the training in a practical environment.

Good Morning Lady and Gentleman, Good Morning Sergeant Reichardt. I can't hear you. Good Morning Sergeant Reichardt, the 21 candidates yelled at the top of their voices.

It is 0500 and I'm happy to inform you that today begins your Land Warfare Training Phase. We do not conduct that training here. We do so, in a beautiful part of California, called Niland. You have exactly 1 hour to pack all of your stuff up and return here with your gear and form up. We will travel by bus to Niland. It takes about three hours so plan accordingly. Niland will become your home for the next 5 weeks. When that is over you will get to spend the three following weeks on a beautiful tropical island. Dismissed.

The bus was ready when the candidates returned to formation, one hour later. Ashley had no idea where Niland California was, or what was in store for them. She sat on the bus next to a guy she had become friends with during the first two phases of BUD's. His name was Bart Narwiniski. Hey Bart, do you have any idea where this place is? I know a little bit about Niland, because a friend of mine went there to an adventure camp. What did he say about the place?

Well, all I remember is he said it was hot. I think the average temperature is above 90 degrees, and the lows rarely get below 50 degrees.

I know that it doesn't rain. I think, if it is known for anything, it is known for its Imperial sand dunes, and the Salton Sea mud volcanoes. Wow, sounds like a real garden spot.

Yep, I think there was an old Army Base there as well. It was called Camp Billy Machen, and I think, the Navy SEALs turned it into their desert warfare training facility. I think it is near a mountain range called the Chocolate Mountains, and sits next to an old military base called Slab City.

Wow, you are just a plethora of fact. Ash, what did you just say? Never mind.

The bus ride was a full three hours, and Bart was right. Camp Billy Machen was in the middle of nowhere, and it was hot, dry, and deserted.

Sergeant Reichardt did not travel on the bus, but he was there to greet them when they arrived. OK line up. Those were the first words out of his mouth.

Your barracks are over there. Men take the door on the left, and Jamison you take the door on the right. You have one hour to settle in. Then be back here in formation. You should dress for a nice afternoon run.

Their introduction to Camp Billy Machen was a 5 mile timed run in 94 degree heat. The remainder of the day was spent in the classroom, with a lot of discussion about intelligence gathering, and structure penetration.

The next day they were formed into two patrols, and spent the day, learning about and practicing close quarters battle tactics.

The weeks started to go by quickly. Ashley was trained to react to sniper attacks, and on how to use edged weapons, such as knives, and other blades.

There was also a significant amount of time spent on hand to hand combat. Ashley was a full 5 feet 9 inches, and she had maintained her weight at between 130 and 140.

She was far from the biggest of the candidates, but she was not the smallest. She could handle herself against most of the men when challenged with one on one competitions. There was no question that she was one of a kind, but there was also no question among her peers that she was not to be taken lightly.

One week was focused on vehicles. SEAL's must be able to drive any vehicle, and they must be skilled in high speed and evasive driving techniques. Ashley was amazed at herself. This was something that she really enjoyed and she was good at it. Perhaps in her next life she would be a race car driver.

To be prepared for anything, they were taught the tactics that small units must use. They included handling explosives, infiltrating enemy lines, recovery (snatch and grab) techniques, and the proper handling of prisoners.

The weather just got hotter, and in at least two of the weeks the average temperature was over 100 degrees every day. SEAL's must be able to survive in extreme environments, and Camp Bill Machen provided that in spades.

A significant amount of time was also spent on field medicine. Each candidate was now fully trained in emergency medical procedures.

The training was the most mentally challenging and physically demanding, that the group had been through. They began with 21 and after the first three weeks they still had 21. There was no question, that this phase was designed to continue to build each of them to give everything they had to both accomplish their mission, and support those on their team.

They were tested in a variety of ways and were taught a lot about land navigation, particularly at night. As was now the normal. Sleep was always at a premium, and the 21 candidates were all able to sleep at a moment's notice.

Ashley guessed that on average, they had slept no more than 2 hours each day during the three phases.

They also spent a lot of time in the classroom, and were taught map and compass navigation and how to gather and process information that would help them to complete their overall mission. The classroom work was heavy and the learning pace required, became faster and faster.

Toward the end of the Niland training experience they practiced the fine art of live fire immediate action drills, which had the teams firing and maneuvering in well choreographed sequences.

The drills were difficult at night. Pop up targets were used, and pop flares with smoke grenades that all were designed to create confusion and chaos, which emulated the fog of battle warfare. At one point, the other platoon became disoriented during the famed gauntlet at Niland. Here the patrols had to navigate a course, with multiple, and simultaneous gunfire hits. This required the squad to analyze, and react to, and suppress the gun fire, and get out of the kill zone. Bullets were flying all over the place, and the platoon had to scream at each other in order to communicate over the noise.

The five weeks went by fast and before she knew it, she and her 20 friends were back on a bus and headed back to the Ocean for the final three weeks of training.

Sergeant Reichardt was waiting for them when the bus pulled into the Naval Amphibious Base at Coronado. Lineup, he said, as they exited the bus.

OK Lady and Gentleman. You are now going on vacation to a wonderful island where you will get to spend the next three weeks on the beach.

Does that sound good to you?. Yes Sir, they yelled. I can't hear you. Yes Sir, they yelled at the top of their lungs.

Good, we have a 60 mile boat ride ready to go for you. We are heading over to an island called Catalina Island.

On the island, we plan to test you to make sure that you

have learned what we want you to learn. Your days are going to become longer, and more work intensive, so I hope you are ready for this special vacation.

Your boat is waiting for you at pier 2. Take your bag with you and run to the pier in formation.

As they approached Catalina Island, Ashley was surprised to see how beautiful it was. The island had a beautiful yacht harbor, that was surrounded by beautiful beach front hotels that were all small and quaint. The small town of Avalon, was no more than one mile in length, but every inch of it was designed for relaxation.

Unfortunately, that was the part of Catalina Island that she and her 20 pals would not see or even begin to enjoy. She didn't know it then, but she was about to be tested beyond anything she had experienced in BUD's thus far.

From the minute they arrived at the SEAL training facility, they were put on a schedule. The schedule was seven days a week with very minimal sleep, all while handling live explosives, and ammunition.

The program was designed to test everything they had learned in phase l, 2 and 3, and it required all of the physical strength and stamina that they could handle.

The days became longer, and more work intensive. On the island, the class practiced the skills they had learned in the third phase. The work was very intensive, and set to mirror the work hours spent in the field. To Ashley, this was the hardest part of her training thus far.

After the first week, Sergeant Reichardt and his trainers, were sitting around one evening having a beer when one of the trainers said, Hey Sarg, I watched Jamison in the Ocean Swim today. She is one strong swimmer and made most of the guys look like fish out of water. Yeh, I know what you mean.

We have one tough woman on our hands. If I were a betting man, I would bet that this woman could possibly become a Navy SEAL. I never thought I would say or see that in my life time. She still has some tests ahead of her, but my guess is she is ready for them.

She shows little emotion and nothing seems to get her. Sometimes I think she has ice running through her veins.

There were three timed events. The first was a 2 mile ocean swim with fins in 75 minutes. the second was a 4 mile timed run with boots on in 30 minutes and the third was a 14 mile run.

Ashley completed all of the tests with no problem. During the second week on the Island 2 more candidates dropped out put their helmets down on the ground and rang the bell. There were now 19 left of the 100 that began and one of them was a women on a mission.

BUD's was finally over. The 19 survivors took the boat back to Coronado. They had all made it, and were bonded in ways that no one could understand, unless they had been through what they had together. They were given two weeks leave to rest between graduation and the next phase of their training. Ashley chose to stay on the base, continue with her workouts but to concentrate on sleep and sunshine.

Graduation was set up in large tent at the Naval Special Warfare Center in Coronado. Each successful trainee was told they could invite friends and family to attend. Ashley called home and her Mom, Dad, Brother and Coach Nancy were on an airplane to San Diego.

Sergeant James called Sergeant Sanchez at the YARD, and told him that Lieutenant Jamison had passed BUD's and would go down in history as the first woman to do so.

He told him that graduation would be in two days at Coronado, and that if he and Lieutenant Commander Cook would like to attend they were more than welcome.

Both hopped on a plane and headed for San Diego. This was one graduation that neither of them were going to miss. The graduation ceremony was pretty informal and also filled with humor. Each graduate had been asked to list their three most memorable moments and the things that were said were over the top. There were all kinds of things said but thinking it was normal to have soiled pants during hell week was at the top of the list.

The commanding officer also made a special comment to all of those in the audience. Ladies and Gentlemen, we are about to witness a bit of Naval History. BUD's is about to graduate its first women. Ashley was asked to stand and when she did the 18 men in her class gave her a standing ovation. It was a moment that Jim, Sarah and Coach Nancy would never forget.

When it was over, Sergeant Reichardt came over to Ashley and said, Lieutenant you are to be congratulated. You are one tough woman, and I'm ready to tell anyone that you will someday make a SEAL team very proud. Congratulations Sir.

To her surprise, Lieutenant Commander Cook and Sergeant Sanchez were there with their congratulations, and both were very proud of her accomplishments.

So the first part of her SEAL training was now complete. Next up, she was to report to the Navy tactical Airborne School in San Diego to begin basic parachute training.

CHAPTER 43

PARACHUTE JUMP SCHOOL

In the past, the Navy sent their BUD's graduates to the Army Airborne School, at Fort Benning Georgia. However, over the past couple of years, the Navy SEALs developed their own Airborne training school. The school is Tactical Air Operations, and it is located in San Diego. So Ashley and her 18 other graduates didn't have to travel to report for parachute training duty.

The training consists of both static line and free fall training. It is an accelerated 3 week program, and like all the other SEAL training it is highly regimented, facilitated by world class instructors, and designed to develop safe, and competent, free fall jumpers, in a short period of time.

To complete the course, candidates must pass through a series of jump progressions, from basic static line, to accelerated free fall, to combat equipment jumping.. The training concludes with a night descent with combat equipment, from a minimum altitude of 9500 feet.

Lieutenant Ashley Jamison reporting for Parachute Jump School, she said to the sergeant at the SEAL check in facility.

The Sergeant looked up and said, so your Jamison. Lieutenant you are slowly developing a reputation. Needless to say, we have had women go through the jump school, but we have never had a women come to the school directly from passing BUD's. You're the first, and I would like to say congratulations on a tough job well done. Thanks Sergeant. I appreciate your kind words.

Here is your orientation packet. We have a saying around here that if your mentally tough enough to make it through BUD's, you are mentally tough enough to step out of an airplane. I hope you enjoy your three week experience with us.

There was a lot of academic instruction, that the SEAL Candidates were exposed to, during the first week of Parachute jump School. They were taught that there are basically three methods of skydiving jumps. The first was Tandem Skydiving. This provides jumpers with an experience to help determine if they liked it or not. This was not an option for the SEAL candidates, so no time was spent discussing it.

The second method was introduced to them immediately. This method was called Static Line Skydiving. Static line training takes longer, than accelerated free fall training. It gives the candidates a slower, more comprehensive overview of how to execute skydiving jumps. They all learned, that when participating in a static line jump that they would connect their parachute to the plane before they jumped. Once they were out of the plane and began to fall, the cord would become tighter until the jumper reaches a certain altitude which causes their parachute to automatically deploy. This occurs when the cord gets the most taught.

Ashley and her fellow SEAL candidates were taught the importance of proper body shape during the skydiving experience, and how to navigate the sky with ease.

They made their first Static line jumps three days into the training. Ashley had to admit that 5000 feet is still 5000 feet, and when she looked out the door of the plane for the first time with a static jump it took her breath away. Once in the air, and in the proper position, she felt free and had no fear. Once the shoot opened and she started to float to the ground, she could see why skydivers love the thrill of the experience.

During week two, the SEAL candidates were taught how to Sky Dive with an accelerated freefall. Here they learned how to jump solo from 10,000 feet. Typically, two instructors worked with each candidate, to teach them the accelerated free fall method.

One of the instructors would hold onto the student until they successfully deployed their own parachute, and then released them and deployed their own. This was a quick, exhilarating way to learn to skydive solo, and allowed each of the SEAL candidates the opportunity to experience longer falls.

There were additional complications for the SEAL team candidates. The main difficulty was they needed to learn to handle both jumps in full tactical gear, including weapons.

It took them some time, and practice, but no one at this point was giving up and almost to a man most felt that they could learn and handle this experience.

By the end of the second week, they had made a number of jumps both static and free fall, and had spent a lot of time learning how to position their bodies to handle the combat gear they would be wearing. Body Positioning was key, as was knowing when to pull the cord.

During week three they were all focused almost exclusively on free fall in full combat gear. They all had completed a number of progressions, from basic static line, to accelerated free fall with full combat equipment. Now came the real test.

Now they were focused on completing night descents with combat equipment on. In to pass the final test they needed to do a night dive with full equipment from 9500 feet.

It was Thursday night, of their final week of training, when they were told to prepare for their night jump. They assembled in full gear and were taken to their jump planes. The test would be a free fall dive from almost 10,000 feet, with full equipment and weapons on. It was a pitch dark night and not much was visible.

There were some lights below, but they were few and far

between. The jump landing zone was outlined to all of them and they were to regroup once on the ground together. Ashley was the fourth one out the door.

It was cold, and there was some wind, but she kept her body in the correct position and pulled her shoot at the proper altitude. She began to float down in the dark. The only thing she could hear was the sound of the wind, as she continued her decent. She could see the ground below as it came up to her very quickly. She positioned her body for the landing, and landed on two feet, but then rolled over on to her side. She could see other members of her team doing the same thing around her.

She gathered up her shoot like she had been taught, and packed it away. Then she headed to the landing zone to assemble with the group. All but one made a successful decent. The one exception occurred when one of the guys hit the ground and broke his ankle. He made the jump so he passed but he would need some surgery and rehab before he continued on with this SEAL training.

So, with the parachute Jump School behind them, they all faced the next phase which was SEAL Qualification Training (SQT). They returned to the training facility at Coronado to begin their next phase of training. They all wore a silver pair of wings to denote their completion of the parachute training phase.

The next phase they faced was a 26 week course that would take each of them from the basic elementary level of Naval Special Warfare, to a more advanced degree of tactical training. SQT was designed to provide all of them with the core tactical knowledge they would need to join a SEAL platoon

The course was designed to teach them advanced skill sets, in weapons training, close quarters combat, small unit tactics, land navigation, demolitions, unarmed combat, cold weather training in Kodiak, Alaska, medical skills, and maritime operations. Before they graduated they would also attend Survival, Evasion, Resistance and Escape training.

The goal was now set.

Graduation from SQT would culminate in the awarding of the coveted navy SEAL Trident and the granting of a combatant swimmer and special warfare SEAL officer title.

Once that occurred, the new SEAL would then be immediately assigned to a SEAL Team and begin advanced training for their first deployment.

As Author and ex Navy SEAL, Dick Couch, wrote in his book "The finishing School" "Navy Seals are courageous disciplined and very highly trained. They prize integrity, accountability, reliability, and commitment to team. They do all these things with a passion and they live in a world where personal honor is as important as professional skill" This is exactly what SQT would be all about and Ashley was about to get the most significant test of her life.

She had always been told if you can get through BUD's you can get through anything. Well Welcome to SQT. It will refine you and turn you into a SEAL or it will break you and send you packing.

Her first surprise came on arrival. For the first time the group of 18 was now spit apart. The officers were separated from the enlisted men. To most it was a sad day. They had spent the last seven months totally bonding together, and rank meant nothing. Now it was being brought into the picture again. The 14 enlisted men were sent immediately to join the next convening SEAL qualification course, and the 3 Officers and one Senior Petty Officers, including Ashley, were to begin a series of training courses to improve their leadership skills. Once they were finished they would join the next class of BUD's, and begin the SQT with them.

It was clear to each when they learned the reason for the split. They were all simply to close. They had been through Hell together, and nothing could separate them, or reduce their loyalty to each other. The only way to insure that military command could continue, would be to separate the team moving forward.

Part 1 of SQT was all about leadership. The goal was to teach the Officers and Senior Petty Officer how to be leaders. Every day began with exercise, but then it was off to the classroom.

Ashley was placed in the Junior Officer Training Course. It was a total of five weeks, and it covered all types of subjects. There were numerous guest lectures, and many of them were conducted by SEAL Senior Officers. The course content covered all kinds of things from Naval History to Enlisted Evaluations.

What became clear to Ashley, was the difference between SEAL command and leadership, and other military branches delegations. Most military Leaders delegate responsibility to subordinates. SEAL leaders see a task, set a plan and solve the problem. Delegation is not the normal manner of course. It is a culture that expects all SEALS to use their training and judgment to solve the problem and get the result desired. It would be typical to hear the command, "Let's make it happen" The team is everything in SEAL leadership.

Senior Officers were brought in to lecture on military fights, wars, chain of command, as well as legal, and administrative responsibilities.

Every lunch was spent with some level of a command officer. Questions of all types were encouraged. Because the group was so small, there was lots of one on one, and individual attention.

Another thing that became clear to Ashley was that the SEAL culture demanded that no member of the team was ever left behind, and that was something that was a given. SEALs were brothers, and they would always come home, even if it was after death. Never leave a man was a commitment that every SEAL knew to be a given.

The family was also important, and the officers were taught what family services were available and how to talk to their team members, who may be in need of the services offered.

There were case study after case study on actual SEAL operations. Nothing was left out. What went right, and what went wrong, was discussed in detail.

Each study was based on actual events that had occurred. None were made up whether it be Somalia or Mogadishu.

The officers were taught to always remember that no one was ever to be left behind, even if it meant risking your own life to insure that the commitment was met. It was simply the price every SEAL was willing to pay in order to bring the remains of their own home. They were reminded that someday it may be their call. If that happened even in the worst heat of battle the commitment would be just that, a commitment for ever and for everyone.

A lot of classroom time was spent learning mission planning, and how to use the software to assist with that task; They learned about the Mission Support Center and how to use it when deployed in the field. The MSC provides task elements with the ability to reach back and interact with rear-echelon support staffs, for logistical support, and operational information on a real time basis.

During the last week of training Ashley found herself back in the field. They were taken to the mountainous terrain, at La Posta, where they were trained and tested in quick reaction leadership drills. They were formed into combat patrols that would last up to four hours and sometimes longer. They experienced quick, hard-hitting drills to teach tactical decision making in an operational environment and simulated combat. It was a very difficult week. It was also not a great week to enjoy a good meal. Ashley learned real quickly what a MRE is. It is a meal that is ready to eat on the run and they were made up of field rations, which were not the most enjoyable to consume when you are being shot at.

In the end, Ashley thought the training was excellent, and that she was much better prepared to lead during difficult battle situations.

CHAPTER 44

THE STARS WERE IN ALLIGNMENT

Following the five week JOT training Ashley received orders to attend the one week range safety officers course and the one week diving supervisors course.

She also was notified that following the Diving supervisors course that she would be enrolled in the Survival, Evasion, Resistance and Escape School. This was the SERE school, and it was required before one could carry the designation of Navy SEAL. The good news was, the course was available before she was to began SQT. In the event that it had not been available, she would have had to attend it after completing SQT.

The first school, range safety officers course, focused on gun safety, with most shooting being done at the gun range. Ashley was a good shot and she had improved her marksman ship over the course of BUD's. She would never be a sniper, but she could handle a weapon with the best of her training team.

During this week, she was also taught to be a range safety officer, which was a skill that she might possibly use during SQT. This training was all done under close supervision, and she had no real problem with it.

The next week was not a problem for Ashley at all. She was back in the water and it was where she felt the most comfortable. During this week she learned to set up a diving evolution, and how to check all divers before they entered the water. This was another skill she knew could be tested in SQT, as she could possibly serve as a supervisor during diving training at SQT even though, she would be in training herself.

Next up was the three week Survival, Evasion, Resistance and Escape course. Ashley had read about this course and some of its history. It was developed by the British out of their experience in World War 2.

They saw that there was a real need to train air crew, and Special Forces, in how to evade enemy troops following bail out, forced landings, or becoming cut off behind enemy lines.

The United States, learned from the British, the importance of this type of training and set up its own Evasion and Escape organization known as MIS-X, based at Fort Hunt Virginia.

The purpose of the program is to provide military personnel, US Department of Defense civilians, and private military contractors, with training in evading capture, survival skills and the military code of conduct.

The Navy and Marine School, was established at a remote Training site at Warner Springs, California.

Ashley was now headed to Warner Springs, California, and was doing so, with some concern. She was now the first woman in the SEAL pipeline to go through this training, and she knew that part of the training would be focused on what to expect if you are captured by the enemy. As the first woman to undergo this type of SEAL training, she couldn't imagine how they were going to handle her.

She arrived at Warner Springs with the gear she had been told to bring. She received an orientation package on arrival, which provided her with a place to sleep with a separate bathroom, but she was told she would not be using it much, as there would be a lot of field work ahead for her.

She read through the orientation material, and learned that the curriculum had three parts to it. Part 1 was survival and evasion; Part 2 was resistance and escape, and part 3 was water survival

Ashley entered the first part of the training the day after arrival. It was totally focused on survival and evasion.

She was taught first about wilderness survival including firecraft, sheltercraft, traps and snares, food and water procurement, preservation and purifying and how to improvise when she didn't have the equipment she needed.

Every day was long, with little opportunity to sleep and when sleep, was permitted, it was generally next to a log in the woods. She learned a variety of new skills, including how to use distress signals wisely, and how to navigate without an escape and evasion map. How to select the best route for escape, and everything she needed to know about wilderness first aid. The training also included the techniques and methods she could use to evade the enemy, and what communication protocols could be used. This entire phase was conducted in a wide variety of climate and terrain.

She finished phase 1 successfully and felt that she had learned a lot. She also found that she was able to deal with herself alone, rather than as a member of the team. The training was a test for her, and she felt good about it.

The second phase of training was resistance and escape. During this phase she was taught how to survive and resist the enemy, in the event of capture. It was largely based on the experiences of past US prisoners of war. It was during this phase of training that Ashley was captured by the enemy, and forced to undergo a simulated capture environment. It was not pleasant, and while her instructors did not do what they said she should expect, they made it clear that being a woman and being captured by the enemy would not be a pleasant experience. This part of the training she would never forget.

The third part of the training, was water survival, and how to survive in all types of water related situations. The training took three days but once again Ashley was in her element and was not concerned about her ability to deal with whatever they decided to throw at her. It was during this training that she was taught how to use aquatic survival gear

There was also a fair amount of classroom time spent on academic skills, which included first aid, tailored to an aquatic environment, communication protocols, ocean ecology and equipment maintenance.

Last and very important, was the **CODE OF CONDUCT.** this training was intended to provide each candidate with the skills needed to live up to the U.S. military Code of Conduct, when in uncertain, or hostile environments.

The code was hammered into every candidates head, and they could all recite it from memory when the training was complete. It said the following:

1. I am an American, fighting in the forces which guard my country, and our way of life. I am prepared to give my life in their defense.
2. I will never surrender of my own free will. If in command, I will never surrender the members of my command, while they still have the means to resist.
3. If I am captured, I will continue to resist by all means available. I will make every effort to escape and to aid others to escape. I will accept neither parole nor special favors from the enemy.
4. If I become a prisoner of war; I will keep faith with my fellow prisoners. I will give no information, nor take part in any action, which might be harmful to my comrades. If I am senior, I will take command,. If not, I will obey the lawful orders of those appointed over me and will back them up in every way.
5. When questioned, should I become a prisoner of war, I am required to give name, rank and service number as well as my date of birth. I will evade answering further questions to the utmost of my ability. I will make no oral

or written statements disloyal to my country and its allies or harmful to their cause.

6. I will never forget that I am an American, fighting for freedom, responsible for my actions, and dedicated to the principles which made my country free. I will trust in my God and in the United States of America.

Those who complete the SERE training are awarded a patch that denotes completion of the course. The patch is said to have the following symbolic significance; The color green represents freedom; the patch is halved with a yellow strip to signify that survival, evasion resistance and escape all require caution, with the knife the basic survival tool; the severed barbed wire represents captivity but freedom regained, the word tiger in Chinese alludes to the Dragons/Tigers legend found on early maps; finally the black surround, honors symbolically those who have died on active duty.

Ashley was relieved when she completed the last day of SERE training and she felt both psychologically and physically exhausted.

She knew one thing, and that was simply, I am never going to be taken as a prisoner of war alive.

On the bus ride back to Coronado, she sat next to her friend Bart Narwinski. Hey Bart, do you have any idea what we are getting into with the SQT now facing us. Not really Ash, but I can tell you that I am damn glad to have SERE behind me and I know one thing for sure and that is I never want to be captured by the enemy. I did not like what I learned about being held a captive, and I'm very glad that they didn't actually make us feel what it would be like to have that stuff done to us. It was bad enough, just to listen to what the bad guys are capable of. I know exactly what you think, and I feel the same way, Ash replied. I don't exactly know what they would do to you as a man, but I got a real visual of what would happen to a women and I can tell you it was not something I ever want to experience.

With the completion of SERE, Ashley knew that she would now face the biggest test of the past 14 months. It was time to begin the SEAL Qualification Training Course.

Back to your original question Ash. Here is what I know about SQT. This course is considered to be the premier training course in Naval Special Warfare. More time, money, resources, and talent, go into this training than any other conducted by Navy Special Warfare. The training is high speed, difficult, and dangerous.

BUD's training was extremely hard, and very difficult to survive, but BUD's simply provides you with an invitation to join the SQT party. Based on the rumors that I have heard about SQT, it is about as far from a party that on could possibly get.

I'm also told that the pace, and professional requirements, are elevated several notches and that as officers our leadership skills will be tested in very difficult situations.

It is a given, that if we cannot meet the standards of this course, then we will never become qualified Navy SEAL's. We have already proved that we are tough, and not quitters, but I'm told that is not enough. We will learn to master the skills required to be a Navy SEAL, and I'm also told that as far as we have come, we are still not at the finish line and there will be those among us who simply don't make the last step.

Thanks Bart. Nice stuff to know but not so nice to hear, With that Ashley put her head back and immediately fell asleep.

CHAPTER 45

SQT CLASS 2-20

Ashley arrived back at the Naval Seal Training facility, which was located not far from the US Mexican border, at the Naval Amphibious Base. On the west side of the highway are the West Coast SEAL teams, and the Naval Special Warfare Center, where basic underwater demolition SEAL training is conducted. On the east side of the highway, is the main part of the amphibious base. It is here, on the northeast side of the base that SQT is conducted.

Ashley reported in and was assigned her quarters. As in the past, she was given her own room and bath, which was always good, but she missed not having a roommate and at least one other woman to talk with.

She knew at this point, it simply wasn't going to happen. As such, she just ignored the issue, and let the problem roll off of her like water off a ducks back.

Seal Qualification training is completed sequentially by class and year. In most years, there are four classes that are put through SQT. In Ashley's case, her BUD's classmates that were enlisted and went directly to SQT were SQT Class 2-19.

So the next morning at 0800 the SQT Class 2-20 met in the SQT building to begin their 18 weeks of training. There were three officers, 1 senior petty officer and 20 enlisted men who had just completed their BUD's training.

Listen Up everyone. Came the voice of Chief Warrant Officer Michael Magan. I am Chief Warrant Officer Michael Magan, and I am here today to provide you with your Seal qualification training indoctrination briefing.

You have a full 18 weeks of training ahead of you, and you have all proved to this point that you are driven and fit, however you are about to be tested beyond anything you will ever imagine. I know that you all can see the goal insight, which is to proudly put on our Navy SEAL Trident, but I want you to know that it would be unusual if you all make it to that point.

As such, pay attention to what I say, because you are going to need all the help you can muster up.

In order to receive your Trident, you are going to have to be at the highest skill level one can achieve at everything you do as a SEAL. You will be tested for the next 15 weeks, both in the classroom and in the field. We expect the same performance and motivation that you gave in BUD's, but twice the professionalism. You must work, and commit to yourself, to improve your skills with every chance you get. In order to be a SEAL, you must be totally skill efficient in order to report to a platoon. You will not pass, if you are not proficient.

I need to get one item out of the way before we begin. I'm sure that you have now noticed that we have a women in this class. Her name is Lieutenant Ashley Jamison. As most of you know, we have never had a women wear the Trident, and Lt. Jamison is the first woman to make it through our training thus far. You should know, that she is here because she has completed everything you have done, and in many instances, she has completed the task better than most. She is an equal in this class, and has been, and will continue to be tested, just like all of you. So be mindful of that, and show her the same respect that you show your fellow team members. Gentlemen, do not underestimate her abilities. Enough said about that.

Here are some things I want you to remember.

- Ask Questions
- Be on time and that means five minutes early
- Be prepared with the proper equipment
- Bring a note pad with you and take notes

You will be tested both physically and in writing. You will be graded on your performance. If you don't pass, you will have the opportunity to find another line of work.

There will be a final examination when the 15 weeks have been completed. You must pass that test,

You will have PT everyday but it is not organized like BUD's. Some days you will be on your own, others we will work together. Stay in shape, both physically and mentally. It is a given that drugs of any kind have no place in the SEAL's world. The same goes with too much alcohol. Be smart and stay focused.

Some of you have been to Camp Bill Machen already. You will have the opportunity to visit that garden spot again, and you will get to enjoy the 13 mile combat conditioning course.

Now, a few words about your attitude. You are preparing yourself for combat. This is not a game and smiles will be few and far between. Your attitude is everything, and will be key to your successful completion of SQT.

Last, I want to mention the word RESPECT. We are respectful of others. If you don't get what that means, then you won't make it through this course. Is that understood? Yes Sir, the group said in unison.

There is one more item I want to cover. Leadership. We have in our class three officers and 1 Senior Petty Officer. Would you all please stand up. These people will be your team leaders for the next 15 weeks. Get to know them, and respect them. Respect is never a given, but I am sure that as the next 15 weeks transpire you will learn to respect everyone of these people. They began with a class of 100 and out of that class 19 made it through BUD's. That includes those standing before you.

Are there any questions? No one raised a hand. OK then, take a five minute break and get back in here because SQT starts now.

That afternoon was spent on case studies of field battles. The class was challenged regarding all aspects of the cases, including what medical procedures should be used on those wounded. It was a full day and Ashley took a lot of notes.

As the days progressed, it was clear to Ash that SEQ was primarily focused on the basics, but that it was designed to take an individual's skill level to a higher plateau. There was also a significant amount of time spent in teams, and Ashley was learning how to lead a team, give directions, and motivate her group.

A great deal of time was spent in the classroom, focused on mission planning and intelligence gathering, and reporting. Most classroom work ended with some sort of test of the material.

Work in the field focused on blocks of training covering the major skills required to conduct SEAL missions. Each block of training was different, but none were shorter than three days. The blocks included Hydrographic Reconnaissance, Communications, Field Medicine, Air Skills, Combat Swimmer, Land Warfare, Maritime Operations and Submarine lock in and Lock out exercises.

The swimmer training was spread out over 25 days. Some of those days were devoted to night dives in a pitch dark ocean. They were all done with full equipment and the group progressed from the basics, to full on night missions with target ship attacks.

Ashley remembered the lock in and lock out training from her midshipman cruise, and she found she enjoyed the water as much at night as she did during the day. It was on one of the night swims, she noticed one of her men having difficulty breathing. She swam over to him and saw what the problem was. It was an equipment failure in his air hose.

Ashley was all over him in a few seconds. She was totally calm and could see that the air hose had a flaw in it, and air was escaping from the hose before it could get to the man's mouth piece.

Ashley turned his air off and signaled to him that she wanted him to buddy breath while she slowly moved him to the surface. The man had held his breath for as long as possible and was just about to drown when Ashley shoved her mouth piece into his mouth and grabbed hold of him. She slowly worked him up toward the surface.

The guy was twice as big as Ashley, but she handled him in the water with no problem. Once she got him to the surface, she moved him to where she thought the submarine was and then told him that she was going to take him down and enter the sub all while buddy breathing. She knew that this would be difficult, and if the guy was at all claustrophobic, it was going to be very difficult. Getting the guy in, and out, of the box would be tough while buddy breathing.

She was totally calm and made sure her man could see that she knew what she was doing. She had no fear or panic in her eyes. She just told him to relax, and stay calm, which he did.

Once she had him back in the sub and with some medical attention, she went right back out, met her team and continued the mission. This was a perfect example of what SEAL's are trained to do.

Her instructor had watched it all, and while not much impressed him, Ashley did on this occasion. He told the story to his fellow instructors over a beer the next night.

During Air week her team had both day and night static line jumps, and a water jump, accompanied by a rubber duck which was a zodiac boat with a motor attached to it. Ashley readied her team for this, and once the boat had been pushed out the back of the C-130 cargo plane along with some specialized gear she and her team followed it one by one. Ashley was first to jump. Once they landed in the water, they gathered up their parachutes, and found the boat. They assembled the equipment they needed and continued to perform their mission.

The mission required that they take their boat and equipment to a small island and using their compasses in the dark, locate the target, and destroy it.

Ashley had been to Land Warfare Training at the training facility at Niland, but she had never had to take on the 13 mile combat conditioning course. Her team moved with her while she led them through each element of the course and her team met all of the timed requirements.

It was at that course that one member of another team said enough is enough. He put his helmet down and rang the bell. He was so near and yet so far.

The days and nights began to blur together and the tests were never ending. Sleep was again at a premium. Ashley stayed focused through it all, and set the pace for her team on the Fast Rope Technique. Here, she was required to slide down a nylon rope for 80 feet using only gloved hands to control her speed. She looked like a pro at this event and even the members of her team were proud of their bosses performance.

The final test at Camp Billy Machan came with the special insertion/extraction exercise. It was here, that Ashley and her team of six, were to be removed from an area too rugged or dense to land a helicopter. It was a miserable experience, but the team worked together to make it out and they were able to avoid the firefight that was planned for them along the way.

Ashley and her team were becoming experts in patrolling, improvising booby traps, stalking, and military demolition. They were so use to practicing with live fire drills that they didn't think much about it. The goal was to be successful with the mission. No time to think about whether the bullets were real or not.

By the time they had reached week 13, Ashley's men had total respect for her and she for them. They were now all brothers and would be for life. Her leadership skills were born from both natural ability and practice.

She had taken notes all along the way and was both mentally and physically up to every challenge that was put in front of her.

The motto, "The more you sweat in peacetime the less you bleed in war" was constantly drilled into their heads. Train as you would fight, they were taught.

The only emotion that was displayed by almost all of the men was the word "Hooyah" which was the universal SEAL response for enthusiasm.

During the final week they were given a written test that covered all of the blocks of training they had been through. Ashley had no problem with any part of it, and finally it was time for graduation from SQT.

She had made it, and along the way had earned the respect of a whole bunch of people.

SEAL Qualification Training graduation was held in the bay of the SQT building. The American Flag was displayed behind the podium. The graduation ceremony was much smaller than her BUD's graduation as was the crowd. There was a smattering of instructors and some active duty friends of the new SEAL's which included two SEAL's from the Yard. Lieutenant Commander Roscoe Cook and Master Sergeant Juan Sanchez who were both in attendance.

There were several team CO's and command Master Chiefs. There were three speakers, all SEAL operators, and all with important words for the newest Navy SEAL's. The final speaker then said, we are here today to recognize these men and I'm proud to say women, at which time everyone in the room began to clap. Yes, I said women. Let me introduce you all to Lieutenant Ashley Jamison, our first women Navy SEAL. Lieutenant please stand up.

Ashley was embarrassed but stood up and blushed which most in the room thought was impossible.

After her introduction, the speaker continued by saying.

Today you will all be awarded the Naval Special Warfare SEAL insignia, the Trident. Since you all have worked so hard to be able to earn it, I wanted to make sure that you all understand what it signifies.

The Trident has been the badge of the Navy SEAL's since 1970. It is the only warfare specialty pin that is the same for officers and enlisted men. It symbolizes that we are brothers and now sisters in arms, that we train together and we fight together. There are four parts to the Trident. Each one symbolizes an important facet of our warfare community. The anchor symbolizes the Navy, our parent service, the premier force for power projection on the face of the planet and the guarantor of world peace.

However it is an old anchor, which reminds us that our roots lie in the valiant accomplishments of the Naval Combat Demolition Units and Underwater demolition teams.

The Trident, the scepter of Neptune, or Poseidon, king of the oceans, symbolizes a SEAL's connection to the sea. The ocean in the hardest element for any warrior to operated in. It is the one in which SEAL's find themselves the most comfortable. The pistol represents the SEAL's capabilities on land, whether direct action or special reconnaissance. The pistol is cocked and ready to fire, and should serve as a constant reminder that you too must be ready at all times.

The eagle, symbolizes the SEAL's ability to swiftly insert from the air. The eagles head is lowered, to remind you that humility is the true measure of a warrior's strength.

Today, you will receive your diploma and there will be a name on it besides your own. That is the name of a teammate who was killed in action. Although you should be proud today of your personal accomplishment, you must always reflect on, and pay homage to, the legacy of those that have gone before you.

With that said, the speaker closed and one by one the officers and enlisted men were brought on stage to receive their diploma's and pins. It was a moment that Ashley would never forget.

Afterwards she met with Lieutenant Commander Cook and Sergeant Sanchez.

Roscoe looked at her and said, "Lieutenant, today you made both of us very proud. You did it. We knew you could and you did. Please accept our heartiest congratulations and welcome to the ball club." With that they both gave Ashley a huge hug. They had done something no one else had ever done. They had recruited and mentored the first woman to become a Navy SEAL.

Ash, we will see you in a little while, right now we know you have something to do. At that moment Ashley and her fellow SEAL's then did what all new SEAL's do.

They left the building on a dead run, and ran straight out to the end of the pier and jumped into San Diego Bay. They then crawled out and striped off their wet cammies. They all had their bathing suits on under their cammies, so it was back in the water for a swim across Glorietta Bay to the Cornado Golf Course. This they did without fins.

The safety boat then arrived with their boots socks and Tee shirts. They quickly pulled them on and set off on a run around Coronado. A simple six miles. They completed their run at Gator Beach on the Pacific Ocean side of the Naval Amphibious Base. There the SQT instructors had set up a barbecue for them with steaks and a keg of beer. Ashley had a great evening sharing stories with Roscoe Cook and Juan Martinez.

The San Diego Papers, as well as the papers at the YARD and the Portland Oregonian. She had just done something that had never been done before and the Navy itself could not wait to put her on display. It was a great day for the Navy, for Ashley and for women overall.

CHAPTER 46

COLD WEATHER OPERATIONS

Ashley and the rest of her graduating class of SQT were perfect examples of no rest for the weary. Two days after graduation, they all boarded a flight for Kodiak Island Alaska.

Kodiak Island, is home to the Naval Special Warfare Detachment Kodiak. The training facility is located at Cape Spruce and that is where they were taken.

Each new Navy SEAL was checked in, and provided with an orientation package. Like the other training facilities, Ashley was given her own room and own bathroom.

The SEAL's were shown where the mess hall was located, and told to be back in classroom 1 at 0800 the following morning.

Good Morning Lady and Gentleman. In all my years as a SEAL, and SEAL instructor, I have never had the privilege of saying that. That is due in part to Lieutenant Ashley Jamison who is our first woman SEAL. Congratulations to you Ashley, and to all of you, for earning your Trident. Welcome to the Brotherhood.

Welcome to Kodiak Alaska. They say once you become a SEAL, your training never ends and your experience over the next three weeks will truly exemplify that statement.

We learned as a result of our fighting in Afghanistan, that cold weather training is an essential skill that all SEAL's must be trained in and learn. We now require that all Navy SEAL's undergo this training. Kodiak is cold, wet and windy, and thus it is a perfect place for you to learn how to operate under miserable conditions.

We are going to teach you how to be winners, even when the weather gets really nasty. You will come to know this experience as cold weather training.

I'm not sure if you had time to walk around outside last night, but if you did, you saw steep cliffs, breaking waves on rocks of all shapes and sizes, and winds that never seem to stop. These elements combine to make for perfect conditions. You will, however, learn to handle snow, and at some point temperatures 50 degrees below zero.

As you can see our training facility is sparse. We have two metal buildings which house our sleeping quarters and classrooms, and we have a galley and a small medical clinic. I'm afraid that is the total extent of the luxury you are going to experience

You will spend the first three or four days of your training in this classroom. You will be briefed on medical issues, environmental issues, and nutritional issues, all as they relate to the cold.

You will learn a lot about cold weather, and how to fight in it. You will be issued cold weather gear and you will learn how to use, and care for it. Your cold weather clothing system is called Protective Combat Uniform or PCU. It is made to keep you warm in temperatures that can reach 50 degrees below zero. Your PCU is made to be layered, and mixed and matched, depending on where you're at and what the weather is doing.

Ashley was not surprised to learn that the clothes issued to her were the same as those issued to her men.

You will also be issued field equipment that we call PEPSE. This stands for personal environmental protection and survival equipment. You will be issued a sleeping bag, a sleeping shelter, boots, balaclavas, ground pads, cooking utensils, water bottles, a portable stove system, several hats and some different pairs of gloves and mittens.

In addition, you will be issued a water filtration system, a pack shovel, and a folding saw. To get around, you will be issued a climbing harness, snow shoes, crampons, and folding ski poles.

You are all used to backpacks but the one you will be issued here is different than all of those you have worn in the past. It is designed to provide you with maximum flexibility, and it allows you to carry up to 80 lbs. It is designed with fins on one side of it and snow shoes on the other side of it.

Last, you will be issued a military assault suit or MAS. This is a lightweight dry suit designed for surface swimming in freezing cold water. It is very tight, and very compact, and will allow you to wear your boots over it.

Just so you all know this is not an inexpensive gear issue. Each of you will total about $10,000 when you have all your gear.

OK. We will be in the classroom for the next few days, and then will take our first overnight venture. It will last three days and two nights, and we will use it to get you very familiar with your equipment.

So the training began and the first venture out was a new experience for most of the SEAL's. Most had never spent a night out in freezing cold weather. It was clear that the training was designed to teach them the skills they would need to endure, and operate, in frigid conditions. The first outing was to teach them about creating a shelter, building a fire and finding food. They also learned how to move through the wilderness without getting lost. Needless to say this was an important part of the training.

Ashley paid a lot of attention to the issue of layering her cloths, and before the first outing was complete, she knew just what to put on to handle the condition at hand. She was cold most of the time, but not to the point of being miserable.

The training was conducted in a variety of environments which contained both forested areas and coastal environments.

The base covered 55 acres on Spruce Cape. The training was conducted throughout the surrounding area, and nearby Long Island.

The overall training course was 28 days and the days went by fast. They moved from the class room to the field, and then back to the classroom. They were taught how to navigate using terrain association, and how to find terrain features on a map. Ashley learned quickly that navigation in the cold wilderness is tough because everything looks the same.

The knife they were issued became one of the most valuable tools they had to work with, and they were taught how to survive with only their knife and a fire.

When they were two weeks into the training, the buzz among the SEAL trainees was about FTX. This was the final training exercise that they would have to go through. It would be the ultimate test for all of them. It was designed to put to use the accumulated cold weather survival knowledge they had been taught. Nobody really knew what to expect, but they all knew that it was designed to be the ultimate test of their knowledge and skill.

In the week leading up to FTX they spent a night building and sleeping in a snow cave on Pyramid Mountain. To get there, they travelled by snowshoe. They used their ski poles to get through several feet of snow drifts, which ultimately led them to the Buskin River. The next drill was one Ashley would never forget.

The instructors requested that each platoon leader march their platoon out onto the frozen river until the ice below them cracked and they fell in. Once they were in the river and submerged up to their necks they had to remain for five minutes in the near freezing water. Once the five minutes were up, they exited and worked in pairs, assembling their two man tents and firing up their stoves to avoid hypothermia.

Ashley had been through a lot, but this was a real test and it was the coldest she had ever been in her life. She led her platoon onto the ice and was the first to fall through.

Ashley's first feeling when she broke through the ice was shock, and then it was as though something was taking her breath away. She later listened to one of the instructors as he told a group of the SEALs what the purpose of the exercise was. It was to teach each SEAL that this is what it's going to feel like when you are about to freeze. It's a confidence builder, to let you know that you can do this, and you're going to be alright in the end.

The other experience that Ashley will never forget was the re-warming exercise. The SEALs were asked to line up on the beach with their skivvy shorts or suits on and wade out into the water. The water that day off Kodiak island was forty two degrees. The SEAL's were asked to wade out up to their necks, and then remain in the water for ten minutes. Instructors and Navy Corpsmen kept a eye on them to make sure they were cold, but not hypothermic. After 10 minutes they were told to get out. They waded back to the shore and recovered their gear and then headed into the brush to get out of the wind. The instructor then told them you have about six minutes to get warm. They called it the six golden minute exercise.

There was a lot of time spent on climbing cliffs, and learning to use rope as a tool to help with climbing. This was not recreational climbing. It was climbing done at night, up and over wet and slippery cliffs. She learned to rappel with her full pack on. She had done it before, but not carrying this much weight. The day Ashley did it, her pack weighted 65 pounds

Finally, it came time for the final test the FTX. This was a 24 hour final training exercise that was designed to be the ultimate test for the SEAL's. It required that they use all of the accumulated cold weather survival knowledge they had developed and use it in a real world scenario.

Evolutions during the FTX included a 500 yard ocean swim

through 34 degree water to a rock beach at dusk, a river crossing via highline and long range navigation through mountain wilderness to infiltrate, and establish covert surveillance of a target site.

Ashley and her 25 SEAL team members did it all, while carrying half of their body weight in gear and weapons.

Meanwhile back in San Diego the new SEALs were about to be assigned to their first Teams and Platoons.

There are eight SEAL teams. Each team has six platoons and a headquarters element. SEAL platoons consist of 16 SEALs, two officers, one chief and 13 enlisted men. A platoon is generally the largest operational element assigned to a mission. The platoon may also be divided into two squads of four elements. Every member of a SEAL platoon is qualified in diving, parachuting and demolitions.

The teams are split between the East Coast and the West Coast of the United States. The odd numbered teams, fall under the command of Naval Special Warfare Group One and are based on the West Coast in Coronado, California. The even numbered teams, are under the command of Naval Special Warfare Group Two and are based on the East Coast in Little Creek, Virginia.

There are other specialized teams of SEALs called SEAL Delivery Vehicle Teams SDVT. SDV teams operate in areas where it is too far out for a SEAL to swim and carry gear. Using underwater SDV watercraft, these teams increase the areas in which SEALs can operated. SDV teams usually deploy from submarines, but they can also deploy from shore based stations and surface ships.

There are two SDV teams. SEAL Delivery Vehicle Team one is based in Pearl Harbor, Hawaii, and operates in the Pacific and Central geographic areas. SEAL Delivery Vehicle Team 2 is based at Little Creek, VA, and conducts operations throughout the Atlantic, Southern and European areas.

At the SEAL Command Center in Coronado, the Senior

Officers were discussing each SEAL candidate by name, and reviewing all of their test scores and training in order to find the right placement for each of them.

Hey Sergeant look who's up next. Let me guess. It is no other than Ashley Morgan Jamison. Yep, you got that right. What do we do with our first woman Navy SEAL and our first woman officer Navy SEAL?

Well, from what I know about Ashley, and what I have read about her, I have a good idea where the best fit would be. She is not only smart, but she is fluent in Chinese and is one of the best SEAL's we have observed when she is in the water.

She also did one of her midshipman cruises on a submarine, and she distinguished herself with the rescue of one of her men and used the in/out drill on the sub to save his life.

I think given the language skill, her familiarity with submarines, and her unbelievable water skills, that she should go Directly to SEAL Delivery Vehicle Team 1 in Hawaii. She is the perfect fit and they would welcome the Chinese Language skill. In fact Mark Price had let me know he would like to have her as his AOIC.

I totally agree with you. They are a perfect match. I will see that her orders are issued and I would love to see the look on her face when she finds out that she is going from Kodiak to Honolulu.

CHAPTER 47

SEAL ORDERS AND HOME LEAVE

Ashley was still shivering when she boarded her flight to San Diego. She had completed her cold weather training successfully, and she and her team, were headed back to Coronado. They arrived in San Diego on time, and were taken by Navy Vehicles to the Naval Special Warfare Center.

Each of them checked in and were assigned a room for the night. They were also handed a package that contained their orders. They would spend one night at Coronado, and then would head out the next day to their new Platoon assignments. They were all excited and as one could expect they were heading all over the place to their new duty stations. They no longer belonged to the Center; They were now platoon SEAL's.

Ashley almost fell over when she read her orders. She was bound for the Swimmer Delivery SEAL Team Once based in Honolulu Hawaii. She knew, based on her assignment, that the team was attached to a Nuclear Submarine but her orders didn't tell her which one. She was to take two weeks leave, and then report to SEAL Team One.

Before she left Coronado the next day for the flight to Portland, she stopped by the check in desk to say goodbye to Sergeant James. Hey Sarg, it's about time for me to blow out of here, and I just wanted to stop by and say goodbye, and thank you for your help and encouragement.

Lieutenant, it has been my pleasure. I am so glad you stopped by, as I want to tell you something. I have watched you perform since the day you graduated from BOT's and I want you to know, that I would be pleased and proud to serve with you any time in the future. You are one strong and talented officer, and I'm sure those who will have the opportunity to serve with, and for you, will be very proud they had the opportunity to do so.

Thanks Sarg. If you're in touch with Sergeant Sanchez or Lieutenant Commander Cook, would you please give them my best and tell them where I'll off to next.

I have already talked to them and told them about your assignment.

Neither of them were surprised with your placement. They were sure that with your Chinese Language ability, and your incredible water skills, that Seal Team One would be a perfect fit.

I think they are right. Best of Luck Lieutenant. Thanks Sarg and goodbye. With that having been said, Ashley grabbed a cab for the San Diego Airport and started thinking about home.

Ashley was in full Navy uniform and it was clear from the patches and pins that were on her that she was a United States Navy SEAL, At the airport some people noticed, but most did not have any idea what the insignias on her uniform meant.

She boarded her plane for Portland and finally laid her head back on headrest to relax. It was a typical West Coast Flight on Southwest Airlines and it was packed.

Ashley had a middle seat toward the back of the plane. It meant nothing to her as all she wanted to do was sleep.

She found her seat and settled in. The plane was full and a guy about 22 years old was in the outside seat and a woman about 65 was on the seat facing the window.

She just wanted to sleep and get the hour and a half air flight behind her. It didn't take more than a few minutes when the young man beside her said, "Excuse me Sir, are you a

Navy SEAL? Ashley was so tired she thought about not saying anything but said, "Yes, I am a Navy SEAL". Thanks for asking

Well Sir, I think I may know who you are. Really, Ashley said. Yes Sir, I live in San Diego and go to the University of Portland and I think I have read about you in the papers. Are you Lieutenant Ashley Morgan Jamison? Yes I am.

Well, my name is Mike Martinez, and I have been reading about you and your accomplishments for some time. I do not want to inject myself into your space but I want you to know, that I am very proud that you have successfully entered the Navy SEAL arena, and will in all probability give a number of women a course to follow that has never been done before. Thanks Mike. That is very nice to hear. But now I need to go to sleep. Ashley did not open her eyes until the plane was on final approach to Portland International Airport.

It was the quickest flight she could remember. It seemed like she just shut her eyes, when the Captain announced that they were on final approach to Portland International Airport.

She had checked her duffel bag because it was just too big and heavy to go in the overhead so it took her a little longer than usual to clear baggage claim. As usual both her Mom, Dad and Brother were waiting for her outside. To their surprise and also to Ashley's they were not the only ones waiting. There were at least five photographers and just as many reporters all anxious to get the story of what it took for a woman to become the first Navy SEAL.

Ashley didn't know what to make of it. The reporters were shouting questions and the photographers, were snapping pictures. She just decided to be herself and show no emotion. She gave her parents and brother a hug and whispered to her Dad, "Let's get out of here". With that, she smiled at the newspaper people and said, I have no comment at this time. Thanks for coming to welcome me home.

On the way home, John said to her, Wow Ash, you are a real movie star. I bet you can't wait for all of the money to start rolling in. Ashley just laughed, and said, John, I would like you to know that the annual salary of a second lieutenant in the Marine Corp is exactly $3,108 per month and it will grow to $3910 per month after three years. There are no bonus payments or stock options. The benefits are good but let me tell you from experience you have to earn them.

My guess is when you take your first job out of law school, that you will triple your little sisters monthly net worth. John just started laughing. They arrived home before anyone asked any more questions. Once they were in the door, Sarah said I have lunch ready for you Ash. When you're ready we are all dying to know what you have been through. We are so proud of your accomplishment, and know that it must not have come easily.

Lunch sounds great Mom and yep, I have some real stories to tell you. Let me put my stuff away and then we can get down to eating.

At lunch, Jim was the first to say, Ash, I have to tell you that you look like you have lost some weight, and yet you look like you are made of steal. Your body fat must be close to zero. Yeh Dad, I have lost some pounds, and there is no question that I am in the best shape of my life. This has been a test beyond my wildest imagination.

I have so many stories to tell you but the bottom line is that I started the process with 99 men and me. When it was over the day before yesterday we were down to 3 officers, 1 senior petty officers and 14 enlisted men.

How did so many get eliminated, John asked. John, they eliminate themselves. Basically those that leave come to a point where they just can't take it anymore. Once they make that decision they placed their Helmut on the ground and ring a bell three times. That is the end for them. I felt really sorry for some that made it through most of the training but then ran into problems. The Ocean took its toll on a number. There are just some people who never get use to the water, and if you have that kind of fear, night diving in the Pacific is not your cup of tea.

Ash, where do you go from here? Sarah asked. Well Mom, yesterday I received my orders. After I get to spend the two weeks at home with you, I am to report to a Navy SEAL unit based in Hawaii.

It is a unit that is attached to a Nuclear Submarine, and so most of the work will start from the submarine in open ocean water. I feel so lucky to get that assignment. I think I now know why. The number one reason was I am very at home in the water and did well in all of the tests that had anything to do with swimming, and second, I am fluent in Chinese. These are the two key reasons I think I got the Pacific Ocean Assignment.

I still can't believe that I am going from Kodiak Alaska where I literally froze my but off, to the Hawaiian Islands and the warm Pacific Ocean.

Why the training in Kodiak Alaska? Jim asked. Well, based on the SEAL experience in Afghanistan, it was clear that SEAL's needed more training in how to fight and win in cold, and miserable, climates. So now it is a requirement of all SEALs to undergo cold weather training. That sounds miserable, John said.

Yes, I have so many stories to tell you but let me give you an example of one part of my training in Alaska. We were asked to leave our equipment on the beach and then walk across a river that was frozen until one by one we fell through the ice. Once we were all in the freezing water up to our necks, we had to stay there for 10 minutes and then we were given 6 minutes to get out, build a fire and get warm. It was not a pleasant experience.

I'm cold just listening to the story Ash, Sarah said. What do you have planned for your two weeks home stay. Well, number one I want to sleep. I plan to see Coach Nancy tomorrow, and see if I can train with Team Unify while I'm home. I need to stay in shape because I have a lot of Ocean swimming ahead of me.

I plan to just relax and catch up with you. Once I leave this time, who knows when I will be home next. I feel lucky to have been granted the two weeks leave before I have to report for duty. Most members of my class were heading out immediately to their assignments.

In my case the submarine that my unit is attached to, is out to sea, and won't be back in for two weeks so it worked out perfect.

Ash, how do you want us to handle the press? We have already had a number of calls come to our home wanting to get a time for you for an interview. I think we should direct all of those calls to the Navy's public relation office. Let them deal with it.

Lunch was great Mom. Thanks very much. In fact, it was heaven compared to what I have been eating over the past three weeks. It is amazing what you can find to eat once the tide goes out, but it is not always the most tasty of meals. I can't imagine, Sarah said.

Now, I'm going to take this uniform off and take a nap. I will see you in a couple of hours, assuming I wake up.

The days passed quickly and Ashley managed to swim every other day and on her off day she worked out in the gym at the Y. She caught up on her sleep, and managed to make it to Killer Burger twice. She also told her Mom and Dad story after story about her training. Neither of them could believe what she had been through.

On her first trip to Killer Burger, she had the **Peanut Butter, Pickle and Bacon Burger**. It was made with 1/3 of a pound of grass fed beef, bacon, peanut butter sauce, house sauce, mayo, grilled onion and a pickle.

On her second trip she ordered the **Fun Guy.** It was made with 1/3 of a pound of grass fed beef, bacon, mushrooms, Swiss fondue, house sauce, grilled onion and pickle. It was good, but she decided that nothing could top the Peanut Butter, Pickle and Bacon Burger. It was becoming a homecoming tradition to her.

In her second week home she managed to make an appointment with her High School Counselor Mrs. Atherton.

Mrs. Atherton welcomed her with open arms. Ashley it is so good to see you and I so appreciate your taking the time to come by.

Wow girl, you have had quite a go of it. If everything I have read about you is true then you are a real superstar.

Let's see, you graduated from the US Naval Academy. You were a four year NCAA swimming champion in two events, you went to the Olympic Games representing the United States of America and you brought home a Gold and Silver medal and then you beat all odds and became a full fledged Navy Seal. Something that No woman in history has accomplished.

In her normal modest way Ashley just said, yes I have had a lot of luck along the way. Luck my ass, young lady. You are one of the most driven people I have ever met, and I'm sure, if I hadn't brought up your accomplishments, you wouldn't have said a word. Ashley just laughed. I suppose your right.

So where do you go from here. I'm off to Hawaii to join SEAL team 1 which operates for the most part from the middle of the ocean, and as such is attached to a Nuclear Submarine.

You're kidding me you actually depart for your SEAL missions from a submerged Navy Sub. Yes, that is one way to put it. My god, the thought of that scares the hell out of me.

Ashley stayed and talked to Mrs. Atherton for about 45 minutes and then she said her goodbyes and headed home. She was glad she had made the contact and was pleased that Mrs. Atherton had followed her career so closely.

The last night before she left Her Dad asked her the question they had wondered about for years. Ash, can you tell me now the reason you selected the Navy Academy and the Navy SEALs? Yep, when I was a sophomore in high school Coach Nancy invited a Navy SEAL in to give us a motivation talk. I was never so impressed with anyone in my life, and I knew then, that I wanted to try to make it happen.

Each step along the way was always toward that goal and I made it. I'm very proud and very happy. I knew in the beginning, and I know now, that it was absolutely the right thing for me. Jim just smiled. Thanks for the answer I have wanted to know for some time. Congratulations on a job well done.

Before she knew it she had said her goodbyes to her family, and was headed to Hawaii on a flight from Portland to Honolulu.

CHATPER 48

REPORTING FOR DUTY SIR

Ashley's flight from Portland Oregon to Honolulu Hawaii was great. She was fully rested from her two weeks at home and ready to report to her first SEAL assignment. She was dressed in full uniform but no one said anything to her.

She arrived in Honolulu international Airport and got her sea bag from baggage and then grabbed a cab to Pearl Harbor. Once there it did not take her long to find the headquarters for the SEAL Delivery Vehicle Team 1.

She went to the front desk and behind it sat a Master Sergeant with a trident pin on his uniform. Good Afternoon Sergeant, my name is Lieutenant Ashley Morgan Jamison and I am reporting for duty. With that, she handed her orders to the Sergeant. He looked them over and then said welcome Lieutenant we have been expecting you and let me be the first in our unit to congratulate you on your SEAL designation. You have successfully achieved something that no woman has ever been able to master and I am happy for both you, the SEAL brotherhood and the Navy in general. It is a major accomplishment which only those who have earned the trident before you completely understand. My name is Mike Johnson and I am the Platoon Chief of our gang of merry men.

Thanks Sergeant, your words of support are appreciated.

Then the Sergeant added, in addition those of us who

spend most of our life in or on the water were very appreciative of your performance in the Olympic Games. Your gold and silver medals were earned and gave those of us who watch swimming something to be Navy proud of.

I have an orientation packet for you but before I send you off to get settled in I need to give you a little history and some specific background on our unit.

As you may know, there are two SEAL Delivery Vehicle Teams. Ours located here at Pearl Harbor and SEAL Delivery Vehicle Team 2 located in Little Creek Virginia.

Our Team is attached to the US Nuclear Submarine USS Louisville SSN 724. She is a Los Angeles class fast attack submarine. Our SEAL team specializes in operating in areas that are farther from land than some of our brothers units. We also use SEAL delivery vehicles that are manned submersible vehicles that help us get to our missions.

The SDV units that we use require that we ride exposed to the water, breathing from the vehicles compressed air or using our own SCUBA gear. We use the Mark 8 SDV It is an upgrade of the earlier Mark 8. It is quieter, faster, more efficient and has a longer range than the earlier model. It is built from aluminum which gives it a sturdier hull and it is roomier.

You will learn all about the vehicles and will be trained to both drive and ride them as a passenger.

As to our team. Your boss is Captain Mark Price. He is a very experienced SEAL and has earned the respect of every member of our team. He carries the designation as our OIC or Officer in Charge. We have a second officer spot that is the AOIC that is your spot as the Assistant Officer in charge. We have a platoon chief which is the role I play and we have a leading Petty Officer. The remaining SEALs are all enlisted all in all we total 18.

Your quarters are in the officer housing structure which is not far from here. The information on your room is in your orientation package. You will have your own room and bath.

Because you will be the only woman you will not have a roommate.

We have scheduled an orientation session for you this afternoon at 1600 with Captain Price.

He will fill you in on everything else you will need to know to get started. You should plan to meet him in our large training room. It is located right here on the map.

As I'm sure you have been told we were all rookies at some point in time and all of us would agree and tell you that it will probably be about three full years before you really feel you fit in.

Once that happens and you will know it, you will have been tested in about every way possible. Your confidence will grow with each new test.

Yes, I have been told that and expect to be challenged.

Ashley found her room which would be her home for an unspecified amount of time. As she walked over to her room, she couldn't help comparing this 85 degree day vs. the Kodiak experience. All she could think was boy am I lucky.

She settled in and put her things away and at five minutes to four she was in the officers conference room where she was to meet Mark Price at 1600.

At exactly 1600 Captain Mark Price walked into the room with a big smile on his face. He extended his hand and said you must be Ashley. Yes Sir, I am Ashley Jamison. It is a pleasure to meet you.

Ashley, I want to ask you what do your friends call you when they say your name. Most of my close friends and my SEAL brothers in training just call me Ash. Then, if it is OK with you, I will call you Ash as well.

Please call me Mark. OK Mark, that's simple enough. I must tell you Ash, that I know more about you than I have about any new SEAL that I have had the pleasure to supervise over the past five years. Like many of us that are SEAL's the story of

Ashley Jamison is something that we have all followed with interest. But that is not how I got my insight into you.

It so happens that one of my best friends and SEAL brothers is Captain Roscoe Cook. Roscoe and I went through BUD's together and also SQT together. He told me years ago that he thought he had his sights set on the first woman that could possibly become a Navy SEAL and by god he was right.

Over the years he has kept me up on your accomplishments, to the point that once I heard that you would be available for assignment I let SEAL command Coronado know that I would be interested in having you as a member of my team.

It just so happened that you had all of the aquatic skills we require at SEAL Delivery and when they told me you were fluent in Chinese it was a perfect fit.

I assume that Chief Johnson provided you with your orientation packet and gave you some information on our structure and how we operate. That he did. He made me feel really welcome and to tell the truth I wasn't quite sure how my first SEAL team would view being stuck with the first woman SEAL.

Well each man will make their own judgments but I can tell you that we as a group are very pleased to have the first Navy SEAL woman as a part of our team and brotherhood.

So, now it begins, your real life training. You will learn a lot over the next couple of years and because of that you will be viewed as a rookie for some time. Gradually you will gain real life experiences and over time you will absorb all of them and see them as the training experiences you need to become a real SEAL leader.

You will be my second in command or AOIC as we will designate you. We are not a formal part of the Navy and I encourage you to get to know each of our men well. They all know who you are but no one knows yet what to expect. Be yourself at all times and ask as many questions as you need to in order to understand the situation fully before you give an order.

What you say and how you say it will be very important in building your overall creditability.

I have a brief meeting scheduled at 1800 to introduce you to our team. Then we will have dinner together.

Tomorrow morning I have an appointment to introduce you to Captain Jason Miles. Captain Miles is the Captain of the USS Louisville SSN 724. The Louisville is based here and our SEAL team is attached to it. The ship has I50 sailors and 12 Officers. You will get to know and meet all of the officers and many of the men who help make our job easier.

After tomorrows orientation and introduction you will begin to train in one of our SEAL Delivery Vehicles.

It is a Mark 8 Mod 1 it has an endurance of about eight to 12 hours which gives it a range of 15 to 18 miles assuming she is fully loaded with our team members.

The less she is loaded the farther she will go. Your training will be conducted by Chief Johnson. It will involved 2 or 3 days of classroom training and then you will be underwater for the next couple of weeks learning how to drive and ride on the thing. We are scheduled to go out on a training mission with the Louisville at the end of the month so you will have at least three weeks training on the Mark 8 before you get to test it in the middle of the ocean.

The Chief will go into detail with you but we use the SDV primarily for inserting our SEAL team to handle covert operations or for placing mines on ships. We also use it for underwater mapping and terrain exploration, location and recovery of lost or downed objects and reconnaissance missions.

This Mark 8's allow us to land on shores inaccessible to a larger submarine and they provide a degree of stealth that is much greater than that offered by small surface craft.

We have you in a temporary housing unit here on the base. It will be good for the next year after which you will in all probably want to get your own place off base. Because we are in Hawaii, you will also get an additional housing allowance but I can tell you from my own experience that housing here is really expensive and as such you should begin to check places out sooner rather than later.

If you see something that you want and can afford it my advice is to take it and move off the base.

OK Ash, any questions so far? No Mark, it seems pretty clear to me. I look forward to meeting the team this afternoon and to learning a lot from Chief Johnson over the next few weeks. Good, then let's take you on a brief tour of our facilities. I want you to see where we eat when we are on the base, where the officers club is and also the gym and workout facilities.

Based on what my Pal Roscoe Cook tells me, you not only spend a lot of time in the water but also in the Gym. That is true. I have spent a lot of time in my life as a gymnast and because I swam the butterfly competitively I have always needed to build my upper body strength.

Makes sense to me Ash. Let's begin our mini tour.

They finished their tour and Ashley had about an hour to herself before she was introduced to the team. She put her stuff away, and then walked around the base a bit trying to get herself oriented. She did see the USS Louisville, it was tied up to one of the submarine piers and on top of it was a Mark 8.

At five minutes before 1800 Ashley entered the large conference room at the SEAL training facility. She was not surprised to find most of the team already in the room. She just smiled and took a seat. At 1800 Mark entered the room and said good afternoon everyone. I asked you to join me for a few moments so I could introduce you to our new AOIC.

Ash, would you please stand up. Everyone I want you to meet lieutenant Ashley Morgan Jamison. To her surprise the men began to clap. All she could say is, "Thanks for the nice welcome".

You have all known that we would have the first woman to

ever wear a SEAL Trident joining us and now she has. I am very proud to have her as a member of our team and from what I know about her she is going to make all of us proud to have served with her. I also know something that you may not know about Ash and I want to give you some advise.

Never and I mean never get into a swimming race with this woman because you're going to lose and one thing we don't like to do is loose. The team just laughed.

OK. Ashley will begin to train with Chief Johnson beginning tomorrow. Some of you will be involved in her training, please tell her everything you can. The smarter we can make her the better it will be for all of us. Any questions?

There were no questions. We have dinner scheduled together in 30 minutes. See you then. The next 30 minutes were spent on introductions and answering questions. Ashley knew from the reception she received that this was going to be a good fit and she was going to enjoy the new relationships.

The next three weeks were spent training on and learning about the Mark 8. The underwater training was done in Pearl Harbor and thus the water was warm and clear which made the training both interesting and enjoyable. Chief Johnson was a no nonsense guy and spent 9 full hours every day working to bring Ashley up to speed. After the second week she was becoming more comfortable with everything and it showed. Chief Johnson just couldn't believe how she was in the water and how calm she was during what many would think was stressful underwater training.

At dinner one night Captain Price asked Chief Johnson, Hey Chief, what's your take on Ashley. Well I've had two full weeks with her and I can tell you she is smart and a quick learner. I can also tell you that the women has ice in her veins and doesn't let anything rattle her. When she is in the water she is like a fish. Every movement is smooth and as such she does not waste any energy.

We even had an incident the other day when a 10 foot Great

White Shark decided to come and check us out. Ashley saw him coming and didn't even flinch. When he got to close she just motioned at him and scared him to the point he decided to go find someone else to play with.

Thanks Chief. All your comments verify what I have heard about her.

CHAPTER 49

ANCHORS AWAY

Ashley and Mark met with the Captain of The USS Louisville, Captain Jason Miles. Captain Miles was a full, four stripe Naval Captain, and had more than 25 years in the Navy. Ashley found him to be very easy to talk with, and someone who had a significant amount of confidence and experience.

Captain Miles indicated that he had orders to get underway with the SEAL detachment at the end of the month, and he expected that they would be a sea for a full month. He also mentioned that the mission was designed totally around SEAL training, and they would be working in deep water both with day and night operations. Captain Miles invited Mark and Ashley to return the following week for a Tuesday night dinner. He indicated that he would have his full complement of officers on board for that dinner, and it would be an excellent opportunity for Ash to meet, and get to know them.

The date and time were set. Ashley and Mark arrived for the Tuesday night dinner. The Captain introduced them to his officer crew. To say that the officers were impressed, would be an understatement, as they all had some idea how difficult it is to become a SEAL. For a woman to have achieved the Trident, they knew, she must be something special. They had all witnessed the SEAL team at work and almost to a man no one wanted anything to do with the tasks they performed on top of or underwater.

It was a very nice evening and Ashley enjoyed it very much. The next day it was back to training with Chief Johnson.

The end of the month came very quickly, and it was now time to pack her sea bag for the trip aboard The USS Louisville. Ashley was assigned to a stateroom, and finally, she had a roommate. Her name was Misty Freemont and she was also a graduate of the Naval Academy. Misty was a full lieutenant and the Weapons Officer on the Louisville.

Hey Ashley, welcome to the USS Louisville, I'm Misty Freemont the Chief Weapons officer aboard this nuclear submarine. Hi Misty, it is great to meet you, and I should tell you, from my perspective, it is really nice to see another woman officer. For the past year, I have been with men only and have had no roommate to talk with.

Well girl, you have got the right roommate, because I love to talk. I understand that you went to the YARD and chose the Marine Corp option instead of the Naval Option. Yes, I wanted to be a SEAL and that was the best way to go about it. Well it looks like you picked the right way to go about it, because, as I understand it, you are first woman to ever make it through.

Yep, that is true. Well, I look forward to catching up later, but right now we have to get this baby underway so I'll see you later.

Ashley settled into the space allotted for her in the stateroom. It was small but still comfortable and it had its own bathroom.

Things began to settle into a routine. For the most part the SEAL's conducted two exercises per day. They were constantly using the in/out entrance and exit from the submarine, and they had exercises both during the day and in the dark of night.

They had been at sea for about two weeks, when the Captain called Mark up and asked him to meet him in the control room. Yes Sir, what can I do for you, Mark said. Mark, I just got a call telling me that there is a very significant Typhoon heading through the south china sea. It is Typhoon Mary. She is packing winds of up to 80 knots and the seas are super rough with 23 foot waves. We have been informed that there is a Chinese Freighter right in the middle of it, and that she is taking on water. We are the closest to her and have been asked to check her out and see if a rescue is needed. I've changed course and should reach her in about 26 hours.

I'm told that the sea is so rough that a surface ship can't get close enough to her to help, so we may need your team to undertake a rescue, if the situation warrants. I will know more as we get closer, and will let you know if we can use your help. I'm told she has a crew of 8. They are all Chinese and no one speaks any English.

Well Captain, I think we can help with the second problem for sure. Ash speaks fluent Chinese, so if we need her to talk with the Captain, we can provide the service.

Thanks Mark, that is good to know.

Mark called Ash to his stateroom and briefed her on what he had just learned. She was comfortable with the language, and if needed, she knew she could be of help.

The next morning Captain Miles called Mark up to the control room. Hey Mark, thanks for coming up. Yes Sir, where do we stand? Well, the storm has not gotten any better and we are heading right into her. How does the sub do when there is a significant storm up top? Well, it depends on a lot of things, but for the most part, when we are operating at normal operating depths, even a large storm on the surface has little effect on us. Now having said that, we know that a really bad storm can affect the ocean as deep as 200 meters down and we know that the salinity and temperature of the water have an effect on how deep the storm moves the water around. In deeper waters, when the temperature changes abruptly it is called the thermocline. The thermocline creates an imaginary line in the water. Below the line, there is little or no mixing of water from above it. We are in warm water here and thus the thermocline is running at about 70 feet deep so I plan to stay at or below that level as we approach

How is the ship doing? I'm afraid it is not doing well and has begun to list to port at about 15 degrees.

I have been thinking a lot about how we can get those men off of that ship and to safely. I'm not sure how to go about it. Do you have any ideas? Yes Sir.

I know this is going to sound crazy and dangerous, but I think it will work. Let's hear it, Mark.

I think we can send six of our team out the in/out box from 70 feet down wearing our closed circuit SCUBA gear. This gear is mounted on the front of our men and is much lighter in weight than having to use tanks. Three of the men would then tie a long nylon rope on to the conning tower of the sub and remain with the sub at that point. The other three will then swim to the freighter, surface and climb up a rope ladder that we will ask be dropped from the deck. Each swimmer will carry two small light weight rope chairs with them. Each chair has a ring on the end of it and it is designed to slide down the rope.

Once that is done, we will have you bring the sub up to the surface for a few minutes while we send each member down the rope on the rope chair. The height of the freighter will give us the downward speed we will need to move the men down the rope. The rope is strong enough to have three men moving on the line at once. Our three guys on the sub will catch each man as he arrives, and get them aboard and inside. Once we have them all inside, we will take the sub back down to70 feet. Our three guys on the freighter will then go back in the water, and using their compass find us by swimming down to 70 feet and then across to us. They will then come back in using the in/out process.

Mark that sounds like a fiction movie, and it also sounds like it will be dangerous as hell for your six men. Yes Sir, but we are trained to be creative and to be challenged. I think it will work.

How are you going to communicate with the men on the ship. Ashley will be one of our team swimming to the ship.

You have got to be kidding, you're going to send that woman out there in the middle of that Typhoon?

Yes sir. She will be the team leader and the lead swimmer. I think you will see just why she wears the trident and is a Navy SEAL. How long do you think we are going to have to stay on the surface? If I'm right we will have them all back in safe in 10 minutes from the time we enter the ship's deck. How will the ship handle the 10 minutes. Well I can tell you we are going to rock and roll. These babies don't like being on top of the water and they really don't like it when the waves are big which these are going to be.

Mark, we are going to be in radio contact with these guys within the next hour. We will need Ashley to help them understand our plan. I will go through the plan with her when I leave you, and she will be on call to come to the control room when you need her.

Mark found Ash and briefed her on the plan he had developed. Sounds like it will test our skill boss. I'm up for a little swim in the Jacuzzi. Let's get our team together and go over the plan. I think that I will send our two best swimmers with you and keep three of our big guys back here to catch these guys when they go on the ride of their lives.

Mark brought his team together and briefed them on the mission. Ashley would be the lead swimmer and would handle all communication once on the ship. She would carry four of the rope chairs with her. One of the swimmers would also carry 4 chairs and the other would swim pulling the rope. They planned to mount floats on the rope to help lift it to the surface and make the pull much easier.

One on the ship the other two members of the swim team would get the rope tied off and the chairs set to go while Ashley informed the crew what would happen next. They would plan to send a man every minute, so the catch group will have one minute to get the guy in front out of the way, before the next on arrives. If all goes well they will have all eight men off in eight minutes from the time the first one takes off.

It wasn't long before Ashley was called to the control room.

The submarine had made contact with the ship and the Captain was on the line. Ashley took over from there. She was confident in her ability to speak and she understood everything the Captain said. She explained how they planned to rescue he, and his men, and made it clear that he needed to get a long rope ladder hung down the port side of the ship to the surface of the water.

She also made sure that he knew, the minute that the divers started up the rope ladder, the Captain was to have all of his crew members on deck and ready to go. They were to bring nothing with them except the cloths they were wearing.

The Captain was obviously very afraid, as the ship was now listing to Port at 20 degrees.

Once she was sure he understood she signed off and said that they would be there to help them within one hour.

She headed below to get her wet suit and equipment on before heading for the In/out hatch. Ashley had seen, and used, the light weight rope chairs in BUD's and she knew that once they got going they were like a high line ride but without a breaking system.

The team was in place when the captain said that they were now 100 yards from the ship. Mark then gave the order to load in the in/out box and head out. The six SEAL's were all about business, and would be, until they were safely back in the submarine.

They got to the storage box and found the nylon rope and chairs they needed. They put the floats on the rope and using their compass headed for the ship. They stayed down at 65 feet because they could tell there would be significant turbulence in place when they began to surface.

They were all strong swimmers, however Ashley's two team

members couldn't help but notice how strong of a swimmer she was, and how calm and relaxed she was as she headed for the ship. They all saw the freighters hull at the same time and Ashley gave them the signal to surface. They did so gradually, and were bounced around a lot on the way up. Her SEAL teammate who had the rope, had his hands full, so she took the four chairs from the other one and told the two of them to handle the rope together. It went a lot easier with two, than it had with one.

They broke the surface of the water and grabbed hold of the rope ladder. The ship was not only listing but it was rolling with the waves so it made the rope ladder climb harder than they had thought it would be. They reached the deck, and the two guys with the rope tied it off and began to rig the chairs. Ashley introduced herself to the Captain and told him what she wanted the men to do.

She then communicated with the Sub control room and told them that they were ready to send the first man. The Captain had brought the sub to the surface and it was really rolling around, but the seals kept the line tight and the first guy was on his way scared to death. They caught him and got him inside with the help of the submarine crew. The next one and then the next one all arrived as planned. Last the Captain was placed in a chair and was sent on his way. When he was successfully in the SEAL's hands Ashley and her two team members, headed down the ladder and jumped into the ocean. The ship was now listing at more than 30 degrees and it was just a matter of time until it went over and began to sink.

The SEAL's knew what effect that would have on everything in the water and they planned to be long gone before that happened. They proceeded down to 70 feet and then using their compass headed back to the Submarine as fast as they could swim. The two guys had trouble staying with her, but they gave it their best shot.

They arrived back, put their gear away in the box, and headed for the in/out chamber. They were back in the sub when word came down that the freighter had gone under. Just another day in the office.

CHAPTER 50

MISSION ACCOMPLISHED

Ashley, and her five SEAL teammates, were back on the submarine when they learned that the freighter had just sunk with everything on it, except the crew, which was safely aboard The USS Louisville.

When they opened the in/out box inside the submarine, Ashley and her men stepped out into the bright light. Both Mark and Captain Miles were there to greet them.

Captain Miles spoke first. I have seen a lot of things in my long and checkered Naval career, but I have never seen anything like that. My congratulations go to all of you on a job well done. Ashley, when you are out and dressed, I need your help with communication with the Captain. He knows he is on a submarine but he is very confused about what is going to happen to he and his men.

Our plan is to get out of this storm and let it pass. Once that happens we plan to go into Subic Bay Naval base in the Philippines and let them off. They will fly home to China from there.

I need you to get them to relax, understand that they are safe, and that we will bring no harm to them. Also, let them know that we plan to get all of them home to their families. Yes Sir. It won't take me long. Would you like me to meet you in the control room. Yes Ash, that would be great. I will take you to them from there.

The Captain left the room and Mark looked at his team and said nice work gang. Just another day at the office. He smiled and left them. The two swimmers looked at Ashley and said, my God boss, you can swim. In fact you pushed us to our limit on the way back. Nothing to it guys, you did all the hard work. All I did was take a swim in a world pool bath and carry a couple of chairs up a ladder. You did everything, while I sat around practicing my Chinese with some guys I have never met. They both smiled and gave her a high five.

Ashley met the Captain in the control room within a half hour, and she was taken to the Captain of the freighter and his men. She spoke to them in Chinese and told them what the Captain had said. They would all be fed and receive warm cloths and then taken to the Naval Base at Subic Bay for transportation home to their families. The relief on their faces was very noticeable. Ashley also told them that if they had any questions she would get the answers for them.

The Captain then said to Ashley in Chinese, we all want to thank you and your men for saving our lives. Without you we would now be at the bottom of the Ocean. We will be forever grateful to you and your team. The Captain went on to say, I have never in all of my life seen a woman that was as brave as you. You were amazing and we will never forget you.

Ashley thanked him, and said that she would also thank the Captain on their behalf.

Ashley left the men and returned to her room. Her roommate, Misty Freemont, was in the room when she arrived. Hey girl, rumor has it that you have had a pretty interesting day.

Yep, I'm sure some would think it was a bit unusual. Well, are you going to tell me about it?

Sure, three of us went for a swim in a large Jacuzzi which one would call the Pacific Ocean in the middle of a Typhoon. We swam underwater at 70 feet down and then swam up to a tanker that was about to sink. We then got to climb up a rope ladder to the ship's deck, while the ship was listing into us over

20 degrees. Once there, we were welcomed by 8 Chinese sailors could not speak English, so I had the opportunity to practice my Chinese. We got them organized, and then sent them down a rope line, which I'm sure, was the ride of their lives. Three of our guys then caught them, detached them and put them in the sub. Once that was done the sub went back down and the three of us had the joy of jumping off the sinking ship and then swimming back down to 70 feet. After that we used our compass to find the sub and here I am. Just another day at the office.

You have got to be kidding me. No that was a pretty accurate summary. I had no idea that you speak Chinese. Yes, one of my hidden skills. Ashley just laughed. In fact I just left the Chinese crew. The Captain told me we are headed for Subic Bay and should be there well after Typhoon Mary passes. We are going to then let our passengers off. I need to coordinate with their Chinese Freight company to arrange transportation for all of them back to China.

The Captain told me he expected to be in Subic Bay in a couple of days. Ash, have you ever been to Subic Bay or the Philippines? No, not even close. Well let me give you a bit of history about it. Subic Bay is no longer an active Naval Base. In its heyday, which was during Vietnam, it was the largest Naval Facility outside the United States. It still has some minimum facilities, so we will be able to get in and get out, but it is nothing like it once was. It borders on a town called Olongapo which I don't recommend spending any time in. It was to Olongapo that all the sailors went during Vietnam days to check out bar girls. I'm told, that if you fell off the small bridge that linked the base to Olongapo, that you would need some 20 different shots. Sounds like a real garden spot. I think I'll stay on the sub.

Probably a good idea. Are you going to dinner now? Yes, I am starving. Let's go together. OK.

Later that evening Mark had a chance to talk with one of the swimmers that went with Ashley to the Freighter. Sam, how was your swim with Ash today? Boss, that woman not only can swim, but she is one cool cucumber. I could not believe how calm she was in the face of some pretty ugly conditions. She also scampered up the rope ladder with no problem and let me tell you, it was not easy. She was able to calm down the Captain and his crew and made it easy to get them hooked up and on their way. If what I saw today is indicative of her abilities, then we not only have a real SEAL on our hands, but we have a potential leader. Jim and I saw her close up, and both of us would agree that her performance was at the top of the class.

Thanks Sam, that is good input. By the way, well done today. It was a very successful mission. Thanks Boss.

The USS Louisville arrived in Subic Bay. Ashley escorted the Captain and his crew to the base headquarters. She had talked to the freight company and arranged for their representatives to meet them on arrival. It all worked out well and Ashley turned them over to the representatives. The Captain thanked her again. She left and headed back to the ship.

The Louisville got underway that afternoon and headed toward Pearl Harbor. On the way back, the SEAL team continued to train. Ashley had lots of opportunity to learn how to both drive and ride in the SEAL delivery Vehicle. She felt very comfortable underwater and the vehicles were easy to maneuver.

When they returned to Pearl Harbor the temperature was 85 degrees and the sky was bright blue. It had been a full month and Ashley was ready to set foot back on land.

She had a couple of days off and decided to use the time to check out the housing market. She wanted an apartment that was one bedroom, one bath and had easy access to the city restaurants. She also wanted a place that had a pool and a relaxing environment.

She did some research and found that for $2000 per month that she could find a two bedroom, one bath unit but if she spent the $2000 on a one bedroom, one bath she could get more of what she wanted and it would be furnished. The problem she had was that her monthly income was $3108 plus her housing allowance that made her income about $3500 per month and $3500 per month was not enough to afford a one bedroom apartment for $2000 per month.

So, as Mark had warned her, housing was expensive and finding the right spot would take some time. She spent the next two days researching and looking at a large number of Apartments. She didn't find anything that met her needs but she was able to locate the area she wanted to be in.

She found that the two areas that met her criteria were the Fort Derussy Beach Park area, and the Ala Wai Boat Harbor area, near Ala Moana Blvd.

She was tired of looking when her two days off were over, but she was pleased that she had found two areas that would meet everything she wanted.

The next two weeks were pretty normal. If she was not training at sea, she was in the classroom learning about this weapon type or that weapon type.

One Sunday morning she was in her dorm room reading the paper with a cup of coffee and looking at the rental adds, like she did most weekends.

This day there was an add that she had not seen before. It said. Studio Apartment available. Ala Wai Boat Harbor location. Honolulu Arms. Pool, view, furnished with easy beach access. $1600 per month.

The unit sounded small but it was a the top of her budget but it was where she wanted to be and the amenities sounded great. Ashley called the number in the add and got the manager on the phone. She introduced herself and ask about the apartment. He told her his phone had been ringing off the hook all morning and if she was interested she would have to get there quick. Ashley told him she would be there in l5 minutes. He met her and showed her the unit.

The view from the front room window was right at the yacht

harbor. The unit was small and as the ad said, it was a studio. The bed folded out of the wall and it had a very small kitchen with a stove, sink, dishwasher, and refrigerator. The unit was simply furnished but the complex had a pool and there was a walking path that led to Honolulu's, Waikiki beach.

The manager, Mr. Piedmont, asked Ashley what she did for a living? She told him she was a United States Navy SEAL Officer stationed at Pearl Harbor. He thought for a moment and then said I think I read something about you.. Are you the only woman to ever pass the SEAL training tests? Yes, that is me.

Well I would be very proud to rent you this place, if you want it. It would be like having a celebrity of sorts within our complex.

Well Mr. Piedmont, I would like to rent the unit but I have one question. My SEAL team is attached to the USS Louisville SSN 724. I don't know when this will happen, but at some point, we will be deployed to somewhere east in the Pacific for at least a six month period. What happens with the unit when I'm gone? Well it is up to you, but I would be happy to rent it out for you on a six month rental if you want. You would just have to let me know in advance.

We have a deal Mr. Piedmont. Thanks for your help. I will write you a check this morning for the first month's rent and for the security deposit you requested. When would it be available for me to move in?

Well Ms..........Just call me Ashley, everyone else does. Well Ashley, I can have it cleaned and ready for you by next weekend if that will be acceptable to you.

That works out really nicely. Thanks Mr. Piedmont.

When Ashley got back to her dorm room she called Mark and said, Hey Boss, its Ash. Guess what? I have no idea why you would call me on a Sunday Morning on your day off. What's up?

Well I took your advice and started looking for a place to stay off base a couple weeks ago and this morning I found a perfect spot.

Where is it? It is a studio located at the yacht harbor near Fort Derussy Beach. It looks out on the harbor and has direct access to Waikiki beach. I'm pretty excited it will be my first real place of my own. The manager also told me he would short term rent it for me when we deploy. Wow that sounds perfect Ash. How much is it if you don't mind me asking? It is $1600 per month. My budget will be a bit tight but I can live with that.

I'm happy for you and am glad you did it. Don't forget to let the base know when you are ready to move out of your dorm. I won't and thanks Mark. See you tomorrow.

Ashley notified base housing that she would be moving out the following Saturday and she started to really look forward to this next chapter in her life.

She had one more week on base and then she would be out on her own.

CHAPTER 51

THE REUNION

Ashley was so happy to have found a place to live off base and she was so looking forward to finally moving into to her own first home that she could not wait for the next week to begin. On Thursday before the end of the week, Chief Johnson came up to her and said, "Lieutenant you don't seem as focused as usual this week. Is something going on that is taking your mind elsewhere?

Great observation Chief, you are right. This week my mind has been in a completely different place than it has been. Here is what has been going on. I have been trying to find a place off base to live that would fit within my budget. And, after a lot of searching, last Sunday I finally found one and got it. I'm going to move from the base into it on Saturday. So by next week I should be back to normal. This is my first place on my own and finding it was not easy. I guess you could say I'm a bit schoolgirl excited.

Well Ash, I can tell you that we have all been through that process, and as I remember, it was real nerve racking. My guess is, you will be happy with what you have chosen, and once your moved in and settled you will be back to normal and focused on our team and nothing else. Thanks Chief. As usual you are the best.

The next day the SEAL team had a very difficult training

exercise and at the end of it Ashley was very tired. She wanted to go back to her dorm room and just call it a night but Mark ask her to go and have a beer in the officers club to evaluate the day's results together.

Ashley was super tired but just said, OK Mark that sounds good.

They walked over to the club together and talked on the way about the day's training. Once they arrived they ordered a beer and continued with their conversation. About 15 minutes later, Captain Miles walked up to them and ask Mark if he could talk with him for a while.

Mark and Ashley were almost done with their analysis so he excused himself and went to join Captain Miles at another table.

Ashley was left sitting at the bar by herself. She was about to finish her beer and head for her dorm room when a voice behind her said "Hey Sailor, can I buy you a beer" She didn't turn around immediately but thought she recognized the voice.

She also wondered who in the heck would call her a sailor. She turned around and almost fell off her bar stool. Standing behind her and wearing Naval Aviator Wings was none other than Ryan Joshua the only guy she had ever cared for during her entire four years at the YARD. She didn't know what to say but she did know what to do. She jumped off her bar stool, gave him the biggest hug she could muster and then gave him a soft kiss on the lips.

Wow, that was the best greeting I've had since I left you at the YARD. Ryan, I cannot possibly say how happy I am to see you. Well, Sailor, you didn't answer my question "Can I buy you a beer"? You bet baby have a seat we have a lot to catch up on.

Ashley ask the first question, Ryan, what in the heck are you doing here? Good question, easy answer. After I left the YARD, as you know, I went to Navy flight school in Florida. There I got my wings and I now fly a McDonnell Douglas F/A-18 Hornet. It is a carrier based jet fighter. Right now I am attached to the

USS Yorktown CV10. It is based here in Pearl Harbor. My tour aboard her is a three year tour and I am about I year into it.

Ash, you have been easy to follow. I'm not sure that any individual from the Academy has had as much press as you since the Academy was first formed. I followed you as you went undefeated in the Patriot League for four years. I followed you through four NCAA Championships and then I watched you perform in the Tokyo Olympics and take home a gold and silver medal wearing a US Navy swim cap.

Then, after all of that, you started making news with your quest to become the first woman SEAL ever and like everything else you have done. You did it. Which means you deserve significant congratulations. Once I read that you had completed your training, I made a couple of phone calls to find out where you were going to be stationed. When I found out you were coming to Pear Harbor to the SEAL delivery team stationed here, it was just a matter of stocking you until I found you. So you're the reason I'm here and why I wanted to buy you this beer.

So this will sound a little mushy but I've been thinking what to say to you when I finally caught up with you. The truth is no one has ever made the impression you made on me, and I have been unable to get you out of my mind as a result.

You may not remember this, but when I was about to leave the YARD we had a very brief discussion about our relationship and what the future had in store for both of us. We both agreed that the career paths we had chosen to pursue just didn't lend themselves to a long term relationship at that point. We both felt it was important to stay focused on our own individual goals and try to achieve them.

Well, what this all is meant to say, is that we did what we said we wanted to do, and we now find ourselves back together again. I have no idea if you have a relationship going with someone but I do know that you're not married yet so I wanted you to know that if you would be willing I would like to start to focus on developing a long term relationship with you.

Ryan, I am completely blown away. The simple answer to your question is I have no man in my life other than those that make up my SEAL team. I have never stopped thinking about you and I remember that final kiss we had before we parted ways. I would love to start to develop a lasting relationship with you and I can promise you that I will work very hard to make it happen. With that she gave him another huge hug. Mark saw the second hug and decided he would wander back over and see what was going on.

Hey Mark, I want you to meet someone that is very special to me. Mark Price, I would like to introduce you to Ryan Joshua. Ryan was the Captain of the Naval Academy Gymnastics Team when we were both at the Academy together. Ryan, Mark is my Commanding Officer. Hey Mark, it is nice to meet you. Ryan I see by the wings on your shirt that you are a fighter pilot. Are you attached to the Yorktown? Yes Sir, I am. I fly an FA 18 Hornet. Nice airplane. Not an easy gig.

I like it, but I would say based on what I know about what you and Ashley do, that my gig is a walk in the park compared to your jobs. Well, thanks but both occupations have their ups and downs.

Ash, I will see you for training in the morning. If you need any help with the move just let me know. Nice to have met you Ryan. I'll see you later.

What's this about moving? Oh for the first time in my life I am getting a place of my own. It is a studio apartment at Ala Wai Boat Harbor. It is small, but it has a great view and easy access to Waikiki beach. I'm moving in on Saturday.

I would be happy to help you if you need it. Thanks, but the apartment is fully furnished so all I need to do is take my stuff from my dorm room here and get it put away in the new place. I tell you what though, by Sunday I should have it organized and the way I want it. Would you like to come over for a bottle of wine and dinner on Sunday. That would be great Ash. Just give me the address and I'll be there when you want. Let's say at 5PM. I have a big day on Monday so let's make it an early dinner. She wrote the address on a bar napkin and gave it to Ryan.

They finished their beer and gave each other a final hug before they headed to their own homes.

The next morning Ashley met with Mark for their daily briefing before they started working with the delivery vehicle. Ash, last night when Captain Miles asked to talk with me it was about our next deployment and the rescue operation we conducted.

He received word yesterday that we will be deploying to the far east in December for a six month deployment. That means we will have a full five months here before we leave and we will have time to plan for our potential missions that may occur when we are deployed. How does that work Mark. Are we told in advance what they may have in mind for us?

Not very often but when we are not facing a battle crisis SEAL TEAM 1 in Coronado manages to come up with some real interesting practice sessions for us. My guess is this deployment will be no different. If that is the case, they will give us some advance notice of what we will be up against, so we can maximize the benefits of our training.

However, I have yet to be on an overseas deployment when we were not asked to perform some sort of clandestine operation for real and I can only assume that we will have something come up that will require we go into action for real.

The second issue the Captain wanted to discuss was to tell me that he has been notified by Submarine Command that the Lexington and her crew were going to receive a formal commendation medal for their efforts regarding the Chinese lives that were saved He was extremely happy and told me that our SEAL team will also receive some sort of commendation, which is really unusual. Apparently the Captain of the tanker that went down could not stop talking about all of us and that the Chinese Government formally sent a commendation request to Naval Command in Washington. So, that is something that rarely occurs. Our team will be really pleased. Mark, that is great news.

They finished their training on Friday and Ash was off for the weekend. She was up early on Saturday morning, and between Friday night and early Saturday morning she had all of her things packed, organized, and ready to go.

She took a cab from the base to her apartment and was met at the door of her place by Mr. Piedmont who handed her a key.

Ashley, just let me know if you need anything and I will see what I can do. Thanks Mr. Piedmont.

She walked in to her new digs and just couldn't stop smiling. Finally, a place of her own. She put her stuff away, did some minor re-arranging, and then did an inventory of what was in the kitchen. She made a list out of the kitchen items she would need, and the basic spices she needed to pick up at the store.

She was within walking distance of a Safeway so it would be easy to pick up the items she needed to stock her cupboard

That night she called home and talked to her Mom for over an hour. She told her about the rescue operation and about the apartment. She also told her about meeting Ryan and that she was going to have him over for dinner the next evening.

She decided to say nothing about the deployment until she knew it was for certain.

When she finally went to bed she was really beat. She pulled her bed out from the wall and was surprised to find it comfortable and easy to make up. She slept until 10 AM the next morning.

Once up she began to think about dinner and cooking for Ryan. She was not a very experienced cook and she needed to make a good impression so the meal needed to be simple and easy.

She had always loved cooking with her Mom using a Wok,

and decided that she would pick one up, and cook in it, for her first dinner at home. She decided on a beef, broccoli, shredded carrot and mushroom stir fry. She would use thin cut Filet Mignon for the meat and she would use Maggie Gins Sir Fry sauce.

Desert would be carrot cake and the wine would be a French Pinot Noir by Nicolas Potel. It was called Bourgogne.

She also decided that she would toast to them before dinner with a glass of Prosecco. She decided to serve it with French blue cheese and crackers.

The last thing she had to think about was what to wear. She only brought two dresses with her and neither were going to work for the evening. In fact, she had not had a dress on in so long she didn't even know if either would fit.

So it was a quick walk over to the mall, and it took her no time to find a short Hawaiian sun dress with tiny spaghetti straps.

It did the trick. She had a swimmers body so finding a dress to fit was no problem.

She was back in early afternoon with plenty of time to prepare for the evening ahead. She looked good and felt even better.

Ryan was right on time. He was dressed in shorts and a Hawaiian golf shirt. He looked great and thought Ashley looked fantastic.

Ashley poured them each a glass of Prosecco and put the French Blue Cheese and crackers out on the table. She lifted her glass in a toast to him. Here is to a guy I am so happy found me and to the beginning of what I hope is a wonderful long term relationship. With that they toasted each other. Cheers Ryan said.

The night went just as planned, they ended up sitting on Ashley's small deck with a cup of coffee before ending the evening. They held hands but said nothing, It had been a wonderful evening and was to be the start of something really great.

ABOUT THE AUTHOR

Stephen A Enna is the author of **THE ONLY EASY DAY WAS YESTERDAY.** He is also the co-author of the eight book Aloha series. Steve is a veteran of the Viet Nam War and was a Lieutenant in the United States Navy. This book was written for his grand children in hopes that it will serve as an example of what they can achieve if they work very hard at it. Steve is married and lives and writes in Northern California.

Ingram Content Group UK Ltd.
Milton Keynes UK
UKHW011824230523
422220UK00017B/69/J

9 781728 321851